Cat in an
Ultramarine Scheme

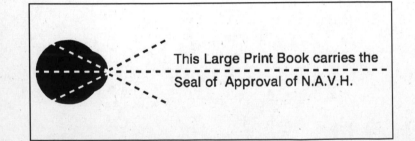

This Large Print Book carries the
Seal of Approval of N.A.V.H.

A MIDNIGHT LOUIE MYSTERY

CAT IN AN ULTRAMARINE SCHEME

CAROLE NELSON DOUGLAS

THORNDIKE PRESS

A part of Gale, Cengage Learning

GALE
CENGAGE Learning

Detroit • New York • San Francisco • New Haven, Conn • Waterville, Maine • London

GALE
CENGAGE Learning™

Copyright © 2010 by Carole Nelson Douglas.
Thorndike Press, a part of Gale, Cengage Learning.

Thorndike Press® Large Print Mystery.
The text of this Large Print edition is unabridged.
Other aspects of the book may vary from the original edition.
Set in 16 pt. Plantin.

LIBRARY OF CONGRESS CATALOGING-IN-PUBLICATION DATA

Douglas, Carole Nelson.
    Cat in an ultramarine scheme : a Midnight Louie mystery /
by Carole Nelson Douglas. — Large print ed.
        p. cm. — (Thorndike press large print mystery)
    ISBN-13: 978-1-4104-3059-5
    ISBN-10: 1-4104-3059-6
    1. Barr, Temple (Fictitious character)—Fiction. 2. Midnight
Louie (Fictitious character)—Fiction. 3. Public relations
consultants—Fiction. 4. Women cat owners—Fiction. 5. Women
detectives—Fiction. 6. Las Vegas (Nev.)—Fiction. 7. Large type
books. I. Title.
PS3554.O8237C279 2010b
813'.54—dc22   2010034077

Published in 2010 by arrangement with Tom Doherty Associates, LLC.

Printed in Mexico
1 2 3 4 5 6 7 14 13 12 11 10

*For Janet Berliner,
a magical writer, editor, and friend,
and, most of all, survivor*

CONTENTS

PREVIOUSLY IN
MIDNIGHT LOUIE'S
LIVES AND TIMES . . .

Ah, me. Here I live and work in the world's biggest and glitziest adult playground, and somebody has gone and turned off the water, lights, and heat.

Well, not literally.

Still, much jazz and razzamatazz has left this jumpin' joint in the Mojave Desert since the economic angst shut down Las Vegas's mad, mad, mad building boom. I am not speaking of any of *my* old joints shutting down, mind you.

Only a couple of years ago the Strip used to be a high-wire act in "construction plaid." What do I mean by "plaid," besides that dead men do not wear it?

Picture this. For months the usual burning blue Vegas sky framed tall, thin, vertical condo towers — "every room with a view" — rising thanks to the high, wide, and horizontal lines of construction cranes.

They are both still there, mind you. Just

11

dormant, sort of like me taking an ultralong Sunday nap.

This halted construction "plaid" has ruined the town's once-so-dramatic helicopter-sweep vista, if you ask me. *CSI: Las Vegas* shows use old stock film when the scripts call for an aerial pan up Las Vegas Boulevard, aka the famous Strip. And the last venerable hotels that would be imploding to make way for the latest multibillion-dollar construction project are still standing proud and being marketed as bargains now that "exclusive" and "expensive" are looking mighty "expendable" in a lot of folks' budgets.

You can get some great deals in Vegas nowadays, and not just at the casino tables.

Ah, almost forty million tourists each year and constant camera crews . . . flashy new hotels rising over the fleshy, seamy side of the Strip. There used to be a lot of fat cats in Vegas.

And one would be me.

I have always kept a low profile for a Las Vegas institution.

You do not hear about me on the nightly news. That is the way I like it. That is the way any primo PI would like it. The name is Louie, Midnight Louie. I am a noir kind of guy, inside and out. I like my nightlife shaken, not stirred.

Being short, dark, and handsome — really

short — gets me overlooked and underestimated, which is what the savvy operative wants anyway. I am your perfect undercover guy. I also like to hunker down under the covers with my little doll.

Miss Temple Barr and I make perfect roomies. She tolerates my wandering ways. I look after her without getting in her way. Call me Muscle in Midnight Black. We share a well-honed sense of justice and long, sharp fingernails and have cracked some cases too tough for the local fuzz. She is, after all, a freelance public-relations specialist, and Las Vegas is full of public relations of all stripes and legalities.

None can deny that the Las Vegas crime scene is big-time, and I have been treading these mean neon streets for twenty-two books now. I am an "alphacat." Since I debuted in *Catnap* and *Pussyfoot,* I commenced a title sequence that is as sweet and simple as B to Z.

My alphabet begins with the B in *Cat on a Blue Monday.* After that, the titles' "color" words are in alphabetical order up to the, *ahem,* current volume, *Cat in an Ultramarine Scheme.*

Since Las Vegas is littered with guidebooks as well as bodies, I wish to provide a rundown of the local landmarks on my particular map of the world. A cast of characters, so to speak:

To wit, my lovely roommate and high-heel devotee, "Miss Nancy Drew" on killer spikes, freelance PR ace Miss Temple Barr, who had reunited with her elusive love . . .

. . . The once-again-missing-in-action magician Mr. Max Kinsella, who has good reason for invisibility. After his cousin Sean died in a bomb attack during a post–high-school jaunt to Ireland, he joined his mentor, Gandolph the Great, in undercover counterterrorism work.

Meanwhile, Mr. Max has been sought on suspicion of murder by another dame, Las Vegas homicide detective Lieutenant C. R. Molina, single mother of teenage Mariah.

Mama Molina is also the good friend of Miss Temple's freshly minted fiancé, Mr. Matt Devine, a radio talk-show shrink and former Roman Catholic priest, who came to Vegas to track down his abusive stepfather and ended up becoming a local celebrity.

Speaking of unhappy pasts, Miss Lieutenant Carmen Regina Molina is not thrilled that her former flame, Mr. Rafi Nadir, the father of Mariah, is living and working in Las Vegas after blowing his career at the LAPD. . . .

Meanwhile, Mr. Matt drew a stalker, the local lass that Max and his cousin Sean boyishly competed for in that long-ago Ireland . . .

. . . one Miss Kathleen O'Connor, deservedly christened Kitty the Cutter by Miss Temple. Finding Mr. Max as impossible to trace as Lieutenant Molina did, Kitty the C settled for harassing with tooth and claw the nearest innocent bystander, Mr. Matt Devine.

Now that Miss Kathleen O'Connor has self-destructed and is dead and buried, things are shaking up at the Circle Ritz. Mr. Max Kinsella is again MIA. In fact, I saw him hit the wall of the Neon Nightmare club while in the guise of a bungee-jumping magician, the Phantom Mage. Neither I nor Las Vegas has seen him since.

That this possible tragedy coincides with my ever-lovin' roommate going over to the Light Side (our handsome blond upstairs neighbor, Mr. Matt Devine) in her romantic life only adds to the angst and confusion.

However, things are seldom what they seem, and almost never in Las Vegas. A magician can have as many lives as a cat, in my humble estimation, and events seem to bear me out. Meanwhile, Miss Lieutenant C. R. Molina's domestic issues past and present are on a collision course as she deals with two circling mystery men of her own, Mr. Rafi Nadir and Mr. Dirty Larry Podesta, an undercover narc who has wormed his way into her personal and professional crusades.

Such surprising developments do not surprise me. Everything is always up for grabs in Las Vegas 24/7: guilt, innocence, money, power, love, loss, death, and significant others.

All this human sex and violence makes me glad that I have a simpler social life, such as just trying to get along with my unacknowledged daughter . . .

. . . Miss Midnight Louise, who insinuated herself into my cases until I was forced to set up shop with her as Midnight Investigations, Inc. . . .

. . . and needing to unearth more about the Synth, a cabal of magicians that may be responsible for a lot of murderous cold cases in town, now the object of growing international interest.

So, there you have it, the usual human stew — folks good, bad, and hardly indifferent — all mixed-up and at odds with one another and within themselves. Obviously, it is up to me to solve all their mysteries and nail some crooks along the way.

Like Las Vegas, the City That Never Sleeps, Midnight Louie, private eye, also has a sobriquet: the Kitty That Never Sleeps.

With this crew, who could?

Chapter 1
Magic Carpet

"Danny Dove really gave you a great view from your bed," Temple told Matt, snuggling into his shoulder. "I didn't realize that, seeing this room from the outside in."

"I'm glad we're both seeing it from the inside out too," he answered. "Sorry we have to do the 'Early Show' routine, though."

"With cable and DVDs, what does it matter? Dinner at eight, movie at nine, and you're on your way to WCOO-FM for your *Midnight Hour* show at eleven."

"Leaving you alone to creep downstairs to your unit, and only a cat for company."

"Don't let Louie hear you describing him as 'only a cat'!"

"Somebody needs to trim his overgrown feline ego. I have to admit that his shenanigans have inadvertently helped save your life, for which I'm thankful."

Matt expressed his gratitude by kissing

her thoroughly enough to make her toes curl. "He's welcome to leave black hairs on Danny's precious damask coverlet up here anytime."

"Not necessary," Temple said. "Louie considers the bed downstairs his."

"You mean, when we marry, we'll have to take that California king-size bed along to our new joint residence?"

Temple understood that the bed she'd shared with Louie — and Max Kinsella — might not make a terrific housewarming item.

"Maybe I'll just take the zebra-pattern coverlet Louie loves and looks so good on."

"I doubt Danny would approve."

"Danny may have updated your monk's cell to an *Architectural Digest* playboy pad, but he's not going to be sleeping in our future house. Have you thought where you'd like to move? Golf course view?" Matt made a face. "Mountainside or Strip view?" He shook his head. "Water view?"

"Wasteful in this climate."

"Church view, like Molina's place?"

"No." He was laughing. "We need to think of other things than moving first."

"Like what?"

"For starters, I have some news."

"News!" Temple muted the movie and sat

up in bed.

"Easy, ex-newshound. It's nothing major. It's actually a bit annoying for a newly engaged woman. I have a week of vacation coming up —"

"And you didn't tell me? We could join Kit and Aldo in Italy!"

"I'm not intruding on someone's honeymoon."

"I'm sure most of the honeymooning must be done by now. They're coming home in a week or so."

"Temple, I can't go to Italy. I can't go anywhere with you. This was set up before we were *us*."

"Oh? So it involves another woman?"

He grinned sheepishly. "As a matter of fact, it does."

"Ah!" Temple inhaled in mock indignation.

"Several, in fact."

"Beast!" She pounded just as mockingly on his shoulder and chest.

"But it might serve our larger purpose very well."

"Larger purpose?"

"Holy matrimony."

"Oh, that's different. Go on. What did you have to keep so secret?"

"It's not secret; I just forgot about it in

the recent excitement."

"*This* recent excitement?" Temple prodded.

Matt ran a hand through his tousled hair. "Not *that* recent. I mean the threats on our lives and our mad, impetuous engagement preceding them."

"Ha! You're about as impetuous as a tortoise, so I believe you when you say this me-less vacation was on the books for some time. Where are you going?"

"Chicago."

"Ah. No doubt you'll be breaking the news about me to the family?"

"Yes, but that'll be the least of my worries."

" 'Worries'? Marrying me is a worry?"

"Not you. The idea. My family saw me as a priest for almost half my life. And it's taken my mother most of my whole life to recover from having me out of wedlock."

"I would have you out of wedlock anytime," Temple said soberly.

"You *are*," he pointed out. "Am I glad I ran into that ex-priests' group when I was helping you investigate one of those murders you feel compelled to help solve. They made me see the spirit of the canon law is more important than the letter of it."

"I keep forgetting I'm a . . . 'near occasion of sin' — isn't that the terminology?"

Matt frowned, sounding stern. "You didn't get that from me. Who told you that?"

"The Unitarian Universalist minister I consulted," Temple admitted.

"You saw a minister, about me?"

"No, about *me.* I needed to know what my being modern about putting the honeymoon before the wedding would do to your conscience. So I'm very happy you'll be seeing the old folks at home next week and preparing them. You didn't have to keep that from me, Matt. I'll understand if they want to reject me."

"No one who knows you would want to reject you."

There was a silence. Apparently, Temple thought, Max Kinsella had, or had at least vanished on her for the second time in their mysteriously interrupted three-year love affair.

"Not willingly," Matt added.

"Remarkably generous concession," Temple said.

He shrugged, which did great things for his swimmer's-strength upper torso, upon which Temple snuggled again.

"Okay. You're out of town for a week," she concluded. "Fans of *The Midnight Hour* will be besieging the station phone lines begging for the voice of their favorite radio late-night shrink. Louie will be hogging the entire other half of my condo bed. You'll be wrestling your large Polish family and pinning them down to offer you independence and support. We'll cope."

"I'm sure *you* will. I'll also be doing a week of *The Amanda Show* live."

"A whole week gig? Not just the occasional hour like you've been doing? And you leave your major-media promotion break to an afterthought? *The Amanda Show* is second only to *Oprah.*"

"Oprah has a huge lead . . . on everything. My relatives do get a huge kick out of me being on TV in their own backyards. I figure that will help them adjust to a soon-to-be married ex-priest in the family."

"Good," said Temple. "I'll try not to solve any murders without you."

Matt checked his watch. "I hate to kick my fiancée out of a warm bed, but the movie's over and I have to get ready for heading over to the radio station."

Temple yawned. "Do what you have to. I'm starting to feel like a lovesick teenager with a curfew," she grumbled. "Home by eleven. Yes, folks."

"I'm sure your parents would be very proud," Matt said as he bent to kiss her good night again, and vanished into the bathroom.

Temple retrieved her clothes and shoes from the bedside and gave a fond farewell look at the fifty-two-inch flat-screen television. She only had a thirty-seven-inch in her condo.

Of course, she also had Midnight Louie, when he deigned to sleep in nights, and he was an extra-large model cat.

Fifteen minutes later she was snuggled down in her own bed, Midnight Louie blissfully on his back on the other side, all four feet splayed in ludicrous disarray. Temple was sure he only unfurled his long, furry, soft underbelly here at home.

The Circle Ritz, like all fifties-vintage construction, was cramped by modern room-size standards, especially in the tiny, tile-lined bathrooms, only a bathtub wide, both of them. Still, Temple loved her petite living quarters. It was like living in a luxurious dollhouse surviving past its time. The thought of forsaking it for another place, for a freestanding house, made her a little sad.

But then, Max had rolled around alone in a big house when he returned to Vegas from his first disappearing act. Maybe it was more grown-up to live in a house rather than an apartment or condominium.

Maybe Temple was finally growing up, not just getting older and wiser.

She scratched Louie's tummy until he yawned to display his vast pink maw lined with white teeth and started purring like a Volkswagen motor.

Nobody who knew her would reject her.

Apparently Max had, despite himself, twice. Somehow Max was still showing up unexpectedly at the most awkward moments. In her mind.

Her heart told her she'd loved Max, but it had always been "despite" circumstances that never stopped keeping them apart. Her heart told her she'd remained faithful to their passionate past for so long, she'd almost missed falling in love with a uniquely wonderful guy who loved her to death. Or rather, until death did them part, and meant it.

That same heart told her that Max would have let her know if he was alive, somehow, if he *was* alive.

And, if not, he was a master magician. You'd think even then he'd have the chops and decency to let her know for sure that he was dead.

CHAPTER 2
HOW GREEN WAS MY VALLEY

"Smog?" Max asked, staring out the Cessna's porthole window as the small twin-engine prop airplane approached Dublin.

"Ireland has smog now? Is that what the Celtic Tiger is thrashing its technological tail about? Is pollution what Ireland's acclaimed economic revival achieved?"

"*Hmm.* The fabled Irish landscape *is* awakening your memories." Garry Randolph leaned forward from his window seat behind Max. "I'm afraid poor old Ireland is the technological Celtic Pussycat since the recession. And, my boy, don't go all dismal and depressive. Can't you see that blur of green meeting the pale blue and pink horizon is nothing so rank and modern as smog, but the legendary Irish mist?"

" 'Irish mist,' " Max mocked. "*You're* resorting to a stage brogue too? I can see why. Green fields and hedges . . . silver ponds and rivers. The landscape below us is incredibly beautiful, an emerald harp strung with silver strings."

"I knew the Auld Sod would bring out the poet in you, Max."

Max snorted in reply. "Bring out the memoryless lunatic, more likely," he added after a moment.

Both men had to raise their voices over the drone of the Cessna's nearby engines, while the cottages and farmhouses — white with dark thatched roofs, like a patch of mushrooms — grew large.

No one could overhear them. The pilot was muttering little nothings about landing to the Dublin Airport control tower, where a man answered in the universal English of pilots, but with an Irish accent.

Max leaned nearer the tiny curtained window to view a lit Christmas tree–shaped grid of landing lights on the ground, pointing arrow-like to the runway. As the plane flew lower, the lights winked red and then green. *Intimations of Christmas,* Max thought, *in an ancient druidic land seen through the mist. . . .*

The pastel dawn seemed a distant dream he and Garry were rushing headlong into. Maybe it was a metaphor for his lost memory, a pale purple haze of terror and delight awaiting him in this beautiful, so-long-troubled landscape.

In moments, runway lights were blinking past the Cessna's miniature window. A smooth landing led to a smoother taxi to a small hangar.

Max sensed that his six-foot-four frame always hungered to unkink from the plane seat and deplane. Here he had to duck considerably to exit, and navigate his injury-stiff legs down a steep, narrow, drop-down stairway.

He groaned at the bottom, waiting for his older, stouter friend.

"Tell me you didn't hire a Morris Mini," Max pleaded, wincing for his recently healed broken legs.

Garry slapped him on the arm. "Am I a secret sadist? Your lovely blonde shrink at the Swiss clinic is, perhaps. Gandolph the Great — never!"

"You *were* a magician," Max repeated. "They are basically tricksters. And someone presumed dead longer than I have been," he reminded him.

"*We* were magicians. Are still. *Aaah.*" Garry inhaled the crisp morning air. "How do you feel about a Ford Mondeo?"

"A Ford Mon Dieu? I've never heard of it. So much forgotten."

"Getting frisky and funny and slightly

profane now that you're on native soil, are we? My good lord, Max, you're back. A Mondeo is the across-the-pond version of the Ford Contour or the Mercury Mystique; the latter name I think better befits our mission. And you as well."

Max spotted the shiny black sedan and nodded glumly. "Serviceable and dull family four-door. Just what old undercover, presumed-dead magicians like us need. Plenty of game-leg room up front, I see."

"Ah, that's the old Max, yearning to go fast and furious. This is a journey into the past. Yours and Ireland's — and Northern Ireland's itself."

"And you naturally thought such a sentimental journey required a car of a funereal color?"

Max was surprised to see the upbeat old man's face grow sober.

"Max, you've just weathered a terrible physical ordeal, one that might have killed another man. And it's an immense psychological trauma to wake up an amnesiac. Yet a worse psychological trial awaits you. Take it one step at a time. You can't make a rabbit jump out of a top hat unless you first figure out how it got in."

"Did I really do that?"

"What?"

"That corny rabbit trick?"

"No, my lad. You used doves. A cornucopia of doves."

Obviously Garry thrived on being mysterious.

Max sighed. "You keep hinting that this land is my land, but I'm obviously as American as hell." Max frowned. "Despite having a knack for vaudeville Irish accents. What kind of an Irish name is *Max*, anyway? It might be of German derivation, like the non-French part of the lovely Revienne *Schneider*."

Garry pursed his lips. "German? No. Never. You're American Irish through and through. We keep this secret also: how you became 'Max.' Your given birth names were Michael Aloysius Xavier."

"Quite a triad of antique saints and one major archangel. That's why you registered me as 'Michael Randolph' at the Swiss clinic! You thought I'd unconsciously respond more naturally to the name *Michael*. How long have I been 'Max'?"

"Since you were seventeen."

"And how did that come about?"

"I rechristened you to save your life."

"What the hell? Why does a seventeen-year-old need his life saved?"

"Because you were a hell of a seventeen-year-old and you got three men killed. They deserved it, and you did it."

Max didn't answer that one. What an appalling past. Garry was right. TMI — too much information. Obviously, he needed to be spoon-fed the ugly truths. He strolled toward the Ford car, limping more than he liked after the flight and landing in the chilly Irish dawn. So an Irishman hankered for sunshine and heat? He seemed to. Or his legs did.

Max eyed the sedan from hood to taillights. "You expect me to drive this thing?"

"Yes, and on the left. It is at least an automatic."

"Even worse!"

"How do you know that?"

Food for thought. "That I prefer to drive stick shift? I don't know; isn't that my key problem? I know the general past. I know what I like. And don't like. I just don't know my own damn past. I can't recall what I did and where I was and with whom. Or whom I hated and whom I loved."

"We know you had a good high-school English teacher."

"Yeah?"

"*Whom* was the proper construction there, and you used it like some men swear. Frequently and fervently, without thinking

30

about it. Relax, Max. Go through the motions and let your old self shine through bit by bit. I'm here. I'm your safety net."

"Why?"

"We're partners. Or were, for your formative young-adult years. I was all the family you had, for a long time."

"After I killed three men. Justly."

"After three men died. Justly."

"I remember a popular song. 'At Seventeen.' It was about an unhappy, awkward girl. What kind of song is there for a guy 'at seventeen'?"

"An Irish ballad. Which is why we're here."

"All the Irish ballads I recall were bloody and sad."

"Exactly. But you're here, mostly in one piece, and too puzzled to be sad. Things could be worse."

Max opened the right driver's door to the Ford Mondeo and eyed the seating and dashboard layout with resignation.

"I drive, old man. On the left, with automatic. You think that will help my memory return?"

"That depends upon where we drive and what we learn when we get there."

"Why the hell don't you just tell me?"

"You're a dubious man, Max. You only believe what you see."

"You mean I'm a magician."

Garry nodded.

"I believe that now. I suppose it's a start."

"A journey of a thousand miles begins with a single —"

"Boring rent-a-car." Max ended the truism. "Hop in and put on your seat belt. I have a feeling this is going to be a bumpy ride."

CHAPTER 3
BROKE NEW WORLD

Temple pulled her red Miata convertible under the Crystal Phoenix Hotel and Casino's shaded entry.

The relentless Las Vegas sun was hard on leather seats and even harder on slightly freckled natural redheads. That was why Temple wore sunscreen daily. Today, she'd added a straw visor with a built-in white cotton headscarf, circa the mid-1940s, tied under her chin.

When vintage-clothing-store-shopper Temple married fiancé Matt Devine, finding "something old" would be a snap.

"Going to be long, Miss Barr?" a parking valet attired in a snazzy bellboy uniform asked.

"Conference with Mr. and Mrs. Big," she said. "Let the Miata cool its wheels in the ramp for a couple of hours, Dave."

"Right," he said, seeing her out of the car and himself in, and enjoying it. "Cool hot wheels."

Temple was the hotel's sole public-relations rep. That got her a permanent parking space and speedy ins and outs. As a freelance publicist, she was always dashing from one client to another, especially if something went wrong, which could be as minor as a short order of folding chairs, or even occasionally something major in the homicide line.

PR was getting tough now. Newspapers were sinking like the real London Bridge in the Arizona desert. Web sites weren't taking up the slack. Vegas's last best bet on mega-million new construction projects was still mostly stalled in midair. Tourism was down, along with optimism. Temple was very curious to see what had amped up the ambitions of Nicky Fontana, Crystal Phoenix owner, and his manager-wife, Van von Rhine.

In minutes she was sitting in the Strip-overlooking executive suite, being told.

"The past," Nicky said, pacing around his wife's ultramodern office.

Like all Fontana brothers — and he had a slew of them — he was tall, dark, and handsome, but Nicky was fiercer than his laid-back bros. "The future is dim, the present is grim. Everybody's talking Depression,

34

although it's only a recession. Why not cash in on what made Vegas in the first place? Our notorious past."

"Retro is Metro?" Temple ventured, eyeing the cool blonde who was his wife.

As usual, Van had a crisp summary of her husband's overheated rhetoric. "Nicky rebuilt this hotel, Las Vegas's first boutique hostelry, from the still-standing corpse of the old Joshua Tree Hotel, Jersey Joe Jackson's rival to Bugsy Siegel's Flamingo. When he talks, I listen. It's the least you can do too."

Nicky paused behind his wife's white leather desk chair, put his palm prints on her glass desktop, and nibbled a strand loose from her perfectly smooth French twist.

"You didn't always believe in my founder dreams, Vanilla baby."

She remained unruffled, even by the use of the first name she hated. Fire and ice worked well for them, Temple had always noted.

"You see," Van told Temple, confirming her observation, "Nicky can sell ice to Eskimos and even get away with mussing my coiffure. Can you sell his hairbrained concept? Granted, his hair is very good. Still."

Temple tried not to giggle. Sometimes spending time with the pair was like babysitting Grace Kelly and Tony Curtis in some never-made sixties romantic comedy.

All ten Fontana brothers were noted for good hair. Only Nicky, the youngest, and now Aldo, the oldest, had married. The other eight remained Vegas's most eligible bachelors, en masse. Even Macho Mario Fontana, the family patriarch, had great hair, high-end, store-bought, and solid silver, the color of the old dollar coins used for some Vegas slot machines until the seventies.

Silver dollars were now history here. And so seemed to be the endless building boom that had produced profitable minarets of condo towers before the current financial unpleasantness. The Crystal Phoenix always moved conservatively and stayed small, so it had deeper pockets than some far-more-famous Strip names.

"So tell me how I'm supposed to make the city's criminal past sexy," Temple told Nicky.

"You don't have to. That's the beauty of my concept." He spread his Italian-suit-tailored arms. "Me."

At the uninterrupted silence, he eyed his wife and hastily corrected course. "Us. I'm remembering what the Crystal Phoenix was almost named if you hadn't had a better idea, Van."

"Way back when we decided against calling the hotel the Fontana?" Van asked, still unsure what her volatile spouse was getting at.

"But the Fontanas are still here in Vegas, and better than ever," Nicky answered.

Temple stayed out of it. This was sounding too marital for her input.

Faint worry lines schussed across Van von Rhine's pale brow like tiny ski tracks. " 'Fontanas' as in your family?"

"*Family* — that's it! She is sharp, isn't she?" Nicky asked Temple.

"Like a Jimmy Choo stiletto," Temple agreed. "I must admit that I'm still just a blunt Cuban heel. I don't get where you're going, Nicky."

"At least you're not a yes-woman." He turned the wattage of his smile on her as he sat in the neighboring chair. "The Jersey Joe Jackson Action Attraction under the hotel grounds has been idle since Vegas decided to forget going 'family attraction' years ago as a bad bet. I say *we* go Family with a capital *F*, as in Fontana."

"Nicky," Van said, "that city mob-museum project goes off and on faster than the semaphores on the Vegas Strip. It got caught in the last election's rebellion against 'pork' and is seriously compromised."

"True. And they started out so coy, calling it the 'redacted' museum. *Redacted*," Nicky jeered. "What kind of word is that? What tourist knows that word? Only English majors. Vegas is not an English-major kind of town."

"*You* know it." Van called him on it.

He shrugged. "I needed to know it to figure out what the heck the mayor was thinking."

"That's a good point," Temple said, watching Van's arched foot in its white patent-leather peep-toe Ferragamo pump tapping the carpet. Her own silver Stuart Weitzman T-strap sandal offered plenty of "peep toe."

She herself and the mostly torrid Vegas climate favored high-heeled sandals and open-toed shoes. Women liked to go bare-legged and show off colorfully painted toes. Or maybe the nail-polished toes announced they were going bare-legged. Temple could remember, as a child, when clingy, bothersome pantyhose was required. Most women had tossed away that fashion "rule" along with strictly prescribed skirt lengths.

Some fashion mavens sneered at white patent leather, but it was hard to come by in shoes and Temple adored it for surviving all extremes of the elements, from heatstroke to flash flood, both possible in Vegas.

Considering extremes, Temple also thought now was the time to pour the oil of PR on the marital CEO waters.

"You're right, Nicky," she told him. "The Vegas powers-that-be have spent almost fifty years soft-pedaling the city's colorful mob roots. The idea of creating a major mob museum here has been floating around for years, but everyone's afraid of that three-letter word."

"When you're afraid of something, you need to face it and flaunt it," he answered.

"Yes, the chamber of commerce types did look silly with that business of blocking out the word *mob* from the Mob Museum title."

"I'm no English major," Van said, "just international business. What *does* redact mean, anyway?"

"Editing or revising a piece of writing for publication," Temple explained. "The museum backers actually crossed out the word *mob* in the title of the Mob Museum. Trying to have it both ways in PR is foolhardy."

Temple quickly printed out the name with a felt-tip pen on Crystal Phoenix letterhead, then inked out the word *mob*.

"Why on Earth, or even in Vegas," Van asked, "create a tourist destination you can't advertise?"

"Why," Nicky asked back, "duplicate what's already there, aching to be expanded and ballyhooed?"

"I agree, but what's already there?" Van asked.

"The Fontana family's mob museum," he answered in triumph.

Silence ensued again. In it, Temple noticed that the hotel cat, Midnight Louise, had either entered on hushed little cat feet or, more likely, arisen from a concealed napping spot in the executive office suite.

She was now sitting demurely at Van's ankles, licking her clawed front toes one by one, grooming her own brand of "peep" toenails, Temple thought.

Although Midnight Louie, Temple's . . . roommate, had inspired this feminine version of his name for this once-stray cat, Louise was smaller than he, with longer black hair. She was just as spit-polished as her larger, buzz-cut, and "butcher" version.

Midnight Louise flicked a paw over one ear, as if cleaning it for better reception. Ears R Us.

Seeing that blot of black on the pale carpet, Temple finally got Nicky's reference, thinking of another glitzier blot of black on the Vegas scene.

"Nicky. You mean Gangsters!"

He nodded, pleased as a teacher with a prize student. "Like gangbusters! You got it, Miss Temple."

Van was puzzled. "That's a small off-Strip hotel-casino setup."

"I've been there," Temple said. "Lots of 'local color' from the delicious bad old days. A string of indecently stretched black limousines always underlines the entry canopy. You'd think it was a funeral fleet. The hotel facade is polished black marble and neon-lit glass blocks. Very Art Deco. The upper stories are capped by a huge neon fedora and gun barrel, both cocked, with veiled red lights visible as squinting eyes in the eaves' eternal penumbra.

"Customers are escorted inside by broad-shouldered men in sinister fedoras who wear pastel ties against dark shirts and suits. 'Le Jazz Hot' and forties swing is on the audio system.

"It's a modest six-hundred-room hotel, but has the four-star Hush Money steak house, Speakeasy bar and restaurant, and a four-thousand-seat theater and gaming casino that's 'raided' nightly by the fake feds. The Roxie, a vintage movie theater, even plays newsreels — about gangsters, of course.

"They have a small museum with gats and getaway cars from the gangland days of old, and up-to-date shopping in flanking wings: Gents and G-Men on the left, with the Moll Mall on the right."

"That does sound like a smart concept," Van conceded, "one that's been totally overshadowed, Nicky, by your brothers' allied and adjacent booming exotic limo service of the same name. Bad misfire. A clever concept lost in the execution."

"Ouch." Nicky mock-cringed. "Don't say 'execution' in connection with mention of the family business."

"Hardly a 'family' business. You've never linked the Crystal Phoenix with your uncle's or brothers' Vegas doings. Smart."

"Yeah, yeah, I'm the white sheep of the family. On paper."

Van placed the flats of both hands on her floating glass desktop and levered herself to her full heeled height.

"Nicky Fontana! You don't mean to say you've been secretly backing your relations' questionable ventures? That is 'Death in Vegas.' "

"I'm saying I have pull with the Gangsters' owners, that's all."

Temple exchanged a glance with yellow-eyed Midnight Louise, who was frozen in mid-grooming, paw lifted, ear cocked. This was hot news.

"And," Nicky continued, "I happen to know this brouhaha about a city mob museum has spurred the owners of Gangsters, the best little undermarketed hotel-casino in town, not the limo service of the same name, to launch a redo, taking and running with the mob theme barefaced, instead of resorting to pussyfooting around and 'redacting' history."

"Oh, my God," said Van, turning as pale as her taffy-colored hair, and sitting.

"Sweet," said Temple. "That publicity campaign could rock."

Even Midnight Louise emitted a surprised little squeak, which only Temple heard.

She had an ear for little nothings of the feline sort.

CHAPTER 4
WHERE LOUIE USED TO . . .

I am sunning my battered frame by the cool aquamarine length of my private pool on the Circle Ritz grounds when a shadow falls over me.

Shadows in Las Vegas are as rare as mint in a marijuana patch, so I know without opening my eyes that something ugly and unexpected is hovering over me.

I snick out all eight of my front shivs without a sound and open one green peeper.

Hmph. A jowly black face with a five o'clock shadow of dog doo-doo brown dominates my field of vision. Same color spats and gloves. Reddened eye-whites. Big white teeth fresh from the dental tech's brushing, but no minty afterbreath. Instead, I sniff the reek of raw meat and desiccated pig's ear, maybe even some pansy kibble product.

Yup. It is a dog. A big 'un. Runs maybe 140, like a middleweight. Makes *me* want to run, but my ribs are still bruised from the derring-do, save-the-maiden stuff at the end of my previous case, and I do not feel like it.

"Dead dogs wear plaid," I say, uncrossing my mitts and preparing to carve a red tartan pattern into his ugly mug.

"I heard you were big for your boots," he growls.

A glob of drool hits my shiny black lapel.

That is it.

I am up on my feet and braced for serious skin surgery. I may be a lightweight compared to this yobbo, but I am faster on my tootsies and have more hidden razors than a pimp with a shaving fetish.

"Hold it, Shorty," the bruiser harfs. "I would love to staple your pinballs to the teak decking, but I am making like a St. Bernard here."

"You are carrying hard liquor?"

"Naw, a message. Okay? Jeez, lighten up."

That is a physical impossibility, both in my coat color and attitude, as both of them are the always-fashionable black. But I sit on my threatened pinballs and wait for this dude to sling some serious trash talk.

"So sing."

He pants out the message in that annoying, excited whine dogs get, no matter how large or small, nearly knocking me over with concentrated drool-breath.

"I am the construction-site watchdog on

some shoring-up work out at Lake Mead, see? So I am patrolling and minding my business, which is being prepared to tear the throat out of any trespassing human, when I am accosted by one of your sort."

I nod, impressed. It would take a lot for even me to accost a Rottweiler on patrol. Whoever is trying to contact me must have stones. And gravel for brains. Or be desperate.

"Your kind is not in my job description," the big dog goes on, "so I let him live long enough to sing a song or two. Turns out he has breached my territory deliberately. I gotta admit I am surprised. He appeals to my sense of duty to the human race . . . the ones who are not violating my masters' territory, that is. I agree that when I am off duty and driven back to town I will take a stroll to this Circle Ritz residence and lay some info on one Midnight Louie. I figure that is you. Cool joint."

Well, now we are chatting as guys will do. I retract the shivs and redact the tough talk.

"Mighty cross-species nice of you," I say. "You ever hear of a dude in your line of work, but a little different? Drug and explosive sniffer. Small fella with a mighty snout. One of those Liz Taylor wrist ornaments. Called Nose E."

"Oh, him. Maltese. About my paw-print size. Yeah. He does not do legwork. Purse-pooch

46

detail. I know *of* him. Smarts and nerve, but not my kind of protection-racket guy. Neither are you, no offense."

"None taken, Mr.?"

"Butch."

Right. "So, Butch, what is the message, and who had the nerve to walk up to you and ask you to play passenger pigeon?"

"The message is that a human body part has turned up in Lake Mead, and someone has to clue in the local constabulary. Apparently you are good at communicating with humans. Me, I do not find it worth my while. I do my job, keep my nose clean, give out my lumps, and gulp down my steak tartar on the hoof or, off duty, as a postwork treat."

"Same here," I growl.

My Miss Temple would be appalled by my demeanor, but guys must intimidate guys.

"I need to investigate this for my own self. Where do I find this snitch of yours?" I ask.

"Hercules Construction project, near Temple Bar, at an eatery called Three O'Clock Louie's."

I nearly do a cardiac swan dive. Every word is familiar, from the site on Lake Mead that by odd chance echoes my beloved roommate's name, to a restaurant that bears a moniker close to my own.

Butch chuckles deep in his massive throat.

"I thought I would shock the black kneesocks off you. This has been worth the hike. My 'snitch' and your contact is the dude named after the restaurant, Three O'Clock Louie."

"My good dog," I say, having recovered. "The reverse is true. The restaurant is named after him."

"Whaddayou know? I figured you were a hairball off the old hide, but I did not know they are naming restaurants after your kind nowadays. It is not as if your old man is the Taco Bell Chihuahua, may he rest in peace and up to his knickers in puppy biscuits."

"Neither are you, buddy. Now be a good dog and tell me when your construction crew is making the next run out to Temple Bar on Lake Mead."

"Temple Bar. Dopey name."

I hold my temper down and my shivs in.

He harfs on. "I am off duty and actually AWOL right now. Just follow me to the yard, and you can hop the next outgoing cement mixer."

"Thanks, but I will hop a gravel truck any day. I do not go for rotating rides."

"Just kidding, pal," Butch says, slavering himself a river on our landlady Miss Electra Lark's new cedar decking.

The sun is pretty high and hot for the haired set now.

This is the worst time of day for a long sweltering drive in an un-air-conditioned truck cab, but duty — and Three O'Clock Louie — call.

Who's your daddy?

I might not have sired Miss Midnight Louise, as much as she would wish to hold that over my head, but there is no doubt I am a nugget off the old noggin of Mr. Three O'Clock Louie, his own self.

CHAPTER 5
SIMPLY . . . ARTISTO

"Don't take my word for the Gangsters' possibilities," Nicky said, now that he had a stupefied and silent audience of two. "I consulted an expert. Exhibit A. Be nice, ladies."

Temple eyed Van. "Did Nicky just tell us to 'be nice ladies'?"

"If so," Van answered, "it isn't going to happen."

By then Nicky had stepped to the office door and swept it open as if pulling back a curtain.

For another stupefied moment a tall dark-haired man in a white tropical suit stood poised on the threshold, looking, at first blush — a very bold blush — like the eleventh Fontana brother.

"I present," Nicky said, "our multimedia artiste, Señor Santiago, direct from Rio de Janeiro."

By then Temple had taken in the glitzy

silver stripes in the newcomer's corona of long, gel-spiked hair and the black silk shirt under the pale suit, accessorized by a flamingo pink tie.

"No 'Señor,' " the vision announced. "I am simply . . . Santiago."

"And who exactly is 'Simply Santiago'?" Van demanded of her exuberant spouse.

Before Nicky could answer, Santiago stepped inside, producing from under his right arm a slim white ostrich-skin portfolio that matched his white ostrich-skin cowboy boots.

"A master of many media and slave of nothing commonplace," he announced. "My curriculum vitae, madam."

Temple watched Van nervously, remembering the last one-named "conceptual artist" to hit Las Vegas. The unlamented "Domingo" had smothered the Strip landmarks in pink plastic flamingos. Not the Crystal Phoenix, however.

The first and foremost temporary environmental art creator, internationally famous Christo of the wrapped South Pacific island and planted umbrella park in Japan, had a lot of cheap imitators to answer for. But, frankly, many of Las Vegas's "new" hotel upgrades and attractions turned out to be temporary, just like the dismantled Jackson

51

Action Attraction several floors below.

Van held up the one slender sheet of paper encased by the luxury portfolio.

"Web site addresses," Santiago declaimed. He didn't seem to speak, but to pronounce. "All relevant information today must be seen, not read. Print is kaput."

"You had to print out this page," Van pointed out.

"Only to show you, madam, what you have at your fingertips, downloaded to your computer screen."

Van turned to view her twenty-four-inch flat screen, blossoming with lavish architectural images of futuristic Brasilia, the first Third World city of the future, dwarfed nowadays by the wonders of Dubai and the Far East.

"You're an architect," Van said, still trying to file her visitor in a logical category.

"I? Santiago? No! Not simply. Architecture is a plebeian art, easily outmoded, hopelessly physical. I created the image collage in three-D, had you the means to view it."

Nicky finally contributed an explanation. "Santiago is a multimedia entrepreneur. What he creates is light years beyond even the two-thousand-four-upgraded Freemont Street Experience downtown in Glitter Gulch."

Van was still clutching the bottom line. "That was a seventeen-million-dollar upgrade, Nicky. We can't begin to compete with that, and especially not during this economic downturn."

"That's just it," he answered. "We need to create only a limited chunk of light and animation for this hotel. It'll be perfect for the Chunnel of Crime underground link I'm planning between the spiffed-up Gangsters and the CP."

"CP?" Santiago inquired politely.

"Where we are now," Temple put in. "The Crystal Phoenix Hotel and Casino."

"Ah. This is reason for the neon Big Bird on the roof," said Santiago. "I can redesign that funky chicken into a swan, a bird of paradise to outdazzle the huge neighboring hotels, and I do mean neigh*borrring*. Santiago and the Santiago Consortium have come to this amusing oasis of entertainment to make fireworks out of these dated light and liquid-animation shows."

"Do you do flamingos?" Temple asked sweetly.

"And you are . . . ?" Santiago asked.

Santiago had not allowed time for introductions, but Nicky recognized sarcasm when he heard it, so he swiftly stepped in as Temple stood to shake hands.

53

"This is our public-relations whiz, Miss Temple Barr."

"Miss Barr," Santiago repeated, with a bow of his zebra-striped mane. He turned to Van, who was no longer stupefied and who had stood to exchange the omitted courtesies. "Señora Fontana."

"I am Van von Rhine," Van responded, retrieving her hand.

"Von Rhine. A German name, surely. Spelled as in . . . rhinestone?" he inquired.

Nicky answered. "Spelled as in b-o-s-s. *Jefe* in your native tongue."

"Chieftain," Santiago said, with a sage nod.

Van just lifted her eyebrows, which were a flaxen blonde, so it was a subtle gesture of polite interest. Boyz might fret about titles; she was interested in authority.

"How did Nicky find you, Mr. Santiago?"

"No, no. Simply Santiago. I am accessible to all at the same level. And so is my work."

"He found me," Nicky said bluntly.

"Indeed?"

Van did not like that, Temple knew, even before she saw the faint parallel lines between those almost-as-faint brows. It underlined the perfumed air of "huckster" that oozed from Simply Santiago like . . . really high-grade motor oil.

"You seem," Van told Santiago, "to have more of an inside track with my husband than I do."

"It's not like that, Van," Nicky said. "I was kicking the idea around with just family. Um, my family, and Santiago had already contacted Gangsters with some redo ideas."

"The Gangsters' contact being . . . ?" Van asked.

"Not me. Aldo and the boys. Gangsters Limo Service has been doing gangbuster business despite the recession. They were wondering how to let that cachet spill over to the boutique hotel. And maybe even the Phoenix, in the most, ah, delicate of ways. Santiago has some killer concepts and execution."

" 'Killer concepts. Execution.' " Van's tone had gone scorchingly serene. "So appropriate to a mobster-themed limo service, hotel, and now our heretofore 'classy' enterprise."

Nicky was a born enthusiast, shrewd but hooked on new ideas, new plans, new people. Also on selling them all to other people, especially his wife. He was not about to be singed by a dose of in-house skepticism.

"Van, baby, this'll be great. Santiago has set up an audiovisual display in his suite that will knock your socks off."

"His suite?"

"In our hotel," Nicky explained. "You don't even have to walk outside to get the full picture."

"The Fontana Suite, I presume," Van said, naming the hotel's prime quarters as she stood. She nodded at Temple. "Come along after you finish that proposal."

Temple watched the trio leave, Nicky holding the door so he could exit last and favor her with a knowing wink.

As soon as the door shut, Temple perched on Van's yummy white leather executive chair she'd spotted Santiago eyeing, and started a Web search, as Van had meant her to stay and do. There was no "proposal" to finish. The subject of the search, of course, was Santiago.

Temple was surprised to find that he was not a flake at first sight.

Simply Santiago was a larger-than-life self-made South American entrepreneur and inventor, the Richard Branson of the southern hemisphere. Born Tomás Santiago in modest lower-middle-class circumstances in São Paolo, by age twenty he'd founded a Web-design business. Now a youthful-looking fifty, he supported projects from slum clearance to advanced communications and the more spectacular art forms, like emo music, futuristic media, and the flashiness of Rio's famous Carnavals.

His trademark white suit, his dramatic face and figure were prominent where big money gathered, at yacht and horse races, international soccer matches, and in Brasilia, the country's ultramodern and also dazzlingly white city. He made the Fontana brothers pale by comparison, and that was going some.

Temple couldn't imagine a more likely candidate to build on Gangsters Limo Service's hip and successful reputation, and upgrade that stylish mob pizzazz to the attached hotel and Las Vegas. In fact, her only question was why such an international bigwig would want to work for a modest boutique hotel.

The answer came as she darkened the screen and rose from Van's desk. Follow the money. That was always the key to motivations everywhere. Vegas's big spenders were strapped for tourists and cash, sitting atop billions of dollars of idled projects. Santiago could make a splash at Gangsters and remake it as a showroom for his gaudy media expertise as well as a more focused and successful enterprise.

Van had wanted Temple's assessment of this guy, his flashy ego, and, most important, his business and personal history. Temple would have to dig far deeper, but on first glance he was the Prince Charming of Chutzpah for good reason.

She headed down a floor to the Fontana Suite, happy she could endorse Nicky's instincts and eager to see what Simply Santiago had to show them.

CHAPTER 6
TEMPTATIONS OF TEMPLE BAR

Max had set the Mondeo's driver's seat in a
position of slight recline to accommodate
his six-foot-four frame . . . if he hadn't lost
an inch or two in height with his leg injuries.
Taking physical stock and measurements
could wait until later.

At the moment, he felt invigorated, happy
he could stretch his spine and legs and be
driving . . . in control and reasonably secure
for the first time since he'd awakened in the
Swiss clinic a week ago, not knowing who
he was.

They drove through a cobblestoned tour-
isty area of shops and art galleries on Dublin's southern side while Gandolph consulted maps on his cell phone.

"Lunch?" he asked, looking up.

"You're not as pretty as my last lunch
companion, but why not?"

"You drive, Max. I'll direct."

"Got it."

"You don't seem to have problems keeping to the left."

"Probably like riding a bicycle," Max said. "Once learned, it engraves itself on your brain."

"Then I'm glad this trip of ours is taking you down an engraved memory lane."

"I can't say I remember this part of Dublin at all, but back then, it was probably shabby and in need of restoration, considering how popular and tidy it is now."

"They say the cobblestones date back to the seventeenth century."

"Our quest hardly needs to look that far backward," Max said, driving slowly to avoid pedestrians.

"The next right will bring us to a car park. Can you walk about a bit?"

"Need to," Max said.

The day sported an encouraging swath of blue sky when they strolled back to the main square. Sunlight gleamed off the paint and chrome of lightweight urban motorcycles herded and chained against a lamppost. It glinted from the clear glasses of passersby. Few wore sunglasses, as Max did. For him, they were an instant disguise and a screen from behind which he could examine the scene and its thronging extras.

"I'd forgotten the first-floor flower boxes,"

Max commented. "The beauteous, bounteous hanging flowers draping every pub sign in the British Isles."

"You do remember that floor levels are counted with 'one' starting above street level."

"Such bizarre small changes of custom," Max said, "but telling. Oh," he added, stopping as he saw where Gandolph was heading, "the lady in red. A bit gaudy, but welcome in a land of frequent gray weather."

The pub ahead occupied a curving corner spot, its sweeping exterior enameled scarlet except for a deep green background at the top, bearing the large gilded letters of its name.

"The Temple Bar," Max read aloud.

Gandolph was silent.

"Can't say I've ever been here before," Max went on. "There's a Temple Bar in London, isn't there?"

"And in Las Vegas," Gandolph said in an odd, cautious tone. "Two, you could say."

"What's with the same name everywhere?"

"Here," said Gandolph, "the tourist guides report that a family named Templeton lived in the square in the sixteen hundreds. Temple Bar in London was a gate to the city in earlier centuries, later becoming part of the four Inns of Court, the city's legal

61

conclave."

"You are a bundle of trivia today, Garry. And what about Las Vegas, which I should remember something of?"

"Temple Bar is a landing on Lake Mead. In the Arizona section, really, but it attracts Vegas tourists."

"I doubt this place does," Max said, after another long gaze at the blazing wall of red.

"Ah," Gandolph enthused, "but the oysters and Guinness are famous here; the music is traditional and free and has won the Irish pub music crown for years; and the 'craic' is unbeatable."

"Craic?"

"The local gossip and josh and chatter, which any passing patron can join into."

"I'd prefer to listen, and be drawn into the food and drink."

By then they'd entered the set-back double red doors and found a tiny free table. Amid the manic music of fiddle and harmonica and drums and the shouted neighboring craic, the pair ordered and ate, imbibing Irish laughter along with the oysters and smoked salmon and Gubbeen cheese and molasses-dark Guinness. They listened rather than talked, for once.

"Was there a reason," Max asked later, as he threaded the Mondeo back through the

Temple Bar area and drove out of the city, "for us to stop there?"

"To fuel up on food and drink and happy music for our journey," Gandolph said, his shrug saying, "Isn't it obvious?"

"And to fuel up my memory?" Max asked.

Gandolph looked over with a rueful smile. "I always have hopes on that."

"So I didn't pass the Temple Bar test."

"This journey is not a test, Max. No pass or fail. Just what is."

Silent but somehow content, he and Gandolph continued north into the fringes of County Fingal, forging into less traffic the farther they went. Above them, massed clouds skated across the sky, creating alternating slashes of sunshine and shadow on the sweeping green and gray-stone countryside.

A Chieftains CD on the car player alternated cheery and soulful Irish folk music, jigs segueing into ballads.

"The song selection is setting the stage for my split personalities?" Max asked wryly.

Garry Randolph looked calm and relaxed in the passenger seat. Gandolph the Great's magician-nimble fingers, though, were tapping the central console in a nervous stutter that didn't quite keep time with the addictively rhythmic Celtic music.

"I'm looking for signs of the careless, passionate young man you were, yes," Garry admitted. "Oh, you fell in love with Ireland when you and your cousin, Sean Kelly, drove from County Clare to Dublin, diagonally across the glorious rolling scenery. Seventeen, fresh out of high school, and on your own. Sean was eighteen. Why did you graduate younger?"

"I can't remember why, or arriving here then, but I must have skipped a year in grade school. Somehow."

"So, you were mature for your age. Yet a bit raw. Socially awkward."

"Got me. You're the historian."

"You were still a virgin."

Max laughed. "What an embarrassing thing to bring up now, Garry. I *know* I'm not anymore, at least, from recent events."

Max's impish grin met Garry's stone face.

"You have no idea who Ms. Schneider really is or what her agenda was, or still might be," Garry said. "You were foolish, Max. That kind of sexual bravura got you and Sean tangled up with the IRA all those years ago when you *were* green and seventeen. You don't need to act impulsively anymore."

"Maybe I did, just then." Max's fingers flexed on the steering wheel. "All right.

You've briefed me on the short form of my personal and professional history with Ireland. I know you entered the picture *after* my dalliance with Kathleen O'Connor and after Sean waited out our tryst in a Northern Ireland pub, which an IRA bomb blew up, and with it my cousin, to smithereens of pint-glass shards and bone while he was nursing a lonely Guinness."

"O'Toole's."

Max flashed him a confused look.

"The bombed pub's name was O'Toole's. Notorious now. Never rebuilt."

"Okay. I can believe the Irish colleen we co-courted was a modern-day Mata Hari playing guilt trips with the pair of us, or even that she hated teenage boy virgins or American naïveté or something enough to set one of us up for the kill and the other for a world of survivor's pain and guilt. I can even believe I tracked the three pub bombers and got them killed in a hail of British troop bullets. Why we're going back to Northern Ireland at this late date I don't get. That's one insane war that's wound down."

"I'm following your instructions," Garry said, "on what to do if anything ever happened to you in the mortal way: find and follow the trail of Kathleen O'Connor, her history and motives. So that's what we're doing."

"The man who wanted that may not be dead now, but he doesn't remember the why or wherefore of such a request. From what you tell me, I'm the one who's left the 'love of my life' in Vegas thinking I've vanished. This . . . redhead."

"Her first name is Temple."

"Even the name is just an improper noun to my blasted memory. Is she Greek or Roman?"

"Neither. One of a kind."

"Well, then, I should definitely be winging back to the U.S. immediately to explain myself."

"Right into the hands of your attempted murderers."

"Not safe there. Not safe here. From what you said I did to enrage the IRA years ago, I shouldn't be here even now."

"Probably." Garry sighed and eased out his seat-belt strap, which cut diagonally and cruelly across a middle-aged girth. "But a promise is a promise."

Max eyed a glimpse of the Irish Sea on the right, glinting like steel gray glass. "Does she have a Web site?" he asked more quietly.

"Kathleen O'Connor?"

"No. This Temple."

"Probably. She runs a freelance public-relations business. I hadn't thought of that. She'd have a Web page. When we get to the hotel we can look it up. No distractions now. We're on the mission you assigned me, and are perhaps half an hour from the Little Flower Convent of Saint Therese."

Max rolled his eyes. "A convent? Don't tell me! The nuns there wear habits to this day, and it's still as Catholic as the Pope. Predictably Ireland, God bless it."

Max noticed Garry's features settling into deep worry lines he guessed were new to those comfortable, intelligent features. Because of him.

"Nothing is predictable in our line of endeavor, Max," Garry said. "Not the present and not the past. Especially not the past. I'll thank you not to swear me to fulfill any last requests in future."

CHAPTER 7
LIGHTS, ACTION

Temple approached the Fontana Suite's double doors, treated like the entrance to a mansion, with etched crystal sidelights and brass torchères, wondering whether to ring the old-fashioned doorbell or just walk in.

An ear-piercing burst of automatic weapons fire first made her jump, then storm through the doors. She immediately leaped down and to the side, tumbling to the floor.

The firing stopped so abruptly that the silence hurt her ears in turn. At least she'd brought her iPhone, if not her purse, with the intention of making some quick notes, and could summon help.

A strange slapping sound came next from the other room. Temple rolled onto her bare, bony knees, not appreciating the cold and rough-textured slate entry floor. She rose awkwardly while pulling her skirt down and tried to tiptoe on her T-strap heels into the marble-floored main room.

Van and Nicky were clapping. Santiago stood near a massive steel-topped table, beaming like a São Paulo noonday sun.

A moderately sized flat-screen TV sat on the burnished metal tabletop, which also supported a fifteen-inch-high cityscape of miniature constructions, an elaborate architect's model.

Temple looked around thoroughly and could see no source for the weapons fire. Apparently a gangland hit was not in progress.

"Won't the tunnel magnify the sound effects unbearably?" Van was asking.

"Totally programmable," Nicky reassured her. "Santiago just wanted to get our full attention."

Temple thought she should declare her arrival.

"He certainly got mine from the hall outside the doors. I thought the Chicago Outfit was back to take over . . . or else it was the feared first terrorist offensive on Vegas."

Santiago spread his white-suited arms like the statue of Christ of the Andes overlooking Rio's harbor. He laughed heartily.

"No, PR lady, it was just me and my media creations. Come closer and see."

That was rather like an invitation from an

albino tarantula, Temple thought, but she walked over the marble flooring to the silken Asian rug to join Van and Nicky at the hypermodern steel-topped table.

She was puzzled that the centerpiece TV screen was only a modest forty-six inches wide. Modest size didn't seem to match Santiago's egocentric, open-armed style. As she got closer, Temple spotted a twinkle in his deep hazel-green eyes. He was laughing at her . . . and at himself and his poses.

He reminded her of Max, wearing his Mystifying Max green contact lenses for disguise and his magic act. Max hadn't done that for ages, concealed his natural blue eyes since then, not since he quit performing two years ago. Temple wondered why her subconscious had resurrected that outdated image. She'd have to do penance and be sure to phone Matt in Chicago tonight. Or at least watch his taped segment on today's *The Amanda Show* at home before bedtime.

"Are you any relation to Flamin— I mean, Domingo?" she asked Santiago.

"That charlatan?" he asked, still laughing. "Only in a gift for thinking big, they tell me. This will be 'big' on a small scale, as you are, Miss Temple, and as is the Crystal Phoenix and Gangsters. Here, Santiago is

70

forced to be confined, in his thinking and the space he has to manipulate. That is what so intrigues me about this project. 'Big is bad' today. Wasteful. Costly. Santiago will make magic on a small scale. See this."

He gestured at the miniature mock-up. Everything displayed was fashioned from white matte board, so it was mysterious and sculptural. Temple moved her spike heels delicately over the thick-piled rug so she didn't turn an ankle. Who could resist 3-D miniatures, so like Christmas dollhouses one had never gotten but had coveted in department-store Christmas windows? A four-boy family wasn't much into dollhouses when it came to the only girl.

"Oh!" Temple recognized a mock-up of the Crystal Phoenix that resembled the Ice Queen's palace from the Hans Christian Andersen fairy tale. That construction anchored one end of the slick silver table. At the other stood another fifteen-story hotel, Gangsters, with low additions for the attached limo service's office and garages. Between them stretched an elongated spiral of white construction paper.

"You must imagine," Santiago said in a hushed, hypnotic voice. "You must imagine this graceful tunnel as belowground, a swift, silent conduit between Gangsters and the

Crystal Phoenix, an underground mono-rail . . . no, an American-underworld horizontal time tunnel."

"A ride?" Van asked, her voice sounding unconvinced.

"No," Santiago said. "A fast car chase . . . with intermissions. What is this wonderful American expression from the gangland days — being 'taken for a ride'? The clients of Gangsters shall have the long-lost experience of that pleasantly helpless, thrilling state so devoutly to be desired."

While he paused to let that sink in, Temple and Van crossed glances. Was this guy selling his ideas or seduction? If a combo, that was in the Las Vegas tradition, for sure.

"So people will be speeding around in underground limousines?" Nicky asked, immersed in the mechanics of the process more than the sensations.

"It may seem so," Santiago said. "The 'limousines' will look like motorcars, like these 'stretch' vehicles, only from the nineteen thirties, forties, fifties, and even sixties. But they will ride like a dream, on rails. On the tunnel walls outside their smoked-glass windows, scenes of iconic American gangster days will unreel before their eyes . . . the Saint Valentine's Day Massacre, the deaths of Bonnie and Clyde and Bugsy Siegel, all the delightfully gory happenings of days of yore. But they will unreel *backward*. It shall be death and resurrection, a theme the very name of the Crystal Phoenix evokes, yes? It will not be morbid, but the happy ending all Americans crave, for themselves and the world. Yes? All people cannot take their eyes off a disaster. All people then hope to see it reversed. The Chunnel of Crime, as you so colorfully christened it, Mr. Fontana, will be the Ride of Resurrection."

"We wouldn't call it by either term," Temple said. "Box-office poison. Just say it's 'Gangsters limos go underground for a thrill ride you can't refuse.' " *Or something,* she thought.

"I like that," Van said, as if relieved to voice a first positive reaction.

"Yeah," Nicky told Santiago. "Temple's a genius at 'spin.' You build it and she'll call it something no one can resist, and they will come."

"Oh," Santiago said, reassessing Temple. "She is a very powerful woman, then. The smaller the explosive device the more concentrated the effect, I have always believed."

"We're not going to have 'explosions' in this . . . attraction," Van said.

"Of course not." Santiago was definite.

"Sounds — yes. Action, motion — yes. Speed — yes. Thrills — of course. But it is all merely show, as you say."

He pointed a sleek silver remote at the hi-def TV. The dark screen jumped into life, a continual sweeping pan of what Temple would call an existential gangster movie — part comic superhero movie, part black-and-white vintage hits and chases, the *Fast & Furious* of mob nostalgia, accented by metallic, symbolic splashes of red, all to a frenetic Carnaval musical beat.

All three stood mesmerized and shell-shocked. Temple was aware of a layer of immense stage-set detail behind the hurtling cars and street scenes and running, shooting figures. There was a 3-D feel, although none of them wore assisting glasses.

"This would require an age limit," Van said.

Santiago shrugged. "The family approach was tried in Las Vegas and failed. As well as impose a dress code on Carnaval in Rio. I would say, what you call PG-13. But no need to worry: this is not a ride for infants in strollers."

"Nor all women tourists," Temple pointed out.

"Women shop and eat in Vegas. Men gamble and seek excitement. Many women too, no?"

His intriguing-colored eyes bored into hers. It was either a challenge or a come-on or an intimation that he knew she was not a stranger to the aftermath of violence, at least.

Oh, yes. Tomás Santiago needed a lot more looking into, a lot more *serious* looking into. Maybe Detective Alch could be persuaded to do that. Or Frank Bucek in the FBI's L.A. office, Matt's former seminary teacher.

Temple smelled something highly fishy about this artsy entrepreneur from the tropics. She knew that many South American cities were rife with crime and corruption. The white suit could almost be a disguise.

"That, my friends," Santiago declared inaccurately, as far as Temple was concerned, "is just the suggested canvas of our new Las Vegas sensation."

She and Van were not "sold," although Nicky was still pop-eyed enamored of the sample show. It had all the action, all the motion of the Dire Straits song "Walk of Life." Temple recalled a line about "Down in the tunnels, trying to make it pay."

Wasn't that the "Talk of Life, and Death," here? Violence and double-talk? Turning the day time into the night? Peddling mayhem, not history.

Temple didn't think shopping and eating would shut up her objections.

"Of course," Santiago said, clicking to another program, "you can't appreciate the three-D of those scenes if you're not riding in the magic limos."

"Magic limos," Nicky repeated. "I like that phrase."

Santiago gave him the exotic-elixir-salesman wink and hit another button on the remote control.

The screen became a black slate of sliding, continuous motion, like the tinted windows of a limo.

"A blank window?" Van objected.

"Ah, yes, dear lady, but it is far from blank. It is a porthole on the past, a magic slate for the future. Behold."

"Behold" the hokey, Temple thought, but even her eyes were glued to Santiago's TV screen.

For a moment the dim windows looked as if raindrops were sliding across their surface at seventy miles per hour.

Then . . . the drops resolved into a human face, a human face under a fedora brim, shaping itself from the curved window into a three-dimensional presence, a recognizable, talking, three-dimensional presence that seemed to leap out of the TV screen into the room with them, the same size as any human present.

Nicky sounded both awed and leery. "Okay, Santiago, I know you're a media wizard, but how'd you get Frank Sinatra to do a personal appearance on your mini movie screen?"

"God," Frank was saying, "where the hell is my regular ride? Look," Ol' Blue Eyes said, staring straight into every eye present. "I appreciate you giving me a lift in your subterranean U-boat here, folks. The Sands goofed on priming my limo, and I gotta get to the Crystal Phoenix for Deano's solo show. Shirley and Marilyn will be there, and we're all gonna have a time of it, right?"

The voice was that resonant speaking baritone heard round the world.

"How did you reconstruct the Chairman of the Board?" Nicky asked.

"Why?" Van asked.

"The mob controlled and socialized with a lot of Italian singers and celebrities in the forties to the sixties because they owned the nightclubs and theaters," Temple answered. Las Vegas history was her business. "Sinatra and Dean Martin outlived the mob-boss era. Remember, JFK was sleeping with Chicago's Sam Giancana's mistress."

" 'Camelot' corrupted. I don't want to remember that," Van said.

"We'll keep the Kennedys out of your zipped-up club-car tour of the 'Chunnel of Crime,' right?" Nicky asked Santiago.

"Of course." Santiago reassured him. "We'll only revive the infamous dead who are well known for their Las Vegas associations."

"What about Jersey Joe Jackson?" Van asked.

"Jersey Joe . . . who?"

"A minor figure," Temple told him, "affiliated with the Crystal Phoenix when it was the Joshua Tree Hotel back in the day."

"What is this 'Joshua Tree'?"

"A big, tree-like desert cactus," she explained. "About as uninteresting as Jersey Joe Jackson."

The first underground attraction had borne his name and gone belly up. Temple didn't want to jinx this new project that Nicky had his heart set upon.

CHAPTER 8
LAKE MEAN

It is about an hour's drive from Vegas to Temple Bar, which is actually in — *shhh!* — Arizona.

State lines are iffy around the meandering shoreline of Lake Mead and the soaring bulk of Hoover Dam. They are easier to find on a map or as the crow flies.

Imagine how thrilled I am to see roadside signs advertising Temple Bar Days, apparently a new annual April shindig. They spelled my roommate's name wrong, though, using only one *r* in *Barr*.

They are always doing that to me as well.

Louis! I see my name written that way again and again.

What do they think I am? A foppish French monarch with a tail of Roman numerals attached to his first name like fleas? I am all-American and the One and Only *moi*, thank you. *Merci. Arrivederci, Roman.*

Lou-ee. That is my name. Plain and fancy.

Capital L, small *o-u-i-e*. Such a meaning-laden name. Except for an *a*, it is a compact and elegant assembly of all the vowels in the English language. A portmanteau name, as the French might put it. Okay. No *a*. But I have always been a *the*, rather than a mere *a*.

The feline PI in Vegas, as opposed to *a* feline PI in Vegas.

I suppose Miss Midnight Louise would take exception to my claim, but she is a rank upstart. I was in this town first and foremost. In fact, the way she tells it, she would not *be* here were it not for me and my unsanctioned love life.

Anyway, all my observations of the physical sort on this road trip are confined to craning my neck at banners visible in the upper area of the windshield. I am a stowaway, riding behind the gearbox amid the perfume of oily rags, dusty boots, and Red Man chewing tobacco.

The radio blares out "Redneck Woman" to match, while I picture what my Miss Temple would think of my current . . . er, ambience. Thus amused, I wait for the driver to gather up his invoices before dismounting. I have about half a second to tumble outside on his work-boot heels before the heavy truck door will bisect me like a bug.

I hover behind his sweat-stained seat, lunging and retreating twice as he remembers another piece of paperwork and turns back to claw it into his grubby mitt.

Although it is only April, every little reek is magnified by the sun's heat beating down on hot metal like it was my personal toaster oven.

At last we both set foot on the desert floor and go our separate ways. He stomps over to a mobile-home office, where the cement mixer disgorges Butch, who immediately trots off on his rounds. I scuttle into the gravel truck's shade to inhale a few deep breaths of the sage and creosote bushes.

The Mojave Desert is not my favorite perfumery, not like a New York New York Hotel delicatessen, say. But I will take Ma Nature over man-made smells any day.

When I edge into the open to explore, I quickly discover that Temple Bar is not the place I used to know.

Oh, the marina and café are still there, and so are the rambling wooden verandas of Three O'Clock Louie's restaurant and bar. But the shoreline boats are bobbing a couple football-field lengths from where they did when last I saw them, and there is a long rambling *bridge* from the highway to Three O'Clock Louie's. Over dry desert!

What the hell — ? Oh. Three O'Clock's does not even look operational. Good news for the café next door scarfing up all the business. Bad news for my esteemed sire of the same name. Butch claimed my dear old dad had sent for me, but maybe his license has expired by now too. Sudden accidental death is not unknown to our kind.

With these dire thoughts, I start padding over the wooden bridge toward the deserted restaurant. I suppose in these hard times many eating establishments have faded away like old soldiers, but I am getting worried about the old dudes who founded and ran this place. Collectively, they were once known as the Glory Hole Gang, and they had "retired" to one of Nevada's innumerable ghost towns before being persuaded back into what passes for civilized society these days.

Come to think of it, I have not heard any fresh reports of Jersey Joe Jackson's ectoplasm showing up in the Crystal Phoenix Ghost Suite either. I will have to get Midnight Louise on that as soon as I get back.

Meanwhile, I have arrived at the restaurant proper, once on the lapping waters of Lake Mead and now as high and dry as an old hippie on weed. The building is shuttered and obviously empty.

So who was around to feed Three O'Clock enough to keep fur and claw together, so he could survive to send Butch for me? Certainly not Eightball O'Rourke, sometimes Vegas PI. Nor his old-time cohorts, Wild Blue Pike, Pitchblende O'Hara, Cranky Ferguson, and Spuds Lonnigan.

I cannot believe all these old guys have just vanished, but they would be living on cactus-spine toothpicks *(ouch!)* and sand had they remained here. I gaze with damp eyes under the veranda tables where I once was wont to lounge, snagging fallen slivers of chicken. Crab. Lobster.

Alas, poor Arthropod, I knew him, shook pincers with him once. Or her. It is hard to discern the fine points with critters that low on the evolutionary scale. You could say we had only a passing acquaintance, but you are what you eat.

I wander to the end of the line, the deck-cum-pier where boats used to anchor and gilt-scaled carp practically walked on water to cadge bread crumbs and popcorn from tourists.

What a fishing hole this was! I imagine how Three O'Clock would hang over the deck rim, batting at a flashing fin. Of course, the old boy was too aged and well fed to hook anything.

If I bend over the wooden edge now and let my imagination out to play, fill the sere sand with sparkling blue water, I can even see

Three O'Clock's white-whiskered black face, the mirror image of mine, reflected back.

How could no one have notified me the old fishing hole was gone? And now maybe my old man has vanished for good.

Then my imagined reflection smacks me one in the kisser.

"Do not gawk, boy!" an irascible voice orders. "You will give away my position. I did not get you all the way out here to find myself scooped up by do-gooders hustling me off to the Big House."

Ah . . . "Three O'Clock? Is it really you? This place is a ghost town."

"It is your daddy, all right, lad," he says, digging in his brittle claws and scrabbling up over the decking to join me on the dried wooden slats. "If you had shown one whisker of concern for your forebear, you would have known the lakeside food and drink biz was taking a dive with the Lake Mead water level. You would have come out here to do an elder check."

"Speaking of 'elder,' where are the old dudes who ran the place?"

"Skedaddled, with the carp and tourists. Even a lot of those boats next door have been foreclosed on."

"The Glory Hole Gang did not take you along when they left?"

"I elected to hide out and keep my hard-won territory, such as it no longer is."

"The Strip is not exactly jumping with joy juice anymore, either," I point out, "but it is better pickings than a marooned empty restaurant. I am sure I could fix you up with one of the Circle Ritz residents."

I frown in deep thought. I do not want the old man on top of me and my doings, and the only sucker-inhabited cat-free unit I can think of on the spot is Mr. Matt's. Given the impending human cohabitation, I do not want a resident parent at my age and state of independence.

"No, no, no!" Three O'Clock is hissing mad. "I am not ready to steal some gullible human's rocking chair and place in the sun. I hear you have expanded your operation."

"My oper— Oh, you mean Midnight Investigations, Inc."

"You can always use an extra quartet of paws and pair of ears, I am sure, son."

"Look, Three O'Clock, as it happens, 'family' business is a lot on my mind right now, but I already have a junior partner. I am not looking for a senior partner."

"Well, I am not looking for a dead body, but I happen to have found one. I would not expect charity or for you to take on an aging relative out of the supposed kindness of your heart. I have brought my own case with me, and it is Murder One."

"Murder One?"

"And a dandy," he says, running a tattered claw through his snow-white whiskers. "Reeks with possibilities."

"Where?"

"Here, of course."

"Here?" I look around. "Deadwood does not count, Dad."

He snorts.

"And those tourists next door look about as lively as any tourists do lately."

His eyes are not the vivid emerald green I possess, but a watered-down version. Still, they flash in the sunlight.

"Care to trot those pampered Vegas Strip tootsies of yours over the dead lake bed? Your old man still can show you a thing or two."

I feel a frisson of interest. It is true that the retreating lake waters might have revealed a sunken treasure. Heck, a fully intact B-29 bomber has rested at the bottom of Lake Mead since an early scientific flight measuring sunspots dropped it there in 1948.

I doubt the lowered water level has given up the ghost that much, but who knows what baubles may have fallen overboard from the thousands of boating expeditions the lake has hosted? Rich dames? Big-time winners wearing gold baubles and bling?

Finders keepers has always been a favorite modus operandi of me and mine.

I shake the dust off my back and follow the old guy's scrawny tail into the pebble-strewn desert that ruled the roost around here until Hoover Dam made the mighty Colorado River into an artificial lake.

Now the water has dried up like the world-wide credit system, a matter of ecology mirroring economy.

I do not know what I expected to see. Maybe carp corpses glittering with solid gold scales. A few diamond rings that slipped from careless hands into the deep blue waters would be rewarding, but it looks as if the metal detectors have already scoured the surface, given the sand is burnished in circles as if a wax buffer had been over it.

So all I see is cracked yellow sand harder than stone and the same old, same old that spells M-o-j-a-v-e Desert. This once-submerged dirt is decorated by patches of burnt brown grass and a few scuzzy green areas, maybe moss where some moisture might have gathered. Beyond it the ringing low hills show a wide beige watermark I've heard called the lake's "bathtub ring." Mostly, the dry land is parched, marked only by the island of an abandoned rowboat trailing a desiccated fuse of rope and some small rock-like hummocks.

Manx, if I had wanted to walk on the moon, I would have applied to NASA!

And if I had wanted to chap my pads, I could have walked the Strip from one end to the other and at least had a few morsels of fast food out of it, either boxed or bagged on the hoof. Or a Paw and Claw dinner of mouse and lizard, not that I eat much that has not been fully prepared and is fit for human consumption these days.

The overhead sun beats down on our black coats. I pause to look back. The ersatz, ramshackle bulk of the restaurant seems far away. Even farther is the sparkle of blue shore and the bob of white boats next door. Add a bit of carp gold, and I would be a happy hiker.

As it is . . .

"Look here, Three O'Clock," I say. "I have developed pretty good distance eyesight from many long nights spent ogling the neon on the Strip. I can see a bright band of blue water that marks the lake's new water's edge. I can see enough sand and abandoned anchors and driftwood and plain old junk to background a *Pirates of the Caribbean* movie. But no hide nor hair of a dead body do I see. So you have no case."

"No?" Three O'Clock does the senior scamper and cackle to a spot ten yards farther on.

I slog over to examine an odd and unpromising "find" about the size of a picnic hamper for munchkins, except it is in no way appetizing.

"Daddy-o," I say, once again adopting Miss Midnight Louise's casual manner of addressing me, "what is this? Some carnival stilt-walker dumped his huge clown shoes and sticks cut off at the calf overboard. Maybe he was giving up the circus and made the grand gesture on Lake Mead. Maybe he was impressing a girl. Humans will do that."

By now Three O'Clock is having a senior tantrum, hissing and spitting.

"Did I sire something with kitty litter for brains? With the eyesight of a bat? The mental acuity of a hedgehog? The arrogance of a hedge-fund manager? Great Bast, help me, boy. You are a detective like I am a Fig Newton! Open your eyes and your mind."

The elderly require patience. I examine the poor old dude's precious find again.

Hmm. It is old like him; no wonder he is so attached. My initial description was not without merit. I sniff the upright sticks. There is a pair. Two. They are broken at the ends and tobacco stained. Or that color. They are embedded in a rock of some sort. Actually it is of a smoother surface and consistency than broken-off rock chunks. It is also the wrong color. Around here rocks are reddish.

So we have brown broken sticks in gray stone.

Three O'Clock slaps me on the shoulder blades as if I need a burping. "Well, Sam Spade?"

I nod slowly. You could knock me over with a carp tail.

"You are slamming homers in the right ballpark, Pops."

Pops? Where did I get that revolting nickname?

"Do not call me that, sonny," Three O'Clock growls. I do not blame him.

"Sorry, um, sire. You speak true. I mean, you are not telling any fibs. In fact, in this case the fibula and tibia are telling a sordid tale all by themselves. I refer to the thinner and thicker set of human leg bones, which appear to have been booted in concrete, hacked off at the knees, otherwise known as patellae, and dumped in Lake Mead long enough ago to melt all flesh from bone.

"You found the bottom of a body, but there's no getting to the bottom of this case. A surviving shoe or footprint has long since deserted that concrete casing. This is an empty shell. Even Vegasset TV-show forensics couldn't come up with anything from this."

"Too bad," Three O'Clock growls, "because *I*

can. Obviously, this was murder by the mob, and the mob has officially ebbed in Vegas since the sixties. These are old bones, boy, and the method of murder is some long-gone gangster's personal fingerprint. Mark my words."

The old boy is right on this much. I am going to have to drag back to town and work hard to influence my usual humans to get the Law out here to retrieve the remains.

Or . . . I turn back to shore and sight along the landmarks so I can lead the bloodhounds back. Also, I need to relocate the old man to an assisted-living facility in Vegas without tipping him off to my ploy.

Elder care is such a drag.

CHAPTER 9
GANGED UP

Temple and her bosses returned to the executive office suite. Nicky planned to show Temple more plans for a revamped Gangsters. Van, looking pale and wan and dubious, opted out.

"Come on down," Nicky urged Temple, as their private elevator sped straight to the main floor.

"The hotel has a Door Number Three?"

"Kinda," he said. "We blocked off the Jackson Action Attraction a while back, when 'family theme park' wasn't working in Vegas."

"Everything is a work in progress in this town," Temple agreed.

"Except your love life, which has finally settled down, I hope."

When Temple started at the reference, Nicky winked.

"Come on, PR lady. I saw you and Matt Devine at Aldo and Kit's wedding. Looks like you two are planning to go forth and do likewise pretty soon." He shook her arm slightly. "Congratulations, right? I'm glad Aldo's going over to the matrimonial side is shaking loose other confirmed bachelors from their routines."

"Confirmed bachelor" was as good a description of an ex-priest as any, Temple decided. Matt certainly had been confirmed.

"We're not announcing anything official yet," she said.

" 'Course not. I just can't help noticing stuff. After the wedding, your aunt hiked her bouquet straight to your hot little hand."

"That Kit. Quite the athlete."

"And I noticed something big and hopefully *not* hot on it."

"You mean this glitzy number?" Temple waved the vintage ruby-and-diamond ring on her left hand. Being bicolored, it didn't scream "engagement" ring. "Matt and I were engaged then, but we didn't want to steal any of Kit and Aldo's spotlight."

"That's a one-of-a-kind stunner," Nicky said.

"Thanks." Temple waggled her ring finger again so he could admire it.

"I meant you both," Nicky added with Fontana gallantry.

She blushed, as meant to.

"You want to watch that nobody steals it," he warned.

Even as she nodded, Temple recalled the unique "unofficial" engagement ring from Max she'd worn for such a short time before it *had* been stolen, and found, and then confiscated. Now the man who'd given it to her was unofficially missing in action. Maybe he'd been confiscated too. Enough bittersweet moment and looking backward!

"Anyway," she said, back to business, "how long have you had this mob theme in mind, Nicky?"

"Longer than I'd care to admit," he said, casting a gaze upward at his wife's office. "Van was the only child of a widowed German hotel hotshot. She grew up in a rotating roster of posh hotel suites and doesn't get the Italian big-family feeling."

"Especially when that big Family has a history with a capital *F* in it."

"Well, yeah."

Temple laughed. "You don't do 'sheepish' well, even though you're the Fontana family's self-described 'white sheep.' You can confess to me, Nicky. You are thrilled as hell to get your entrepreneurial teeth into a mob-themed upgrade of Gangsters before the city powers-that-be even get off their conservative duffs."

"They've committed twelve mill to it, but they're waffling all over the Strip and the media. Now it's a 'law enforcement' museum, so no official toes get stomped on. The public doesn't want political correctness in Vegas. They want a free-for-all. You have a taste for the jugular too. Admit it, Barr. You live to scoop the competition."

"I do have TV reporter roots, from back in the day when news had to be vetted and reliable and wasn't just an Internet streaming-of-consciousness."

"So. We're both on the side of old-fashioned values," he said with a conspiratorial grin. "Family on my end, and a publicity-snagging public-relations coup on yours."

"*Legitimately* publicity snagging."

"Right," Nicky said. "Legit. That word is engraved on the Fontana family escutcheon."

"Uh-huh. Like the Fontanas have a stone shield somewhere that's engraved with the family coat of arms. That's for European aristocracy dating back to the Middle Ages."

"I know what the word *escutcheon* means. Jeez. Give me some credit. We have lots of Fontanas beyond the middle-aged, some in the Old Country still. I guess you could say our coat of arms is etched on our epidermis.

95

Me and my brothers all get the family tattoo when we turn twenty-one. Wanna see?"

"I can wait," Temple said, although wildly curious about the exact location and design of the tattoo on all ten Fontana brothers. She would think they'd have individual druthers.

She imagined that her aunt Kit, latest Fontana family in-law with her recent marriage to Aldo, knew more than she ever would on the subject. And would never tell . . . without the investment of a whole bottle of wine. Which might be fun.

"Say," Temple said, "where are you steering me? We're not going underground to the former Jackson Action ride site?"

"Nope. Not yet. We're hitting the hotel bar. I have some folks I want to take a meet with."

"You are beginning to sound more and more like an escapee from *The Sopranos*."

"Gotta get in the mood and the mode," said Nicky, expertly steering her through the milling crowds, which were milling a bit less these days. "We need some extra oomph and publicity bad. With all this talk about an official mob museum, if we can move fast enough, I figure we can steal the thunder and produce heat lightning of our own."

They had reached the Crystal Court bar,

a tropical paradise of flora and fountains and bright sparkling water and crystal chandeliers.

Nicky's light touch on Temple's elbow escorted her through a scattering of chic cocktail table setups to a parlor palm—shadowed corner booth so low-lit she'd need a seeing-eye dog to get back there on her own.

That traitorous thought made her look around guiltily for Midnight Louise, but if the ladylike black cat had followed them to this conspiratorial corner, she'd be invisible.

Temple felt totally undercover. Even the usual tabletop glass candleholder was shrouded by a net of black widow veiling.

"Ah. Mr. Nicky Fontana and Miss Temple Barr bestow their presence. Welcome to our reunion conference."

A dapper little man stood to greet them. From his white-banded black fedora to the red carnation in the lapel of his pin-striped gray suit, he looked the mobster-movie fashion plate.

"Nostradamus," Nicky exclaimed, "I didn't expect you here. I haven't laid anything resembling a bet since I married Van."

"Not to worry, Mr. Big Shot. A bookie seeking bets I am not. Mine eyes have seen the glory of the fabled desert gang. Old times pass, but can come back around like a favorite boomerang."

Temple eyed the five old men seated in the semicircular leather booth. She'd heard lots of stories about them, and now, bad luck had certainly "boomeranged" them back into the bosom of the Crystal Phoenix family. Their quirky faces resembled a line of English Toby mugs, except their heights weren't uniform like the character barware, but as jagged as the Specter Mountains around Vegas.

"I think you know our history consultants, Miss Barr." Nicky grinned at the fivesome settled onto the booth's leather upholstery.

"Gracious," she said, feeling the need of a genteel expletive, "it's the Glory Hole Gang, live and in person, every last man."

The grins spread.

"Miss Barr," Eightball O'Rourke acknowledged with a nod. "We're wedged in here too tight to stand like little gentleman, thanks to our larger brethren."

He remained wiry and cue-ball bald. She had seen the most of Eightball, so she racked her brains for the other guys' handles, and colorful nicknames they were.

Next to O'Rourke sat another half-pint, Wild Blue Pike, the longtime flyboy. He still flashed sky blue eyes and a shock of snow white hair. Spuds Lonnigan, main cook at Three O'Clock Louie's restaurant on Lake Mead, remained a generously built man with growing gut and thinning hair, as did Pitchblende O'Hara. Cranky Ferguson, on the other hand, was as lean and lanky as an uncooked spaghetti noodle.

Temple recited each name as it came to her, and she nodded at each man, amazed to recall them rightly. What a PR ace she was! Then she realized the Glory Hole Gang members were just too durn colorful to forget. She had to grin back at them. It was like seeing your favorite grandfather after too much time between family reunions, although it had only been a couple of years. The pace of life in Vegas and the massive number of people who came through the toddlin' town could still amaze someone used to dealing with conventions of twenty thousand attendees and more.

"Set and chat awhile," Eightball urged.

Nicky and Temple took the end seats. Nicky ordered beers all around, except for a white-wine spritzer for Temple. The youngest Fontana brother was the perfect host. He'd long ago noted that her "working drink" went light on alcohol.

Temple flashed him a smile of thanks and turned back to the assembled two hundred years of Vegas history seated beside her.

"What are you boys doing here?" she asked, falling into Mae West mode, although she was far from the "Dolly Parton of the Thirties." Somehow vintage Western dialogue went with the Glory Hole Gang like neckerchiefs and dust, both the desert and gold variety.

"I thought you were running Three O'Clock Louie's restaurant on Lake Mead," she added, letting them tell her that it was kaput.

"The water done petered out on the restaurant at Temple Bar, Miss Barr," Spuds said with a sad shake of his balding head. "We was high and dry as Noah's Ark aground on global warming."

"Ah . . ." Temple had read and heard of Lake Mead's shrinking shoreline, as drought dried up its waters, but out of sight, out of mind. She'd forgotten about Three O'Clock Louie's at her namesake Temple Bar, a longtime mark on the map, but not as long as it had been a River Thames landmark near the London Inns of Court.

"Omigosh!" She stared at Nicky as it sunk in that natural ills often caused financial ones. "That's why the Glory Hole Gang lost the restaurant?"

"Jest our customers, ma'am," Pitchblende

100

pitched in. "Not much to gaze out on as they et but sand and desolation. We was used to living in ghost towns, but tourists kinda want water features and lots of local color and no two-block walks over sand dunes to get to their eats."

"Next place over is still afloat," Cranky Ferguson grumbled. "I think they paid protection to the Guy Upstairs to keep their waterline from wastin' away."

"Vagaries of nature," Nostradamus put in, "are as cruel as odds at the track, but a little birdie —"

"A scavenger crow, no doubt," Eightball put in.

"— tells me that the Glory Hole Gang is coming back."

"Right on, Nostradamus!" Nicky's clap on Cranky Ferguson's shoulder raised a puff of sand dust. "Three O'Clock Louie's is coming back, better than ever. What do you guys say to a new location?"

Nostradamus had been standing by, but now he tipped his hat. "I see there's hefty business on the table, so I must amble on while I am able."

The Glory Hole Gang nodded the bookie good-bye, then hunkered down for serious talk.

"Thing is," Nicky said, "I recalled the

operation and want to make Three O'Clock's into a franchise, starting with a flagship restaurant at Gangsters and then going national. After all, the ex–Glory Hole Gang has a colorful early Vegas history, and we can theme the menu to those exciting days of yesteryear."

"That's the concept," Temple asked, "a restaurant?"

"Just one aspect. After all, the Strip Hilton — all that's left of Bugsy Siegel's first Flamingo motel-casino — has Margaritaville. Maybe we'll have Mobsterville. Reposition the name. The old-time 'Families' are as much a 'cultural brand' as Jimmy Buffet's Island paradise."

"That's *in*genious, Nicky," Temple said, "but I'm not quite sold that it's *genius*. 'Life is a beach' is a universal longing. 'Life is a bitch' — maybe not so much."

"Naw, it's true. The Wynn Hotel has gone with a Sinatra theme for its priciest restaurant. Think the *Ocean's Eleven* film revival. Nowadays it's George Clooney instead of Rosemary Clooney and Bing Crosby. Hip, socially concerned, but with a huge wink at our origins. Transparency, right? Today's political buzzword."

Temple laughed. "You're a marketing chameleon, Nicky. Just like the mob."

"The mob," Cranky scoffed. "They were a bunch of punks. Overestimated in the Vegas early days, mainly for notoriety."

"Frankly," Nicky said, "Bugsy had the vision. The big mob boys didn't get it. Jersey Joe Jackson followed in Bugsy's footsteps with his Joshua Tree Hotel-Casino, but they had limited eyesight. They thought motor lodge, not hotel, and would have been astounded by the mega-hotel concept that lines the Las Vegas Strip nowadays. When the mob went corporate, Las Vegas spread its wings. Sure, folks alive today waltzed around the mob fringes, and pockets of the protection racket exist, but now, enterprise has to go mainstream or die. You can't have ordinary people hurting and be commercial. That's why this economic tsunami is so disastrous."

"It sure baked us outta business," Spuds Lonnigan said. "What's our comeback restaurant shtick here at Gangsters?"

"Speakeasy's south. Way south. Underground, in fact, with no pesky problems with Mother Nature," Nicky assured him. "I'm talking the look of a Prohibition Palace. Knock three times to get in. Bootleg liquor, prime stuff. Guys and dolls. A little gaming. A menu that's a history of Vegas influences, Spuds, from lowbrow to high-hat. People will be greasin' palms to get low down with the Glory Hole Gang and its members' authentic ambience and cuisine celebrating the good ol' bad days of miners and mobsters. What do you think?"

"Brilliant," said Temple. "If the Feds don't raid you, I can sell it until doomsday."

Hands came up simultaneously to burnish grizzled jaws.

"We're basically desert rats," Cranky Ferguson noted, " 'cept Eightball here got a city PI business going. Sure, we pulled that silver-dollar heist, train robbery stuff from the old days. You think you can sell us as city slicker mobsters?"

"Rat Pack," Nicky pounced. "Only ahead of your time."

They squinted dubiously, en masse. That was a lot of experienced doubt.

Temple knew her Vegas history. The famous Vegas Rat Pack had begun around the twin stars of Humphrey Bogart and Frank Sinatra in the fifties. Bogart died that decade, so the sixties became a second-stage Rat Pack heyday, with a nucleus of Frank Sinatra, Dean Martin, Sammy Davis Jr., Joey Bishop, and Peter Lawford. Marilyn Monroe, Angie Dickinson, Juliet Prowse, and Shirley MacLaine had been "Rat Pack Mascots" at various times.

The men's solo Vegas acts intermingled improvisationally, and they moved on to costarring in films, most notably the original *Ocean's Eleven*. Nobody today could bundle that particular magic act of personalities and talent, so the Rat Pack, which never admitted to or liked that name, were now all dead but immortalized, despite the mob aroma that hallowed the singers. Sinatra had known Giancana too. Vegas tribute Rat Pack groups had abounded in recent years.

"It could work," Temple told Nicky after long thought, "if we resurrect Jersey Joe Jackson. He was the real deal, a founding figure like Bugsy Siegel, but mostly forgotten. He was also a member of the original Glory Hole Gang, wasn't he?"

"A rat," Wild Blue Pike said, spitting into his palm to be polite in front of a lady, i.e., Temple. "He hid the money from our silver-dollar heist for his own self. Left us grubbing a living in ghost towns, hiding from the law for forty years while he built the Joshua Tree Hotel to rival Bugsy's Flamingo and then presided over its decline."

"The Joshua Tree couldn't keep up with the times," Nicky added. "Jersey Joe ended up being the last resident and dying in the abandoned hotel. You guys later helped find one of his silver-dollar stashes in the desert and turned them in."

"It's a great story," Temple decreed. "The whole Glory Hole Gang saga. Rags to riches to rags. From ghost towns to gangsters to tourist mecca. Nicky and I just need to lay it out new, polish it up, and the publicity will come rolling in."

She glanced at him. When Nicky nodded, she stood.

"Is the Ghost Suite on seven still unlocked?"

"Sure," he said. "Every time we try to lock it we find it open again. No sense messing with a ghost."

"I'd like to go up there and give a ghost lockjaw," Cranky Ferguson muttered, making a fist and punching the air.

"It's no ghost," Wild Blue scoffed, "jest broken tumblers. I can take a look at the lock mechanism."

"No," Temple said. "Midnight Louie and I have no trouble coming and going up there. Maybe we can recreate the suite in Gangsters Hotel. In fact," she asked Nicky, "don't the two hotels' back property lines abut?"

Nicky looked abashed. "Uh, yeah. I believe they might."

"No wonder you can do an underground linkup, for the . . . Chunnel of Crime,"

Temple said.

"Chunnel of Crime! Yeah," Pitchblende O'Hara said, gulping the rest of his black and tan. "Love that. We *were* miners. And the old-time speakeasies favored basement and even cavern locations. When might you get working on it?"

Nicky shrugged. "Already cleaning up the area and installing a few surprises. Depends on when the boss lady okays the link from the Crystal Phoenix end."

"So you old-timers also think it's time to 'come clean' about the city's mob past?" Temple asked.

"Nicky did when he reinvented the abandoned Joshua Tree Hotel Jersey Joe built before he went bust. He was a new generation pioneer," Spuds Lonnigan said. "He did everything on the up-and-up, but on a manageable scale, and look how well the Crystal Phoenix is doing. Now that Vegas construction is in the doldrums, labor and materials are cheaper. Time for reinvesting in the future."

"By harking back to the past," Temple repeated.

"You can't move forward if you don't look back and put the past to rest," Eightball O'Rourke said.

Temple felt another little Ghost Suite shiver.

How could she put her past to rest if she never found out what had happened to Max?

"We'll talk more about it," Nicky said, rising to see Temple off. "You and me," he added with emphasis.

Temple wondered why the Ghost Suite mention had made him uneasy. In fact, something about this meeting struck her as slightly "off." Maybe that was her. They'd talk later, as Nicky had said. Meanwhile, she needed to refamiliarize herself with the Crystal Phoenix's most unsung tourist attraction, a famous ghost in supposed residence.

A shiver waltzed down her spine again. Gee, the air-conditioning was frigid in these Strip hotels, even during a recession.

She wasn't afraid of ghosts. Was she?

CHAPTER 10
SPOOKY SUITE

What had passed for a Las Vegas suite in the 1950s was not square footage in the thousands, as in high-roller-suites today.

Still, the brass numbers on the door reading 713 were shined to a spit polish, and Temple knew she'd find the interior dusted and tidy. She doubted Jersey Joe Jackson had done household chores. A Crystal Phoenix maid must pay a daily visit.

She turned the doorknob and pushed.

Yup. Walk right in. Sit right down. Wait for an apparition.

The room didn't smell stuffy and closed, either, although the wooden-slatted blinds were drawn almost shut against the exterior glare. She walked to the elaborate gray satin drapes that framed the double window. Her fingertips found not a fleck of dust in their sculpted folds.

Her spike heels left faint pockmarks on the flat, tightly woven floral carpeting, marks that disappeared even as she watched. That was the most ghostly effect in the suite she remembered from a couple of social visits.

Midnight Louie had been the Phoenix's "house" cat even before he had crossed Temple's path at the Las Vegas convention center and they had ended up finding a corpse together. If there was any "ghost" of a past occupant here, it was the big black cat's. Nicky and Van said he'd loved to sleep in the dim, undisturbed vintage elegance of the Ghost Suite.

She couldn't find a trace of him anywhere. So much for the Phoenix's self-appointed "watchcat."

Temple smiled as she sat gingerly on a chartreuse satin upholstered chair. As usual, her feet just grazed the floor. She frowned to notice a short black hair on the arm. According to legend, Jersey Joe Jackson's ghost had silver hair to go with a faint, silvery outline.

If Gangsters Hotel-Casino was going to have a Jersey Joe Jackson memorial suite, it would have to up the square footage and all the forties bells and whistles. Sheer size was a Vegas landmark now.

She shut her eyes, envisioning elements. Maybe a silver-dollar theme. The gambling chips should mimic them. And the under-ground tunnel between the two hotels, Gangsters and the Crystal Phoenix, had a Prohibition-era feel. Santiago wasn't pro-posing a ride, really, but an *experience.*

Why had the mention of physically linking the two back-to-back properties above-ground made Nicky nervous? True, the rears of Vegas's major hotels housed a lot of mundane service areas, but it was wasted space, above- and belowground. Temple had a feeling the Fontana family was finally making a more public move with its Las Vegas interests, and Nicky was uneasy because Van wouldn't care for that. Temple thought of the Fontanas more as local color these days than ghosts of a mobster past. After a certain length of time, notoriety became nostalgia.

She liked bouncing ideas around up here. The old-fashioned suite's stillness worked on her like the cool-down ritual after a yoga-Pilates session, lying on a floor mat with a scented cloth over her face and the instruc-tor intoning a relaxation ritual.

Why not a . . . Ghost Suite Spa at Gang-sters Hotel? Ultra–New Age, right? Up to the minute with a vintage forties ambience. What scents would evoke the 1940s? Some-thing exotic and South American, maybe, like the Big Band music of the era. And the decor then had thronged with large, exotic, fleshy blossoms, like Peruvian daffodils and giant orchids and calla lilies.

*Oop*s, that made her think of the Blue Dahlia supper club and Lieutenant C. R. Molina as Carmen, crooning out an alto version of "Begin the Beguine." Oh, they had to use that song on the Gangsters Casino playlist. She adored the lushly Latin song of frustrated passion, so complex and compelling no musician could play it from memory, without sheet music, not even Cole Porter himself. He'd composed the song at the Ritz Hotel bar in Paris, the same one Princess Diana had left before her fatal crash. Wow. Come to think of it, Carmen Molina could kill that song.

Lieutenant Molina was not a relaxing thought for Temple, not even distanced by her torch-singer persona. Nor was Diana's crash. Temple always found her mind segueing from high style to extreme mayhem.

Think spa. A deluxe, woman-only spa, she told herself. Female guests loved pampering. Temple pictured attendants in pale, draped pseudo-Greek gowns. That was a forties look. *Ooh.* Better idea: *male* attendants in short, draped Greek-god togas in the outer areas. *The outer areas of the spa, not the outer areas of the attendants,* she was thinking.

Caesars Palace had cornered the market on the splendors of antiquity on the Strip and Flamingo intersection for decades, but it was solidly Roman. A touch of Greek would be refreshing. Cultural. Hot.

Then there was the tunnel. Always an attraction. People subconsciously adore that rebirth effect. An old-fashioned "ride" wouldn't have worked. Too many average Joes and Jills nowadays felt they'd been "taken for a ride" by their mortgage companies, bankers, stockbrokers, employer 401K plans, greedy CEOs, and even Uncle Sam.

But when a ride was not just a ride, but a "ride . . ."

According to the preliminary figures Nicky had flashed along with the architectural plats for the two properties, Gangsters Limo Service was one of Vegas's top off-Strip attractions. The concept was raking it in like the 11:00–2:00 A.M. wait line at the Flamingo's Margaritaville. Had Bugsy Siegel only known that a beachy Cajuncroon guy could be a meal ticket in Vegas, he would have wasted away in Jimmy Buffetland with a margarita headache rather than end up wasted in L.A. with two bullets zapped through his skull. There she was, back to gangland violence again.

Okay. How would she sell Nicky's new idea?

You go to Gangsters or the Crystal Phoenix hotels and you get a real "ride," speeding limos trekking tourists back and forth through the underground tunnel past *Pirates of the Caribbean*–like vignettes of mobsters at play and pay from B to C, Bugsy to Al Capone. Anything mob would flash past your tinted glass "mobmobile" . . . Chi-Town, the Big Apple, the Big V in the Mojave. Inside you'd be sipping champagne and gulping Glenfiddich. Outside you'd become a spirited-away witness to the bloodiest crimes of the mob era, a *CSI* tech on speed. Hot cars, hot crimes, hot times.

Did she have a commercially twisted mind, or what?

What would Matt think?

Nowadays? He would totally get it.

And Max?

He would think she was unsafe at any speed, as usual.

But surely not as much as *he* would be, if he was still alive.

Again with the macabre thoughts!

A ghostly waft on her calf made Temple jump and look down.

A black cat was waiting to cross her path.

Not Louie. Midnight Louise was standing at her feet, swishing her plumy black tail. Midnight Louise's coat was far too long to have left the skimpy black hair on the chartreuse chair, though. That was a souvenir of Mr. Midnight himself.

Temple had to wonder if he still visited here, and visited Midnight Louise, here. The female cat had not been in sight when Temple entered. She'd looked the place over.

Temple studied the closed door to the hallway. It didn't look completely closed, but she had drawn it fully shut.

Someone had let the cat in after she arrived.

Midnight Louise was the house cat now; maybe she'd made a deal with the house ghost. The suite was always on the chilly side, and now was no exception. Goosebumps stippled Temple's arms.

She picked up her tote bag and walked out the slightly open door into the hall. She turned back to see Midnight Louise curled up on the (warmed-up) chair seat she'd left. The blinds seemed slanted at a more-open angle to allow light to stripe Louise's languid form. The gray satin drapes on the left where the blind cords would be were stirring, almost taking shape as if someone was hiding behind them. . . .

Temple pushed the suite door almost shut, just enough for a cat to paw ajar and get out.

Five steps down the hall, she heard the gentle click of it closing.

Not her business.

CHAPTER 11
MERCILESS TENDERS

"Woo," Max mocked as he stretched to full length outside the Mondeo's driver's side door and took a long look around. " 'I dreamt I went to Manderley again.' "

He smiled at Gandolph, who got the Daphne du Maurier reference right off.

"So you remember the creepy manor house in that forties suspense movie? When I see iron gates and red brick grandeur, I always wonder, mansion or prison?"

Max studied the place.

"The Convent of the Little Flower looks more forbidding than one would think from the quaint name. Good thing we stopped for lunch and a chance to fill our bladders with ale and empty them. I bet the nuns inside could make a hardened felon piss his pants, if I recall my fleeting memories of the good sisters in grade school."

"You once told me the grade-school nuns were Old World, even in Wisconsin. And that the Christian Brothers ran a tight ship in your high school too."

"Apparently they did, if Sean and I graduated as virgins. He died one too. Poor bastard." Max sighed. "That was the purpose of Catholic same-sex education. Worked for quite some time, until the free workforce dried up."

Max momentarily shut his eyes. Behind his studied cynicism, an image was assembling in pieces like a torn photograph. Gap-toothed twelve-year-old grin, a freckled face growing angular with hints of a man's strength. Sean. As redheaded Irish as a leprechaun. Max was Black Irish. Dark hair, no freckles sprouting in sunshine as freely as mushrooms do in the shade for him. Always a flat-black dark seriousness beneath any age-appropriate banter. Temper. An icy vengeful temper that gives nothing away, and no quarter. And never forgets, without the intervention of amnesia . . . even now.

That surge of teenage memory and emotion shook him. If he was getting pieces of himself back, he couldn't control them as he'd probably learned to by age thirty-four, the hard way. He'd have to recall and reclaim every stupid, vain, idiotic, maybe crazy puzzle piece and subdue it again. Apparently Michael Aloysius Xavier Kinsella had been that obsessed. Apparently Garry Randolph, Gandolph the Great, cared enough to do his very best to fulfill that man's crazy boyish bequest.

Max clapped the old man on the back. "You've teased your audience-of-one's attention to the breath-stopping point, Gandolph. Show me the payoff behind the facade."

Sister Mary Robert Emmet was older than God, who was older than Earth.

She wore a long black gown, and fanciful arrangements of starched white linen surrounded her face and shoulders, but the "penguin" look framed features worn with incalculable worry.

"Perhaps Mr. Randolph told you, Mr. . . . ?"

"Kinsella."

A slash of sunshine flickered on the shadowed terrain, a smile.

"Irish, then. But American too, by your accent. I am something of a museum curator here at the convent. I am the 'media liaison,' God help me. I don't even know what media is — are? — these days. Mr. Randolph swore to me on the tenets of his Lutheran faith, sadly disused, that what I

119

have to impart is key to the salvation of your soul."

Max wanted to blush. This situation was quite impossible. Damn Gandolph and his sometimes almost-Irish way with words. Max wasn't sure he had a soul, or that it could be saved. This ancient nun, for all her weary sorrow, had a tried sort of innocence he found impossible to dismiss with mockery.

"I'd be honored if you'd suspend your rules for my benefit," he said with a courtly bow. He was tall enough to pull off a bow even nowadays. And magician enough. "I can't guarantee a saved soul, but perhaps a soothed one."

"Very wise, young man. Salvation is not up to us. Only the effort. Well, what I am going to show and tell you was mostly before my time and place, thank God, and there is much denial even to this day. No institution — political, military, or religious — seems free of the cardinal sin of pride."

Max was glad she wasn't a priest, because he'd have to confess that he was jogging partners with that particular sin. He'd detected it in himself several dozen times in the week or so he remembered in detail. It had tempted him to sleep with a woman, fornicate, they'd call it here. Pride had helped him survive, though, and now it urged him to control his remaining slight limp as their footsteps echoed down a long wood-floored hall.

Sister Mary Robert Emmet, named for the Virgin and a long-ago "martyred" Irish patriot hung for his freedom fighting, led them down halls paneled in coffered, worm-eaten wood, then over tiled floors, through echoing rooms barren as very old buildings are, so that even antique luxury seems penitential.

Max felt panic rising, as if he were tunneling into a burrow of old-fashioned confession boxes or torture chambers. Even without much of a memory, he'd considered himself a modern man, a strong and clever man, a man who could cope. All that bracing outer ego was melting away. He was a kid again, facing the clawed fingers skittering from under the bed, the darkness in the corners of the closet, the King Kong in the basement, the mouse gnawing at his brain while he dreamed. . . .

Sister Mary Robert Emmet led them to a walled exterior garden, devoid of everything but the green moss that cloaks every stone in Ireland.

"This is where they found the bodies,"

she said in her lilting Irish croon, as if recit-
ing playwright Sean O'Casey at a wake.
"Almost a hundred and fifty in unmarked
graves. All women and girls. Ireland has
long been a killing ground, and this is one
of our hidden holocaust sites. The other
wing of the . . . house . . . was the orphanage.

"Who knows where those unwanted babes
went, into what situations, good or bad?
Here the unwed mothers and the girls who
were thought to be ungovernable were
buried alive for years and then buried in
unmarked graves when their eternal sentence to Mother Church was done. They
were considered sinners or bound to be
such. Their names were changed; they were
lost to kith and kin, and they served God as
scullions and laundresses, paid almost nothing and punished for merely being, while
the convents thrived on the labor of their
salvations, until these lost ones died, unrec-
ognized even then.

"These grounds, of which there were
many in Ireland and all over Europe, were
called Magdalen asylums or houses or
laundries, and they persisted until the current century, Mr. Kinsella. Until past the
millennium. Certainly until you, Mr. Randolph says, came here as a boy in search of

the troubled but colorful legendry of the Auld Sod."

"Oh, my God," Max said.

Sister bowed her head. "Mr. Randolph said you are afflicted with memory loss, that you have forgotten much of your personal past and even some of the world's. I pray you may forget or at least forgive this piece of our common world."

"Is that all you can do, pray for forgiveness?"

"I'm stationed here to pray daily for the dead, not for myself."

Max could only look to his current guide, his past mentor.

"And Kathleen O'Connor?" he asked, afraid.

Gandolph must have primed the place's sister-keeper well. She continued without question of hesitation.

"She was doubly cursed — or blessed — to be here, as they thought at the time. She was both an adopted 'orphan' child of a Magdalen laundress and in her turn an 'incorrigible' girl resident of this place. The records show they gave her the name Rebecca. She gave up a baby to the orphanage when she was sixteen. How she'd managed such a scandal under lock and key remained a mystery. She 'escaped' when she was seventeen."

Max could understand why.

He wanted to turn and scrabble away screaming at what that short history of one young woman would mean to anyone who encountered her ever after.

Kathleen O'Connor's body lay buried in a potter's field in Las Vegas, but surely her unbroken but mangled spirit must haunt this place eternally.

CHAPTER 12
MEOW MIX

There is no such thing as an old cat's home, unless you consider being dropped off at an animal shelter with a murderous overpopulation problem or abandoned on the street to be a nice retirement package.

I am not exactly a kit myself, but Three O'Clock has gotten a lot more creaky about the pins since last I saw him.

"What made you think you could stay at the old restaurant?" I ask him as soon as we are tucked away among the black video-camera cases in the back of the Channel 6 van. "That joint looked closed. Why did the old guys not forcibly take you with them when they decamped?"

"Because I did not want to go and I got 'lost' on purpose," he huffs, trying to get comfy with his chin propped on a case.

We share signature white whiskers, but I notice his black muzzle is surrounded by tiny white hairs. From my own mirror-checks, which I do on the sinktop on my way out the open Circle Ritz bathroom window at every opportunity, I am still matinee-idol black haired from stem to stern, save for the almost undetectable occasional white hair every dude and dame of our color sports.

The old man's muzzle is starting to look bearded, like Hemingway's. I only wish he had a superlarge fish to share with a landlubber offspring.

Alas, now Three O'Clock has no sea and no fish to shepherd, with the lake and the lovely golden shoreline carp it used to boast doing a disappearing act.

"Where are you taking me?" he snarls. "I told you I am doing fine on the next-door leavings, and I wanted to watch *CSI* in action on my turf."

"Your 'turf' is a dried-up wasteland."

"So is yours."

"But mine has neon and foot-long submarine sandwiches and Bette Midler."

A rough stretch has Three O'Clock's chin seeming to nod agreement. "Bette Midler is all right. You cannot eat neon, and foot-long-anything foodstuffs are more than I care to tangle with at my age."

This talk of fast food has my mind revving up. What to do with the old folks is the conundrum of the era, especially as the population of old folks is growing by leaps and bounds. Or by creeps and pounds.

I climb a few boxes to curl my shivs around the van's rear window slit. I see we are getting into serious traffic. Time to bail.

"Come on, Pop," I urge as I clamber back down. "Time to rock and roll."

"You young folks still into that racket?"

"You betcha."

I eye the silver tangle of aluminum tripods stacked behind the driver's seat. We need to distract our chauffeur just enough to slow down but not enough to crash and burn. It is a delicate operation, and my current partner is none too reliable. Who would think I would actually wish for the presence of Miss Midnight Louise and her nubile climbing skills?

"Okay, Daddy-o. You are going to climb that silver metal tree while I get behind the wheel."

"There is no way to climb that mess, son. I will just end up in a tangle of clattering pipe."

"Exactly. Mount Charleston it is not, but you still have built-in pitons and can make quite a mess and commotion of it."

"I see. You want a distraction."

"Duh."

"Why did you not just say so? I was attracting thrown tin cans on the backyard fences while you were just a gleam in my old lady's eye."

With that, Three O'Clock rousts his own twenty-pound, leftover-pumped bulk over the camera boxes and leaps like a sumo wrestler for the tripods. Immediately the unseen driver starts muttering and pumping the brakes.

By then I have scaled the vinyl back of his seat and landed in his lap, tail faceup and claws thigh-side down and snapping into place like a staple remover.

The screams are awesome.

I fight to unsnag my valuable shivs as the driver simultaneously slams on the brakes and puts the gear into park, opens the door, and grabs the lapels of my furry ruff.

We hurl outside together into the merciless sunlight as horns bellow and traffic screeches to a stop. The scene causes him to release his grip. I roll under the stopped van, pleased to see Three O'Clock slithering onto the doorjamb edge and then the street.

"Psst!" I say, sticking out a paw to gesture him under the undercarriage.

He slinks into the shadow beside me.

"That guy took some really primo footage of me and thee hamming it up over those Lake Mead bones," Three O'Clock protests. "Your escape plan has delayed getting our mugs onto the evening news, where they belong."

"Relax. There will be some exchange of this and that information, then all these hot steel boxes will get rolling again. Meanwhile, you and I can leapfrog from shady spot to shady spot and leave this mess behind."

"Your 'shady spots' could start mowing us down any 'leap.' We are not frogs."

I agree that there is not a lot of "leap" left in Three O'Clock Louie, but I have enough hiss and vinegar for the two of us. I soon prod the old dude out of the street and onto one of my routes to the Circle Ritz.

"This is worse than our recent trek across half of Lake Mead," he starts complaining. "I did not want to leave my old hangout even when my humans pulled up 'steaks.' I hid out until they gave up coming back out and trying to lure me away with the daily special."

"You are a stubborn old cuss."

"I am not going to give up my independence. Besides, during the last days they converted to an all free-range, organically grown menu. Those chickens must have had leg muscles the size of ostriches'. And, as far as I know, vegetables are only good for encouraging five-year-old human kits to run away from home. I had never been offered so much dry, twiggy, dirt-dusted chow in my life. Now you are dragging me across a concrete desert. With no food or water in sight. You are a cruel cat, my son."

I cannot claim that shade and watering holes

exactly dot the city landscape if you are not near a major hotel. Sure, I know Three O'Clock has not got much stamina and has already been sore-footedly tried today. For once, I am completely perplexed. Where to park the old man until I can reunite him with his geezer gang?

I need to find someplace soon.

Meanwhile, the Las Vegas sun is boiling high above us in a clear blue sky, soaking into our pure black coats, making our pink tongues roll out like red carpets and our tenderized pads to crack and burn like well-done strip steaks.

Manx! Even my ability to come up with similes has shifted into survival overdrive. I cannot believe that shepherding only one elder could be so taxing.

I am glad that . . . oh! Of course.

Obviously my brain has been fried on Lake Mead, along with the rest of Three O'Clock Louie's lost and lamented cuisine.

"Come on, Daddy-o," I urge with a growl. "I have just the retirement pad for you. Only a few hundred more steps."

Argh, matey. Yo-ho-ho, and a cache of cement booties.

Frankly, my feet feel like they have been cast in hot concrete and my legs worn down to the bare bones by the time I herd Three O'Clock through a stand of oleander bushes into a delovely clearing dominated by my favorite fast-food restaurant, a big brown Dumpster.

"Have you taken me in a circle, Grasshopper?" Three O'Clock asks out of the side of his mouth. Who would have thought the old man had so much sarcasm in him?

"This looks like the abandoned restaurant you just rescued me from. Only I do not get a lake view."

"Such as it was," I point out. "I do not believe your vision was keen enough to enjoy the distantly sparkling ripples."

"My eyes are a durn, er, sight better than yours, lad. Who spotted those pathetic bird bones sticking up out of the lake-bottom sand?"

"Who moved mountains to get them discovered by human movers and shakers?"

"Humans are a cruel breed," he says, shaking his grizzled head. "They toy with their kill. I have heard that all my life, but until I saw the pathetic pair of leg bones sticking out of the concrete ball like plant supports in an empty flowerpot . . . The poor victim was poured into his fatal cement footwear while still alive, you know. Vicious breed, humans. And you lead me into the heart of their darkness here in Sin City."

I sigh. "We are speaking old-time gangsters, or someone modern who was trying to emulate them. I am sure my friend the coroner, Grizzly Bahr, is even now dating and dissecting the whole gruesome mess down to the DNA."

"They have an ursine coroner here? That is open-minded. I am impressed."

I sigh again. My old man is not the only one who has chewed through a dictionary or two in his day.

"The name *Grizzly* is a nickname, Daddy-o. His surname is spelled B-a-h-r. No genuine bears work for the Las Vegas forensics department."

"Bahr, eh? Related to your cross-species lady friend? The one you sleep with?"

"You have been living with professional bachelors too long out at Lake Mead. You should be so lucky to have a human fan who has a lakeside recreation area named after her, although I think it was just a weird coincidence."

"I see another weird coincidence," the old guy says, jabbing me in the ribs with a jovial mitt of half-unfurled claws. "Who is that hot babe I see sniffing along the Dumpster edge?"

Can it be? Has Ma Barker, his old inamorata and my old mama, edged into sight just at this convenient moment? Manx! The sire's eyes must be broken if he considers her a "hot babe," although I will take any happenstance luck I can right now.

I look where he is leering.

Horrors! Double horrors.

What is Miss Midnight Louise, my detecting partner and stridently proclaimed daughter — therefore the old guy's granddaughter, no less — doing here?

I was hoping to arrange a meet between Three O'Clock and Ma Barker and gang. Not between the Senile and the Nubile.

"She is fixed," I hiss in his somewhat battered ear.

"I do not care who she is fixed up with, I am tossing my whiskers into the ring for that chick."

What a cluck!

"She is also *kin*," I add, emphasizing my point with a cuff of shivs to the jaw.

"These things are hard to trace among a nomadic kind."

"Make one mew out of line and she will perforate your liver from the outside in. Trust me, I know this kit."

"So you want to keep her to yourself."

This is seriously not true. "She is a business partner, and that is it."

"Oho."

Before I can argue further, a low and hackle-

133

rising growl from the oleanders behind us delays further discourse. Then comes the reading of the riot act.

"You two roadkill bums can forget drooling over anything you see," Ma Barker glowls. "This is *my* gang's territory, and you are trespassing. I can scar your behinds with my initials and give you a sex-change operation before either one of you drifters can muster a rusty shiv."

Meanwhile, Miss Midnight Louise has scented our presence and is heading our way at top speed, claws kicking up asphalt like it was unclumpable litter-box sand.

"You take the spitfire up front, and I'll reverse to face the hellion at our rear," Three O'Clock says.

What is a parent for but self-sacrifice, right? Except I am the one sacrificing my most vulnerable end. Papa is literally saving his ass.

I comply, knowing Ma Barker will recognize her baby boy from any angle and Miss Louise has already ID'd Three O'Clock as the stranger on the block.

"You are in bad company, son," Ma Barker growls at my rear. "Who is this aging sack of hairballs you have been foolish enough to bring here?"

Meanwhile Louise continues her liberated

she-devil act. "Freeze, stranger! Do not turn around to face me or you will be looking up Eye Patches Are Us on the Internet."

"He is just a homeless guy I found out at Lake Mead," I say, not ready to make introductions under the circumstances. Family reunions can be so difficult.

"We are all pretty much homeless, except for you," Louise notes.

"Have a heart," I urge. "He is a relative."

"I object," Three O'Clock growls. "The one behind me who bedazzled my old eyes with her cute not-interested act is too good-looking to be a relative, and the one in front of me now is too ugly."

I squeeze my eyes shut, awaiting Three O'Clock's instant annihilation.

"Say," hisses Ma Barker, "my raccoon shiner does not permit me the crystal-clear vision of my youth, but I am old enough to know you are not so bad yourself, stranger."

Huh?

Miss Louise goes whisker-to-whisker with me to whisper, "What can Ma Barker be thinking?"

In a moment we, gasp, then know.

"You remind me," Ma Barker says, "of a smarmy, swaggering, swell-headed young tom who used to come around when I was more receptive to gentlemen callers."

"I was all that," Three O'Clock admits proudly, "except I do not know 'smarmy' from blarney."

"They are the same."

Ma Barker's right mitt clips him a smart one in the chops. And possibly the loins. She always excelled at one-two punches.

At any rate, Three O'Clock rolls into a ball, spins a few times, and ends up back on his pins three feet away.

"Can that be you, Pool Hall Polly?" he asks. "I recognize the English."

Ma Barker bats her eyes like a baby doll, including the one that is still at quarter mast from the raccoon incident.

Louise and I exchange a shocked stare and back off to let this play out unassisted.

"So," Ma says, "sonny boy managed to catch up with your mangy hide. What are you two bad boys up to now that you have twice the chutzpah and half the brains?"

"We are working the case of the truncated shin bones, doll."

I wait to see Three O'clock caroming off the back wall of the police substation that is now Ma Barker's hideout.

Instead, she rubs back and forth on the base of the oleander bush. "So you want in on our boy's private-eye business?"

"No way," Miss Midnight Louise snarls.

"Right," I second. "It is bad enough I got saddled with a girl. I do not need a geezer."

"Pipe down, junior," Three O'Clock says, "and let your elders settle this."

"I am not a 'junior,' " I point out. "And you better act more humble if you want to get bed and board at Ma Barker's headquarters. She runs this outfit."

"Really?" Three O'Clock noses toward Ma Barker. "I have been retired from the nautical life in Puget Sound for a couple of years, but if you have need of an enforcer . . ."

"We are all enforcers here," Ma snaps back. She eyes me and wrinkles her sparse vibrissae, which are whiskers to veterinarians and others in the know. "So you want to hang around for old times' sake? I can put you on probation."

"Probation? I ran a fishing trawler. I was the skipper's right-hand catch-inspector. Then I retired to Vegas and got a food inspector job with the Glory Hole Gang out at Lake Mead. I should be *consigliere* here, at least."

"This is a street gang, Three O'Clock, not some fancy-schmancy operation."

Ma ambles over to me and Miss Midnight Louise.

"So, Grasshopper. If the old guy stays, I will have to call you disgusting pet names, since the 'Midnights' are getting a bit thick around here."

"I am Louie," I snarl. "He can be Three O'Clock. *Capiche?*"

"Whatever, you two can duke it out. Meanwhile, who is going to do the honors?"

"There is any honor around here?"

"I mean introduce your partner to her new grandfather."

Louise's baby yellows get moon size. She had not followed the family resemblance to its logical conclusion — her. *If* she really is my offspring.

Even now she is arching her back and shaking out her shivs to make sure Three O'Clock knows he is not top dog around here.

CHAPTER 13
DEM OLD BONES

Temple left the Crystal Phoenix with her head still whirling with empire-building ideas.

Give Nicky Fontana credit: the boy could dream. He was her age, just pushing thirty-one, but CEO of her only permanent contractual client. Van was an amazing executive and executor, but Nicky had the cockeyed vision it took to take Vegas establishments to the next step.

And this time, Temple would be an idea girl from the ground up . . . or down, if the plans to reimagine the underground spaces were as open-ended as Nicky said.

Underground. Underworld. That was so postmillennial and perfect. Dark, daring, and cooool, man, cooool.

She wanted to tell someone. She wanted to tell Matt. And maybe her Aunt Kit Carson, who — oh, rats — was honeymooning in Europe with her first and postmenopausal husband, Nicky's eldest brother, Aldo. Sixty is the new forty-five, and so was Aldo. Go, Aunt Kit!

The red Miata wove through the packed Strip traffic like a computerized sewing machine on zigzag. Temple refrained from cellphoning while driving, but her mind rehearsed what she'd tell Matt when she called him tonight.

Temple's head was still bursting with wild ideas when she came home to her quiet Circle Ritz condo. She'd been too busy to check with Matt in Chicago earlier. He was used to her calling him because of her erratic freelance schedule.

She plopped down on her soft living-room loveseat, kicked off her Weitzman spikes, and kicked her bare heels into the luxuriant long fibers of her faux-goatskin rug. Then she grabbed the remote just in time to catch the opening of the six o'clock news. Matt was in a two-hour-later time zone, so she had time to chill, shower, and change before calling. More construction defaults and lower tourist numbers still made the news, along with a murder-suicide in Henderson, but the feature story tease was on "cannibal cats."

Ick!

They even ran a five-second close-up of a

poor, starving stray kitty gnawing on some bones.

Temple averted her face, but not before the cat's color registered.

Black. And big.

The whiskers were an unusual pure white.

As long and straight as kabob skewers. *Uh-oh.*

Temple programmed her recorder and slipped into the kitchen to pour a glass of red wine. No, white. She might see something startling enough to cause a spill on her off-white couch. Forewarned was forearmed. Or four-armed.

Why would *her* Midnight Louie be making the evening news munching on bones? He had a perfectly fine full bowl of Free-to-Be-Feline dry, vitamin-packed, politically correct cat food in his kitchen bowl at this very minute. "Full" was the key word.

Oh.

The nightly news had perfected the art of tease. Between every boring roundup they flashed footage of a black feline muzzle and sharp white fangs snapping at the jagged ends of what sure looked like bones. Temple gulped wine.

During commercial breaks, she checked every cat hiding spot in the two-bedroom unit and shouted from the tiny balcony. No

Louie anywhere. Had the trespassing cats on the news been taken into custody?

She opened and checked every last kitchen cupboard and refilled her glass with red wine.

The sacred sports and weather sections were coming up. If the cat story didn't run soon, it would never run. Had she missed it during a commercial break?

An insect brushed her arm. No! Louie's white whiskers.

He had just lofted over the sofa back to sit beside her. Must have come in the guest-bathroom window she always left ajar.

"Louie! You had me going. Where have you been?"

But his green eyes weren't turned toward her. They were focused intently on the TV screen. His whiskers twitched as he settled into his haunches.

"Now here's a gristly tale," the female half of the anchor team intoned with relish, "better fitting Halloween than spring break. Animal lovers attending the Temple Bar Days annual festival at the Arizona area of Lake Mead called animal control to round up a couple of feral cats scavenging for food dangerously near the lake's sadly lowered edge and not far from the defunct Three O'Clock Louie's former lakeside restaurant.

The foraging felines eluded capture, but the animal-control people found they had been snacking on a gruesome discovery."

The camera pulled back to show crime-scene tape circling the littered lake bottom, then zoomed in on an odd formation.

"Yes, witnesses said the object of the cats' interest appeared to be a pair of snapped off human leg bones mired in rock. Arizona police authorities are mum about the find, but the area is only an hour's drive from Las Vegas, and the remains have been sent to the city coroner's facility. Could stray cats have unearthed the remains of some early Vegas crime figure who had been given the concrete booties treatment and dumped in Lake Mead decades ago? Crime historians must be scratching their heads and searching their archives. Meanwhile, the carnivorous kitties made their getaway and are still at large."

"Carnivorous!" Temple accused her seating partner, then imbibed more wine and reconsidered. "Of course all cats are carnivorous. They said 'cannibal' first! That's all wrong. I am so mortified. I recognized your white whiskers instantly, of course. You are grounded, my lad. No more open window for you."

Louie yawned.

"I'm going right now to slam it shut. See!"

He rolled over onto his substantial side to flash his fangs as he nibbled at a clawed toe.

Temple did as she had promised and returned triumphant.

"Did you hear that? Shut. *Two.* Cannibal cats, plural. So who was your accomplice? The other cat?"

Louie remained mum. And way too calm.

Temple sighed. "Three O'Clock Louie. Of course. Why the heck and how did you get way out there? Arizona, for Pete's sake. I suppose gnawing on human bones can't be considered cannibal for a cat. Oh."

She punched the cell phone's auto-dial to try Matt at his Chicago hotel number. "Our fiancé is going to be so disappointed in you, Louie. Old bones. Criminal bones. Gangster bones. What a news hook. Wonder who it is. Was.

"Bet the Glory Hole guys might have a clue, but who would even remember them to ask? This is a Temple Barr exclusive. Where the heck is Three O'Clock now, huh? You didn't just leave your *compadre* to the coyotes and animal control, did you? No, of course not. He's probably wherever that gang of feral cats that hung around here for a while went. And are you sharing that info with your loyal bed partner? *Noooo.* Just

144

you wait. You are confined to quarters, mister, but I am going to be out on the town and on this first thing in the morning like a . . . carnivorous cat."

And, Temple mumbled to herself, *since when had there been an annual festival on Lake Mead with her name on it?*

For a PR person to miss her own publicity was really humiliating.

CHAPTER 14
MEDIA DRAW

Welcome home to the conquering hero.

I guess not!

Here I have been through a fatiguing trek to Arizona, for Bast's sake, not to mention my roommate's namesake place and event on Lake Mead, and I am scolded and locked in like a juvenile delinquent.

It would not sting so much had I not gotten a similar dose of dissing and moaning at my last stop before this.

The locked window does not curl my whiskers.

My Miss Temple flatters herself that I need her arms and two opposable thumbs to fly this coop whenever I please. The living-room row of French doors has horizontal pulls and latches that a kitten could open with its milk teeth.

The lamented, but perhaps not late, Mr. Max Kinsella had often warned Miss Temple about the doors' flimsy security, but she had relied too much on my crime-fighting presence to take him seriously.

So I can blow this joint anytime I wish. It simply suits me to make like a couch potato and rest my burning pads for a while. Also, to run the watershed events of the past several hours through my weary brain.

Of course it was up to me to mastermind and pull off the "cannibal cats" routine. Three O'Clock had neither the imagination nor inclination to bestir himself, once I'd gotten myself out to Lake Mead and eyeballed his "find," his "case," his dubious "murder victim."

Say it turned out to be Jimmy Hoffa. Now that would make multimedia news.

I have no such expectations, but I know that if I can rouse human interest in this odd piece of found art I can get us air-conditioned transport back to civilization. Obviously, the old dude cannot hoof it, or even move fast enough to hitch it.

My plan is risky, but the best ones always are. I mentally replay my favorite moments.

First, I pick up my sandy toes and trot to the neighboring hash house that is still solvent. The closer I get, the more succulent is the sniff of rare hamburger and well-done anchovies on pizza. My kind of buffet table.

Right now, though, I am only pretending an interest in the quick-fried cuisine. I am trawling for a sucker, preferably a kid or a middle-aged lady. Dudes are useless for my purpose.

I glance back to mark the spot I want to aim at by the black lump of Three O'Clock's form. The sun is getting hot, and I do not want him to cook more than the ground beef here.

My nimble mitts quickly spar with my cheeks, giving my snappy white whiskers a tangled and bedraggled look, then I roll over in the sand several times before hitting the asphalt surrounding the café. *Yowsa!* Hot on the bare tootsies.

I suppose I could say I then "hotfoot" into the restaurant "like a scalded cat."

No. I am too cagey for that. I duck under the nearest vehicle, where the tarmac is shady and cool. By darting from shade to shade, I am able to approach the exterior tables that afford a nice view of the sandy lonesome that used to be lakefront.

Perfect.

I scoot under the first family-of-five table I can spot. Even more perfect! There I peruse four sets of legs and a child's seat with kicking tiny tennies barely below chair-seat level.

The sweet sound of kiddie fussing whines above my head. Below I see two sets of large ugly tennies and two sets that barely reach the floor, one accessorized with Hello Kitty pink anklets.

I manage not to toss my cookies at the sight of this supercute kitty face swinging in duplicate so close to mine.

I brush my furry puss on the slender bare leg between anklet and shorts.

A small face ducks under the table level, as if searching for something dropped. The mouth makes a silent elongated O.

It disappears, and a French fry plops down beside me. The grease smell almost knocks me over, and the big dollop of attached tomato ketchup could make an Italian greyhound nauseous. I pull back my whiskers and harf and garf the fry down, even though it is death to my cholesterol count.

Another follows. This one I grab and retreat out of reach to eat in patented Hungry Stray Kitty behavior, which says: You feed and I will eat but Touch Not the Cat.

By then the smallest foot set is beating its heels on the chair legs and screaming up a storm. I must say not even a Siamese cat can compete with a human toddler for range and screech effect when howling.

I look up from burping after downing the second fry to see my Hello Kitty friend crouching on the wooden boards, a grease-stained napkin tucked like a hobo's kerchief into her ketchup-stained little hand. I even sniff hamburger.

Good girl!

No one is watching as I lure her tidbit-by-tidbit down the few steps and onto the parking lot. Now I am simply picking up the latest offering, another fry, and moving away, hunching over it, watching her approach. Just as she gets within reach, I pick up my fry and retreat.

Nothing is as determined as a nine-year-old animal-loving kid attempting to feed a poor, starving stray kitty.

I have her out on the Lake Mead sandlot and halfway to Three O'Clock's position before the howling heel-kicker can take a breath for another two-minute aria.

Of course every eye in the place has been surreptitiously glued to the screaming Mimi, and the mortified parents are totally concentrated on trying to stifle the sound without doing anything that would bring in the child-protection agencies.

Meanwhile, they fail to notice that Daughter Dearest is decamping on the trail of a no-doubt filthy, diseased, or even rabid stray cat.

I hate to play on my kind's totally bad rap or the touching humanity of children, but private dicks are always being forced to cross moral lines, if you go by the books and movies.

By the time I hear the hue and cry raised back at the restaurant veranda, Hello Kitty has forgotten feeding me and is busy watching Three O'Clock wash his whiskers beside the bizarre leg-bone setup.

Shortly after a half dozen hysterical people have assembled, my friend Hello Kitty is snatched up, up, and away, and cell phones are put into instant service.

My major hope is that the angered villagers do not get lethal and decide against leaving stray cats and concrete-imbedded leg bones of unknown origin to the authorities.

Thanks to the urgent lobbying of our friend Hello Kitty Anklets, the hysterical adults are persuaded to withdraw and leave bad enough alone.

Luckily, what is left these days of the electronic media arrives first to get the money shot: Three O'Clock and I licking our outstanding whiskers over the macabre mortal remains.

(I had a devil of a time convincing Three O'Clock to smack his whiskers. He said that was rude and the act of a "whippersnapper."

I said, "No, it was the act of a whiskersnapper.")

My next challenge was arranging for us to snatch a ride with a TV-station van back to Vegas, undetected, and before the well-meaning animal-rescue folks took us for mere stray cats and tried to "save" us.

Sigh.

Now my Miss Temple has again tried to "save" me from myself by locking me in. She thinks.

I tell you, being a superhero of your species is very frustrating work. Pleased to have finally safely stowed away Three O'Clock — for his sake and that of Greater Las Vegas — I now have a chance to rest my weary feet and mind, eat something that is not greasy, but desert-dry, like Free-to-Be-Feline, and catch a few Zs. As in Zorro! *En garde,* world!

CHAPTER 15
THE GUGGENHEIM OF
GANGSTERS

Las Vegas had its "whales" — big spenders who dropped millions on the gaming tables and were treated like sultans for it.

It also had its architectural "whales" — hotel-casinos lined up along the Strip, each one grander and more expensive than the next and inevitably sliding into "old-hat, second tier" as heaver behemoths sprang up along the eternally elastic Strip.

Yet Vegas had always sported the more budget-minded hotel-casinos among the major glamour-pusses, and smaller outfits had also thrived just off-Strip.

Temple was surprised the next day when Nicky collected Van from her literal ivory tower and herded her and Temple and the entire Glory Hole Gang into one of the Crystal Phoenix complimentary airport vans.

First of all, Van didn't normally "herd." Secondly, Temple had never ridden in the hotel's vans and appreciated the navy blue Ultrasuede upholstery and soft piped-in music. The regular airport round-trip was short, but Vegas traffic could be balky.

Even here Van's white-glove service showed.

As did her impatience as she tapped one Italian designer pump on the immaculate navy blue carpeting.

Temple, meanwhile, was as excited as a kid heading toward Disneyland. You could live in Vegas and never visit the Hard Rock Hotel, for instance, or even Circus Circus on the Strip. She'd only thought of Gangsters as a limo service with a cool office-cum-parking lot with hot-and-cold-running Fontana brothers running it in turn.

Perhaps the Fontana boys and their cool Italian tailoring had distracted her from looking up any farther than six feet something.

For there'd always been "some building" towering behind the enterprise, and she knew Gangsters was a hotel-casino with some intriguing attractions, but Temple had only visited it a couple of times when funny-man Darren Cooke had appeared there with tragic results in her case called "Flamingo Fedora." So she'd never really checked it out.

Now she was craning her neck so hard as they approached the car services' headquarters that the seat belt threatened to decapitate her. Short women often felt more threatened than safe-guarded by vehicle seat belts. Temple was beginning to think the auto industry had it in for anyone under five feet four.

Gangsters was another relatively "short stack" hotel, like seven-story Bill's Gamblin' Hall, once known as the Barbary Coast, nestled on a Strip corner dominated by towering properties. Bally's and the Flamingo were on its east side, and Caesars Palace and the Bellagio across the Strip.

Gangsters Hotel-Casino had capitalized on a reputation as a well-kept secret. It was only a block off the Strip and eight stories taller than just plain Bill's.

As Nicky and the whole Glory Hole Gang hustled to help her and Van down from the high-step-up vehicle, Temple glimpsed an edge of unlit neon sign atop the building that looked as high-profile as the Hard Rock Hotel's iconic guitar and thrusting, neon-fretted neck.

But first Temple needed to get her feet on the ground, and when she looked up to human height again she was greeted by a reception committee of eight Fontana brothers arrayed on either side of a suggestively red carpet, wearing not their usual sherbet-tinted summer suits, but pink pinstriped navy suits with black silk shirts accessorized with *Miami Vice* neon-colored ties, ranging from peach to turquoise to hot pink to cobalt, melon, and purple.

Van bowed her flaxen-haired head, perhaps the only female on Planet Vegas immune to the conjoined attractions of the brothers Fontana. That was probably from having been married to the youngest, Nicky, and the absence of the eldest, Aldo.

The middle of the pack seemed more like clones, but Temple had always found that the Fontana brothers' biggest charm, their unanimity. Somehow it made their high spirits and good looks less overwhelming.

As they extended their welcoming, finger-spread "jazz hands" of Broadway dance ensembles to the visitors, the Glory Hole Gangsters do-si-doed down the red carpet in their battered cowboy boots, well-worn jeans, and plastic mother-of-pearl-buttoned plaid shirts.

It was desert western versus Vegas dude.

"Love the suits," Eightball O'Rourke said. "I can't give up my jeans, but I'll do the shirt and jacket with my bolo tie."

Nicky had escorted Van and Temple by

the simple gesture of extending both arms, so the women inspected the honor guard from vastly different points of view. Van was theme-hotel executive, dubious to her pale pink–painted toenails.

Temple was curious down to her "Tara O'Hara Scarlett"–painted toenails just what Gangsters would reveal beyond this production-number greeting. Obviously, some remarketing renovations had already been done.

What the interior revealed was Macho Mario Fontana, the boys' uncle, who had dyed-in-the-DNA-authenticated mob roots, as a tour guide.

On his pasta-enhanced rotund form, white pinstripes looked like parentheses with a stutter, but they matched the silver streaks in his Men's Spare Club toupee.

Temple couldn't help thinking had his suit stripes been horizontal . . . they'd have resembled vintage prison stripes. Perfect uniforms for the parking valets. No. Bellmen. The valets would be both male and female here, Bonnie and Clyde types.

She knew this was Nicky and Van's job, dreaming up revamped hotel themes, but she had so many good ideas. This was her best job assignment in aeons.

Their party turned a lot of heads. Nine of the ten Fontana brothers and their Uncle Mario would anytime, even without eight of them attired in Broadway-musical gangster suits. The Glory Hole Gangsters were older and shorter and less natty, but no less interesting. Van and Temple could toddle along ignored, which suited them, because it allowed for a sotto voce tête-à-tête, to combine both Italian and French phrases.

"Nicky is really jazzed on this Gangsters redo," Temple started, stating the obvious.

"And it *is* Nicky, solo," Van replied. "I had no idea. Obviously the brothers had been cooking this up since their custom limo service became such a famous local attraction. I *am* worried that the accentuated "mob" theme is going to focus too much attention on Nicky's Family connections."

"The consensus," Temple pointed out, "is that the mob 'went corporate' in the seventies, and any remaining shenanigans are shadows of their former selves."

"I know. But the Fontana name carries overtones of the old days."

Meanwhile, Temple had been taking in the usual casino trappings. "This place always came across as old-fashioned and intimate and has a ready-made vintage gangster ambience. Oh, look! I love that the shopping marquee reads the 'Moll Mall.' Don't you?"

"I don't quite get it," Van said, trailing Temple to the brightly lit tunnels of shop windows sparkling with feminine glitz.

"You grew up in Europe, so you wouldn't know the reference, but Americans would. A 'gun moll' was a gangster's girlfriend. Usually her clothes were brighter than her I.Q."

"Wasn't there some civil unrest in Africa decades ago, before the Tutsi and the Hutu? A bloody uprising of natives who were called the Mau Mau?" Van asked.

"Exactly. Almost everybody younger than a stereo system has forgotten that, but 'Moll Mall' has that same ring of madness, only it's all us riled-up female shoppers."

"I'm not much of a shopper," Van noted.

She doesn't have to be, Temple thought. The more money a woman has, the less she likes to join the shopping scrum to hunt for bargains and "perfect little" thises and thats. Temple could see that women and shopping are like men and sports: both are self-expressive, energetic youthful hobbies that become sporadic spectator sports as one gets older and tired and more responsible.

Of course, Temple *herself* was aeons away from any of those last three things.

A sharp whistle — not a wolf whistle — turned Temple from her chance to educate Van on conspicuous consumption that was more conspicuous than costly. Most of the biggest and choicest Strip hotels sold only luxury goods in eerily quiet, elegant shops far from the madding crowd.

Gangsters was clearly not that kind of place. Nicky's urgent whistle alone showed that.

Van turned slowly, like the Queen Mary, annoyed by the streetwise hailing.

"The Mob Museum," Uncle Macho Mario Fontana mouthed reverently from the bottom of an escalator flanked by neon cityscapes of Chicago.

"Not likely to be on the level of the Guggenheim at the Venetian," Van suggested under her breath as she and Temple hustled through the milling gamblers. "This is going to be a bigger disaster than the revamped Aladdin was, but I suppose Nicky wants gainful employment for his playboy brothers."

"They *have* made a lucrative go of the limo service," Temple said.

"What have we made quite a go of?" the nearest brother asked.

It could have been Armando. Or Ralph. Their white straw summer fedoras made the look-alike clan even harder to distinguish from one another. What part of tall, dark, and handsome is a hallmark?

"The museum is up here," Macho Mario gestured from twelve smooth-gliding steps above them. "Watch yer high heels, ladies. We don't want any unfortunate accidents at Gangsters."

Nicky had waited to swing onto the moving stairs behind Temple and Van. "Don't worry," he advised, "I've got your backsides."

Van visibly bit her tongue, while Temple was tempted to turn around and stick hers out. Nicky was in an ideal position to be cheeky and knew it.

At the escalator's top, Temple wasn't surprised to spot a lavish 1930s-style movie theater blinking its neon-bulbed marquee at them like a flirtatious chorus girl's false eyelashes.

The name between the blinking lights read *The Roxie.*

"Oh," Van said, impressed for the first time, "an American movie palace."

The graduated triangle of Art Deco columns thrust up in step-pyramid glory. Its towering central spire was silhouetted against a twilight-azure sky darkening to a navy blue dusted with golden stars, a sickle

161

moon serving as the dot on the spire's exclamation point.

They followed the red carpet through the lobby populated with black-and-white human-sized cutouts of the great gangster noir movie actors . . . James Cagney and Edward G. Robinson, Humphrey Bogart and Ida Lupino, Robert Mitchum and Barbara Stanwyck.

Beyond the double doors with the porthole windows, tommy guns rat-a-tatted and car brakes screeched as men groaned and women screamed. It sounded as much like a shooting gallery as the Santiago-occupied suite at the Crystal Phoenix had, but when two Fontana brothers swept the doors open, the movie "screen" before their eyes was a cutout set that they could walk right through.

Then they were strolling ill-lit alleyways littered by fallen bodies, with wax figures in trench coats huddled over submachine guns and a sound track blaring out threats and counterthreats and lines of immortal gangster-film dialogue, like "You dirty rat."

"*Dis* is where the latest find will be," Macho Mario said, adopting Chicago-style mobster diction like a theatrical pro.

"Latest find?" Van asked.

"Yeah. The body part that just surfaced

from Lake Mead, now that the dried-up fringes uncovered some dirty work."

"Surely," Temple said, "the police wouldn't release —"

"Vegas is not just some one-Bugsy burg," Macho Mario said. "We have a Madam Tussauds wax museum in town. There are these mortuary artists or whatever from the morgue to the Madam's working here. Macho Mario does not wait for things to become public domain. My domain *is* public. *Voilà!*"

Well, Temple thought, *according to legend, the old-time gangsters did carry submachine guns in violin cases.* She supposed that implied some "culture."

Macho Mario whisked a black trench coat from what seemed a nearby hunched figure to reveal a display pedestal surmounted by a Plexiglas box. Through the clear plastic, one could view a glob of coagulated concrete from which two splintered shin bones stood up like giant toothpicks in an aspic of solid cement oatmeal.

"Oh, my God," Van muttered, "shades of the Black Museum."

"Black Museum?" Macho Mario was gratified by the reaction to his prize. "I like that title. This is just a mock-up of the latest body parts found in Lake Mead, but it

163

will be in Gangsters upgraded Black Museum. Oh, wait! We gotta make clear we're not celebrating black gangsta rappers. Boys, isn't that going to be confusing?"

Yes, Temple thought, as the Fontana brothers rolled their eyes in unison.

"The Black Museum I was referring to," Van explained, "is a very old, private, and venerable museum kept at Scotland Yard in London."

" 'Venerable'?" Macho Mario rolled the word on his tongue like Mama Fontana's world-famous pasta sauce. "That means fancy, right? Scotland Yard? That's Sherlock Holmes stuff, right?"

Van absorbed Macho Mario's further questions with inarticulate disbelief, while her husband placed a quieting palm on his uncle's well-padded suit shoulder.

"Yeah," Nicky said. "Pardon my wife's shock. She's a tender blossom, reared in Continental girls academies. The Black Museum hit her at quite an impressionable age. The museum is this 'little shop of horrors,' you could say, at Scotland Yard headquarters. Few outside the constabulary get in to see it, but her daddy was a major hotel manager —"

"Like you." Macho Mario nodded seriously.

"Like me and Van. Only in London. Her father got them an 'in,' because this place is famously hard to get into."

Macho Mario's manicured hand lifted like an upscale traffic cop's. "Say no more. That happens with them fancy French restaurants in Paris. You gotta reserve months in advance by letter. Now that is class. The Eiffel Tower joint at the Paris Hotel on the Strip is classy, but a letter in advance is real class."

"Real class," Nicky repeated. "And e-mail may do it nowadays. You must remember that Van's father was German."

"Sorry," Macho Mario commiserated with Van, who was now biting her lip from either fury or laughter. "Italian is much better."

Nicky soldiered on. "So Van was just twelve when they had the tour, and there was a pedestal like this one, with a clear cube atop it, only it was actually really thick glass."

"This Plexiglas here is better than glass." Macho Mario rapped thick knuckles on the surface, making an interior liquid quiver creepily. "It's lighter. More modern. More expensive. Not breakable."

"Absolutely, Uncle Mario."

"I buy the best."

"Of course, but back to the Black Museum," Nicky said.

"Did it have all these lights and sound effects, eh? Like a gangster movie?"

"No," Van finally said, speaking for herself, "it was just a series of offices then, really, with some framed Jack the Ripper notes on the wall, an acid murderer's claw-footed bathtub, and tables of confiscated homemade weapons, including Freddy Krueger's clawed gloves from the American horror film series, with human blood on the razorblade nails."

"Yeah? I'm impressed. That Freddy the Ripper! What a hit man! Dressed up like a movie creep and doing the serial-cutter crawl through London."

"That's not what made the biggest impression on Van," Nicky said.

"Nor the Victorian Inquisition–like S-and-M machinery," Van muttered under her breath to Temple, whose eyes widened.

"What in that office suite of horrors did impress you so much, little lady?" Macho Mario inquired delicately. "A knitting-needle murder weapon?"

"No, Uncle Mario," Van answered as coolly as only Van could. "It was the glass display cube so like this one, also filled with some liquid or other."

Macho Mario glanced at the concrete-booted shinbones. "Death by water would have kinda terrified this guy before his end came," he said. "I can see how it scared a little girl like you."

"Nicky said the exhibit made the 'biggest impression' on me, not that it scared me."

"No?" Macho Mario managed to sound both condescending and dubious.

"No," Van said. "Something floated in the liquid, which was evidently a preservative: a severed human arm. Cut off here." The edge of Van's pale hand gave a light karate chop to her own upper arm. "Severed across the humerus bone. It had been floating there, flesh and fingers and all, for decades."

"Ew," somebody said, behind the inner circle gazing at the impaled bones.

Temple turned, surprised to find the speaker had been Spuds Lonnigan, the Three O'Clock Louie's cook.

"I'll never be able to boil another soup bone in my kitchen life," he went on. "Why would the Brit cops have a severed arm on display?"

Van smiled. "They had crime scene fingerprints that they thought would match a German perpetrator. So they wired the Berlin police to send them the man's fingerprints."

"The man in question," Nicky said, "happened to have been killed in a police shootout, so the German police cut off his right arm, packed it in dry ice, and shipped it to Scotland Yard."

"But —" Macho Mario was almost speechless with confusion. "Why the whole arm? Why not just the hand, which would be, uh, cheaper to ship?"

"Teutonic efficiency," Nicky explained, straight-faced. "The Black Museum guide explained the matter that way. Why skimp on body parts when you could as easily ship an arm as a hand. You'll understand why I don't cross my wife, Uncle Mario."

"I guess not!" He wiped his palms nervously on his pant seams.

"A gruesome little trophy, this," Temple agreed, gazing upon their own similar artifact, "and it has a genuine Las Vegas connection, likely mob. Until someone knows who and why that guy's feet were encased in cement and dropped like an anchor in Lake Mead, though, it doesn't command a lot of media interest. And that's what you need to launch the announcement of a redone hotel."

"You're a snoop sister," Macho Mario told Temple, with narrowed eyes. "You figure all that out."

Eightball O'Rourke stepped up beside Temple. "I heard some long-gone mobsters favored the 'Lake Mead footbath' as a way to dump rivals or turncoat associates. That was in the forties, before the place became a tourist draw. So anything in the way of evidence on this guy's bones was probably eaten away decades ago."

"On the other hand," Temple said, "solved cold cases are a hot ticket in both fact and fiction now. I'll check with the coroner's office. Forensics is much more sophisticated, and ID-ing a long-dead body would make a bigger tourist draw."

Nicky surveyed the surrounding vintage cars and blown-up photographs.

"Great stories make museums, not exhibits," he said. "We need to bring everything alive."

At that moment, a figure in a huge photograph stepped away from the wall and sprayed the onlookers with . . . the neck of an electric guitar, as a sound track played screaming riffs, and the static photographs started streaming past as if everyone present was riding a carousel.

Which they were.

Even Van lost her composure enough to reach for Nicky's support, at the same instant chrome stripper poles shot up from the floor, ready to be grabbed for balance. Nightclub booths also levitated around the moving circle's edge. The Fontana brothers gestured the others into seats, then swung round the poles and seated themselves.

Santiago in his white pseudo zoot suit with his hopefully unloaded vintage tommy gun leaped between the rotating booths into the carousel's center like a ringmaster.

"Sound," he shouted into the din. "Motion. Surprise. This must look like a traditional museum but become an 'amuseum.' An amusement park that does not 'park' itself but takes you, the viewer — the 'amusee' — places."

Temple grabbed hold of a cocktail-table edge. The entire exhibit area was slowly screwing itself down to a lower level, the surrounding walls changing into black-and-white movie scenes, with Edward G. Robinson barking threats at the circling party as anonymous punks in trench coats and fedoras sprayed crescendos of gunfire into their midst.

There was only the slightest jerk as the elevator floor reached the lower level and stopped turning.

Leggy cocktail waitresses with aprons as small as their bar trays scissored their fishnet-hose-clad gams to the tables, setting down drinks in vintage lowball and small martini glasses.

Temple tried to name the drinks. The first

to come to mind was . . . an old-fashioned. She thought she recognized some gin rickeys and Singapore Slings.

A flat-screen TV menu materialized from the middle of each booth's table, flashing movie scenes of the available drinks clutched in some long-gone movie star's black-and-white hand.

"Disneyland for adults," Van declared, sipping her — Temple checked the flashing "pages" of filmed drinks — Tom Collins. "Everything's animated." Van eyed the six frozen-faced beauty-queen waitresses floating drinks down to tables occupied by the men in the party, while Santiago explained their video menus to them. "Except for the eye candy."

"Gangsters gotta have that," Nicky said.

"Vegas too." Van glanced at Temple and sighed. "What do you think?"

"This is just the first stage Santiago proposed," Nicky said. "It can always be redacted."

Using that ridiculous word made Temple and Van laugh in tandem.

"We can always 'redact' Santiago," Van added.

"Meanwhile," Temple suggested, "let's see what other media magic tricks he has to show us. I do like the sinking cocktail bar.

Very post-*Titanic.*"

"Uncle Mario wanted a bank of Marriott-style bullet-shaped glass elevator cars with tufted white satin-lined doors to reach the underground level," Nicky admitted to the women's groans, "so I vote for the cocktail carousel myself."

By then Santiago had reached their booth and swung into his sales routine.

"This is only a crude approximation yet. The Speakeasy bar and restaurant will be under the area of the hotel we just left. That offers necessary ventilation and crowd-control possibilities in case of disaster. This descending carousel is the cocktail area, of course, and beyond us, in the dark, Gangsters limos on rails will await passengers desiring an exciting trip to the Crystal Phoenix.

"These elderly gentlemen are becoming quite animated about the menu possibilities. Apparently, they have actually drunk some of these amusing old cocktails."

The Glory Hole Gang members were indeed hashing over future entrée names on menus, and Temple was dreaming up a theme of bullet-hole-riddled online pages, with sound effects and videos, and Van's face was still paler than her hair.

"Trends change constantly in the hospitality industry," Van said at last. "What's new quickly becomes 'old hat,' and what was forgotten becomes the new favorite. For a while."

"Why, Miss von Rhine, could you possibly be talking about Santiago's multimedia inventions?" the man himself asked.

"Eventually," Van said, with a softening smile. "Everything moves so fast these days."

"One would hope *values* would not," Santiago said.

The word seemed odd coming from such a flamboyantly shallow persona, Temple thought.

Still, every artist in every media had to be a one-man or one-woman show these days, on the Internet, on Facebook, on Twitter — "on" all the time, everywhere. She'd even heard Matt complaining that the radio station wanted to move him "onto YouTube and beyond" their Web site.

"Let me show you," Santiago suggested, "the darker possibilities ahead."

His gel-slicked hair reflected the motion in the wall-cast videos as he nodded into the unlit direction of the proposed Chunnel of Crime.

As they walked forward, out of the elevator-cocktail area, work lights hanging above them glowed into life as they passed.

That caught the eyes on the cocktail carousel, where Nicky's brothers were content to sit and sip and flirt with the waitresses dressed in pointy, short, and skimpy, patented Rat Pack sixties style. The Glory Hole Gang, though, couldn't resist exploring the unknown dark for possible treasure. They deserted their drinks and came clattering after the disappearing party of four. So far, the lower depths of Gangsters were just that: a crude basement tunnel hacked from limestone.

"Love the ambience," Nicky said. "Raw, real. We'd want to keep the earthy stone walls, dirt floor, dim lights, the sense of a primitive flouting of the supposed order and law above. Bathtub gin. Sin."

"Nicky," Van asked, "have you been tunneling through from the Phoenix already?"

"Ah, call it an investigative sampling," he answered.

"Call it chutzpah," Van said tartly. "So . . ."

She turned to the Glory Hole Gang, who'd regarded her with elaborate and even fearful courtesy since the introductions at the Crystal Phoenix. ". . . Am I to understand you five would look favorably upon reinventing Lake Mead's popular Three O'Clock Louie's restaurant as Three

174

O'Clock's Speakeasy subterranean bar and restaurant down here?"

"Ah . . ." Spuds, the short-order cook, rubbed his palms on his jeans' side seams. "Yes, ma'am. All that deep frying is hard on the epidermis. I would be beholden if I could try a more varied and European, but kitschy, cuisine. I am a big fan of Julia Child and Wolfgang Puck. Something, uh, high-end, I mean. And fun."

He winked, looking like Long John Silver in chef's clothing.

Van blinked.

She turned to Temple. "Am I right in believing that your PR genes are eating all this up?"

Temple went with the flow. She rubbed her palms together, flexing her fingers and flashing her long, strong natural fingernails, painted Hyper Hussy Red, which was a bit toned down from her Scarlett-Woman toenail color.

"Yes, ma'am," she decreed. "I could make this concept pop on YouTube, Facebook, Twitter, and every surviving newspaper on-line. *Baaad* is good. I'm thinking a downloadable temporary-tattoo page."

Van's delicate brows frowned ever so slightly. "Why the tunnel and riding the rails?"

175

Nicky, as usual, had an answer. "The average tourist can't afford to rent a Gangsters limo for the whole evening. This way they invest in a kicky new-old drink and get a shot of speed and nostalgia in one bolt."

"What about ventilation? Regulations? You're talking an underground fast rail operation, no matter how short the distance."

"We can handle it, Van," Nicky urged. "We have the underground, Jackson Action Haunted Mine Ride okayed on the Crystal Phoenix end, and the rails are already laid. That's why I brought in Santiago. He's first and foremost a renowned and innovative architect. We're lucky he's interested in our rather limited project."

"Nonsense, Nicky," Santiago objected. "Las Vegas is a petri dish for architects. A playground. Anything goes."

"Say," Wild Blue Pike exclaimed as a new work light revealed more tunnel, "this sure reminds me of our mining days working the Silver Spoon out near Rabbit Hole Spring, don't it, boys? This tunnel safe?"

"Of course." Santiago was offended. "Everything above us and to the side has been shored up by steel struts. These 'walls' you see are concrete and stone aggregate, troweled on like hand-sculpted walls in houses. It only seems to be natural stone."

"Waal, this don't seem all that natural," Cranky said, approaching a section.

He pulled a metal measuring tape off his worn leather belt and rapped it on the ersatz stone.

A small hollow knock sounded.

CHAPTER 16
A RAT IN TIME
SAVES NINE LIVES

Needless to say, I am always "all ears."

And I am not alone. At the moment.

Miss Midnight Louise and I have been exploring the tunnel from the Crystal Phoenix side. "Spelunking," I believe they call it.

I call it "looking for Elvis."

Of course, I do not tell Missy Louise that. She is most skeptical on the subject of Elvis. She would better believe me if I said that Michael Jackson had appeared to me in the tunnel created a few seasons back. Actually, since that was named the "Jersey Joe Jackson Action Attraction," I would not be surprised if the King of Pop had popped in to visit the King en route to rock 'n' roll heaven.

I must say I am glad that a major concert career is not in my past or my future. It seems to be a fatal job choice.

This subterranean rendezvous was Miss Midnight Louise's idea. She hissed the suggestion in my ear during the brouhaha of the

Midnight family reunion at the police substation, whilst my parents (her grandparents) were squaring off.

"I have been eavesdropping in the Crystal Phoenix executive offices," Louise informs me as we amble along in the almost-dark, following the steel tracks of the defunct Haunted Mine Ride portion of the attraction.

I spot a faint glow far ahead of us, but I do not wish to mention any lights at the ends of tunnels, because (1) it is a cliché, and I am nothing if not original, and (2) that has become a phrase synonymous with moving on to another existential plane, like death, and I do not intend to use my battle-sharp shivs for plucking a harp quite yet.

"Eavesdropping is admirable," I admit, "and one of our species' finest skills. The human observer sees us as flicking our ears against the incursions of vermin, when their banal maunderings are the object of our interest."

"It is not very banal around the Crystal Phoenix of late," Louise says dryly. "Not with Mr. Nicky and Miss Temple around to cook up new promotional schemes. Miss Van von Rhine and I have our mitts full keeping the lid on."

"Never fear. I am here to supervise now."

Miss Midnight Louise favors me with the sight of her tail high-flagging it ahead of me down the Chunnel of Crime-to-Be.

I remind myself that we are possibly — even probably — related and follow her in what you might call a disinterested way and I might call a darn shame.

The overhead work lights remind me of a night game of baseball or some other entertainment where human and feline interests meet. I must say the human recreational propensity for chasing balls of all sizes, from tiny golf ball to big basketball, is one of their most endearing qualities.

Even as I muse, Miss Midnight Louise can be seen to stop suddenly ahead.

She crouches and freezes.

I trot to catch up to her, but just as I arrive she bounds away.

I am too old to fall for this game!

I bound after her to the section of wall where she has landed.

Alas, by the time I hit the wall, she has bounded on, and I bounce off rough concrete like a Ping-Pong ball. Not the kind of sport I had in mind — me being the thing that is smacked, whacked, and dribbled.

(In fact, a bit of unleashed drool from the impact is now meandering down the hairs of my chinny chin chin.)

I pause to hastily tidy my moustache, shocked to see Miss Midnight Louise shooting along the base of the wall some thirty feet away. Luckily, she stops to start digging frantically, so I am able to come abreast of her.

Will I deliver a verbal thrashing!

Before I can get my growl wound up, I hear heavy footsteps approaching.

"Dig, you old fool!" Miss Midnight Louise admonishes *me,* when the snit should be on the other mitt. "They will never get the idea unless we ham it up like crazy."

I agree that humans can be unbelievably dense, but am myself a bit puzzled.

"Dig!" she orders. "Unless you want your roommate to walk right past the entrance to the third tunnel."

Third tunnel? What are number one and number two . . . ? No, I am not referring to the coy way people describe the major variations of dog doo-doo and dog dewatering.

We have tunnels from Gangsters and the Phoenix meeting in the middle.

Third tunnel?

I see only a crack in the seam where dirt floor meets plastered wall.

Then a small furry head pokes through.

I need no further invitation to scrape away with all shivs going like a circular saw. No dirty rat is going to move in on my territory, which is anywhere I happen to be.

"Louie!" a familiar oncoming female voice

calls in shock behind me.

"Louise," calls an even more shocked male voice.

"Dig until we bare dirt," Miss Midnight Louise hisses into my ear hairs until they tickle. "They will not get the picture unless we draw out every last detail."

"Must be mice," I hear Macho Mario Fontana say, dismissing our prey.

Mice? My well-placed spitball would handle mice. We are talking bigger game here.

"Is the bigger one our Three O'Clock Louie?" I hear chubby Spuds Lonnigan inquire in a slightly breathless wheeze.

He is a fine one to mistake me for my older, fatter father! That is like the potbellied stove calling the cattle black. Or some such phrase.

I hear a sharp squeal from within the wall and see that Louise has pinned a long, hairless tail with her fanned front shivs.

"Rats," my brilliant Miss Temple points out. "We will have to fumigate. No way Gangsters can run a restaurant down here until the entire rat population is completely eradicated."

Murderous little thing, is she not?

That's my roomie!

I lay a big mitt over Louise's dainty one and pull back with one powerful jerk, revealing the entire rat. Case closed.

Before I can do a karate chop to the neck,

the rat's racing claws kick something big and dusty out of its hole right into our faces.

We sneeze in tandem, our claws relaxing in one uncontrollable reflex moment.

Rats! Exhibit A is history. We step back, boxing our nostrils and vibrissae free of some pretty well-aged dirt and sand.

My Miss Temple approaches on her hind claws, aka spike heels, and bends to pick up the trash. Humans, even the best of them, are hard to figure sometimes.

It is obvious that Louise and I deserve to be picked up and made much of for our valiant effort to seek, find, and agitate vermin. Not that we would accept such namby-pamby fondling even when well deserved. We are professionals. Just buy us a steak and salmon dinner and call it quits.

Miss Temple unfolds the wad of paper.

"This looks like . . . a stock certificate."

"Yeah?" Nicky asks. "That's worth about a penny these days."

Miss Van von Rhine stretches out a hand. "Let me see."

The light is dim, but long, tall Pitchblende O'Hara steps up and produces a tiny high-intensity flashlight.

"This and a Swiss Army knife are always in my jeans," he explains.

Miss Van von Rhine quirks a smile at her

confident spouse.

"You'd be wrong, Nicky. This isn't as old as it looks, and it looks less like a stock certificate and more like a bearer bond."

"Bearer bond?" Miss Temple asks. "Is that worth anything?"

"Ten thou," Mr. Nicky says, taking it to stretch the crumpled paper smooth, "to anyone who holds it in his hand."

"Or hers," Van says, taking custody.

Girls can be so possessive.

CHAPTER 17
LOVE CONNECTION

It was early evening by the time Temple returned to her Circle Ritz condo. She was still a having a brain attack that made her stomach turn cartwheels. What an amazing turn of events! What a PR break, if she handled it right.

She had to slow down and think. She had to call Matt.

First, though, she had to take a shower and blast the plaster and limestone dust off her epidermis and out of her hair. The showerhead installed over the vintage bathtub was a fancy chrome "waterfall" type, expensive and European-made. Its warm, tingling downpour rinsed her right off. Yup. She was enjoying one of Max's upgrades of the premises. She so did want to wash that man's memory out of her hair.

Perhaps only leaving the condo that had initially been "theirs" would end the unwanted memory reruns. Matt's unit was too small for two, though. Unless Electra would let them remodel two units into one, they might have to move out. Darn. Rip Midnight Louie from his charming Circle Ritz home? Unthinkable!

Temple, now double-wrapped in a huge Crystal Phoenix bath towel (perk of the job), padded barefoot and dripping into the main room. She threw herself down on the living room couch and picked up her iPhone to dial Matt's cell phone. No answer.

He often turned it off when traveling, perhaps the only annoying habit he had. When Matt was on camera on a major TV talk show, he sure didn't want a ring tone broadcasting over the air, even though Temple had installed Leonard Cohen's awesome "Hallelujah" and it was pretty playable.

She left a message, part love note and part incoherent job report, disappointed. Matt always had long business dinners at fancy places when he was in Chicago, so they often didn't connect until midnight or later.

Temple couldn't wait that long. She was bubbling over with ideas and anxieties (wasn't that always the way?) and needed to run them by someone she could trust. What she was planning was risky to the point of being a hokey failure, but her job depended on selling her bosses and the public on her thinking. A consultant always needed someone close to consult.

Matt's room phone rang and rang.

She tried the cell phone again. If the dinner ran late and the wine had been primo, she knew Matt would call her on the room phone from bed. He knew she liked to wake up to his voice, and while it wasn't totally phone sex, it was sweet-little-nothing sex that left them glowing and intimately connected, long-distance.

Matt's experience hosting *The Midnight Hour* radio call-in program had made him a sex symbol to thousands of women, and Temple had that smooth baritone on personal speed-dial. She indulged in a little shiver that cooled down her overactive brain.

Temple kept her old-fashioned line phones because they were cozier to cuddle up to and she used a headset on her cells for business calls. She didn't want to get brain cancer from long cell phone calls. Well, it could happen! Besides, her long-time bedroom phone was shaped like a red spike-heeled shoe and she'd never give it up.

Temple jumped up and went to her tiny black-and-white kitchen that would wake up a narcoleptic. She opened the refrigerator and stared inside, then did the same with all her cupboards. She hadn't eaten dinner but she was too jumpy to find anything appetizing . . . except her absent fiancé.

Back to the living room to scan the day's newspaper.

She jumped up again in five minutes and did an all-room under, inside, and above search for Midnight Louie. At least she could *tell* him her plans. He listened with remarkable attentiveness and intelligence and only yawned occasionally during her monologues.

But the only black body hairs and rare white whisker she could find were throwaways. Who knew where he'd gone after the hubbub in the Chunnel of Crime-to-be?

Back to the kitchen. Caramel corn. No! Blueberry yogurt. No. Try the phones again. No answer.

She finally went to bed without supper, all alone without her iPhone. She found a terrible sixties movie on a bottom-feeder cable channel and watched it until her eyes crossed and her nerves flat-lined and . . . she went to sleep.

The old-fashioned ring from the bedside phone gave her the expected but still pleasant little shock.

"Oooh, is this my secret midnight caller?" she cooed into the shoe phone's toe, only then realizing something might have gone wrong at the Phoenix and midnight was prime time there.

Matt's laugh was low. "Hi, Lolita. This is Lonesome calling. You sound all sleepy and warm."

"And I'm only wearing a towel."

"You just showered?"

"No, hours ago, but I went to bed early just so you could wake me up."

"I could wake you up a lot more if I were there."

"I *know*. So it was a late dinner? I left messages on all your phones."

"The cell's on off in my jacket pocket, but I saw your red light blinking on the hotel phone the second I got in. You must be ready for business."

"For you, always." Temple let her voice exit intimate mode. "But I really do have business to talk over with you."

"So you've been so frantic to reach me just for . . . business?"

She started to explain, but he interrupted.

"Actually, Temple, I might have some work stuff to discuss with you before this trip ends. So what's up besides me?"

"Oh, really? You just made me forget what I was going to say."

"Small chance. I can hear your PR vibes revving up even now. Spill."

"Okay. I've got this really wild idea for promoting Nicky Fontana's mob-style update of the Phoenix ex-underground attraction and Gangsters Hotel and Casino. Guess what we found in the under-construction tunnel connecting the two properties today?"

He knew better than to guess and she rattled on.

"It's so incredible. Midnight Louie and Louise found it, chasing a rat into a hole and digging out an old bearer bond for ten thousand dollars!"

"Louie stuck in a paw and pulled out a plum?"

"Financially speaking. Van said bearer bonds *never* lose their value. Whoever holds 'em can cash 'em."

"I imagine Louie and Louise were relieved of their find?"

"They may be smart, but they don't have bank accounts. Van has the bond now, but one of the Glory Hole Gang thought the side wall was hollow in one spot, and the workmen went at it with pneumatic drills and the Glory Hole Gang grabbed pick axes and the noise and dirt were atrocious, but they uncovered a buried vault door right in the middle of the tunnel! I mean a bank-style, heavy-metal vault door. Locked. Can you imagine if the vault is stuffed with bearer bonds and silver dollars?"

"Big news," Matt agreed. "What are you going to do with it, Ace?"

"The workmen chipped away all the concealing construction and I got this idea."

"Obviously."

"Given the legends about the Phoenix's own Jersey Joe Jackson hiding stashes of cash and silver dollars in and around Vegas, I want the workmen to open the vault in full media presence. The public loves the idea of buried treasure, so the 'opening' should bring out all the syndicated media from Los Angeles as well as all the usual suspects in Vegas. Nicky could not buy better exposure. But I need to get the whole setup together really fast. What do you think?"

"I think you're brilliant. If anyone can pull this off, you can."

"It might be a real tangle who gets the money, but that's up to the powers-that-be to decide."

"True, but *I* think you should get a bonus."

"Bonuses are good. That would help with

the bridesmaids' costs for the wedding."

"Bridesmaids, plural? You *are* planning on a big production."

"I *always* plan on a big production, keep that in mind."

"I do, I do."

"And that's what you'll be repeating at the altar. Gee, I hope I'm not biting off more than I can chew here."

"You're talking about the unveiling of the vault again, I hope."

"Yeah." Temple suddenly felt a nasty, aching gnaw in her stomach. Cold feet?

"What's the worst that could happen?" she asked him.

She answered her own question before he could.

"The worst that could happen is that vault could be absolutely empty."

"I'll say a prayer that it isn't," Matt promised.

"Thank you, Matt!"

The Deity having been invoked, they wound up the conversation with a few innocent but extended good-byes, and Temple hung up.

The gnawing feeling in her stomach wasn't cold feet about anything. Apparently her nervous fit was over. She knew her course.

She jumped out of bed, heading for the

main room and the kitchen.

She was starved! Starved for . . . blueberry yogurt with a crisp topping of . . . caramel corn.

CHAPTER 18
WHOSE VAULT IS IT?

Temple found it impossibly nerve-racking to have all of Fontana, Inc. peering over her shoulder, including Van von Rhine.

Not that Temple's shoulders were broad or high enough to keep a grasshopper from kibitzing over them.

"You're sure we went with the right announcer?" Van asked.

Underground, in the hard-surfaced tunnel, her hushed whisper carried as if she were yelling through a megaphone.

Not to worry. The announcer was absorbed in fussing with the tiny earphone in one ear and eyeing himself in a mirror the prop girl was holding up.

"Is this all the camera-power opening Bugsy Siegel's vault could pull?" Macho Mario Fontana demanded from behind Temple's other shoulder.

"It's all the major stations as far as L.A. and several national news feature shows, including *Excess Hollywood*," Temple assured every Fontana ear within hearing, which included Nicky and eight of his brothers, who formed an impressive crowd on their own. "Everybody's pooling camera teams now. Recession."

"Recession!" Macho Mario ridiculed. "In my day we had goddamn real Depressions, not these pansy recessions."

"Watch the political correctness," Nicky growled.

"Now I can't even say the word *Depression?*"

"It's the flower thing, Zio Mario," Julio put in as the second-oldest and therefore bravest nephew on site.

"I will call a g-d daffodil a daffodil. And who is this limp-wrist holding the microphone? I wanted someone with authority, like Robert Stack or Charlton Heston."

"They're dead." Julio broke the news.

"No kidding? And they didn't even announce it on TV? The world is going to the bloodhounds."

Temple didn't want to admit she shared the paterfamilias's anxiety.

She'd wanted Geraldo Rivera, but he'd been booked.

At least she'd found someone who remembered who Geraldo Rivera was.

Basically, this job required a huckster who deeply believed in his own seriousness.

Meanwhile, the pneumatic hammers drilled into the rock surrounding the massive metal door of the vaunted "vault."

Rock shards littering the packed dirt floor and the support structure's wooden ribs made this section of tunnel feel like the belly of a petrified whale. The vault had been sited halfway between Gangsters' and the Crystal Phoenix's stoutly supported tunnel of fauxrock mine walls bolted into strong concrete beneath.

Everybody present wore hard hats, including the videographers toting large cameras on their shoulders, giving them *Alien* monster silhouettes.

The Phoenix's section had built-in temperature controls, but this new area was the last freshly excavated bit from the Gangsters side and oddly combined hot and cold spots. It felt dank, but also steamy.

Temple figured a little sweat added to the ambience, and it certainly made the drill operators' tan, muscled, bare arms look wrestling-ring ready. Two of the four videographers were female and were not missing panning the local color.

Somehow Crawford Buchanan, self-proclaimed local "personality," radio vagabond, and perpetrator of cheesy events usually involving underage females, was the exact right figure to ballyhoo the forthcoming mystery revelation. His short stature, black suit, and gel-slathered, black-streaked white pompadour made him an "anti"-Santiago. It also brought a funereal gravity to an operation that threatened to reveal . . .

"Bugsy Siegel's vault, folks. This massive rusted steel door has been dated to be at least forty years old," he shouted into the mike over the racket of spitting faux rock and concrete.

"You know the story of Al Capone's Chicago vault, found decades after his death and famously broken into on live television with Geraldo Rivera at the microphone in nineteen eighty-six. No? Forgotten about that? Let me fill you in."

Buchanan began pacing in front of the looming steel vault door.

"Capone took over the Chicago Outfit in nineteen twenty-five, before Vegas was a glimmer in the mob's eye. He was a primo mob boss. He planned the Saint Valentine's Day massacre and ran the operation from a suite in the Lexington Hotel until he was arrested for income-tax evasion in nineteen thirty-one. Capone was kaput."

Temple was wishing by now that Crawford

was kaput. Every bit of this exposition could be cut, and probably would be.

"So, folks," Buchanan continued, "the old Lexington Hotel was long overdue for renovation by the eighties. When a surveying crew comes in, what do they find? A series of secret tunnels. Yes, folks, tunnels just like this one linking Gangsters with the far older former Joshua Tree Hotel-Casino, where Jersey Joe Jackson holed up until his death. And in those Chicago tunnels, they found escape routes to local taverns and brothels. They even found a shooting range! And rumors of a secret vault beneath the hotel." His radio baritone deepened into a thrilling basso: "Just. Like. This. One."

Crawford straightened his slight frame even as his voice grew deeper and more powerful.

"By then, Geraldo Rivera himself was kaput. He'd been fired by ABC, but he cooked up a comeback broadcast, a two-hour live special program of opening that vault. Thirty million people and standing-by IRS agents and a medical examiner watched, breathless to find Capone's buried riches or bodies.

"Inside the finally-opened vault? Nothing. It was empty, but Rivera's career was revived.

"And, don't forget. This is Vegas, babies! We've already had a notorious vault excavated and found it stuffed with treasure, if not bodies. Vegas's shady founding father, Benny Binion, had a son named Ted, probably killed because of a massive vault buried in the desert, which authorities opened on his death in nineteen ninety-eight. The vault was . . . crammed with six tons of silver bullion. Six tons! Not to mention scads of chips and paper currency and piles of uncirculated mint Carson City silver dollars, more than a hundred thousand, worth millions. And that was only a decade or so ago."

This recital was actually causing some onlooker jaws to drop, including Temple's. She glanced around. Even Santiago's eyes were glinting with speculation. This tunnel was his playground at the moment. . . . Might he find more vaults?

Maybe there *was* something fabulous inside this vault.

"Remember," Buchanan egged on his now-actually-spellbound audience, "for the last century, Vegas remained a playground for outlaws, from train robbers to mobsters to corporate shysters."

Buchanan was in full flight of fancy, covering all bases.

"This is not Al Capone's vault and maybe

not even Bugsy's vault, but it may be Jersey Joe Jackson's. He died supposedly broke, atop this very 'hunka hunka burnin' hidden treasure. Remember? One of Jackson's reputed stashes of mint silver dollars worth millions was discovered a few years ago deep in the desert. Imagine what the cagey old fart would have buried in his own back-yard!

"We're talking fast-buck operators from the Vegas founding era, when Bugsy and his Jersey-Joey-come-lately desert empire-builder pal, Jackson, were putting up the Flamingo and the Joshua Tree Hotels," Buchanan went on. "We know Bugsy was shot dead in his girlfriend's Beverly Hills living room, but Jersey Joe literally faded away in Vegas, just a few hundred feet from and above this very spot. He died in a modest suite in his abandoned Joshua Tree Hotel —"

Temple considered it a Howard Hughes story gone very wrong, much sooner.

"— a hotel now risen from the ashes as the glamorous Crystal Phoenix."

Temple also considered that finding that desert cache unfortunately unmasked Jackson as a cheating member of the Glory Hole Gang of prospectors.

The surviving gang members were all on

site now, grizzled and creaky but still possessing camera-ready grins. Their colorful, Old Vegas presence had really helped roust the media for this admittedly hoary and hokey stunt à la Geraldo's highly hyped *The Mystery of Al Capone's Vault.*

Sensationalism was the name of the media game in print or on film these days, and retro was popular . . . again.

Macho Mario had made it plain to all comers that he was personally hoping that the opened vault would reveal a scantily clad pinup-girl poster on the inside of the door, number one. Then a fortune of some kind.

The surprise existence of the vault was genuine. It predated the Crystal Phoenix excavation and was located beyond the area the hotel had cleared. Although a rat hole circled it, the vault door was sealed tight as a submarine's engine room.

Temple would forgo pinup girls, but some souvenirs from the *Titanic,* say, would be most welcome. Even some more vintage silver dollars. Jersey Joe was rumored to have had more than one stashing spot, and the area above them had been raw desert back in the fifties.

The shrill drone of the drills slipped into another range of shriek.

With a crack, the locking mechanism gave way. The metal door's huge hinges slipped, sending up clouds of stone and metal powder from the surrounding structure.

Fontana brothers frantically clapped the dust from their immaculate silk-blend dark suits, now the same pale color as the powder.

"Pay dirt!" Crawford Buchanan bellowed, pushing Pitchblende O'Hara and Wild Blue Pike aside to jerk on the gleaming brass spoked wheel that would open the door.

Nothing happened. He jumped up and down on the spokes like a monkey on a stick.

Nothing moved.

"Now, there," said Macho Mario, his stocky figure in Fontana signature threads pushing to the fore, "I'm head of the family. I'll do the honors."

He grabbed the huge loosened wheel and tugged. Then he grunted and twisted. Finally, he fell back, panting.

"I thought you cut through the lock," he yelled at the sweat-streaming workmen who had dutifully ebbed aside to let the big shots claim the glory.

Everyone stared, stymied, at the metal powder-dusted door.

Then, while no one was trying, it slowly

edged ajar four inches.

"Jersey Joe's ghost!" Crawford shouted. "Human hands were not touching the handle just now. I was watching and swear it."

Absolutely true. The hovering videographers focused for a close-up of the waist-high mechanism.

Temple's brow crimped with consternation. This was a great effect, but someone must have engineered it. There would be hell to pay when the media realized that. Being short, she looked down, wondering if a concealed chain of some sort had been attached to the door base.

A motion at the door's very bottom caught her eye. A black cat muzzle retreated from the opening.

No, Temple thought. *Impossible. Midnight Louie had "nosed" the metal door open? From the* inside?

She watched his black form slip out and vanish unnoted among the videographers' jean-clad legs as they jockeyed to film the ajar door, not the exiting cat.

Nicky took matters into his hotel owner's hands and stepped up to jerk on the immobile metal spokes with both fists. That old Fontana-brother magic still worked. The bank-vault-thick door groaned open with a clank befitting Marley's ghost . . . and out came . . . walked . . . another black cat, to Temple, anyway, the first giant step for cat-kind to all the other witnesses.

Midnight Louise sat in the opening and yawned.

"Someone's already breached the vault," Eightball O'Rourke accused. "This isn't any debut opening. It's a setup job." He glared at Crawford Buchanan.

Temple pushed to the forefront, even though she might accidentally and unprofessionally appear on camera.

"This vault was not accessible beforehand," she insisted. "We checked it last night and again this morning."

"Stop the fussing and see what's inside," Eightball O'Rourke urged. "You folks call yourself media, but you don't have the curiosity of that little cat there. Now that's better, but don't trample her. That's the Crystal Phoenix mascot."

"Midnight Louise?" Van von Rhine's soprano suddenly cried into the milling people and rising dust. "Don't hurt her!"

Temple herself was pushed aside by Crawford Buchanan as he elbowed through the narrow opening. She didn't see Louise underfoot anywhere.

"I got it!" Buchanan crowed, his voice

echoing off metal. "I'm inside. *Whoo!* What a rank whiff. I sure hope paper money doesn't mildew. Get me some light here."

In seconds, the press of light-bearing workmen and videographers had pushed the heavy door open wide and rinsed the dazzling silver metal interior with light.

It illuminated a room-sized empty safe, all right, except it wasn't empty.

Gasps echoed in the sodden air.

"Let me out!" Buchanan ground the Cuban heels of his pimp shoes into Temple's tender instep as he stampeded past. "It smells like a cat box in there."

By now everyone had stopped crowding and yelling in the opening.

By now every eye, human or mechanical or digital, had fixed on the rotund corpse of a man in white tie and tails who lay oddly but stiffly splayed on the red satin lining of his evening cloak on the safe's steel-gray metal floor.

His white gloves, cane, and a top hat that lay on its glossy black side were arrayed near his pale, bloated features.

"What a rip-off!" someone yelled. "It's a wax dummy."

That certain "someone" had been Crawford Buchanan.

As usual, he was terribly wrong.

Someone else had to do something. Temple guessed it was up to her.

She stepped forward, ripped the mike from Crawford's clammy yet clutching grip, and considered bending down to press her fingers against the formal gentleman's carotid artery just above the high starched collar.

Overkill, so to speak, she decided.

Obviously, the man was as cold and un-moving as a still photo, yet definitely not made of wax. He was dead. Morally, ethi-cally, spiritually and physically, positively and absolutely, undeniably and reliably and most sincerely . . . dead.

Shock had turned everyone present into stone. Then the videographers all rushed forward, grunting to seize the best camera angle.

A wall of expensive dark tailoring materi-alized in front of them, blocking Temple from being overrun. A six-foot wall of gangster-suited muscle between her and a media feeding frenzy was even more wel-come than silver dollars.

When she spoke she knew she was heard but not seen, and that was fine with her too.

"I'm sorry, ladies and gentlemen of the media. We need to clear the scene and call the police. No more filming."

Like a row of ultradressy football linemen, the brothers Fontana swayed en masse this way and that to block all camcorders and cell-phone cameras.

One cell phone bobbing up and down was clutched in Buchanan's pasty hand.

He, unfortunately, was definitely and indubitably not dead.

CHAPTER 19
ROAD TO RUIN

"This whole blasted island is only the size of Wisconsin."

"Indiana, actually," Gandolph corrected.

Max knew he'd sounded cranky just then and had deserved correction for that, if not his geography. His whole body ached from a mere three-hour flight and now this drive across half of Ireland. If he took a wrong turn and needed to reverse direction, his shoulders ached so much he had to turn the car around in several moves on the narrow road. So much for the aftermath of grand gestures. He found it easier to admit to being a mental grouch than a physical one. Call it the *House* syndrome. Wait! That was a television show popping up in his memory. Old or new?

Gandolph must have put up with a lot from him, because he continued speaking in a calm, professorial way. "Ireland is a small nation; always was, Max, but it always loomed large in your personal history."

"Where am I actually 'from,' Garry?"

The older man sighed. Older people often did that. Trouble was, Max was so inclined himself these days.

"Your birth family was . . . is . . . in Wisconsin."

" 'Birth' family? I'm adopted?"

"No, not at all. After Sean's loss, you adopted a number of foreign lands, a different future, and a different family, which you constructed piece by piece. It was all your choice. Forced upon you, but a choice, nevertheless. A hard choice. Especially for a boy, not a man."

Max stomped on the brakes so the modest family car, the Mondeo, did a dramatic TV-chase U-y. Only when they were facing the opposite direction on the deserted country two-lane did Max realize his immature gesture might have strained an older man's neck. Good thing they'd left the major highway, the "colorfully" (not) named M1, to find a quaint place (or a good bush) for a rest stop.

"Sorry," Max said. "I'm acting like an ass."

Garry blinked, then chuckled. "So what's new? Glad to see the old form is still there."

The man Max still often thought of as Gandolph the Great massaged his nape. He wore a soft wool scarf over his suit jacket. Garry Randolph, past seventy, had far more reason to ache than Max did, or at least to complain about it.

"Why," Max asked softly, "do I get the idea you know me way too well?"

"Somebody has to, Max. You've always been Mr. Mystery to everybody who cared to know you."

" 'Cared to know' me. Am I that bad?"

"That . . . demanding. Never more of anyone than of yourself."

Gandolph — and Max now focused on the older man as a magician in the classical sense of a mage, like the wizard Gandalf his stage name played upon — shook his head.

"You're a hard case, Max Kinsella, but hard times made you so. Why do you think we're following the sad trail of Kathleen O'Connor?"

"She's an irresistible siren, that girl renamed Rebecca. I remember the movie."

"Just the movie? There were several TV versions as well."

"Rebecca was a beauty, but she was an evil woman, a manipulator, a man-eater," Max said.

"Granted. Notorious women leave longer legends than noble ones."

"And dead before the novel began, yet she

had more vitality even when dead than the novel's pallid nameless heroine."

"That was the point, my boy. Evil can be not only attractive but vital. Some women are poison."

Max glanced at his mentor as the accelerating Mondeo clung to a curve. "You have Revienne in mind?"

"Don't you? Oh, what a lovely candidate for a femme fatale. Blonde. Beautiful. French, but don't forget she's half German. Easy for her to be at war with herself. I know nothing about this woman, Max, except her impressive résumé as a psychiatrist. When I discovered she was associated with the sanitarium I whisked you to in desperation, I seized upon her services. I knew every step of the way it could all have been set up by whoever attempted to kill you back at the Neon Nightmare club in Vegas. Or not. It's hard to believe any man would encounter two she-devils before he was thirty-five."

"And Kathleen O'Connor was indeed demonic?"

"After our visit to the Convent of the Little Flower near Dublin and a glimpse into its presumed impious prisoners, wouldn't you have been?"

"Unbelievable how past wrongs keep rais-

211

ing their monstrous heads. I remember reading about the Irish institutional abuses a decade ago, and here they are making headlines again."

"Victims never forget. And . . . it's easier to track records, and people, now."

Max glanced at the open netbook on Gandolph's lap. "You find anything online on Kathleen as opposed to the downtrodden Rebecca?"

"Kathleen O'Connors are as common as grains of sand on a beach, in Ireland or out. We'll have to rely on personal interviews with old enemies. Next stop, Belfast and any ex-IRA men we can turn up."

"You're sure they're 'ex'? I do remember headlines about pub bombings and outrages against innocents in my vague 'way back when' youth."

"You don't remember family? Where you lived? Wisconsin? A street? The house?"

"Pieces. As if Picasso had played *Guernica* with images of my past. A long empty echoing hall, in a school or possibly a church. Snow covering a looming pair of fir trees in a front yard. Concrete stairs and a metal railing to a white-painted door. Midwestern, it looked. I felt more at home on the Alpine meadows, come to think of it."

"You were on the run. That's been half

your life, the most recent life. No faces from your past haunt you?"

"No faces. It's as if someone had erased the most intimate parts of my memories."

"You're sure Revienne didn't drug you? Hypnotize you?"

"No. How could I be sure she didn't? I stayed off the pain pills and injections in the Swiss clinic as soon as I was conscious, but anything could have been pumped into my mind or veins before that. My apparent memory loss could be totally induced."

"That's the Max I remember. Always suspicious."

"Not a fun guy."

"Not now. You used to be amusing company."

"I don't know whether to be relieved or insulted. When did we stop keeping company?"

"Just over two years ago. We split up when you got the Vegas hotel job. You'd met Temple Barr in Minneapolis, and it was love at first sight."

"Wasn't I . . . more careful then?"

"Not about her. You whisked her away from her native city and family to live in sin with you in Vegas while you headlined a magic show at the Goliath. I, and our employers, understood you deserved a life.

Hiding behind the magician persona had always been a natural cover for you. I was relieved we both seemed to have 'retired' due to true love, and I resumed my long-ago hobby of unmasking fraudulent psychics."

"A contradiction in terms, isn't that last?"

"So I've always found, but I have hopes. Anyway, your redheaded girlfriend got involved promoting a hokey Vegas Halloween séance in which I was playing the undercover patsy . . . and you came along eventually to safeguard her, so I had to fake my own death."

"A true Gandalf."

"I've always been Gandolph. What do you mean by true?"

"The book! Even I remember *The Lord of the Rings*. You took your stage name from the wizard Gandalf the Grey, right? He appeared to die in the novels and then came back."

"Really? Sounds more like your role in Las Vegas, if you ever revisit the place. That 'revival' thing is just a bizarre coincidence. I didn't actually read the books. Do you know how long each of the three is? I plucked the Gandalf mojo out of the popular-culture air ages ago. My last name was Randolph. I needed a 'magical' moniker. 'Gandolph.' "

Garry chuckled and patted the hair at his temples. "Time did make me 'Gandolph the Grey,' though."

Max chuckled too.

Chuckled. His mood was improving. No wonder he'd partnered with this guy.

"This route doesn't seem familiar," Max complained ten minutes later. "Sean and I had to have taken the M1 heading north before."

"It shouldn't," Gandolph said. "Times have changed. I'm tracking our route on a Yahoo! map on my computer. The M1 wasn't much of anything when you and your cousin made your way north. How? Hitch-hiking, perhaps? Once you had ID'd and targeted the three IRA members who'd blown up O'Toole's Pub and killed Sean, among six other victims, my job was to recruit you and get you off the island and onto the Continent for concealment and training. You were on the IRA's most-wanted list for years."

"When did that change?"

"Officially? Ages ago, as international grudges go. Since the Good Friday Agreement was signed by the British and Irish governments in nineteen ninety-eight, most of the politically motivated violence tapered off. International repugnance for the horror of nine/eleven finished off the 'Troubles' the way hundreds of years of relentless hatred and undying hope could not. The IRA has evaporated except for last-gasp 'alternate' groups. Recently, Belfast was named the safest city in the UK."

Max snorted. "My memory is dysfunctional, not my nose for political hatred. The English have tried to destroy the Irish for almost five hundred years. And vice versa. Enmity is in the blood."

"Quite true, Max, but it can't compete with fundamental Islam's jihad against Christian nations, for longevity. Give the Irish credit for knowing when they're outgunned. At any rate, Belfast is the new tourist hot spot."

"That bridge toll I paid near Drogheda?"

Gandolph nodded. "That was for crossing the Bridge of Peace. Less than two euros a car. You didn't even notice."

"It was a bloody highway toll. They're as common as grass."

"Exactly. We've crossed the border. You didn't notice the changes in signage."

Max looked around wildly. "It can't be that simple. I may not remember much, but even my aching bones know that."

"It won't be simple," Gandolph said, "but

it at least will be possible now."

Max spotted a pub sign. The place was stage-Irish rustic and called Durty Mulligan's.

"That looks like a fine place to get stewed," Max quipped.

Gandolph ran a vein-knotted hand through his pepper-dusted white hair. "Ah, it's like old times again, without the imminent danger."

"Are you sure?"

Gandolph shrugged. "No one's had time to fix on us and figure out our mission. For now, we can eat, drink, and be merry, eh?" He eyed the attractive pub that had probably been put up five years ago.

"And you can catch me up even more on my forgotten past," Max said.

"I said 'be merry.' Time enough for business when we're back on the road."

Once they were seated over a pint in the Belfast pub, though, Gandolph revved up his computer.

"We should have been doing this in the Temple Bar area of Dublin," he said wryly.

"When I didn't even know who she was and that we'd had a . . . serious connection? Even smacking me in the face with her name in foot-high gold letters didn't trip my memory trigger. You'd think if our love affair was that intense, I'd remember it.

"And *why* do all these things come wireless nowadays?" Max asked, unable to keep an irritable edge out of his voice. He felt both antsy and reluctant. "It's intrusive, and we could be tracked."

Did he *want* to see the Web site of this "Temple Barr" in Dublin's fair city or Belfast or anywhere on the globe? If she was his "lost love," he had forgotten that fast enough to sleep with a sleek, mysterious blonde of the possibly traitorous sort, who could have seduced an alpine walking stick.

So all he'd get out of perusing his past now was looking at a woman betrayed, thanks to His Truly. Or Untruly, rather.

Garry . . . Gandolph, starting to look familiar and trustworthy, was as eager as a boy, though, bringing up the "Web page" as if unveiling a magical feat. Even Max knew the old guy was behind the times, more at sea at these tech things than how Max himself would be with an intact memory. His rush of affection made plain that he needed to keep that superior knowledge from his mentor.

Temple Barr, a memorable name for a PR woman, had chosen to use a Web site photo of herself taken against the huge stone creature statues on the floor of Vegas's McCarran Airport. Max was shocked to instantly identify the place, but not the person. What kind of a cad was he?

"She's . . . cute," he couldn't keep from commenting in his dazed monotone.

Gandolph laughed. "*Damn* cute. What a disappointment, Max! You're making the same first-glance mistake most people do about her."

"I don't think I ever did 'cute,' even in my right mind."

Gandolph turned the laptop to eye the image. "Then your right mind is an ass. I never worried about you sleeping with her. That Continental blonde . . . pretty poison maybe."

Max spun the laptop to face himself again. "Pretty cute," he said on second look. "Nice hair. She looks . . . petite."

"Natural redhead, but she's toned it down since I last saw her. Or you did. Five feet zero. You can see the high heels."

Max hit Alt + to focus close-up and personal.

"Great ankles, not to mention arches curved enough to turn foot fetishist for."

"Max!"

"Just saying I do find her attractive in some ways."

"You're not a foot fetishist."

"Could have fooled me." He worked his way up the close-up image like a street-corner Romeo. "Sweet figure, if you like miniatures." While Gandolph cradled his unbelieving head with closed eyes in his hand, Max finally focused on the face and smiled. "You give up too soon on people also, Garry. I see it now. Smart. Feisty. Tenacious."

Gandolph glanced over.

"She's a pistol, isn't she?" Max suggested.

"You haven't completely lost your mind."

Max nodded. "Not yet." He hit the Alt — until Temple Barr became fairy-tiny on the sterile, hard-surfaced, long-shot background of McCarran Airport. "She's far away and long ago, Garry." He sighed. "I feel nothing earthshaking. I feel nothing. 'It was in another country. And besides, the wretch is dead.' " He paraphrased a famous line from the Elizabethan play *The Jew of Malta*.

"I won't allow you to become so cynical, Max. I know you're directing that quote back on yourself. The original line was, 'the *wench* is dead.' So you're really talking about the late Kathleen O'Connor, once aka Rebecca. I assure you that Temple Barr is far from dead and far too many aeons away from being a mere 'wench' to be forgotten so easily. I'd bet she's not given you up for dead, either."

"You mentioned I had a rival there anyway."

Garry took back the laptop grimly and typed a few short letters into the search engine. He turned the resulting Web page and image back to Max, who rolled his eyes.

"Pretty too," he said acerbically, eyeing Matt Devine's professionally taken head shot on the WCOO-FM radio Web site. "They make a photogenic match. Miss Temple is way better off without me and my bum legs and blasted mind. Shut this damn thing down, and let's get deeper into the new, PR-polished Belfast you've been bragging about."

Gandolph held the laptop open despite Max's thrust to close it.

" 'Pretty too.' Can't disagree. Handsome and a really nice guy, from what I've learned. Matt Devine, radio advice personality. Maybe you're doing the noble thing by leaving them to their own ignorant devices. . . ."

Max snorted with disdain.

"Ex-priest . . ."

Max's eyes narrowed with disbelief. "This smoothy media personality?"

"And relatively recent knifing victim of

221

Kathleen O'Connor, henceforth christened Kitty the Cutter by your ex, the 'cute' redhead."

"Kathleen was in Las Vegas?"

"Looking for you. She never succeeded. You found her, dead, first."

Max said nothing. Until . . .

" 'Kitty the Cutter'? The redhead's got a quick mouth and mind on her. The ex-priest didn't kill easy?"

Gandolph shook his head. "Glancing wound. Kitty was looking for you and found you too elusive. So she found him."

"So. My mea culpa. Again. He bled for my sins. He should thank me. A scar makes him much more interesting. 'Kitty,' " he repeated, finally laughing. " 'Kitty the Cutter.' I like that little redheaded girl."

"You always did."

"And she liked me?"

"She did. Maybe still does, although you appeared to run out on her for an inexcusable second time." Gandolph glanced at the screen. "He was a good priest, from what I learned. Left formally, and celibate."

"In his . . . what, early thirties? Isn't that too Sleeping Beauty to believe?"

"Believe it. I'm guessing he loved Temple from the moment he met her. It was first love on his part, but you were in the way."

Silence. Then . . .

"I'm not now, Gandolph. I'm here in bloody Belfast, which I'm willing to bet hasn't forgotten me, although I've forgotten it. Blood feuds die slowly. Someone, some entity, just tried to kill me and failed. Several times. If I don't find the hit man or woman, or them, I might as well be buried at the nearest graveyard to Temple Bar in Dublin, and you can write Sean's name on my tomb to put a just and bitter end to our 'graduation' trip to Ireland. *Ire* means 'rage,' doesn't it? A fitting English name for a blasted country."

He glanced at the laptop, which his mentor had finally shut off and closed.

"Why show me these losses of the recent past when I'm knee-deep in the bloodier past?"

"A reason to live?"

Max let his jaw drop. "My supposed girl is seeing, maybe even planning to marry, a man, a freaking ex-priest, who took the heat for my sins like bloody Jesus Christ, and you think *that* will inspire me with a reason to live?"

"A reason to revenge, then, maybe."

"We're in the right bloody country for it." Max stood. "Can we go on to the hotel now?" He glanced at their semiempty plates and the last strands of beer foam webbing the bottom of their pint glasses. "I've had all that I can stomach."

Gandolph nodded, took up his laptop computer, and walked.

CHAPTER 20
HOOPLA AND HOMICIDE

"And the point of this so-called media gathering was purely publicity?"

Detective Ferraro was "middle" everything: height, weight, age.

Now he was putting on a show of being middling patient with the situation, but just barely.

He'd ordered everyone present in the tunnel at the time the body was discovered into separate rooms at Gangsters, since it was the closest premises to the "crime scene."

As far as Temple could calculate, that was a cast of nine indignant Fontana brothers plus their uncle, Macho Mario; a death-pale Van von Rhine; four panting media videographers; three gawking workmen; a happily flushed Crawford Buchanan, sure to appear on evening news hours nationwide, not to mention YouTube. And her. The cats — and rat — appeared to have been overlooked, as usual.

"Did you recognize the deceased?" Ferraro asked now.

"No," Temple said, "but I didn't get a good long look at him. Also, he was lying on his back, so the body and face were foreshortened."

Detective Ferraro's basset-hound dark eyes looked up from his lined notebook pages. "Would you like to see a photograph? One should be posted at the morgue shortly. I can e-mail you the photo number."

"No. Really. I'm pretty sure I don't know any portly men who wear white tie and tails, nor of any Vegas act using them, although I'm not up on every last Cirque du Soleil production, particularly the sex one, *Zumanity.*"

"Too much information, Miss Barr." Ferraro's mustache quirked with distaste. "I wasn't really asking your preferences. I was being polite. What is your e-mail address? Please examine the features of the deceased when they arrive and let me know."

She accepted his card. Technology was getting creepy. First it had been regarding the corpse through a small window with draperies, then it was looking at a photo, then the photo was e-mailed fresh from the morgue to your queue for the final indignity of sitting cheek-by-dead-jowl with Nigerian solicitations, fake PayPal fraud warnings, and chain letters that would consign you to hell if you failed to pass on a soppy hard-luck story to ten of your closest friends. Who had time for that number of intimates these days? Temple didn't even know a fat man in evening dress found dead in her very own stunt safe.

"You are the person primarily responsible for everyone else being there?" Ferraro asked.

"Uh . . . yes, I suppose you could say so."

"And you're responsible for the presence of mob and muscle."

"Mob and muscle?"

The mustache quirked again. Maybe a sense of humor hid behind Ferraro's clenched, refreshingly unbleached, beige front teeth. "The Fontana family and that highly photogenic drill team. You pick those particular construction crew members?"

"As a matter of fact, yes, but it was purely random."

"The random factor being . . . ?"

"Uh, they were working on the actual project."

"And?"

"Good tans, skimpy T-shirts, impressive, uh, tool belts."

"Thought so. You manipulated this event

and staged the scene. Why wouldn't you have also arranged to have an overdressed corpse appear inside this empty, useless safe?"

She was speechless. She was so used to dealing with Molina and the homicide lieutenant's favorite detective team of Su and Alch, she wasn't accustomed to being considered a serious suspect.

"What are you implying?" she asked, wondering if she should shut up and get a lawyer.

"That you hired the corpse for this gig."

"Hired a corpse? That's not possible."

"It is if he was alive and you had him slip into the safe before lights, action, and camera time."

"But the door had to be drilled open."

"Maybe. Maybe it was all a media setup gone wrong."

"Not 'maybe.' It *is!* This kind of publicity is not helpful, believe me, detective. And if you don't believe me, which I see you have no reason to, ask Dr. Bahr, the coroner, when the deceased died. The smell was ripe enough to indicate it was at least overnight. No sane patsy would sleep overnight locked in that rank, dark safe, even if there was some way to open and close it before today. Which there wasn't."

"And how do you know that?"

"Of course we tried to get into it before we arranged for a formal 'opening ceremony,' so to speak."

"So you were willing to risk revealing whatever was in there?"

"Whatever *wasn't,* detective. I knew, we all knew, it was probably just an empty safe someone had installed for who-knows-what reason. Making a big deal of it à la Al Capone's vault was a joke. A harmless media 'event' in a city known for being over the top."

"You consider murder a joke, ma'am?"

"No! A body was the last thing anybody expected to be in that safe!"

"Was there anything you thought might be in it?"

"Maybe . . . It was a long shot. Maybe some old silver dollars."

"The Jersey Joe Jackson part of the 'joke.' "

"He was real, and he did bury a lot of stolen silver dollars around town and in the desert years ago, some of which were found and turned in. That's one Las Vegas legend that's true."

"It would take a lot of nerve to ask the media out for a safe opening that might or might not contain some silver dollars."

"Yes. That's my job."

"To have a lot of nerve?"

Oh, how she wanted to snap back: "Yes." That was not smart.

"To ask the media out."

Actually, they'd gotten a sensational story out of it. Temple's stock would be high with them.

With the Las Vegas law . . . not.

"Don't you have friends at the Las Vegas Metropolitan Police Department?" Van von Rhine asked, pacing her pristine office.

Nicky was still at Gangsters, waiting with his uncle and brothers during their separate interrogations by Detective Ferraro's partner.

"Ah . . . acquaintances," Temple told Van. "I can call . . . one . . . to check on the progress of the case. He's a great guy, but when it comes to department policy, I can't guarantee Detective Alch will tell me the weather."

Van was not appeased. "I knew flaunting the family's . . . Italian . . . connections would go terribly wrong. What was Nicky thinking?"

"How to cheaply enhance a venue during an economic meltdown by appealing to public curiosity. Gangsters eternally fascinate the public. Rap culture was built on reinventing it."

"We don't need our own *Ocean's Eleven* through *Thirteen* happening right here beneath the Crystal Phoenix."

"That is kinda cool," Temple remarked. "It hadn't occurred to any of us."

"What?" Van paused. She moved like a harried executive, but her face and mind were cool and collected.

"The *Ocean's Eleven* parallel. The ten brothers and their uncle. What happened to their father, by the way?"

Van's delicately glossed lips vanished into a straight, stressed line. "Shot down when Nicky was still a preadolescent. The 'last hit' in Vegas. His grandmother had made a legitimate fortune on a pasta factory. *She* underwrote the Crystal Phoenix. Now all of it's endangered, thanks to this angel-hair-pasta-brained publicity scheme of his."

"Maybe not."

"A body in a hidden vault beneath the juncture where the Crystal Phoenix and Gangsters property lines meet? An underhanded criminal alliance implied between the two hotels? A *secret* vault? Only a few silver dollars may have been found under the body, but they raise the shady ghost of Jersey Joe Jackson, a founding spirit of the

Crystal Phoenix. We are ruined, Temple. It's just a matter of time."

"What if the body could be tied to another gang, something very far from gangsters?"

"What do you mean? How? You're a wizard at manipulating events, but I don't think a dead guy who could sing Italian opera can be wished away."

"Something about the body, the way it was . . . arranged, rang a bell with me."

"Publicity at any cost?"

"No, I'm thinking of a secret society."

"Oh, great. Like the Mafia?"

"No, a mystical secret society called the Synth. I'm serious, Van. The way the body was laid out was ritualistic."

"Well," Van said bitterly, sitting on her immaculate white leather chair, "I guess you know more about crime and bodies than the average hotel executive does."

Temple understood her frustration. She was worried sick about Nicky and his brothers and had no way to help them.

Temple sat and leaned forward over the glass-topped desk. "It was more the way the red lining of the cloak was arranged. You noticed that the body's flung-out arms and legs made something of a star shape?"

"No. I wasn't close enough to see, but now I will imagine that, which is worse."

"The police are going to zero in on the contortions, but that wasn't the bizarre part."

"If you say so, Temple."

"It was the cloak lining. I knew it reminded me of something, some weird shape I'd seen before. Then I realized I was remembering an *outline*, not a piece of flagrant cloth, and I'd seen it at the site of an unsolved murder, of a professor at the university campus."

She quickly sketched the configuration of a forgotten constellation's major stars on Van's pristine notepad.

"Our dead body is part of a serial killing?" Van demanded.

"More like a sequential killing, I think. Anyway, once I get a chance to check my records, I can tell you whether the poor guy's cloak is a dead match to Ophiuchus."

"Off-ee-YOO-cuss? I have some background in the classics, but . . . is this name of a lost Greek play? *Off-ee-YOO-cuss Rex?*"

Van had wanted Temple to smile after all these grim events, so she did.

"No, Van. It's the thirteenth sign of the zodiac."

"I'm a little superstitious, so I know there are only twelve signs of the zodiac. I'm a Virgo."

"And I'm a Gemini. Traditionally. Yet, in December, the sun passes through the constellation of a man twined by a serpent. But this interesting pairing doesn't name a sun sign like the constellations of Libra and Virgo and Gemini do. As far as I and some interested parties were able to determine concerning the death of the professor, the star positions of Ophiuchus resemble a distorted pentagram and are a mystical symbol of the mysterious Synth."

"That sounds . . . truly ominous, Temple."

"Actually, it gives me a good angle on current events and a possibility of diverting police and media interest to individuals and enterprises far removed from Fontana family affairs."

"That," said Van, "would encourage me to regard this Ophiuchus entity as a friend of the family and make sure Nicky gives you a raise."

CHAPTER 21
WHEN A BODY MEETS A BODY

I have not had occasion to explore the bowels of the Crystal Phoenix since the Jersey Joe Jackson Action Attraction ceased to be attractive. My solo return to the scene of the crime puts me in a reminiscing mood.

It seems like only yesterday that the "new" Vegas promoting "family values and entertainment" fizzled like a glass of lukewarm iced tea at a stripper joint. Vegas hastily returned to soap-opera status: The Luxe and the Lustful.

I found it rather poignant when the underground mine-ride cars vanished, leaving only unused tracks in their wake. This area was now a dead-end destination, no longer a rowdy, raucous place a guy would expect to encounter fun and profit.

This subterranean sweatbox had a lot of history before it was resold as an entertainment venue. A gang of would-be heisters had used the tunnel for a robbery scheme but was undone by my able sleuthing work, thanks to aid from the world of Elvis-imitators, now called "Elvis tribute performers."

The actual King and I crossed paths here a few times, his path and presence being totally ectoplasmic. I find it interesting that the only individual in my circle of acquaintances, human and otherwise, who has also apparently had an encounter with the ghost of Elvis is Mr. Matt Devine, the former priest.

I believe my species has a special connection to the spiritual, hence our gift of nine lives. Or so. I am now working on the "or so" portion, which is why I sincerely hope my assumptions are true.

Mr. Matt never claimed to see Elvis's ghost. There was merely an anonymous caller to his radio advice program who seemed to sound exactly like Elvis. This fact was vetted by Mr. Matt's ex–seminary mentor now in the FBI, namely Mr. Frank Bucek. These "mentors" are apparently important folk in younger lives. (I would not know, given my mama was forced to train all of us kits on the street and move us on ASAP.)

Anyway, the world is full of would-be Elvii. Las Vegas particularly attracts the breed, and tourists have been married by "Elvis" almost since the King's death more than thirty years ago.

Maybe that is what Elvis and Mr. Matt have

common. They both performed marriage ceremonies, one more religiously than the other. Now Mr. Matt is eager to move on to taking vows instead of administering them. I must admit he and my Miss Temple make a photogenic couple, but I and my Miss Temple also look good in pictures, together or apart.

I have no intention of letting my significant other of the human sort leap into matrimony without me as a codicil.

As I understand it, a codicil is not anything fishy, but an add-on to legal matters, marriage being one of them. I plan to be the codicil on bedroom protocol. That is, I will retain my bed-snoozing rights so long as I can stand what else may go on there. I was not born yesterday or even a couple leap years ago.

I have a lot to muse on these days, what with the wholesale way my Miss Temple has swapped suitors without even consulting me. That has made me reconsider our relationship. I am thinking that I need a pre-nup for myself, and fast.

While I am so doing, ambling along the abandoned mine-ride tracks by the dim illumination of work lights, I run into an immovable object.

A moment later I am whisker-dancing in the dark with a stranger.

This is nothing new for a dude about major

resort destination, even in these depressingly financially flat days.

Visions of Satin from the Sapphire Slipper chicken ranch in the next county, or Topaz from the Oasis Hotel setup down the Strip, dance a heady tango in my noggin.

Alas, my impediment, like the sleek Topaz, is black-furred and female, yet, by the twitching of my nostrils, I can tell it is only my partner in crime solving, Miss Midnight Louise.

"What are *you* doing down here again?" we croon in simultaneous challenge.

"The Crystal Phoenix is my turf now," Miss Louise growls.

"This is my crime scene. I was here first, and my resident human has a big new project going here for the owners. That trumps your paltry claim of possession of the premises. Millions are at stake."

"Millions of fleas, if your unsanitary hide is involved," she sniffs. "You have been hanging out more with the feral gang than I have."

I did say she sniffed, and you can take that literally.

"I receive an herbal repellent from my mistress in my daily food to handle that sort of infestation," I say.

"But you rarely eat the Free-to-Be-Feline she uses as a staple because you are politically incorrect in your most primitive appetites. Thus, you are unprotected."

"Not true! I am the most protected tomcat in town! Unlike most cowardly human males, I have chosen to have 'the surgery.' "

"While knocked unconscious," she jeers. "You were kidnapped by that airhead actress Savannah Ashleigh and returned to your mistress in a satin pillowcase bearing her initials. I am amazed her plastic surgeon only did a vasectomy and a tummy tuck. He could have done a sex-change operation."

I had never considered that possibility and feel slightly faint from the thin air in this deserted section beneath the hotel grounds.

"At least I am not an 'it,' " I lob back. My powerful serve of sarcasm silences my mouthy self-described "daughter." Youngsters. No respect for their elders, even when they are trying to label them as delinquent dads.

Now that the formalities of our unexpected encounter have been observed, we sit and get down to business.

"I agree that you must solve this case to protect your mistress's financial interests," she concedes. "Just get straight that your land is now my land and I have the Fontanas to protect, so I will be a participating party in any investigative shenanigans you and/or she might get up to, high or low, at the Crystal

239

Phoenix and its environs to the property lines, above- and belowground."

"Jeez, Louise. Have you been consulting a lawyer?"

"I thought you tacked an 'Esquire' onto your name on occasion."

"My degree is in street smarts."

"Mine as well, and far more recently than yours. What do you think of this scheme to link the Crystal Phoenix with Gangsters?"

"Not much. The CP has a solid-silver rep as classy. This mob stuff could tarnish what Miss Van von Rhine and Mr. Nicky Fontana have so carefully built."

Louise is not buying my dire scenario.

"The Fontana brothers, sans Nicky, have built the exotic Gangsters Limo Service into a popular Vegas brand, though," she ripostes. *Ow!* Her ripostes end with pretty sharp punctuation marks. "Even the mayor wants to loosen up the Code of Silence on the city's mob roots. I thought you would approve of your human associates getting the jump on the city-hall bunch."

"When those guys are nervous, there might be reason. First they called it a mob museum. Then they called it a law-enforcement museum. They are fudging the facts so much they would look good accessorized with nuts and marshmallows."

"Are you always thinking of your next meal, Daddy-o? You could stand to lose a few fat rolls."

"Bulging muscles, my girl. Now that your 'furomones' have been 'fixed' you simply cannot tell the difference between a male at the peak of his powers and some fuddy-duddy fixee."

She shakes her head. "I am done trying to urge you to a healthier lifestyle. I do have news that tops your latest Elvis sighting."

"That was some time ago. The Memphis Cat has not deigned to show himself this trip through the belly of the beast, so I am most interested in what your insights are."

"I paid a recent visit to the Crystal Phoenix's so-called Ghost Suite."

"Ah, old seven-thirteen. A most provocative number for a hotel room. And who did you find there? Or should I say, what?"

"Miss Temple Barr, for one."

"Really? I thought she was on the scoffer side of matters paranormal."

"She was using the peace and quiet to muse."

I nod sagely. The presence of Miss Midnight Louise, my possible number-one daughter, brings out the Charlie Chan in me.

"She also was using it to mourn, I believe," Miss Midnight Louise adds. "I do not think that

241

is healthy."

"*Hmm.* You mean she was contemplating the absence and likely death of Mr. Max Kinsella. You were there when he hit the Neon Nightmare wall on that sabotaged bungee cord. A savage end to a most civilized magician."

"You believe you can see Elvis and yet you think a seasoned performer like Mr. Max would use equipment he had not checked for flaws?"

"Perhaps someone compromised the cord after he had launched. That Neon Nightmare club is a maze of secret passages and rooms. The cord required an anchor at the top. I recall shenanigans of a similar sort at the New Millennium Hotel and Casino, which shortly after put an end to that treacherous lady magician Shangri-La."

"Does that not make your nether appendage twitch just the slightest bit? These *two* acrobatic acts afflicted with lethal malfunctions?"

"Which 'nether appendage' do you refer to?" I ask, deadpan.

"The one that is long and useful for balance," she snaps.

Yup. Literally snaps. I avoid her daughterly snit and let her fangs close on a whisper of my retracting whiskers.

I am still quick on the draw both fore and aft.

We hunker down to resume civil discourse.

"You have made a decent point, Louise. There has been a lot of lethal aerobatic hanky-panky at major hotels lately. Reminds me of the dead dudes found in the spy spaces above the Goliath and New Millennium gaming tables a year or two ago."

"Phhhtttt!" she says. "Those were not spectacular deaths of professional performers. The victims there were small-time law-breakers."

"Does that not sniff more of 'mob' activity than the Cases of the Plunging Performers?

"Please, Perry Mason," she says, "let us not get illiterate about it."

"Perry Mason novels are very literate," I protest.

"I was referring to the Case of the Repeating Initial Title Consonants. I believe you are guilty of that very thing sometimes. Now I know where you get it. Perry Mason, indeed. I am no Della Street."

"No, you are not. You are more what they call 'proactive.'"

"Thanks, Pop. It makes me sound like a variety of yogurt, but I realize that you meant to be complimentary."

CHAPTER 22
GUESS WHO'S
COME TO DINNER?

Temple was surprised to have been invited to Van von Rhine's office for a one-on-one.

Van without Nicky was like latte without coffee. Puzzled, Temple hoped the couple's differences in enthusiasm for the Gangsters redo hadn't gotten serious.

She settled into a chair facing the desk. Van didn't look ruffled.

"How is everything going?" the boss lady inquired, sticking a Montblanc pen into her blonde French twist.

The effect reminded Temple of a geisha girl, although Van was anything but.

"Frankly," she answered, "we've got a bit of a mess. The police are pretty annoyed by the drama of a mysterious, anonymous man in formal dress dying in a hidden vault in an uncharted tunnel beneath major Vegas Strip attractions. The civic mob-museum committee has been threatening to 'commandeer' the entire vault for the city's 'vintage law-enforcement' exhibition."

"Amusing," Van said, sounding anything but amused. "Obviously, that death scene is the last thing the police want. They're clearly out of their depth, excuse the expression. Everything the Phoenix had planned has ground to a costly halt. We need that murder solved."

"Yes, ma'am," Temple said.

Van sighed and retrieved the pen from her coiffure.

At that geisha moment, her Asian personal assistant knocked on the door, then entered.

Tommy Foy had seen Temple in. He knew the women were simply noodling around on Crystal Phoenix matters and therefore interruptible.

"Miss von Rhine," he said, "you wanted to know the moment your foreign visitor checked in. Her luggage has been taken to the Crystal Cascade Suite, and she is here."

"Wonderful," Van said, standing. "Show her in." She smiled at Temple. "This is a friend from my European upbringing, visiting Vegas out of the blue. I'd love you to meet her."

Van was literally bubbling over. It reminded Temple that career women like them didn't have much time to nourish female friendships. Associations, yes.

Temple, the only girl in a family of boys, felt a pang that she had no best gal friend in Vegas. Van was an employer, after all, and Electra Lark, a landlady. And, gosh, who next came to mind? Her nemesis, homicide lieutenant C. R., aka Carmen, Molina. Was that pathetic!

Temple turned to greet the newcomer with a warm smile.

Oh, wow. Supermodel tall, slim and sleek. Blonde like Van, only not like Van. *Zorchy*, used to be the word. Cool, blonde, and hot, the type that always made Temple feel like she was on loan from the Girl Scouts to the local high school. Or college. Or TV station job.

"Revi!" Van exclaimed, coming around her desk to grasp expensively suited arms and to brush cheeks. "So amazing to see you again."

"And I, you. I see so few from Saint Moritz these days."

"A girls academy in Switzerland we both attended," Van, always the perfect hostess, explained to Temple. "And, Revi, this is the hotel's ace public-relations expert, Temple Barr. My school friend, Revienne . . . Schneider, is it still?"

"Yes, of course," the blonde said, with the faintest of accents. "You also work under

246

your maiden name?"

"Of course," Van said.

Well, Temple thought, 'Revi' had neatly dodged the issue of her marital status. Bet *she* knows Van's married surname to an *F,* as in "Fontana family."

"Revienne is such a lovely name," Temple noted. "I've never heard it before."

"Yes," Van agreed. "It's French, but totally unique. It comes from the word *return,* and here she's returned to my life. I wish I had such an evocative name."

"Now, Van," Revienne said, "I've always found your full name enchanting. I do understand why you dislike it, though." The woman sat in the chair next to Temple and arranged her long legs into a paired, high-fashion-model side slant. "I use mine in full form now."

No more girlish "Revi," she was saying.

In fact, Temple had a rough time envisioning the newcomer as ever having been an awkward adolescent. Revienne wore a mossy green silk suit that had to have been purchased in a major European capital and which fell into expensive, unwrinkled folds fresh from the transatlantic flight.

"No time to psychoanalyze me at the office, Revienne," Van said, donning her impassive executive mask for a moment, in fun. "We'll dine after you've rested. What brought you to Las Vegas so suddenly?"

"I'd been promising to do some lectures for a friend from Lyon. He's had a visiting professorship at your branch of the University of Nevada here. Hugo Gruetzmeyer. He thought a local case might intrigue me. But, Van, I caught some disturbing buzz on the Internet after the flight."

"You're talking about the Crystal Phoenix," Van said, her blue eyes sharpening. "So, this is a business, not a pleasure trip. What *is* your business then?"

Temple would not have wanted to be under Van's suddenly suspicious gaze. Her hotel and her husband's family were the center of a sensational murder case. Even old school friends needed to prove themselves for suddenly showing up.

Revienne shrugged her wide, expensively clad shoulders. Her quick gray-eyed glance summed up Temple's position and temperament as if taking a psychic temperature.

Temple felt as cautious as Van did. This woman was as quick and subtle as she was smart, in both meanings of the word.

Revienne spread her long, graceful fingers palms up, in a gesture of charming surrender. Temple noticed she wore no rings, not from a man and not from Revienne to

Revienne. Temple instantly remembered Matt's glamorous engagement ring on her third finger. She'd certainly come to take it for granted and sometimes wondered if it was too much bling for a petite woman. Now it felt like a glitzy weapon blinking out a Morse-code message: Don't tread on me. I have backup, lady.

It was weird this woman got her and Van's hackles up so fast. They were equally protective of the Crystal Phoenix, perhaps, and even more protective of the Fontana family males, as well. Temple did have some best pals in Vegas, she realized. They just weren't girls, but an updated rat pack of cool guys and one big beautiful black cat named Midnight Louie.

Revienne gave a single breathy laugh, part apology, part peace gesture. "I realize, Van, and Miss Barr, you need to be sensitive about negative publicity right now. That's why I'm here. To help. Professor Gruetzmeyer called on me because certain aspects of the tunnel vault death might relate to my experience. I know you have the legendary *CSI* filmed here in Las Vegas, but that is television-show razzle-dazzle, as you say in this country. I am a respected psychologist on the Continent, and beyond — England, the Mideast . . ."

"Not in the U.S.?" Temple asked.

"Not . . . yet. Though I very recently worked with a most challenging and unforthcoming American. You are a wary people, I must say."

"These are wary times," Van said.

"Exactly. I do have experience in cases involving terrorism."

"Perpetrators or victims?" Temple asked.

"Both," Revienne said.

"This has nothing to do with terrorism," Van said. "We have one unidentified man, in formal costume yet, dead and likely murdered in an abandoned part of the hotel property. If we hadn't been, er, excavating for a new attraction, no one would have known."

Revienne gave Temple an amused (possibly condescending) glance. "I take it your publicity efforts devised the live taping of the old vault being opened. I never heard on any news source that anything besides the dead man was found inside."

Temple tapped the sole of her high-heeled Nina sandal on Van's cushy carpeting. "No news is bad news when it comes to publicity. The Crystal Phoenix is getting as much buzz as the Wynn or the Venetian now. If you manage to solve the death, it'll make a super exhibit in the new Mob Museum at

250

our affiliated facility, Gangsters."

"Spin," Revienne mocked. "You Americans are experts at it until you become entangled in unexpected outcomes."

"You French, on the other hand, are experts at food, wine, and tomfoolery."

"Tom whom?"

Van laughed. "*L'amour,* illicit love affairs, Temple means."

"Ah," Revienne said, nodding her perfectly windblown, shoulder-length Bed Head. "Is love ever truly illicit?" She nodded at Temple's ring finger. "You are tying yourself to one man — always risky. An impossible dream, perhaps?"

"Not really," Van said briskly. "You'll meet my husband at dinner, if you can rest sufficiently to be up and about then."

"Oh, I slept on the plane. Like a baby." She stood, all five-nine of her on four inches of Christian Louboutin spike-heeled leather.

"Barbie goes supermodel," Temple muttered under her breath, as Van ushered her friend to the office door.

"What was that, Temple?" Van asked, coming back.

"Your friend could be a supermodel."

"Not really. They're even taller and thinner." She sat in her chair and swayed it from side to side. "I suppose we could use the help of an internationally known psychologist, but Revienne has become rather tiresomely perfect."

"She wasn't always like this?"

Van shook her head in its polished blonde-satin helmet of elegant hairdo.

"Those exclusive girls schools in Switzerland? We were all offspring in the way of our wealthy parents, parked there to learn how to look and act healthy, wealthy, and wise. We were mental messes, Temple, and Revi— Revienne — was just as fragile and confused as the worst-off of us. My father was a widowed hotel executive who changed temporary residences and lovers almost as frequently as the maids changed sheets. He had a semilegitimate reason for dumping me. Revi's parents had a stable luxury flat in Paris. They dumped her because she witnessed her younger sister's suicide."

"Oh, my gosh. That slick woman?"

"That woman." Van nodded grimly. "We were all isolated, ignored, and mad as hell. Revienne may look smooth and successful, but that's what we were trained to do. A renowned psychologist? Yes. But we all learned to put on a good front at school, and unless something dramatic happened to shatter that psychological shellac, which

252

we all hid behind, she's not the paragon she seems."

"What 'shattered' your 'shellac'?"

Van looked startled. "You think mine did?"

Temple nodded. "You kept the hairdo and the manner, but you snagged the first Fontana brother to break the family front and marry. I'm happy to say my aunt was the second. How'd that happen?"

Van smiled and spun her fancy executive chair all the way around, like a kid on a ride. "Nicky. He broke through. Never underestimate the persuasive power of a Fontana."

"I wouldn't," Temple swore, standing. "If your old school friend and her professor friend want to investigate the death, we can't stop them. I have some suspicions of my own and will follow them, solo, if you don't mind."

"Not at all."

Temple opened the door to leave.

"But," said Van, "don't hesitate to call on all the resources of the Crystal Phoenix, which are mostly Fontana brothers."

"Aye, aye, ma'am." Temple grinned as she shut the door on Van.

She'd like to see Revienne up against a Fontana brother.

Not literally, however.

CHAPTER 23
BAHR BONES

Temple wasn't a habitué of the local morgue, but her size-fives had visited the low-profile building a time or two.

"Dr. Bahr is expecting you, Miss Barr," the receptionist reported in a happy chirp.

Temple knew she was a nice break in routine, being alive and not being a grieving relative or in a helping profession.

"Thank you, Yolanda," she said. A savvy PR person always reads name tags and uses first names to establish rapport.

The door to the morgue's inner sanctum — and here that cliché phrase really resonated — opened, crammed full with burly Dr. Bahr in his white lab coat.

His surname, tall bulk, and untamed, curly, reddish gray hair had earned him the "Grizzly" nickname. Also, like most medical examiners, he dealt with death and the dead in a matter-of-fact, sometimes wickedly humorous way.

"Come in, come in," he greeted her, the soul of professional conviviality. "You are looking very lively," he confided as he showed her into an empty conference room.

The vanilla-bland Formica tabletop and surrounding black chairs could have been in any business office.

"Let's see today's shoes," he suggested before they sat at a pair of meeting corner seats. "Oh, the dead will like that open-toed look, especially the bloodred toenail polish. Tagless toes are a big turn-on here."

"High praise," Temple said, putting her perpetual tote bag, this one red patent leather, on the empty chair seat next to her.

"You could almost smuggle out a body in that giant bag, Miss Temple."

"I'm here on behalf of Gangsters renovated mob museum, but I am not their 'bag' lady."

"You are nobody's bag lady," he said gallantly. "What exactly can I do for you?"

"Did you ID the vault victim?"

"Ex–Vegas magician named Cosimo Sparks. Bizarre death."

"How did he die? I found the body. He was in formal dress, and I didn't see a mark on him but the studs on his shirt front."

"Sure one of them wasn't a stab wound?"

"That would take a pretty 'anorexic'

weapon."

Bahr nodded. "Like a supermodel in spikes. I can't leak any more confidential info, except to say there were odd hesitation marks. Usually stabbers overdo it, over and over again. Sparks' wounds were an odd combo: A half dozen trial cuts — hesitations — then a bold killing stroke, one clean, deep drive to the heart. An angry, powerful, but initially timid murderer."

"Glad he or she was long gone before I got there," Temple said, with a mock shiver. "Okay, I could also use any details on the Lake Mead . . . find. That would be super helpful."

"Ah, yes, a cold case. I can spill my guts on that one. Just a figure of speech. So you are intrigued by our old pal 'Boots.' Too bad he's too dead to enjoy having a lovely young lady like you on his case."

"You have a name for him already?"

"We always nickname our corpses for in-house reference. Numbers are so impersonal."

" 'Old pal' is not a total figure of speech?"

Grizzly pouted his lips and shook his head. "Those leg bones are eligible for AARP, at least."

It took thirtyish Temple longer than usual

to get his meaning. "Oh, fifty years old or more."

"That's going by what's left of the leg bones. The only parts of the feet and boots that didn't decay, dissolve, or were eaten are some scraps of the soles. Cowboy boots."

"I suppose many men wore cowboy boots out here in the forties and fifties."

For answer, Grizzly shifted in his chair and stuck out a foot.

Temple glimpsed a stitched, pointed black toe.

"Not necessarily just them," Grizzly said, stating the obvious.

How could she have omitted checking out footwear just because it was on a man, and a respected professional man, an older man!

"My bad," Temple admitted. "Those are mighty good-looking boots."

Grizzly shrugged. "The higher heels and steel arches support your feet when you're standing over a cold body all day. You gals aren't the only fashion victims. Besides, height is a psychological advantage."

"Don't I know it," Temple said glumly, thinking of the perfect Revienne Schneider.

On the other hand, Kitty the Cutter wasn't more than five-three, to hear Matt tell it. He was the only man to have seen her alive and in person, and then again, among the naked and the dead, here, where she had finally been both.

Wow, Temple realized, *Max and Matt are the only men who've seen both Kathleen O'Connor and me naked. Not* a happy thought! Thank goodness women today didn't have to marry any man who'd seen them naked.

This place made her mind run in wild, morbid veins. Veins! *Oh, no.* No wonder Grizzly and his staff practiced black humor. The mind loved to play gruesome tricks on itself. Maybe it was the notion of all the naked corpses concealed here in window-less rooms and on sheeted gurneys.

"Would you like to see him?" Grizzly asked.

"Him?"

"What's left of Boots."

"Ah, sure." She could check that the wax replica — taken from a photograph someone had obtained illegally at the morgue, prob-ably a Fontana brother, and she did not want to know which one, ever — was ac-curate. "If it's all right for a member of the public to view the body."

"Sure. I have lady 'cozy' crime writers in here every month. They are much cooler with it than some of those male slice-and-dice thriller authors. I do have to make the ladies promise not to eat and drink during the autopsy, though."

"Not a problem with me," Temple said as she rose to walk in his boot tracks back into the hall and then into an area of shining stainless-steel walls, gurneys, tables, sinks, and instruments. All that wall-to-wall steel reminded her of the fatal vault.

At the door Temple donned latex gloves and a Plexiglas face shield with the coroner.

Everything smelled fine, but on every inhalation she expected a hint of decay. The suspense was really hard on one's breathing rate.

Coroner Bahr didn't notice. This was his daily arena, and he was busy commanding it.

"I had the remains brought out for you. The TV stations were satisfied with the discovery footage. You can't beat the human interest of those cats sniffing around old Boots here. I knew you'd want to see the real thing, sans snacking pussycats."

Temple's stomach finally reacted and sky-dived. She wasn't going to admit she knew those "cannibal" cats, especially that she often shared a bed with one. TMI.

Bahr's large, latexed fingers pulled a sheet back from a beach-ball-size lump that looked a lot larger than the "appetizer with toothpicks" Louie had uncovered.

That was because a "doily" of caked lake bottom had also been excavated with the concrete and leg bones in place.

Grizzly smiled fondly at the mess. "Makes me feel like an archaeologist for a change. Ah, the good old days of crime, not drugs and bodies in the street, but bullet-riddled bodies dumped in strange and secret ways."

He picked up a surgeon's scalpel and used it as a pointer. "I decided to chip my way in from the rear. If there were any footwear remnants, the heels would be the easiest to uncover and offer the most information. As it happened, I struck pay dirt."

"Literally."

Humming relevant bits of the old song Temple recognized with a sinking heart as "Clementine," as in ". . . was a miner, forty-niner," Bahr produced a steel tray that clanked with the moving metal on it.

Temple peeked. It wasn't a rolling bullet, but something both bulkier and thinner.

"Silver?" she asked. "You hit silver?"

"Yup."

"That's a mighty big tooth cap, Dr. Bahr. Boots must have been a giant."

His laughter rang off all the surrounding stainless steel. "Most amusing. And apt. I hadn't thought of it that way. No, Miss Barr, since we are being formal, it is not a tooth cap for a giant. It is a cap of sorts, and it is — *ta-da!* — signed."

"Dentists do that, don't they, with fillings?"

"True, but let's drop the orthodontic comparison, unless you wish to posit that the victim had a set of choppers in his heels."

Temple bent to study the find close up. "Oh. There are two! Nested together."

"Simply a convenient storage option. Let me . . . unnest these lovely twins. . . ."

"I'm stumped," Temple admitted, after he had done so, looking at the odd silver shapes.

" 'Stumped,' " Grizzly echoed, eyeing the truncated leg bones. "You will force me to hire you just for the very punny commentary. Quite unconscious, of course."

Temple rolled her eyes. "Do you have any idea who this guy was? Besides a marked man?"

"He certainly was a heel," Grizzly mused.

Temple stared, still stumped, at the silver shells. They still reminded her of dental caps. She mulled the coroner's broad hints.

"I'm shocked," he prodded. "It's right up your alley."

Temple knew that shocking and awing

261

civilians was Grizzly Bahr's favorite pastime. No one would have dared to nickname him if he didn't relish word games. He was right. That was right up her alley, along with "spin."

Spin. Wait! She took the odd artifacts from his hands into hers and . . . spun them.

"Caps, or taps! Taps come on shoes. But this guy is getting called Boots. Aw, cowboy boot heels, high, wide, and handsome! These are sterling silver boot-heel caps.

"Hi-ho, Silver," Temple finished up by quoting the Lone Ranger. "Away!"

"Very good. Care to examine them further?"

"It won't hurt the evidence?"

"We've already tested and photographed them for the Hall of Exotic Evidence Fame."

Temple let her curiosity loose.

"These marks aren't concrete damage or sand crust. They're . . . engraved."

"En-graved," he repeated, going off in wheezing laughter.

"A stylized leaf motif. Looks Mexican."

"*Very* fancy."

Temple knew enough to look for marks on silver, at least a "925" for sterling silver content.

She turned the heel caps around, wondering what kind of guy was secure enough to flaunt these things, besides a Fontana brother. *Aha!* On the inside of the heel cover just under the sole. Very discreet, but a complete artist's stamp. Who and where. Not Taxco, the sterling silver Mexican stamp of the mid-nineteenth century, but . . . Hollywood. Of course. Singing movie cowboys were peaking then — Gene Autry, Roy Rogers. Outfits were extravagant.

And . . .

"IOHLANDMADE . . . CALIF . . . HOLLYWOOD . . . STERLING," Temple read.

"*Whew.* This is real signed silver," she added. "And collectible. And it might even be traceable, if you find an expert on cowboy boots of the period."

"Just what I thought," Grizzly said, beaming. "The faded first letter of the name is *B,* as in Bohlin. And I'm counting on you to find that expert, Miss Vintage Rag Wearer."

"I've been a little busy for vintage collecting lately," Temple said, frowning.

Literally "losing" one boyfriend and getting engaged to another didn't leave a girl a lot of shopping time, unless it was for a shrink.

"But you know the vintage scene," he said.

Temple nodded. "I know the scene." Even better, the Internet probably knew it too. She could hardly wait to track down this late, great Hollywood artisan.

"Hold your horses," Dr. Bahr said as she turned to leave, lifting a gloved palm.

She'd forgotten to lose her accessories.

Temple was into vintage, but latex gloves and a plastic visor weren't her idea of going-to-tea wear, and she was happy to leave them. They made her sweat. She wasn't eager to linger, but Grizzly Bahr held up another steel dish, and these contents *did* roll around.

Temple peered inside. "Silver dollars! You have no idea how these might connect —"

"I have plenty of idea. These were evidently once bolted onto the rotted away boot sides. Too bad they aren't nineteen-thirty-four San Francisco mint dollars, worth a bundle today. Still, Boots appeared to be a silver-lovin' dude."

"Did they call guys 'dudes' back then?"

"Sure did. There have always been dudes. Do silver dollars mean something to you more than a gleam in your eye? They were once more common than fleas here in Vegas and were melted out of existence by the thousands every time silver prices went up."

"I know," Temple said. "The last big silver-dollar roundup and meltdown was in the seventies, when the Texas millionaire H. L. Hunt cornered the silver market and drove the price so high my spinster great-aunt sold the family silverware. Hence I inherited stainless steel."

"Minting of silver dollars stopped in nineteen thirty-five," Bahr said, "so this guy could have snagged these from then until the seventies. His bones say he was last running around about nineteen fifty, give or take a few years."

"But his footwear says there may be a motive for his murder some folks still alive may know about."

"It's always better to consult the living," Grizzly Bahr agreed. "Better hurry, because this guy's peers would be getting so up there in age, St. Peter might be already reaching down for them."

CHAPTER 24
SYNTH YOU'VE BEEN GONE

I decide I must take the lead with Miss Midnight Louise as decisively belowground as above it.

"I must admit that this space just cried for something dramatic to happen in it," I tell her. "I had a tad of trouble finding a way into the underground tunnel from Gangsters, which is a chichi little venue that could use a dash of Fontana makeover magic, so I went back to the Phoenix, and underground there. Worked like a charm, so, all in all, I would be able to give my blessing to this Chunnel of Crime notion. Linking two enterprises in these days when people want more for their money is a good idea," I pronounce.

"Three," she says.

"I beg your pardon?"

"Three."

"Three what?"

"Three venues."

While I am still blinking like a blind bat at

what she is implying, the little minx adds the codicil.

"I did not 'amble over' from the Crystal Phoenix," Midnight Louise explains, with a quick smoothing of what bristles pass for her eyebrows. "I walked, all right, and the route was subterranean and a bit tight at times, but I came from the underbelly of the Neon Nightmare."

The Neon Nightmare club? Where the cabal of disgruntled magicians known as the Synth keep secret meeting rooms? Where Mr. Max just tragically crashed and maybe died not two months ago?

You could knock me over with a magic wand.

Luckily, Miss Midnight Louise is not packing any, but she cannot smother a huge smirk as she starts grooming spidery cobwebs off of her whiskers.

While I have resigned myself to letting Miss Midnight Louise lead when it comes to exploring the third and most secret underground tunnel in this below-street-level maze, I had not counted on the pathway being so paltry.

"Hurry up, Pops," Miss Louise is nagging from ahead of me, like Charlie Chan's number-one son.

Fact is, I cannot!

The passable concrete area around the

vault is a glorified rat maze, and the human-fist-size rift at one dark corner of the vault opened up by a small earthquake or construction vibrations is mouse-size to me.

In fact, delicious as my surprise exit from the opening vault door was, I was so low to the ground, the cameras overlooked me and Louise entirely, and I nearly lost my midsection coat from my innards being squeezed through the raw-metal-edged hole.

Now we must retrace our path around the vault exterior. It has been jolted into rubble by the recent tawdry pneumatic drilling on the front door, so it is an even tighter squeeze for any creature other than a snake.

Fine for a sylph like Miss Midnight Louise to wriggle through when she is all of nine pounds soaking wet.

I am a feline of size. I do not "wriggle" like an earthworm; I "bull" my way, like a dozer. (Not the kind that sleeps, I hasten to add.)

So there I am having clods of stone and sand kicked up into my face as I follow the narrow path she has forged.

Ah! At last! We get into man-high territory, if the man were on his knees. It strikes me that this tunnel is a recent and inexpert excavation.

Sneezing out a cloud of stone powder, after much circuitous footwork, I finally follow Miss

Louise into a large and thankfully finished piece of manmade construction, what is certainly a rarity in Las Vegas, which is built on concrete foundations — a basement.

While I enjoy a coughing break, the kit is pacing ahead of me, twitching her front and rear extremities. By extremities, I am being literal: not legs, but vibrissae and tail. Yes, the rear member whips up more dust for my sensitive sinuses.

Only a few dim work lights, aka classic bare lightbulbs, illuminate our way into what turns out to be a vast space.

Before long we encounter the massive figure of a martini glass. By then I could use one. Miss Louise has leaped atop the toe of a high-heeled sandal that would really ring my Miss Temple's chimes.

All of these items are made from a giant fretwork of wood and steel or aluminum supporting milky glass tubes in Rube Goldberg–style rat-maze arrangements, i.e., like a really complicated maze for giant rats.

Manx! I would not want to meet the rat large enough to run this junkyard maze, but . . .

"Hey, Louise! Any one of these big retired neon signs would make a great jungle gym for Ma Barker's gang behind the police substation. They are just wasted down here."

"At least they are not fading in the acid rain

and sunlight UVs at the neon graveyard top-side," she replies. "But I like your idea. Maybe you can manipulate your red-and-cream roommate to claim one of these mementos when we bring the Neon Nightmare crowd down."

"Uh, we are bringing a nightclub crowd down?"

"Of course. Not the customers, but the Synth set. No human would find or follow that rat tunnel around the vault to trace the passage from the Crystal Phoenix underground to here."

Now she tells me! So I have started this crawl by personally enlarging with my body a tunnel made by and for desert rats. Think about it! I look around for some rat on whom to take out my angst, but I find the place as quiet and still as, well, a graveyard.

Meanwhile, Miss Louise has sashayed into the pale spotlight of a work light.

"Remember when Mr. Max as the Phantom Mage hit the nightclub wall upstairs and was carted out of here as DOA?"

"Um, I would hardly forget such a disaster."

"Remember that I promised to kick major butt around here?"

"Yes, but that is your general modus operandi anyway."

"General Modus Operandi is about to breach

enemy headquarters. Want to tag along, Daddy-o?"

I slink along after my number-one (and only, that I know of) daughter.

In my heart of hearts, I realize that my devotion to my Miss Temple and her affairs (I am not just speaking of Mr. Matt here, but her life-threatening murder investigations) has made me a trifle derelict in pursuing the trail of Mr. Max Kinsella.

This might have been a wee tactical error. He is the primo international undercover cat in our circle of human acquaintances, and it is never wise to underestimate what he might be up to and who might not like it.

Oh, rats!

Thus I find myself tailing a *girl* to the scene of the crime! I mean, a girl other than my Miss Temple, who is always sensitive to my contributions and appreciative and a pleasure to tail.

The Neon Nightmare, as Miss Louise and I — and Mr. Max before us — have discovered, is designed like a pyramid-shaped wedge of Swiss cheese. It has more hidey-holes than Cab Calloway did. Okay, that is an abstruse reference. I am an abstruse kind of guy. Mr. Cab Calloway, being a musical black cat of the human persuasion back in the Jazz Baby age, was noted for his vocal chorus of "Hi-de-hi, hi-de-ho." Hidey-hole. Get it?

So "Hi-de-hi, hi-de-ho" is all I can mutter to myself in consolation, as I follow Miss Midnight Louise through a long and winding upward path of hidden hallways and cubbyholes toward the lofty peak of the pyramid, where the conspirators who call themselves the Synth maintain a private club so tony that Sherlock Holmes's older smarter brother, Mycroft, might feel at home there, save that there are at least two women members we spotted on an earlier occasion.

Every door looks like a jet black wall in this magical maze, and every opening is operated by pressure hinges. Push and release; the hidden latch pops the door ajar.

Those of my breed have no trouble being pushy, and I, at least, being exceptionally big and strong, can leap high enough to select floor designation buttons on even the highest hotel-tower elevators.

On the other hand, such gymnastics need to be accomplished on the sly, without human witnesses. They could cause comment and sudden attempts to capture a trick cat like myself with a camera, if not a strangling grip around the throat.

Luckily, the designers of Synth headquarters played it cute and placed many of their pressure points *below* the usual human hand level. Of course both Miss Midnight Louise and I remember this ploy. There is a bit of kerfuffle as we nudge shoulders to each command the active role here.

My longer reach wins out but at the cost of a nick in my sensitive sniffer.

"Sorry, Pops," she hisses. "I did not see your prominent nose in the dark."

The door has opened without a sound after the initial click, so I stand back to let her enter first.

She gives a surprised purr under her breath, mistaking my holding back for courtesy. Hah! It is only seasoned break-in strategy.

She, being practically anorexic from scarfing up Chef Song's low-fat, low-cal Asian delicacies at the Crystal Phoenix koi pond, requires a less-ajar door to enter. I, being majestic in size, push in after her, thrusting the door open farther. I immediately whirl to nudge it shut, but delicately, though there is little light to admit from the dark passage.

There! We are once again closeted with the same cast of characters, plus a couple more, whom we had intruded on before Mr. Max's tragic accident-cum-assassination attempt.

They are not acting the usual calm and smug, though, but riled up like a school of flesh-eating piranhas feasting in a diet spa's hot tub.

"You incompetents," a voice with a stagy echoing tone admonishes so passionately, the hair on both Miss Midnight Louise's and my backs rises as if we had been attacked.

It is the same eerily altered human voice I have heard through the Cloaked Conjuror's whole-head mask and used by protected witnesses on TV true-crime shows.

"Sparks is dead, and you have no idea how, who, or why," the man goes on.

"And," the second newcomer adds in an echoing, possibly female voice, "you have no idea where our 'investment' has gone."

I am not being specific about the description of these Jill-and-Johnny-come-latelies because they wear long, concealing cloaks and, of all things, full-face Darth Vader–type masks!

I nudge Miss Louise in the shoulder, but she is gone. Even with my superior vision, I cannot see her. I give the kit credit for stealth. She has probably established a listening post under somebody's floor-length dark robe, a delicate operation for one with her longer coat's tendency to tickle human skin.

"Listen," the dark lady known as Carmen says.

I have eavesdropped on this dame at Synth Central before, but every time I hear or see this Carmen chick, I get a jolt. That is the same first name the *C* in C. R. Molina conceals. The unsmiling homicide lieutenant only goes by that moniker when she is undercover, kicking back as the Blue Dahlia nightclub's blues singer. Not that she has had any time free from kicking ass, including her own, lately.

Of course, there are other Carmens in the world, just as there are other Louies. We are just the most important ones in Vegas. But I digress. The wrong Carmen is still yammering.

"We are not responsible for Cosimo's wandering or death," she argues. "Why would any one of us trail him to that vault and draw every eye to all of us? It is bad enough that the two hotel excavations met in the middle at our ground zero. You would think they knew what they were doing."

"Exactly," says Vader One, pacing like a caged member of my actual breed. "Things could not have gone worse for us. Using that aged vault was folly."

"Benny Binion's son Ted had a treasure vault buried in the desert," says a tall, unmasked man who must be in the Synth.

"This part of Las Vegas is not desert and has not been since a few years after that vault was built," Vader Two points out, "probably by the colorfully named Jersey Joe Jackson."

His spooky, gender-altered tones drip sarcasm like rattlesnake venom.

"First the Phantom Mage dies," Vader One ticks off on a forefinger, which makes me suspect she is female. We guys do not "tick off," unless it is making someone else mad. "Why?"

The lady known as Carmen stirs uneasily on Cosimo Sparks's vacant easy chair, which she has apparently claimed since his death. The slinky Carmen stirring is quite a show, but neither Darths, nor Miss Midnight Louise, I am sure, is properly impressed.

"You do not know for sure, do you?" Vader One demands. "This is not a game of make-believe for magicians. Your creation of the Synth was a brilliant ploy, but you magicians tend to be all show and no go, as they say. You were always the facade for the real operation, and you would have been rewarded by having your revenge on the hotels and venues that ousted your tired acts years ago."

A buzz of protests has as much effect on the two interlopers as if the resident three-some had been flies.

"Spare us," Vader Two says. "We want to hear your theories, not excuses. There is too much at stake."

"Well," says the heretofore-silent, turbaned medium, whom I remember has taken the show-cat moniker of Czarina Catherina, "lords and masters — or lady and master — we have been holding the fort here at the Neon Nightmare waiting for you to give the word for the moment we would astound Las Vegas and the nation . . . and you have been as quiet as mice."

What an insult to those who would masquerade as the mighty feline hunter species! Of course, humans are not built for imitating us. They have lost the ability to kill for their supper and also to tease adoration from those who are willing to serve them.

"Where is the money?" Vader Two demands.

"We do not know!" Carmen says hotly. (There is no other way this femme fatale could possibly speak.) "We do know when the economic crash made the mortgage on the Neon Nightmare unfeasible. We were all dipping into our own reserves to pay the monthly fees, even as our club's bar tab plummeted and the loss of the Phantom Mage as a draw also killed our bottom line."

"Ah." Vader Two purrs almost as convincingly as Miss Midnight Louise. "Now we hear a motive for why Cosimo Sparks, your senior Synth member, could have gone rogue. You cabal of failures could not pay the rent."

"Mortgage," Czarina spits back. "We were buying the building. It is not our fault. Our combined assets now couldn't get enough credit to buy a busted magic wand. The entire country was caught napping. And the world."

"Stop whining," Vader Two says. "We have always operated as a shadow group, with our own shadow economy. Your end of the deal was to hunker down at the Vegas base, guard our tangible assets, and prepare to unleash your illusionary skills when called upon."

"So," Vader One adds, "our amassed-over-the-years assets are either gone or are on the verge of being discovered by the authorities, and your leader is not only dead, but attracting the exact kind of attention that none of us can afford."

"All heart, right?" the medium asks.

"Even worse," Vader One goes on, "news of this long-secret operation in the making is now running like wildfire through the Continent, stirring up old enemies the Synth was created to confound."

"We are here," Vader Two adds, "to untangle your mess and find out why Cosimo Sparks was killed, not because we care, but because the secret stash is gone. We are here to follow and find the money, the bearer bonds, the cash, and the guns."

Guns?

Oh, my. We are not in the audience at Amateur Night anymore.

"Obviously," Vader Two continues, "you have a spy in your ranks. Or did."

Czarina sits up straight. "You are accusing Cosimo of being a traitor? Now that he is dead and cannot defend himself?"

"He has no need to defend himself, because he *is* dead," Vader Two observes coldly. "And we thought you had dealt with any traitors in your midst when the Phantom Mage hit bottom. Nice spectacular end, by the way. Should have discouraged other weak links, but apparently Sparks —"

"You have no idea whether Cosimo was a traitor or a victim," the Synth man declares.

"Do you?" is the icy retort.

A silence holds during which you could hear a cat scratching at a flea.

Luckily, Miss Midnight Louise's constant fishy breath from her high-end Asian cuisine, and my own personal magnetism that repels all vermin as if by magic, have kept us from any such rude personal grooming impulses at the moment.

Obviously, none of the Las Vegas branch of the Synth had considered that Cosimo Sparks could have died a traitor.

"While you lot are examining your consciences," Vader One says, "and hunting traces of your brains, we will be watching all of you and the case with keen interest."

279

"We have kept our eyes too closely on the international situation," Vader Two further notes, "and left you to your own sorry devices, relying on your self-interest to keep you out of trouble."

"Alas," Vader Two purrs again, overdoing it this time in a poor imitation of the real thing, "that approach has not worked. You can count on being the objects of concentrated but hidden observation from now forward."

"What can we do?" Czarina wails. "Cosimo is dead, and the rest of us might swiftly follow."

"Consult your crystal ball," Vader One snarls, sweeping the long cloak back as if brushing them aside so swiftly that the heavy faille material hisses. "Perhaps it has more intelligence than your conjoined brains."

I am only able to avoid their dramatic exit and accompanying foot stomps by sucking in my stomach and flattening against the black wall.

Another long silence commences, which is unfortunate because I cannot let my breath out until they start yammering again, and the longer they do not, the more certain my breath is to release in an audible windstorm *whoosh!*

Perishing from self-strangulation is considered pretty kinky these days, and I have no wish to succumb to something the tabloids would have a field day with.

"What nerve!" Carmen finally says, standing up to pace, whipping her own silken cloak around as stylishly as the recently departed Darth Vaders. "They play the long-distance puppet masters for several years, holding us back from our big, uh, reveal, as they say on the extreme-makeover shows, and then dare to blame us for Cosimo's death."

"Ah, those extreme makeover shows have moved from facial reconstruction to major house renovation," the Synth man points out.

"I do not care about any of those stupid shows, Hal Herald! Apparently you have no better things to do than watch them. I am thinking about the magic show of the century we were planning for Las Vegas."

"Last century or this?" Czarina asks dispiritedly, which is a rather sad condition for a medium. "We have been involved with these mysterious money backers almost that long."

"You did not see this coming," Hal points out.

"Please," Czarina urges, "we do not need to quarrel; we need to solve Cosimo's murder so we can get the foreign investors off our backs."

"What about the Phantom Mage's 'accident'?" Carmen asks. "Or was it murder?"

"Did any of us do it? What about Cosimo?" Hal continues the questions.

"You mean we might have a serial killing go-ing on?" Carmen demands.

"He wasn't one of us," Hal notes dismis-sively. "Just a hokey half-acrobatic magic act that gave a few thrills to the drunken postmid-night crowd. He did no real magic."

"As if 'real magic' is on any of our résumés," Czarina finally jibes back. "You and Cosimo and the other old-timers, like that Professor Mangel, might have wanted to diddle around tracing magical, mystical schools of history, but we were always a cadre of dreamers and schemers. I happen to think the schemers had the right idea all along. Looks as if Cosimo was more on the schemer side than anyone thought, and maybe the Phantom Mage was too."

"You are not going back to that old notion that he was Max Kinsella?" Carmen asks.

"Kinsella vanished about the time the Mage crashed, did he not?"

"Yeah, but that was a pattern with him," Herald points out. "Nothing new."

"Maybe the reason was new, Hal."

"That is crazy, Czarina. The Mystifying Max lost his Goliath gig. He may have pretended his contract just expired, but so have all our contracts expired as our venues dried up here in Vegas. Siegfried and Roy were retired by tragedy. Cirque du Soleil kicked the pants out of magic acts, face it. Dumb as the Phantom Mage's act was, at least he was in the bungee-jumping, costume-wearing vanguard. We're —" he snaps a flat disk on the mantel into the magnificence of a classic magician's "topper" — "old hat."

It is enough to pull a tear out of an aged duct. Not mine, mind you.

"Lance Burton just re-signed for several more years at the Monte Carlo," Hal notes.

"But not thee and me," Carmen says. "Oh, poor Cosimo. Who'd want the old man dead? And why?"

"We are a threat," Czarina intones in a dire alto voice almost as spooky as the strangers' masks.

"So we had hoped," Hal replies. "I think the Synth was just another Vegas scam. Something to keep us busy and hoping for a second coming, like the millennium nuts. Only we're magic nuts."

"You believe the Synth's House of Ophiuchus was a delusion? It has killed four people so far," Carmen points out, "maybe five now, including our colleague. The cloak beneath his dead body was spread in the celestial shape."

"Ophiuchus is a forgotten constellation, Carmen," Czarina says. "I do not think I can believe in the stars any longer. Unless it was a meteor like the Phantom Mage. He certainly put stars in *your* eyes."

"A pose," Carmen says haughtily. "I am not so easily impressed."

"There was that intimate parting note from Max Kinsella," Herald smirks, "before the Phantom Mage fell to his death. Maybe he was leaving you in both personas and *you* cut his bungee cord. A woman scorned . . ."

"Silly accusations!" Carmen objects to Herald's jibes with a shrug and a dramatic spin to the hidden door. "This has not been a productive assembly, except for those foreign Synth members showing up. I wonder what they really want from us. We would be better off going to ground separately, or assuredly we will be pestered whenever we meet here until those interlopers leave Las Vegas. I am not going to accept any masked individual who knows how to breach our club rooms as a Synth member."

"You did accept Max Kinsella and the Phantom Mage as just that," Czarina singsongs to Carmen's departing back.

I leap aside as the woman's knee nudges the door's pressure device and she vanishes into the dark beyond.

So I am left with two grumbling Synthettes and Midnight Louise.

Wait! Where is Midnight Louise?

The room is dim, and our kind is adept at the magic of blending into the background so we are not noticed, but even I have not noticed Louise for too long. You would think I would relish a vacation from her constant demands, and of course I do . . . but not when I do not know her whereabouts after we have dropped in on a sinister cabal of magicians.

Has she been kitnapped to play some moth-eaten top hat's up-popping bunny rabbit? What a comedown for a born predator.

While I worry, I stir like a vagrant draft along the floor, brushing pant legs and robe hems of the remaining two Synth members. Miss Midnight Louise is not hiding out under anything human or inanimate in the room.

What a puzzle. What a worry.

Did not master magician Mr. Max Kinsella disappear from this very place only a couple months ago? Are not Miss Louise and myself the only investigators who have kept a weather eye on these shady characters? Should I stay to investigate this obvious hotbed of past and future villainy, or rush off and return to the Crystal Phoenix to assist my Miss Temple, who has her hands full with an awkward murder related to this very place and present company and does not even know either one exists?

And what of my missing . . . uh, partner?

Surely, the scrappy little thing can take care of herself for once without me. To hear her tell it: *Surely, Daddy-o dude. Chill.*

Still, having the whole long-lost family now reunited on the streets of Las Vegas puts me in a pickle. I am only one individual. I cannot protect everybody at once!

Everybody at once . . . That reminds me of an old Las Vegas legend needing resurrection. One for all and all for one. The Rat Pack is dead; long live its successor — the Cat Pack.

CHAPTER 25
A GHOST OF A CLUE

Temple sat in her Miata outside the coroner's facility, inhaling the smell of sunwarmed leather to erase any rubbery, plastic, formaldehyde or decaying odors that might have clung to her clothes. She still didn't understand how the significant others of morgue workers ever got used to what had to come home with the job.

One odor she couldn't escape: this case reeked of Jersey Joe Jackson and his silver-dollar hoards hidden in the desert around the Joshua Tree Hotel he founded, which desert had become a sprawling city. From the macabre skeletal remnants exposed on the bottom of Lake Mead to the chubby, sad, clownlike, overdressed corpse inside the abandoned underground vault, it all came down to a Las Vegas legend of crime — Jersey Joe Jackson and his silver empire.

Temple decided that communing with a ghost was impractical. What she needed was witnesses.

She revved the Miata and squirted out of the morgue's parking lot onto Pinto Lane and then Charleston Avenue, buzzing by vintage-clothing stores as if they were in the city dump. The Blue Mermaid motel whizzed by on her left. Down the street stood its inspiration, the Blue Angel. Temple had heard that the graceful female neon figures atop their respective motels were inspired by Disney's Blue Fairy from the classic animated feature *Pinocchio.* And she knew that a woman designed the Blue Angel, Betty Willis, who also came up with the iconic and still-standing "Welcome to Fabulous Las Vegas" sign that "said" Las Vegas all over the world. Go, Betty!

Temple never saw the "Virgin Mary blue"–attired mermaid or angel figure without thinking of Matt. He'd first sensitized her to the religious significance of that particular hue of blue, which Temple realized echoed the shade of a Tiffany's jewelry box, of all things. Temple had a sudden inspiration. Her wedding attendants would wear VM blue! That ought to please Matt's Chicago Polish-Catholic relatives. Her Unitarian and Lutheran relatives would never guess a thing.

Wait! *Who* would be her *attendants?* Matron of Honor, Aunt Kit Carlson Fontana, of course. Bridesmaids? She didn't have a sister or many female friends close enough to pay for a VM-blue gown and an airfare to Chicago or Minneapolis.

Aha! Matt had a young Chicago cousin, Krys. And there was Temple's oldest brother's daughter, Tabitha. What about Mariah Molina, if her mother would let her? *Heh-heh.* That would so get her mother's goat and also help Mariah's self-esteem. She was getting taller and leaner and needed to get over her teen crush on Matt. Watching him get married ought to do it. On the other hand, Matt in a tux was not a discouraging sight. . . .

Three bridesmaids seemed plenty, but Temple could picture all eight eligible Fontana brothers as groomsmen in pale formal attire, morning coats out of an Oscar Wilde play — to die for! Obviously a . . . summer wedding. So she needed five bridesmaids more by then. Her mother would be over the moon. Only one daughter, one mother-of-the-bride dress. Temple would manage it, the whole schmear.

Okay. Matt's best man? He was short of relatives too. Maybe his birth father? Yes. Full circle.

Wait another minute! Temple was blue-skying the future when the present was a tangle of Las Vegas's perpetual reinvention woes and bizarre deaths and buried secrets. Didn't the past just always have to keep cropping up that destructive way?

She directed the Miata down the Strip and then off it, to Gangsters.

A parking valet in a Bonnie Parker beret offered to care for her car in the most personal way, with assurances it wouldn't get hit with any nasty G-men bullet holes.

A Fontana brother had been alerted to escort her inside.

Temple shifted through her brain cells to identify the brother. The feature-shading fedora didn't help. The Fontana did, though.

"Call me Ralphie the Wrench. We've all got new mob handles. Nicky's idea."

"Sure thing, Ralphie. I need to consult with the Glory Hole Gang. Where are they hanging out now?"

"The executive chef's suite. It's got a whole new test kitchen, but it's also a bunkhouse. Nicky calls it that so they don't feel it's charity. The fellas are too old to be off on their own, except for Eightball, who is not about to give up his little house from the old days and his PI license."

By then they had passed through the *ka-*

ching chatter of the casino area to the elevators.

Ralphie the Wrench continued to play tour guide en route to the tenth floor. "Work on the Speakeasy's bar and restaurant layout and the Chunnel of Crime is pretty intense, so the GH guys are mostly in the suite these days, menu planning."

Ralphie pulled the latest fancy phone from his pin-striped breast pocket and rang up ahead of them, explaining afterward to Temple, "Even really old bachelor guys are not tidy enough for lady visitors without warning."

Always the gentleman mobster, Ralphie the Wrench knocked for Temple, escorted her inside the suite, checked that the residence was fit for the presence of a lady, and then left her to her mission.

Pitchblende O'Hara was lounging on the huge upholstered conversation pit, wearing a flour-dusted apron and drinking a Red Bull. He jumped up at Temple's arrival.

"I'm the designated welcoming committee, Miss Temple. Gollee, you look fresher than one of Spud's French pastries right from the oven. We are gonna call them Bonnie's Bits."

"Well, maybe I just look flaky by now," Temple said, waving good-bye to Ralphie as the door closed on his pin-striped back. "I need to talk to all of you. Can the kitchen crew put the experiments on heat-lamp warming and come out for a few minutes?"

Pitchblende rose and beat it back to the kitchen, drawing Temple's attention to his size-thirteen feet in battered Roper boots. Serviceable, not fancy, and probably resoled and resewn a number of times.

Their well-worn clothes told the tale of the Glory Hole Gang's obscure, last-but-not-best decades living in a ghost town until drawn into Vegas by another, earlier search for Jersey Joe Jackson's silver hoards.

The first Glory Hole Gang member out of the kitchen wasn't one.

Santiago bustled through.

He looked flustered to see her, but no more than she to see him.

"Ah, Miss Barr," he said. "You have caught me. The sublime scents of the test kitchen penetrate to my suite next door, and I cannot control myself. Thanks to my neighbors, I'm indulging a fascination with genuine western barbecue." He lifted a blue-and-white-checkered linen towel that added a smoky, spicy tang to the air, which had Temple's stomach ready to growl. "Not my usual fare. They are going to call it Smokin' Smothered Sirloin on the menu.

Gentlemen, as usual, my gratitude and compliments to the chefs. Miss Barr."

With a bow, he was out the door. He must be a barbecue fanatic to eat it in that white suit. Temple smirked to have seen a smudge of deep burgundy sauce on the edge of his pristine white sleeve cuff. Simply Santiago was simply . . . a freeloader.

"He's been in and out like a boarder with a tapeworm," Pitchblende complained, "slinging those fancy compliments like they were hash. I think he was afraid our fixin's for the new restaurant would not be tony enough for his high-tech 'installation.' But we use the best aged beef, and those South Americans know prime steak when they taste it."

"Howdy, Miss Temple!" The next kitchen émigré was Wild Blue Pike. The old man had the face of an aging angel, amazingly unwrinkled and pale. Maybe he was into Oil of Olay. He would have looked innocent in any lineup, with his lush white hair and distance-focused blue eyes.

Spuds Lonnigan came clunking out, wiping his wet hands on another checkered linen towel. Cranky Ferguson was munching on one of those flaky French pastries too delicate to put down, but he carried a saucer under it to catch crumbs.

Eightball O'Rourke exited the kitchen last. *Whoops!* He was *not* the last. A large black cat, not Midnight Louie, ambled out, tongue working some dropped morsel out of his long white whiskers.

"Three O'Clock has moved in?" Temple asked, pleased. "I thought he wouldn't let you guys near him when you left the restaurant at Temple Bar."

"Ah, he jest visits for the chow train," Cranky said with a dismissive wave of his hand. "He's like your house cat, a will-o'-the-wisp."

"Not in girth," Temple said.

"None of us are wispy these days," Spuds said, " 'cept Wild Blue and Eightball."

"And our Miss Temple," Eightball loyally pointed out. "I noticed," he added, "you been admiring our footwear. There a reason you want our feet all in a campfire circle?"

Eightball was not a man to be fooled.

"Absolutely," Temple said. "I confess. I was sizing up your feet."

"And . . . ?"

"You've always worn cowboy boots?"

"Hell, yes," said Wild Blue, "even in my flying days."

"We don't say 'hell' in front of ladies," Cranky warned him.

"It's okay now," Temple countered. "I'm

294

here to examine your boots, which is not a very ladylike pursuit."

"Phew," Pitchblende said. "You shore don't want us to take 'em off before suppertime."

"Sit down and make yourself at home," Eightball urged. "You can eyeball our foot-leather better close-up."

Temple smiled and pulled a folder out of her ever-present tote bag.

"I'm trying to solve the identity of the Three O'Clock Louie's once-submerged corpse."

Wild Blue winced. "Poor guy who was et away almost down to his anklebones? Those Lake Mean carp were hungry suckers, even when our restaurant was still going. Hate to think what they did before there were piles of tourists to feed 'em."

"More like piranha," Spuds agreed. "Say, we could serve catfish and call it something like Cannibal Catfish."

"So you saw that TV news piece. How about Capone's Catch of the Day?" Temple suggested.

"More refined and Frenchlike," Eightball agreed. "But how come our boots are suspects? Forgive me, Miss Temple, but even we can't string out a pair of boots for more 'n twenty years' wear. That Lake Mead dead guy musta passed back in the glory days of the forties and fifties, because as Las Vegas heated up as a tourist destination, you did not wanta pollute the wonders of nature they could be bussed out to, or have an indiscretion caught on a boat anchor and causing consternation."

"Gotta give whoever dumped that body in concrete booties credit," Cranky added morosely. "Didn't get found until Mother Nature sucked all that H-two-oh outta the lake."

"You guys go back that far, along with Jersey Joe?"

"Yes, ma'am, 'cept we are all still alive. Living out in the desert keeps all that carbon monoxide from the Strip out of a man's lungs," Pitchblende said.

"Did Jersey Joe get too big for his boots when he stole all those silver dollars you all found? Did he dress like a dude?"

" 'Course he did." Eightball snorted.

"You woulda thought he was the second coming of Roy Rogers," Spuds said. "Bolo ties with western suit coats. Boots pointed enough to make a horse run away from him."

"So he went 'Hollywood,' like the movie *Melody Ranch*'s singing cowboys?" Temple asked, to make sure they were talking the same language and style.

"Oh, yeah. Got way above us and hisself." Wild Blue said. "Dollar cigars. We didn't figure it out at first, where he got the money. Thought he won it gambling, or one mob or the other was backing him. He always had big plans."

"We had Jilly to raise, number one," Eightball said gruffly. "That changed our dreams of hitting a strike at an old mine. We only did that train robbery to get a fund for our girl, and when we found all the silver dollars gone from our mine tunnel, we figured at first other prospectors took 'em, not one of our own gang."

"JJ was a disappointment," Cranky said. "But he was long dead and gone, and the Joshua Tree Hotel and Casino was a wreck no one wanted to take on, by the time Solitaire Smith and that tourist gal stumbled on one of JJ's new hiding places for the silver-dollar hoard."

"We'd been hiding out all those years from that robbery, and turns out it wasn't necessary. The dollars were only worth anything to those 'numisintist' people."

Temple couldn't help smiling at Spud's mangled version of the word.

The Glory Hole Gang had all been roped into being stepfathers for Eightball's orphaned granddaughter, and dreams of riches and glory had faded with their quirky responsibility for a young girl. Jill grew up looking out for her gang of uncles. Now she was Mrs. Johnny Diamond and lived on a lavish ranch that the Crystal Phoenix's never-fading ballad singer kept as a retreat after his nightly shows.

The whole Crystal Phoenix family, Temple knew, would be devastated if any of these old guys had anything to do with killing the sunken soul Midnight Louie and his daddy had found on the bottom of Lake Mead.

"So," she said, taking a deep breath. "Did you know anyone else in the old days who could have afforded a custom pair of silver heel-capped cowboy boots signed by a master silversmith out of Hollywood named Bohlin?"

She tossed the close-up photo of the maker's stamp onto the coffee table that centered the sprawling conversation-pit sofas.

And all conversation stopped.

Every last man stared at the black-and-white photo as if it were an eight-foot-long rattlesnake sunning on a hot rock six inches from their cowboy-booted ankles.

They should have been safe from any poison, but just seeing the possibilities made their blood run cold.

"Oh, man," Pitchblende wailed. "I saw those things fresh outta the box. Real fine box, with all this girly tissue-stuff wrapped around them for shipping."

"Darn and definitely darn," Wild Blue pitched in. "He did leave town without notice."

"Forever," Cranky intoned.

"I thought it was another fast deal down Arizona-way," Eightball said.

"He never did like water," Spuds mourned. "Only in his whiskey."

Temple sat still and silent, realizing she had kicked off a wake.

For Jersey Joe Jackson? Didn't seem quite right.

CHAPTER 26
MOTORPSYCHO NIGHTMARE

Max dreams and knows it.

He's riding a sleek silver motorcycle.

Through the Alps.

Revienne Schneider is riding pillion behind him, clinging. She is not the clingy type.

If this weren't a dream, she'd be hurling Freudian interpretations his way.

Motorcycle, symbol of freedom. Alps, symbol of hubris and danger. She would yank him off his electro-glide high horse, bring him down to Earth.

So he knows dreamland is not throwing the sexy, brainy shrink at him, but someone else, the visceral, gut-wrenching shrew who is riding behind him in Revienne's intellectual sheepskin clothing. Riding him.

Rebecca was a spoiled, conniving bitch in the famous novel of that name. And dead.

Now he sees the woman passenger's long black entangling hair whipping around his face like a mesh mask. The burr on his back is Black Irish, just as he is. Thorny. Dogged. Just as he is. Deceptive. As he can be if he has to. Hate filled, as he never was, unless it was at himself.

Maybe *that* is the key to Rebecca. Her hatred was always self-directed, and turned outward.

Whatever the truth, he knows what she is. A revenant, a haunting dream. A nightmare is always a dark female ride for him.

He dares to pity her. And feels steel spurs in his side.

The tarot card reads Strength. Who is compassion and light.

He is the Magician. Who is action and power.

His dark rider is . . . Death. Who is dark and sometimes welcome, which is light.

Rebecca. Kathleen. Kathleen O'Connor. Kitty the Cutter.

The odd card in the deck, the Hierophant, with the stage name of Gandolph, rises with a staff, barring the middle of the steep, dark road. A ring glints into the air, all gold and twisted like the worm Ouroboros, the serpent swallowing its own tail, that ancient symbol of eternity. Its eye is shimmering like an Australian fire opal, which is a symbol of hope and purity.

A lost engagement ring. "Engagement" being action and power, as well as passion and commitment.

He wants to ditch this monkey on his back, this entire magical, mystical motorcycle ride.

And he does. The motorcycle lies on its side, smoking tires spinning. He bends over to brush a long, lusterless lock of hair back from the pale face on the ground . . . and recoils.

The face is a map of decaying fungus, iridescent with rot.

He is up and running. Down a dark, deserted road, naturally.

Not so naturally. He's running toward something, a black pyramid topped by a rearing stallion etched in flaring neon light.

It's her! The real nightmare. The steed the fairy-tale knight urged up the glass mountain again and again, as he failed to surmount it again and again. To win the princess.

He understands that dreams are often the outpourings of subconscious punsters, like the literal nightmare. He's got a split mind, both creator and hapless creature of himself, of his banged-up mind.

Then he's running through a place he knows, the neon-sign graveyard in Las

Vegas, faded in the sterile sunlight, larger than life, clownish. All bones and no flesh . . . flash.

As if turning on his dismissal, the world goes from sun soaked to black velvet painting. There is noise, music, as loud and raucous as the blazing neon images clashing all around him.

He is plunging down a dark rabbit hole, swinging out over an abyss. Instead of crashing down into the blur of life and motion and light below, he swings into an angular zigzag of a tunnel, running again, bouncing off the reflective black walls.

Then . . . it all opens up again into light, the warm glow of lamps against the darkness, and the whole cast is onstage, in costume, posed for a vignette fit for an Addams family portrait.

He can finally stop running, trying to escape, because he knows and can name each face.

This is where he was led and to where he has to return.

He assumes a confident persona, donning his own costume.

Flames flicker against the soot-blackened walls of a fireplace, but their red and yellow tongues are too regular to be real, and they flash a spark of gas-fed electric blue. Yet their false heat warms the room's cherry-wood paneling and highlights tufted leather couches and Empire satin-and-gilt chairs.

"Czarina Catherina predicted you'd never come back to us, but Carmen always knew you would," a portly man in white tie and tails says as pompously as the White Rabbit, speaking from his position of power standing alongside the fireplace.

From his tone, Carmen is the handsome Spanish woman in her thirties lounging on one of the black horsehair-upholstered chairs. Her clothes and coloring are a study in black, white, and crimson. The name pricks Max.

Max bows to her acknowledgment, then turns to the other woman present.

This is the usual "medium," a woman in her fifties or sixties, blowsy and exotic in her own commanding way, wearing a gold lamé turban and caftan, with a name as fussy as she is. Czarina Catherina.

She speaks in a surprisingly deep yet quivery voice. "Carmen said you weren't dead."

"You commune with the spirit world," he answers. "What do they say?"

"Imposter," Czarina Catherina charges, her voice thick with accusation. "Max Kinsella fled the Neon Nightmare the night the Phantom Mage fell to his death at that very club. Why would a murderer return to the scene of the crime?"

Before he can answer, she adds, "Besides, you don't at all resemble the Mystifying Max."

He turns to where she is staring and finds his entry door has become a floor-length mirror.

Dreams will do that: go out of their way to seal off any logical means of escape.

He sees four people behind him, the two women and the formally attired man he suddenly knows for a stage magician who'd worked years ago as Cosimo Sparks. The second man is tall and dark-haired and so familiar-looking. It is Max Kinsella, looking as intense and secretive as the poster for his stage show. His long-retired stage show.

So who is the star of this dream, the man facing him in the mirror?

Max feels a strangling spasm of disbelief.

Sean stands there instead . . . as he'd never lived to be: tall, broad, and husky, the curly red hair now auburn and spiky with some trendy gel, grinning like a death's head come back to life.

While Max stands gaping, Carmen slinks up behind him to curl crimson-taloned hands over his shoulders.

"Don't go so soon," she croons in an Irish

accent. "We're just starting. Do you like my engagement ring, darling?"

He stares at the huge fiery opal framed in diamonds. He'd given someone a ring like that, but it had been smaller, finer, more tasteful. Exquisite.

"It's synthetic!" he protests. "It's not real."

Next his dream self would be shouting, *You're nothing but a pack of cards!*

With that thought, he meets Sean's hazel eyes in the mirror and watches them darken into expanding pupils, a pair of emotional black holes to suck his sadly split selves into their own heart of darkness.

CHAPTER 27
SILENT PARTNER

"Not Jersey Joe," Eightball O'Rourke quickly assured Temple. "He could wear a suit and would go so far as to don a black leather bolo tie when business called for it. We found it pretty fancy, but he was all for building something that would last, like Bugsy."

"Not his goldurn wardrobe," Wild Blue agreed, picking up the photo of the silver boot-heel stamp.

"Aw, it destroys your faith in humanity all over again," Pitchblende said mournfully. "Our old pal Boots Benson musta been in on sneakin' off our illegally obtained lucre and squirreling it away for Jersey Joe. Just another dirty rotten desert rat."

"Now, maybe not," Eightball opined, sitting forward on the oversized yardage of couch. "Maybe our restaurant out at Temple Bar was settin' atop the answer to our busted lives of crime all the time, buried under fathoms of silent Lake Mead water."

"Our mascot, Three O'Clock, has snagged carp out there," Spuds Lonnigan said, with a shudder. "That could be the seventieth generation of fish that nibbled on Boots's bones. How long do carp live, anyway?"

"Longer than we'd think," Cranky Ferguson answered. "I'm guessing twenty-five to fifty years in places where there ain't predators, and carp is not a prized game fish unless it's a real huge one."

Temple had sat openmouthed during this conversation, but she shut it fast when she realized all her companions were versed in the sport of fishing.

"No," Eightball agreed, "it's your largemouth and striped bass, channel catfish, crappie, and bluegill you want at our southern end of Lake Mead. Tourists have fed the shoreline carp to overstuffing for decades. So I agree, several of those suckers could have nibbled on Boots's sunken chest. Yo, ho, ho."

"That is so gruesome," Temple said. "I knew there was a reason I didn't like sportfishing."

"Boots is gone," Eightball told her. "Weren't pretty, but now we know where, thanks to you."

"I need to know why," Temple said.

Eightball shook his head and regarded his pals. "Just like my granddaughter, Jilly, at age six. Why, why, why." He turned to Temple again. "You and I have done some private-eye work, and we know murder always boils down to motive and method."

"The method in this case illuminated the motive," Temple said.

"How so?" Cranky asked.

"It's such a classic mob ploy," she explained, "encasing a man's feet in concrete and throwing him off a pier."

"Yup." Wild Blue jumped into the discussion. "That was a big city mob method. They had a lot more water at hand — New York Harbor or Lake Michigan in Chicago."

"That's right," Temple said, getting into the ghoulish groove. "A lake for body dumping was a novelty in the desert. Lake Mead's artificial. When did it — ?"

"Oh, young lady," Pitchblende said, "the big Depression, of course. Hoover Dam was one of the few things that damn-fool president did to help folks get work. His first reaction was to laugh the whole thing off as poor folks not wanting to work enough. Building that dam backed up the Colorado River, and then you got the lake."

"Nobody much cared about that big old watering hole in those days," Spuds said.

"Nobody much cared about any of this until Bugsy Siegel tried to sell the area as a resort to Hollywood folk."

"What I'm getting at," Temple said, "is that Boots Benson went missing because he'd been murdered in this spectacular, brutal, big-time mob way. I'm thinking his death was mostly meant to be a message."

"Yeah, but if nobody knew he'd been killed, much less that *way,* what was the point?" Wild Blue asked.

Temple glanced at the photo of the maker marks on what was left of Boots's footwear. "Maybe someone got all modern and took photos of Boots's going-away launch. Maybe someone else was told and shown what happened to Boots."

"That's it!" Cranky Ferguson slapped his tobacco pouch down on the coffee table, making them all jump. "That's why Jersey Joe got so quiet and dodgy with us all about where the train-robbery silver dollars were hidden and what was going on in town and when we could expect to get some of our cut."

"He kept stalling us," Spuds put in, "and stalling us, saying it was needed to put up the Joshua Tree Hotel and Casino."

"And that put you all off?" Temple asked.

"Sure," Wild Blue Pike said. "We expected

to wait to get something back on our investment. The Joshua Tree was the whole purpose of the stickup. Train robbery was pretty rare by then. We had it all figured out how to separate the silver cars and shuffle 'em off on a side rail and keep movin' them along from spur to spur track. We didn't wear bandanas on our faces and pull guns or nothing. I kept track of everything from the air, before and during and after, from my biplane."

"Why'd you think the Crystal Phoenix put the Haunted Mine Ride in the Jersey Joe Jackson attraction, girl?" Spuds asked. "During those early construction days, rails ran right nearby. We were miners, for mercy's sake! We just excavated ourselves under the hotel-to-be property and scooted those silver-dollar-loaded cars down there and covered up the shaft."

Temple's mouth was open again.

"Only we ended up *getting* the shaft," Wild Blue complained. "Nothin' we could do about it. Jersey Joe seemed to have spread the wealth from there, to hiding places in the distant desert and right under our feet, and nothing we could do about it but stew."

"Then the lost vault was real?" Temple asked.

"Sure." Eightball shook his head at that

311

latest travesty. "It was real hard to keep our composures, watching that sucker getting opened in front of God and TV cameras and that weasely Crawford Buchanan and fancy man from down Rio way."

"Looks like that dead magician fellow inside got the same shaft we did," Pitchblende said, puffing on his now-smoking pipe.

"What if the vault had been loaded to the gills with silver dollars from that robbery?" Temple wondered.

Eightball chuckled. "That's been dead to us for decades. Those ill-gotten gains are too infamous to do anybody any good now. 'Cept gettin' new greedy fools killed. Poor Boots started the chain letter of deceit from hell, and Jersey Joe was the next recipient."

"So you're thinking Jersey Joe never gave the mob the money, but he never had a worry-free day in his life from then on," Temple said.

"Yup." Cranky had returned from the test kitchen with an opened longneck. "That's why he never faced us guys again."

"Maybe he thought you'd get the 'concrete bathtub' treatment like Boots if you were linked to the robbery," Temple suggested.

The stunned silence showed they'd never thought of that.

"Jersey Joe was cheatin' us because he was *protectin'* us?" Pitchblende asked in slow, four-four time.

"He didn't live much of the high life after the Joshua Tree went up," Temple pointed out. "After all, he's famous for what he hid and *didn't* use. And, Eightball, didn't your granddaughter, Jill, find some of the stash?"

"Yeah, that was a fluke," Eightball said, "and by then any money we couldn't give Jilly for college and such was moot. She was already grown."

"But she's played the World Championship Poker game," Wild Bill pointed out, "and is the top-ranking female. Wouldn't have happened if she hadn't grown up playing Gin Rummy and Old Maid and poker with us old coots when we were all hidin' out for years in that ghost town."

"I guess," Eightball said, beaming even as he shrugged at their ward's accomplishments.

"And now," Temple pointed out, "the very drying up of Lake Mead that revealed the resting place of your old associate, Boots, is putting the light of day on the puzzling actions and motivations of another old associate who may have betrayed you all for your own good."

Eightball considered, nodded his head,

then glared at her.

"You are an inveterate and unreformed Little Mary Sunshine, did you know that, Miss Temple Barr?"

"Not really." She cringed a bit inside. These guys had endured forty years of deprivation, loneliness, and justifiable anger. Who was she to put a better spin on it?

"Get a whole round of those beers, Cranky," Eightball ordered. "We need to drink a long-delayed toast to Boots Benson and Jersey Joe Jackson, may they finally rest in peace, boots and bolo tie together, and to Miss Temple Barr: may forever she wave, at Lake Mead or elsewhere, wherever it's needed."

CHAPTER 28
AN INSPECTOR CALLS

When Temple told Van she'd work on the death in the vault solo, she hadn't realized how really solo she was these days.

She was used to a sounding board, but Max was as gone as a Las Vegas tourist on a three-night jag. Now Matt was in Chicago, doing a daily live *Amanda Show* gig and having serial dinners with his relatives, especially his wary mother and his newly discovered birth father.

"I'll do some groundwork for you flying up with me on a later visit," he'd told Temple on the long-distance phone call when she checked in from her car. "I understand you'd want to have a formal wedding in Minneapolis or Chicago for both families, but mine is a mess right now. I don't want their ancient issues clouding the biggest day of our lives. Believe me, I've seen how a couple of feuding family members can make a wedding into a battleground no one will ever forget, including the happy couple."

Temple had nodded, though he couldn't see. She'd witnessed that too, had attended wedding receptions where pregnant brides' bitter fathers had too much champagne and blabbed their daughters' condition to all and sundry, or where best men had needed to confess during the wedding toast that they'd known the bride "in the biblical fashion." Or worse.

When Temple returned to her Circle Ritz condo, it was quiet and empty, and she realized that would drive her nuts. She went to the spare bedroom to use the desktop computer and did a search on Revienne Schneider and Professor Hugo Gruetzmeyer. She no longer Googled. She used Bing.com because that encouraged her to shout aloud, "Bingo!" when she hit pay dirt and found something.

Pay dirt, she mused. That was a gold miners' expression, and if anyone should take it seriously, it was the old guys who made up the Glory Hole Gang.

Hmph. Maybe she *wasn't* solo on this investigation. They had a lot at stake in settling matters and getting their restaurant underway at Gangsters. Their brainstorming session today had put a new light on some very dark issues in their lives and given her a lot more to think about regarding current deaths and disappointments.

Why hadn't she thought of them sooner, instead of moping around feeling that forties song staple, lonely and blue?

Cheered, Temple dove into the many sites mentioning Revienne Schneider. She found nothing about her family, but plenty on that Swiss private school. Then the Sorbonne in Paris, then a gap, then graduation from Sigmund Freud University of Vienna and Paris, and an impressive portfolio building to a crescendo of 165,000 Web mentions.

Apparently, Revienne Schneider had been a girl wonder right out of PhD school, working with damaged young women all over the Continent and Ireland.

Mention of that island nation always chilled Temple's blood. It had spawned Kathleen O'Connor, she who'd ruined the lives of Max and his terrorism-slain cousin, Sean, and who'd seduced Max into a future of regret and undercover counterterrorism.

Now Temple was chilled to the bone to read of the awful Magdalen institutions, where young women were given a life sentence of drudgery and incarceration. Verbal, physical, and sexual abuse thrived among such an isolated and helpless population, as it can in private families as well.

In comparison, having four slightly bullying, obnoxiously superior older brothers didn't seem like much of a problem at all.

The former reporter in Temple was working up a righteous rage, but the Magdalen atrocities had long been revealed, though the hidden sins of the Roman Catholic Church in that regard persisted the way Wall Street CEOs' unbelievable millions in "bonuses" persisted after the entire country's economy crashed in 2008.

You had to admire Revienne for wading into that cesspool of damage with her fresh shrink credentials and, well, media-ready personal attributes. This woman definitely looked "Illegally Blonde."

Jeesh, thought Temple, staring at another image of Revienne, designer-suited up and sleek, *what is it with these European femme fatales?* Thirty-seven, single, dedicated to her work. It didn't seem . . . natural for a woman this attractive to have no marriage history or romantic links, but she was a Frenchwoman. She'd have no trouble connecting with men wherever she went.

Temple wondered why this perfect, and even selfless, career woman gave her the creeps. A big black bar flashed across the screen and slapped Revienne Schneider right in the elegantly aloof blonde kisser. It was a furry tail.

"Louie! You scared me. When'd you get home? And from where? And why are you playing computer-screen smackdown with the beautiful blonde stranger in town?"

He hunkered low on the desktop, covering Temple's notepapers and pen and a quarter of the computer keyboard. He began grooming his slap-happy paw and purring loud enough to imitate a queen bee hive.

"Apparently," Temple said, "you don't like gorgeous blonde interlopers on our crime scene, either."

Louie just yawned to show his carnivore-red mouth and flash his white baby-shark's teeth.

Temple was still mooning at this image of tall blonde perfection when her old-fashioned doorbell rang. Avon calling? Maybe.

Right now she was about convinced that finding the right facial foundation might make her look taller. She padded barefoot to the entry hall, and voilà . . .

"You!" Temple was sorry she'd answered her doorbell, though it was too nice of a one to ignore. Now she wished she'd just stood behind the closed door, enjoying a long, sonorous melody of bells until her visitor had given up and gone away.

Unfortunately, her visitor was not the type to give up and go away. Ever.

"I thought my life had been too blessed to be true lately," Temple grumbled as she stepped aside for Amazonian homicide officer C. R. Molina, in the extenuated flesh. And wearing flats!

"And here I thought we were drinking buddies," Lieutenant C. R. Molina said, crossing onto Temple's black-and-white-tiled entry-hall floor with her giant Big and Tall Women low-heeled loafers.

Flatfoot was *right!*

Even without high heels, the homicide officer still towered over her. Well, why not? Temple not only went mostly barefoot at home, she knew she looked particularly shrimpy at the moment, wearing her longest T-shirt belted as a short knit dress.

Molina was eyeing Temple's bare pink toes with their scarlet nail polish looking like blood drops on the black-and-white checkerboard of cool marble.

"So that's your secret to stomping around on spikes all over the Strip. At home you're a closet toe nudist. Even Mariah had more 'toe' at age nine."

"My toes are off-limits. How is Mariah?"

"She's fine. I understand from Van von

Rhine that you've recently met an old school friend of hers, Revienne Schneider."

"Just in passing in Van's office. Why on Earth would you be interested in Van's European school friends?"

"So you'd never heard of or met this woman before?" Molina asked.

"Nope. Why'd you ask about her?"

"After the body in the vault — oh, Lord, that sounds so Agatha Christie! — everyone new at the Crystal Phoenix is a person of interest to the police. Detective Ferraro has his hands full with the cast of dozens on the scene. I decided to consult your friends and business associates in the Fontana crime family. They were quite forthcoming about such exotic recent imports as Mr. Tomás Santiago and Miss Revienne Schneider."

"Santiago was Nicky's find," Temple said, taking the chance to defend herself while she had it. "The body in the vault was a freak accident, I swear. I didn't do it to drum up publicity for the hotel, and I don't think Crawford Buchanan did it, even though he deserves a murder rap, and I am totally cooperating with Detective Ferraro and any minions he may have, because the Crystal Phoenix really needs to shut this incident down."

"Not a stupendous opening stunt for a

mob museum," Molina agreed, eyeing the pale living-room sofa for big black blots with claws in residence.

"Santiago is, unfortunately, all for real," she went on. "His avant-garde architectural work is well known and respected internationally. Revienne Schneider shows up as a world-renowned expert in her field. Her only flaw — Well, I looked as hard for some as you probably did, but I found only two things awry."

"*Two* things! What a relief." Temple sighed.

"One would think an international expert doing a workshop at a local university would be a much ballyhooed event on the Web site, at least, if not in a course catalog. Not so with Dr. Schneider."

"Van seemed to be hosting her at the eleventh hour too," Temple noted.

"She'd come here directly from Zurich, which is not her home or office base."

"But she and Van attended a Swiss prep school. They would have Swiss friends in common."

"Being a proud graduate of Our Lady of Perpetual Mercy in East L.A.," Molina said, "I wouldn't know about Swiss prep-school friends. Interpol tells me there was some sort of recent upset at an Alpine Swiss clinic. Dr. Schneider left abruptly and notified the clinic later from Zurich that she wouldn't be returning."

"Maybe the visiting professor here needed her to bail him out."

"So you don't find her presence just before the murder was discovered to be suspicious?"

Now was the time for Temple to blab or babble about the Synth and the forgotten thirteenth sign of the zodiac and the suspicious shape of the victim's red cloak lining.

Yeah, Molina would really crack the whip and have Ferraro follow those lines of inquiry.

"This is clearly a local affair," Temple said. "Weird but all too local. That's Vegas."

Molina eyed Temple hard, then nodded her satisfaction.

"Good," she said, plopping down on the cushions like she owned the place. "I'll take something cool and slightly alcoholic. Don't fuss. Whatever's handy."

She smiled and lifted the strong, dark eyebrows Temple had always thought were in desperate need of plucking. On the other hand, the Brooke Shields look had worked for her for years. So . . . Molina was *working* her, Temple?

Think again. She banged around the tiny kitchen that suited her just fine and returned with two tall, festive glasses filled with something the color of watermelon juice.

"Pretty pale sangria," Molina commented, taking a sip.

Temple sat on a chair at the end of the glass-topped coffee table, checking to see that her no-sweat, absorbent stone coasters were out. As usual, what was left of daily newspapers these days littered the coffee-table top. NO PHOENIX REVIVAL ACT FOR BIZARRE BODY IN HIDDEN HOTEL VAULT was the gripping three-line head over the one-column front-page teaser story for a more-detailed inside report.

"Front page," Molina commented. "A publicist's dream. Unless the topic is anti-productive. What is this stuff?"

"Newsprint? How soon they forget. Oh, you mean the drink. It's not like I keep a fully stocked bar."

"What is it?" Like all homicide detectives, even off-duty Molina wanted answers, pronto.

"Crystal Light cherry pomegranate with vodka."

"Not bad." Molina nudged the paper away to uncover a coaster, as if delicately unveiling a dead body . . . or a cockroach. She put the glass down.

Temple took a big farewell gulp of hers

and did likewise.

"Relax," Molina said. "I'm not here about your current problem. I'm not even surreptitiously examining the premises for symptoms of Max Kinsella."

" 'Symptoms'? Like he's a disease?"

"Not still contagious by now, I hope. No," Molina mused, "I'm convinced I no longer need to worry about him, and you certainly don't, not with another man's engagement ring on your left hand."

No . . . not until Molina bopped over and got overly cozy with Temple's spiked Crystal Light and seemed about ready to drop a bombshell.

"By the way . . ." Molina shifted on the sofa.

Was she going to draw a gun?

Temple's paired bare knees pressed together until the bones ached. What was going on here? Really?

Molina thrust a hand into her khaki blazer pocket and pulled out a . . .

Plum?

No, a plastic sandwich baggie wearing a narrow white label.

Temple eyed it as if a tarantula crouched inside.

"You'll recognize this," Molina said, tossing the baggie onto the bed of newspapers on the coffee table.

Temple reached to take another sip of her cherry-pomegranate-vodka cocktail. Did the baggie contain drugs? Was she being set up? Was she paranoid? Yes! She picked up the plastic baggie.

Something heavy sagged down in one corner.

Too heavy to be a tarantula.

But not too heavy to be a shock.

Temple heard her own voice echo as if she were speaking in the Chunnel of Crime. "It's the ring. My ring."

"Right. Kinsella's ring, which the late magician Shangri-La conned you out of during her magic act way back when."

"You . . . said it was police evidence, that you had to keep it."

Molina shrugged. "I suppose it still might be police evidence, but you're engaged to Matt Devine now. And Max Kinsella is . . . apparently long gone. Shangri-La's dead. So it's my call."

Temple tangled her bare ankles together. Her toes barely touched the long white fur of her fake-goat-hair area rug under the coffee table. She was just too damn short.

Since her clamped knees made her skirt into a secure little hammock between her thighs, she peeled open the bag's zip-strip and worked the ring into her palm. She remembered telling Max that opals were unlucky, but he had laughed at the idea.

Oh. Seeing it again was like viewing a full moon for the first time. This was a particularly vivid, fire-laden stone, the whole sky's worth of aurora borealis captured in a knuckle-sized square. Wasn't that just like Max? The diamonds framing the opal twinkled in obeisance to the central stone. This ring wasn't as antique or expensive as the ruby-and-diamond Art Deco showpiece she now wore and adored, but it was unique and exquisite.

It brought back the magic of Max, and the knowledge that he was utterly gone, even as far as his archenemy Molina was concerned. Temple was surprised Molina hadn't croaked, "Come . . . bite," in a hag's voice just now as she offered the ring to Temple.

Temple gazed up into the homicide lieutenant's eyes. They were as vividly blue as the Morning Glory Pool in Yellowstone Park — which was brimming with poisonous sulfur.

Molina's expression remained the usual law-enforcement-personnel noncommittal blank.

Temple was equally determined not to

327

give an inch, or even a centimeter of opal.

"If you can give this ring back to me now," she said, "you didn't need to keep it as 'evidence' all this time."

"No. No, I didn't."

"Then that was mean."

The schoolyard epithet sank deep between them like the opal ring had weighed in Temple's lap. Impossible to ignore.

"Yes," Molina said, her hands jamming her blazer pockets, her front teeth biting her barely lip-glossed bottom lip. "That was mean. I have been a mean girl."

"And you're giving it back now because . . . you think Max is dead!"

"Maybe," said Molina.

"You *know* Max is dead!"

"I don't, and I'm not sure I'd believe it if I did hear it. Max Kinsella, dead or alive, has nothing to do with my bringing that here."

"Why, then?"

"Shangri-La is dead. The case is closed, and the wench is dead." Molina shrugged. "No reason to keep it."

"I can't wear it!"

"It's a keepsake, then. I certainly don't need it cluttering an evidence locker."

"This little thing?"

"Any little thing," Molina said, smiling wryly.

Temple inhaled but didn't say anything, after all.

Molina sipped her drink. "This is pretty good, amazingly. You have a gift for the impromptu."

"So do you!" Temple charged back, eyes flashing. "You just show up, brandishing my engagement ring?"

"Hardly an engagement ring now," Molina said.

"Why now?" Temple demanded.

"It was an excuse to talk to you."

"You've never needed an excuse before."

"I've never needed your 'expertise' before."

"Which is?"

"You . . . appear to be something of a better judge of men than I am. Except for Matt. He's golden, as we both know."

"Mostly. He's human too."

"Apparently, I am not."

What a confession! Temple felt they really ought to be seated in a bare little room with a two-way mirror somewhere. Molina wanted something from her. Molina was flashing something that looked a lot like . . . humility? Vulnerability? Oh, happy day!

Temple took up the gauntlet and sipped

329

deliberately. Damn good cherry-pomegranate-vodka cocktail. If aspartame is your aperitif of choice.

"What are you not being human about?" Temple inquired.

"Our main topic. Men."

Did Temple ever dream she would see the day she and Molina snuggled down with booze to discuss men? No.

"Which men?" Temple asked. "If you're going to grill me about Max again . . ."

"No. Max Kinsella is a dead issue."

Temple cringed. "An official declaration?"

"Totally personal. Or don't you think I have a personal view?"

"I think it's all been personal about Max."

Molina actually winced. "He's such a natural-born suspect, even you have to admit that. If he was always the counterterrorist operative you claim, that would draw official suspicion, even subconsciously."

"Maybe," Temple admitted. "So it's Max you want me to dissect."

"Actually, no. I say he was a likely suspect. You say I was persecuting him. He disappeared, probably happy to not be a bone of contention any longer. No, let Max enjoy his anonymity. I'm more interested in knowing what you think about Dirty Larry."

"Huh?"

"Dirty Larry Podesta. You've seen him around crime scenes. The recovering under- cover guy."

"You mean 'Dirty Blond' Dirty Larry."

"If you say so. So you think *blond* means 'dumb'? You're marrying a blond."

"Do I have to call him Dirty Larry? It's so seventies."

Molina cracked a smile. Vodka will do that to even the most poker-faced person. "Yes, he does seem out of some Steve McQueen time zone, doesn't he?"

"I thought you liked him."

"I have associated with him. Or, rather, he has associated with me. What do you think?"

"He's not your type."

"Do we know what is my type?"

"I guess not," Temple admitted. "You are an enigma wrapped in a torch singer hiding behind a madonna."

"We ought to tip a glass more often." Molina tipped hers, but Temple noticed her vivid blue eyes were completely focused.

That was the problem with striking eyes. Temple's were a changeable blue-gray, which allowed her to play vague or steel- sharp.

"Dirty Larry." Temple savored the theatri- cality of the nickname. "Did he decide to leave the undercover detail, or was he shuffled out?"

"The records on that are vague."

"Suspicious in itself. Your impression?"

"He showed up suddenly. I could have been flattered. Or I could have decided I got a rash of unknown origin."

"So you never trusted him."

"I never trust anyone."

"That is sad, Carmen."

"Did I say we were on first-name basis, Temple?"

"You gave me a ring, Carmen."

The lieutenant burst out laughing. "I would hate to play poker with you, I'll give you that. Look. My personal and professional life is a mess at the moment, admitted. I bet you'd be busy loving that, except you can't admit how worried you are about your missing ex, even with the upscale brass ring from another man on your third finger, left hand. I can't admit how wrong I probably was about your ex, which makes him the elephant in the room. But we aren't the type to go around blindfolded discussing elephants when we can be doing something productive, are we? Is Dirty Larry dirty or not?"

"He could be. You don't invite hangers-on, and he's sure stubborn about that."

"Exactly," Molina said. "I've watched him

as much as I can with a mystery stalker intruding now and then into my house, and my teenage daughter acting out, and me trying to push an invisible man into a corner, where I'll probably end up getting myself trapped."

"I'd lose him," Temple said. "Personally. Watch your back, but lose him."

Molina nodded and lifted her glass. "Any more where this came from?"

"If you want Crystal Light and no-name vodka, you have hit the mother lode."

Temple bustled off to refill their glasses. She made Molina's heavy on the vodka, hers on the Crystal Light. Did she think she could outdrink the Iron Maiden of the Las Vegas Metropolitan Police Department, or Carmen the bar singer, or whatever role Molina was going to whip out of her blazer today? Not without playing a bit dirty. Dirty. The word of the hour. Maybe.

"So," said Molina, when Temple had returned with the drinks reloaded. "You've disposed of Dirty Larry as a bad idea whose time has not come. What about . . . Detective Alch?"

"Really? We're supposed to discuss him, as what? A detective? Or a favorite uncle?"

"Your opinion, your choice."

"He's kind of like me," Temple said

thoughtfully.

Molina almost spit out her drink in surprise. "How in the world?"

"Fiercer than you'd think."

Molina thought about it for a long while, then nodded grudgingly. "My best man."

"Are we still speaking professionally?"

"Your choice."

"Solid-gold veteran," Temple declared. "And . . . a bonus: he gets girls."

"How do you mean 'girls'?"

"All ages, all stages."

"He has an only daughter, grown," Molina confirmed.

"Ah! And a wife?"

"Ex-wife."

"Somehow I don't get someone leaving him."

"It was the other way around, but it wasn't his fault."

"No. It wouldn't be," Temple said. "Does Alch know you're such a fan?"

"Probably, but he wouldn't think much about it. Does he know *you*'re such a fan?"

"Did I say that?"

"He's your right-hand man. I say that."

Molina nodded and sipped. "And Rafi Nadir."

She didn't phrase it as a question, but Temple realized it was the one "burning" question Molina actually wanted someone else's opinion on.

Wow. Had Rafi supplanted Max as the object of Molina's obsession? Was this progress or regression or just plain human?

Temple went for shock value. "Max didn't think much of him."

"Kinsella knew him?"

As if there were another Max in this town for either of them. Temple noticed Molina was back to last names, a way of dehumanizing people.

"Max ran into Rafi when your ex first came to Vegas," she explained, "and was working temporary security jobs around town."

Molina raised her eyebrows expectantly, but no way was Temple going to turn this into a discussion of Max's various efforts to protect Temple and investigate traces of the bizarre cabal of magicians known as the Synth.

"He found Rafi bitter and biased and just plain bad news." Temple spotted the slightest hint of a wince in Molina's features, which she hid behind another sip of sweet-and-sour vodka pop.

Molina was forced to interrogate further. "Later you, as Zoe Chloe Ozone, were so warned off the guy that when you teamed

335

up with my daughter at the *Teen Idol* reality-TV house, you both got crazy cozy with Rafi Nadir, of all security personnel to turn to with a murderer on the premises."

"Sounds nuts, doesn't it?" Temple said with a sober sip and a smile. "Zoe and Mariah were just crazy mixed-up teen kids, right? Actually, Rafi proved pretty perceptive in that house of pop-culture horror and murder. He looked out for us both."

"And got close to my daughter under false pretenses."

"Did he even know he had a daughter then? I don't think so. They just naturally clicked."

"Oh, my God! You've been encouraging their unlikely relationship just to bug me."

"It's never been about you, Carmen Molina. That's like saying you were chasing Max's shadow all over Vegas for a murder rap just to annoy me. Other people are living their lives naturally, without it being a conspiracy you need to bust."

Temple sat back. "Yes, I've decided that Rafi isn't so bad. You're just mad because you've come to the same conclusion *after* Mariah and I did. And ditto for Max. You're fresh out of personal villains, unless Dirty Larry cooperates and turns out to be a pimp or something."

Temple wasn't sure whether Molina was going to explode, stomp out of there, arrest her, or . . . laugh.

"You *are* fiercer than you look," Molina said, shaking her head. "Good thing you plied me with vodka doubles so I'm in a good mood. No. I don't need any personal villains. Or heroes. I just wanted to make sure *you* weren't getting back at *me* for pursuing your apparently heroic ex-boyfriend by foisting the villainous Rafi on me."

"It does seem you underestimated each other back when you were young and foolish. Rafi does seem to have reformed enough to earn a shot at fatherhood, and Mariah deserves to know who he is. She likes him, you know."

"Yes, I know." Molina put down her glass. "There are right psychological moments, though, and legalities to consider."

"If you managed to work those out by the junior-high father-daughter dance this fall, that would be nice. Matt is dying not to have anyone depend on him to be an official 'father' anymore."

"He's not around right now?" Molina looked up at the ceiling that was the floor to Matt's upstairs unit.

"In Chicago on a working vacation, actu-

337

ally. He has family there."

"Really? Oh. Of course. That pond-slime stepfather he tracked here had to have left other disenchanted souls behind in Chi-Town. Now that Matt's past family issues are resolved, I'm sure he'd make a great real father. Mariah likes *him* too."

"Not that way, mama. And you're prying. . . . We haven't even set a date and place for the wedding."

Molina stood. "So it's anti–Dirty Larry and pro–Rafi Nadir. Pro–Max Kinsella, as always, and pro–Morrie Alch. Interesting. I wonder which of us has been taken in the most? By whom?"

"Ourselves?" Temple offered, standing too. She was determined to reduce the tall police lieutenant's degree of "loom."

Molina didn't answer but pulled a cell phone from her blazer side pocket.

"You're calling in reinforcements?"

"I'm calling a squad car to drop off a driver for my vehicle. I'm not getting behind the wheel after drinking those 'Vodka Surprises' of yours. Nice try. We'll have to do this again some time. Enjoy the old bling. I'll see myself out," Molina said. "Thanks for the drinks."

Temple blinked and took a deep breath after her front door closed on Molina. She had a valuable Tiffany ring to return to a plastic baggie.

She would not try on Max's ring to see if it still fit. It would. She would not try the ring on to see if it threw bolts of reflection around the room like it used to. It would. She would not play with the ring, admire the ring, or touch the ring to see if she still felt regrets for Max Kinsella.

CHAPTER 29
RINGING ISSUES

So my Miss Temple just sits there on our living-room sofa, as if lost in a dream, turning the plastic baggie and Mr. Max's opal ring around and around in her hand.

She does not even move when we hear her front door open and close.

Ooooh, that Miss Lieutenant C. R. Molina has been a *mean* girl. Humans! They claim not to use tooth and claw as we four-feet do, but even a so-called "nice" gesture can come with a fierce bite, a "kick" like the firing of a gun.

I can see that my Miss Temple has no idea where she should put this ring. It would look tacky on her third finger, right hand, although the jewelry biz is busy marketing a "right hand" diamond ring as every woman's necessity, to up sales.

Even I know that two major pieces of bling on the same person's petite ten fingers is tasteless. I know my Miss Temple's scarf drawer is not lucky for ring storage, not after Mr. Matt found Kitty the Cutter's worm Ouroboros ring inside, and no one can figure out how it got there. The evil K the C had stolen the tail-sucking snake back from Mr. Matt after forcing him to wear it as a sign of her murderous power over everyone he knew.

"Wait a minute!" Miss Temple shouts.

I jump slightly at the racket, but at last my roommate has leaped into action. She has stood to yell after the long-gone Molina.

"You must be off duty if you're drinking, even if you can get a driver home. Giving this ring back is not an official act."

Nice point, but the door is shut and Molina is out of hearing range. Only I am here to get the message.

Miss Temple sits again to squirm on her uncomfortable side chair, and so I come out of hiding to loft onto the empty sofa she is leaving vacant for me.

I can read her mind like it was pile of tea leaves.

She eyes the anemic pink liquid and melted ice cubes in her glass, obviously wondering if maybe she had imbibed more hard liquor than she realized. She looks puzzled and a little sad.

At last she looks up and spots me. Now is

the time for some distracting action on my part!

But which part?

I leap onto the sofa arm so I have an artistic pedestal and begin sucking my rear-toe hairs. This is quite the athletic feat. I know I look a little silly and that therefore Miss Temple will find me talented and endearing and forget her woes. As they sing: "Pack up your troubles in your old kit bag."

I am certainly an old kit.

"Oh, Louie," she says, totally won over by my native charm and cute little nibbling acts. "You must have been hiding in the spare bedroom until the fuzz was gone, or until your toe fuzz needed a grooming. Now, do not fall off the sofa and hurt yourself."

As if I couldn't do a double axel on the way down and land with all four sets of shivs stapled to the wood parquet floor!

Of course I do nothing of the kind to damage the décor, but I give my Miss Temple one of my best world-weary, totally superior glances. She had never heard me come in, has no idea that I have seen and heard the entire scene. I can go barefoot around this place too, so she will never hear me sneaking up on her.

She smiles gratefully at my presence.

"Louie," she says, "you are the only male in

my life I have no worries or doubts about whatsoever. Unless you fall off the sofa arm."

Oh, please. The one to worry about is she herself.

After all, I had returned to my center of operations and paused to check in on my Miss Temple, only to find her entertaining the enemy. Cordially. With powdered drink mix and hard liquor.

I suppose my antipathy to Miss Lieutenant C. R. Molina is nothing personal.

She has her job to do, and I have mine. We both nail crooks, and her way is a lot less personal than mine usually, because she has underlings.

Yes, yes, you could argue that because I am a prominent member of the Feline Nation, the entire population of humans become my automatic underlings.

But there is a communication disconnect, so I am forced to exert precious time and energy in leading these self-involved and inarticulate creatures down the most logical garden path. Certainly they chatter a great deal, but much of it is meaningless.

At any rate, Molina, as my roommate and her intimates so abruptly call her, has not been on any personal crime-solving trail, nose to the groundstone, until she recently got too nosy about where Mr. Max Kinsella kept a safe house in Vegas and she broke the law by breaking and entering.

Miss Midnight Louise witnessed the whole episode, so we had plenteous blackmail material to hold over Molina the next time she came around bullying my Miss Temple about the whereabouts of Mr. Max Kinsella. Of course, it would be troublesome to manipulate what we know into public awareness, and now here is the dreaded Molina sharing alcohol content with my Miss Temple.

One never knows when or by whom the sanctity of one's home will be violated. Mr. Max had a way of breaking and entering as an expected unexpected guest. That method had much in common with my comings and goings, plus it gave my Miss Temple the frisson of unpredictability. We suave dudes know how to keep a dame interested.

Big Mama Molina apparently just rang the doorbell and walked right in. So crude and rude!

I eye the abject form of a plastic baggie on the sofa. A lowly commercial object representative of our plastic culture nowadays, which I might sometimes allow to entertain me for a few moments while my shivs staple holes into it until its ziplock closure begs for mercy.

Now it is weighted with a small object that would make it quite bat-worthy, even for a dude of my serious size and dignity. Unfortunately, I recognize a precious object and know better. I edge near to examine this item, once stolen and held for ransom, to refresh my sometimes delinquent memory.

It is a subtle, fiery gemstone set into a white-gold circumference small enough for my Miss Temple's size-five feet and fingers. She wears the same size in shoes and rings, which is handy for dudes who wish to shower her in Jimmy Choos and Fred Leightons. (She has, however only one each of these two gentlemen's high-end foot and finger fripperies, and many of her shoes nowadays are from resale shops.)

Again seeing my Miss Temple's long-withheld keepsake of Mr. Max and what harassment she must put up with in his absence only makes me more determined to settle the hash of these Neon Nightmare Synth people and solve the tri-venue tunnel murder all to my mistress's greater glory and ability to further lord it over the official fuzz, like Miss Lieutenant C. R. Molina.

Miss Temple has always been right. The Molina eyebrows are way too furry for a lady.

CHAPTER 30
BREAKFAST OF CHAMPIONS

"I've had a breakthrough," Max told Garry Randolph at breakfast in the hotel the next morning.

"What?" Gandolph, startled, sprayed the word into his cup of morning hot chocolate.

Watching him mop up the ring around the cup, Max felt the painful nostalgia of finally surprising the man who, he guessed, had always surprised *him,* at least during his vulnerable younger years after O'Toole's Pub.

"Freud was right," Max opined. "Dreams are the key. At least mine were. I've recovered some pretty vivid memories from before my engineered fall at the Neon Nightmare. I dreamed a whole cast of characters. Old-school magicians or charlatans . . . Cosimo Sparks?"

" 'Old-school' is right. Cosimo was strictly minor, even in his heyday. Retired to Vegas from better days in the Midwest. Did social-

346

club benefits and auctions. Thought when they said how the mighty have fallen they meant him. A stumble maybe, but his career successes were mostly in his own ego."

"Carmen?"

"Ah. Your type, right? Femme fatale. Poisonous young thing, once. When I was still working, which is several years ago, as you know, she tried to seduce me into replacing Gloria Fuentes as my assistant. Indeed! Give up a trained veteran who still looked PDG."

"PDG?"

"Pretty damned good. At my age, you appreciate women who manage that, and some do into their nineties now. It's in the head," he said, tapping his right temple. Max winced, sensitized to the word *temple* now. "Anyway, I don't dump a loyal partner for a few crow's-feet when I'm all over sags and bags."

"That's so encouraging," Max said.

"You just twinkled, wicked boy! Making fun of your old partner in a double-edged way. Go to it! That's the spirit. 'Curse, if you must, this old gray head. . . .' "

"Enough, 'Barbara Frietchie.' I had that poem in grade school too. From what you tell me, we both honored our 'country's flag,' as in that old poem, more than the average."

"Charmin' Carmen." Gandolph mused. "That moniker came later when she conned the guy who made a mint becoming the Cloaked Conjuror into taking her on. Ramona Zamora was her real name. Oh, she was tasty, though. Nineteen and hungry. But what was really in it for me to dump Gloria for a young thing but a few blow jobs and a kiss-off?"

"Garry! Have I ever heard you talk that way before?"

He had the grace to look apologetic. "No." He rubbed a hand over his weary features, giving them a passing face-lift. "I used to respect women more, and the world."

"Didn't Gloria die?"

"Hardly. She *was killed* last year. Only fifty-eight. Police couldn't find her murderer right away and probably retired the case. Woman accosted and killed in a parking lot. It's the major unsolved cliché crime of our time."

"Helluva time," Max muttered.

"Don't let me hang up your dream memories. I can't believe your subconscious has dredged up those familiar names from *my* days of yore. I helped you set up the Phantom Mage persona and act at the Neon Nightmare. We knew the Synth members met there, or even owned the place, but you never reported names back to me. Just questions about the Synth, which I'd never heard of before. Who else has your memory conjured?"

"Czarina Catherina, the usual fake medium in a fake turban."

"Oh, I'd exposed her years ago in Cleveland."

"More details about your unsuspected sex life, Gandolph? Really, I'm still too young for such confessions."

"I exposed her as a fake, bilking people out of money for 'messages' from dead loved ones."

"You don't think one can get messages from dead loved ones?"

Gandolph glanced at him with worried eyes. "Occasionally, there are cases and mediums that seem . . . actual. What do you think you saw in your dreams last night, Max?"

"I think one of the four Synth members present is still a mystery to me, because I saw myself in a mirror, and I was Sean."

"You recognized him, and them. A giant step forward, Max."

"Really? I saw Sean as the full-grown man he'd never lived to be."

"You think he's 'haunting' you?"

"I think he's always haunted me, but we don't know for sure, do we?"

"I do know you were that rarity in Irish-American family life — an only child."

"So Sean and I must have been more like brothers than cousins. The same age. What do you know of our families?"

"The cold facts. Nothing personal. Sean was part of the usual large brood. He was a gregarious, charming boy, from what I gathered, but immature. Unlike you."

Max laughed. " 'Gregarious.' Why do I know that's not me?"

"You were always the 'run silent, run deep' sort, Max. Charming too, when you found it useful. And cursed with maturity."

"Even about girls, women? Even about revenge?"

"Why do you think *you* ended up with the enchanting Kathleen O'Connor, who was an 'older woman.' Technically?"

"I don't know. I saw her dead in my dreams, just a swatch of her face on the dark ground, no features. She'd have been in her early twenties when we met, and she already had been through hell."

"Twenty-three to your seventeen. A huge gulf at those ages."

"Gandolph!"

"Yes, Max?"

"Her mother was condemned to a Magdalen house, and she in her turn. She was an unwed mother by her late teens. What happened to her infant?"

"Adopted out? Could have died during childbirth. Teenage mothers —"

"God! Don't tell me we need to look for another lost soul!"

"I don't know, Max. It doesn't concern us now. If getting pieces of your memory back means you're going to obsess about Kathleen O'Connor again, all right. I can live with that, as I did before. But we don't have time to hunt younger generations of old losses. The burying of the terrorism hatchet so long impaled in this island seems to have released some collateral mischief. That's why our old enemies are talking to us. They want what we know."

"What I know is cobwebs and night frights."

"Perhaps more than that, behind the veil?"

"I saw a ring," Max remembered. "An unlucky opal ring. The seductress in the dream, your real-life Carmen, produced it for me, but I declared it synthetic. Like dreams, like my not-quite-teen angel, Kitty the Cutter, like God knows what else is synthetic."

" 'Synthetic,' Max? An odd word for a

dream."

"What? Dreams don't come in three syllable words? Mine do."

"Listen, Max. We're playing a cat-and-mouse game with these 'retired' Irish operatives. They want to know something from us or they'd never cooperate. We desperately need to know what, and what not, to tell them during these upcoming negotiations."

"I get it."

"No, you don't. Even your dreams are trying to tell you. We've been tracing the vague trail of a conspiracy, or cabal of individuals, many of them magicians or former magicians, and unsolved murders in Las Vegas."

"And we're now in Northern Ireland, because . . . ?"

"Because it may have started but not ended here. You dreamed up the word *synthetic*, clearly referring to what these magicians call themselves — the Synth."

"Sounds like they suffer from a lisp."

"This is not funny, Max!" Gandolph's fist hit the hardwood arm of his chair. "This is not a holiday jaunt." He rubbed his banged fist with the other hand, brows forming an anxious knot above the bridge of his nose. "It's obvious your subconscious is trying to break out of your amnesia. Going back to the scenes of your youth might leapfrog a lot of time and pain. So might this."

Gandolph spun his laptop so Max could see the drawing of a city map split by mostly red and green blocks of color covering innumerable neighborhood names.

"The Orange and the Green sides," Max guessed. "Orange, east; Green, west. When's the Broadway musical coming?"

"This 'tune' is too bitter to play in America. To this day," Gandolph said, "this is a land packed with atrocities vividly remembered on both sides of Belfast and both sides — south and north — of the island itself."

"And you hope my and the nation's toxic history might stir my memory in a way happier places wouldn't?"

"Something is stirring." Gandolph shut the laptop, locking away the hundreds of lethal neighboring borders invisibly marked on half a million Belfast minds.

Max shook his head. "Sean and I came wandering north into Protestant Ulster during the thick of the 'Troubles,' didn't we? American-Catholic lambs to the slaughter house. That was stupid."

"Yes, it was. That's the first thing you admitted, after the pub bombing."

"You're not going to fill in the blanks for me, are you?" Max asked.

"No, Max," Gandolph assured him. "Your memory will either kick-start itself here in this traumatic place, or it won't. Best to know as soon as possible which is the case. The city has changed, and you need to."

"How has it changed, other than being a tourist and travel hot spot?"

"Oh, can't you sense the raw energy of a bad place turning better? The locals boast that tourists want to come here. Peace and prosperity are their Horsemen of the Post-Apocalypse. What's more, they've made a point of saying that a visit to Belfast will reveal far more about the British and Irish psyche than visiting Dublin or London will. We're staying in the gentrified city centre, in a decent hotel chain.

"Even better for our purposes, the peace has made access to information on past skirmishes and fighters on both sides of the conflict easier. The government offices we need to visit are nearby, and so are the . . . unofficial sources I've contacted. My recent quest to investigate Kathleen O'Connor and her involvement in the 'Troubles' back then and her whereabouts now has attracted serious interest."

"Dangerous interest?"

"We won't know until we go through the motions, right?"

Max finished his coffee, stood, and stretched without comment. "A middling hotel, huh? These beds are going to be murder on my legs and mobility."

"If that's the only variety of murder we encounter here, I'll be happy."

The morning was late enough that Gandolph rushed them off to an appointment he'd managed before leaving Zurich. Belfast's city centre was obviously a work in progress, Max noted. Grand piles of Victorian architecture jostled glitzy new development. A border of frayed older structures betrayed the ongoing "urban renewal" process of a downtown business district anywhere in the U.S.

They were headed to a Victorian pile. No elevators to mar the vintage grandeur. Max had to suffer managing a long, stone, internal staircase worn swaybacked in the middle, and a long, echoing hall before arriving at an office higher than it was wide or broad. For all the exterior stateliness, this grandly high-ceilinged room broadcast an air of desertion, except for the two London Fog–coated middle-aged men awaiting them across a hard-used wooden table.

A dark, noisy, smoky pub would have been a far better setting for this meeting of obvious law-enforcement types, whether they were still undercover operatives or not. The guidebooks said the pubs weren't uneasy ground in Ulster now. No one wanted to remind the tourists that now packed them of frequent pub bombings in the pre-peace days.

Inside the huge building, the temperature seemed lower than the brisk, fifty-degree air outside. Max's legs and hips ached as if they'd been encased in ice water for hours. Maybe he'd grown too used to Las Vegas heat. He'd bet that little redhead would have warmed him up; "cute" didn't rule out hot.

The two waiting men unconsciously rubbed their bare hands together for warmth, then exacted army-green file folders from their cheap, scuffed briefcases. Gandolph had brought a well-used black case of his own.

Max decided to cast the men opposite as familiar actors to tell them apart: an innocently nondescript Kevin Spacey and a young Brian Aherne, burly and buzz-cut.

"This is the O'Toole's Pub survivor, Mr. Randolph?" the Kevin clone asked, nodding at Max without greeting him, as if he were still a minor who didn't require being consulted. Insulted, yes.

"Not a survivor," Max corrected. "I was nowhere near when the bomb exploded. I'm a surviving relative of a victim."

"A fine point," Brian noted. "Are you always so scrupulously accurate, Mr. Kinsella?"

There was no point denying who he was here. For all he knew, he "owned" one of those inch-thick file folders of hidden history.

"You'd have to ask Mr. Randolph," Max said. "My condition —"

"— is damn unfortunate," Brian erupted. "Not much exchange of anything here. We hold all the 'cards' " — he gestured to their files — "and you lot want all the old information."

Gandolph had somehow pulled out his own file folder. Everyone noticed it at the same time, as if it had blossomed on the creased and nicked oak. The retired magician's sleight of hand had sufficed to startle the two world-weary agents. That was a fine edge of advantage.

"We discovered," Gandolph said, "where Kathleen O'Connor came from, which may explain a lot about her."

"Kitty," Max said, before he knew it was coming out. "Kitty the Cutter, we called her in Vegas."

The Northern Irishmen couldn't hide their eyebrow-raising surprise at that declaration.

"That's just what we don't have," Kevin said. "Where she came from and where she went. The mayhem she wreaked in between, yes. We're bloody experts on that."

"She's dead," Max said harshly.

"You have proof?"

Max licked his lips and glanced inquisitively at Gandolph. "I don't even know why I said what she was called just now."

"Who was the 'we' who called her Kitty the Cutter?"

"I don't remember." Max refused to involve another innocent bystander like the Vegas redhead.

"What was the reason?"

"Ditto," Max said. "I'm like that nowadays. Sorry, gentlemen. I know it's a bore. It bores the hell out of me too."

Another silence. This one lasted.

"Lad," Brian, the older man, said softly, "everyone who ever saw Kathleen never forgot her. Everyone mentioned what a beauty she was. Elizabeth Taylor with ultramarine eyes instead of violet. I don't think even amnesia is an excuse for forgetting that."

"Beautiful?" Max was apparently the one

358

man who forgot all but an anonymous wedge of the temptress's face, but he guessed she'd used colored contact lenses to produce those unearthly deep blue-green eyes no one forgot. "She killed my cousin and two fistfuls of innocents along with him."

Eyebrows lifted again.

"How much did you fill him in?" Kevin asked Gandolph.

"Not that much. You need to understand he was almost killed in Las Vegas less than two months ago and escaped another attempt on his life in the Alps just this last week. He got himself to Zurich with two barely healed broken legs and what wits he has, memory or no memory."

"I remember the common things of our lives and times," Max said. "Just not my own damn history before I awoke from a coma a couple weeks ago."

"So you think O'Connor's dead?" Brian prodded. "We'd have to see for ourselves to believe that. She's had more lives than a witch's cat. She seems to thrive on trouble, other people's, and exploiting it."

Max buried his face in one eye-shading hand. They'd take it for stress. He was really trying to block out this torn photograph that had appeared in his dreaming mind's eye: a pale white cheek on the dark ground, the just-recalled eerie green wink of a nearby cat's reflective eye, a whole lot of disbelief on his part, and . . . guilt? Regret? Savage satisfaction? The exact emotions were as fugitive as his memory.

"We now know why this woman was so lethal," Gandolph said. "I made these notes from our visit to a former Magdalen asylum on our journey from Dublin."

He handed over a printed copy. Max thought he must have used the hotel's business travelers' setup. Dangerous, even printed direct from his laptop.

"Magdalen asylum? Sweet Jesus!" swore the younger man, Kevin. "She was kept in one of those places? No wonder."

"She'd be young for that," Brian mentioned, troubled, "even given her thirty-nine years or so."

Max sat dazed for a moment, struck by the Irish lilt on the words *thahr-ty nigh-en.* It was hard not to imitate the tongue-misted accent that was like a lullaby for his troubled mind, maybe because he and Sean grew up in Catholic schools and churches where some of the older nuns and priests still kept a bit o' the brogue.

"Forty?" he asked. "Kathleen would be *forty* now?"

"About that," Kevin agreed.

"And she's still wanted?"

"If she was involved in that pub bombing fiasco, yes." Kevin consulted some pages. "Three loyal IRA men were named, and run down, thanks to an American kid named Michael Kinsella. 'Cousin of one of the victims.' You say you can't remember being that young and fierce?"

Max shook his head violently to expel the image of a dead woman's pale cheek. They took it for a simple no.

"You can't remember," Brian said, "but we've got many more files on her suspected activities. If anything here helps you recall anything we could use . . . ." They passed him a couple of files while pulling Gandolph's paper pile to their side of the table. It felt like the exchange of human hostages in paper-doll form.

Max flashed Gandolph a glance. They didn't know about his Mystifying Max magician persona, then, or of his undercover counterterrorism work. If they still wanted information on Kathleen's later activities, it might explain why someone still wanted to kill him.

Was it only about revenge for stalking and finding those IRA pub bombers all those years ago? Vengeance didn't have a half-life, like nuclear waste did.

Max nodded agreement and pushed back his chair, liberating his legs from under the cramped table.

While Gandolph gave thanks, set up another appointment, and made farewell noises, Max tried to avoid hobbling to the door with the old-fashioned transom window above it. His body was dreading the long walk and then the worn, perilous stairs to descend, but his hopes were clutching at the files he'd turned to jam into Gandolph's case. He'd need both hands free for the stairs, but at last his mind was liberated from day-to-day survival issues and could exercise its memory.

There had to be something more to the attempts on his life than ancient history, Ireland's or his. Something as contemporary as last month or week.

Chapter 31
The Vegas Cat Pack!

A seasoned sleuth senses when too much is going wrong and it is time to call in reinforcements.

Much as I am concerned about Midnight Louise's puzzling disappearance from the Neon Nightmare's secret maze of club rooms, I know I need to put executive decisions in motion before looking into her whereabouts.

I leave Miss Temple's quarters and ratchet my way down the claw-marked slide of the Circle Ritz palm tree trunk to hit the hot parking-lot asphalt at a jog. I handled a murder case once, in the desert, for a coyote clan, and learned something from the lesser species: the endurance possibilities of the so-called dogtrot.

After my recent stint with the dance competition at the Oasis Hotel, I have also mastered the fox-trot. So I am now well seasoned with a new feral canine flavor — *carrrumba!* — and am perhaps the fastest so-called domestic cat on four feet in Las Vegas.

A secondary advantage to this pace is that my natural black sole leather is not getting singed as badly as it would on naked paving materials in this climate. Ordinarily, I can travel from scant oasis of shade to oasis of shade, be it of greenery or Detroit origin, but I do not have the time now to take a zigzag route.

Who knows what those Synth freaks would do in the Satanist way if they caught an eavesdropping quadruped of midnight hue?

Speaking of such a dastardly situation, I am now entering the Men in Beige zone and need to tread extra carefully. One does not go rushing into police custody, even if they seem friendly. Often they have extradition agreements with the local Animal House of Blues, aka the city pound.

This particular police substation near the Circle Ritz seems to have been civilized pretty well. Officers Shrimp Combo and Miss BO, short for Bicycle Officer, are fast-food aficionados. Not the ubiquitous doughnut, mind you, but a heap of protein in a slick waxed wrapper on a bed of mushy white bread that can be torn off and distributed to our feathered friends, who appreciate not being the Catch of the Day at these McDonald's moments.

(Normally, I do not resort to brand names other than the occasional Las Vegas landmark, but in this case the fast-food place is a mere two blocks away. Also, I am well aware that chichi modern narratives are now fashionably littered with the best in clothing and cuisine. So far, my works have only contributed my roommate's shoemeisters to that trend, except for a few painfully fashionable details from Mr. Max's recent grueling European fling, which is entirely in my collaborator's materialistic hands. You will note those episodes are decidedly and solely inhabited by bipeds and are the poorer for it.)

"Mr. Midnight, sir!" My advent through the cloaking oleander bushes is joyfully hailed.

I brush off my shoulders from young Gimpy's greeting. He can certainly hurl himself over a lot of ground on those three legs. I straighten him up by the scruff of the neck. He wears a sporty striped suit that serves to downplay his handicap. It is bum luck to be hit by a car when you are a homeless kit and no one is around to get you to the hospital, so you lose your misshapen foreleg in a charity ward months later.

However, misfortune leads to improvisation, and little Gimpy could eke out enough free food to swamp the whole clowder, like Oliver Twist beseeching "More" from the local church choir instead of a villain of the piece.

As it happens, I have set up the entire Ma

Barker gang pretty sweet here at the police substation, which I am peacefully explaining to Gimpy when a sharp-nailed mitt curls into my thick shoulder pad.

"The youngster does not need to hear your fairy tales," Ma Barker spits. "I am the one who copped to this location, and now you have burdened me with my ex."

"It is only a temporary thing," I say quickly. "He has had a retirement gig as a restaurant mascot, but these trying economic and eco-logical times has erased his last employment situation."

"Great Bast, son! You sound like one of those boring talking human heads on the nightly news. Forget the philosophy. When do I lose the loser? I already gave him the first heave-ho ages ago."

It is trying to hear one's sire discussed in such scathing terms. I fluff up my ruff and get to the point.

"The old guys who ran Three O'Clock Louie's at Temple Bar on Lake Mead have snagged a hot new venue."

"Is a 'hot new venue' something edible?"

"It will be: Three O'Clock Louie's Speakeasy subterranean bar and restaurant at Gangsters, the underworld departure point for Vegas's coolest high-speed underground mobster run."

"I am confused here. Is this a seafood

restaurant? With lobsters?"

"Naw, Ma. Not lobsters, *mobsters* that run with gangsters. Kinda like you," I add slyly. "Gangsters Hotel and Casino is amping up its theme with an expanded mob museum and cosmetic redo."

"Oh. Are any female mobsters represented in the Gangsters renovation?"

"Ah . . . I am sure your namesake, Ma Barker, will be represented, and an immortal gun moll or two."

She seems "mollified" by that and adds, "I must confess that the human Ma Barker did precede me on the planet by a few decades. So. Three O'Clock is now again leading the life of Riley at a new human feeding station, and outta my hair. I know he took off for somewhere."

"I promise, Ma. Meanwhile, my humans are facing a three-pronged Death Challenge. I need twenty-four-hour, around-the-clock operatives to cover the Crystal Phoenix, Gangsters, and the Neon Nightmare, along with some layabouts in the tunnel that is the immediate scene of the crime. So far."

"You have Midnight Louise already at the Phoenix."

"Bast be good," I mutter, disturbed by having found no trace of Louise here at clowder headquarters. I would not expect her to be slumming, but where can she have gone from the Neon Nightmare, and where might she now be? "I could use a couple more there. It is a big place."

Ma cocks her whiskers at a pair of ninja-black shorthairs enjoying a Big Mac for two.

"These are your half brothers. Having Louise look-alikes on the grounds will be good cover."

"Smart thinking, Ma."

"I will 'smart' your ears if you condescend to me again, boy. I happen to have a lot of 'midnights' in my gang, so I can send a couple more to cover the Neon Nightmare. It is a rough place, I hear, and I do not let my people tackle gin joints like that without my personal supervision. Where will the duffer go? You need anyone out at Lake Mead?"

"Not now."

Her yellow eyes bore into my green ones. At least I got my Black Irish coloring of black hair and green eyes from Dad.

"Might as well assign the Old Man and the Sea to Gangsters, where he belongs now."

"The sea?" I ask.

"Me. Ma Barker. The mother of all mothers. Mother Ocean. Mother Hell-on-Claws. I gotta itch to see this Gangsters operation. See if it gets the Ma Barker seal of approval." She slashes a foreclaw in the sand. "See what kind of cushy gigolo job your so-called father has got himself now."

Three O'Clock and Ma Barker back on the same turf together again, after all these years. It kinda makes even a street-tough dude choke up . . . with horror at the prospect of the two of them mingling with the ex-prospectors of the Glory Hole Gang.

I fear my esteemed parents will require a referee, not a job assignment.

CHAPTER 32
BOTTOMING OUT

"Where can we meet," the man's deep voice on the phone asked Temple, "where nobody we know will be there?"

" 'We'?" Temple asked, still blinking from the recent departure of Rafi Nadir's long-ago ex-girlfriend.

"Well, not your alley cat and me."

Temple glanced to see if Midnight Louie had sensed himself being dismissed. Yup. He had no doubt left the premises by the open-bathroom-window route she had reinstated. As the sole resident second-story man now, he was a frequent patron of the exterior high road provided by an old, leaning palm tree trunk.

Her mind snapped back to her caller. "You and me lunching together, alone?"

"Yeah. I thought you'd decided I don't bite."

"But . . . why? Why the secrecy?"

"I'm not Mr. Popularity in some quarters.

And the why is . . . personal. Do I have to send an engraved invitation?"

"No. I'm just . . . surprised. Ah, are you off work? How about a picnic in Sunset Park today?"

"Picnic? Sunset Park? It's long after lunchtime."

"I know, you're not the picnic type. That's why it's an ideal locale. We'll call it a picnic supper. I can't imagine anybody we know loitering there after working hours on a weekday. And nobody can eavesdrop on one of those well-spaced picnic tables. How about six P.M. near the parking lot? We can hike to a likely spot from there."

"Not if you're wearing the usual spikes."

"You shouldn't be surprised at what I can do in high heels by now."

His laugh sounded relieved. "Naw, I wouldn't. *Ciao.*"

Good golly, Miss Molina, thought Temple as she hung up the phone. *Good thing Matt's out of town.* Rafi Nadir was still a slightly sinister presence on the Vegas scene. Then she imagined how Molina would react to Temple having a private *picnic* with her long-ago live-in and giggled all the way to the kitchen to look up man-size-sandwich possibilities.

She arrived at the parking lot ten minutes

early, raised the Miata's top, and locked the car, then sat on the hood with her insulated lunch and tote bags, swinging her feet, realizing she should have asked the make and color of Rafi's car.

What would he drive? Molina had that awful aging Volvo. About as sexy as support hose. Rafi . . . let's see. He'd been on the skids, working temp security details, until he got that security job at the Oasis.

He'd quickly become assistant security chief and had seemed so solid-citizen lately that even Molina had thawed toward him. She'd thawed toward Temple too. Toward everybody but her teen daughter, Mariah. There she was Mama Bear in every sense of the word.

Poor Mariah, having a homicide cop for a mom! Mothers of teenagers had reason to be paranoid to begin with, and the Molina household had been violated by a stalker. At least Mama no longer thought that had been Max. As if he would have to force himself on women and Temple would be going with a guy who did! Molina was right. She was a horrid judge of men.

"Sensible shoes," a deep voice said behind her, breaking into her mental tirade.

Temple looked over her shoulder to see

Rafi standing at the Miata's other front fender.

"Thanks," she said, eyeing her broad-based but insanely strappy red wedge sandals. "For me, they are."

She was about to hop down when Rafi came around and took her hand, quite the gentleman. He was about six feet, swarthy, around forty, wearing the usual black jeans and boots, not cowboy, and a black T. Just a regular guy. He was also carrying a cooler and incarcerated Temple's insulated bag of sandwiches in it as soon as she was on level ground.

"How'd you get here?" she asked.

"Parked across the road and walked in."

Meanwhile they were pacing along the hard-packed red clay hiking path toward the concrete picnic tables. Quacking ducks swam near the small artificial lake at the park's center, when not beak-diving for snacks or waddling after bread-carrying tourists on the grass.

Temple was used to taking long steps to keep pace with Max's six-foot-four stride. Nor was Matt an ambler. She may have worn high heels for business since college, but she'd never been a tiny-step totterer.

In three minutes she and Rafi were settled at a picnic bench under the concrete sun

373

shelter. He'd brought bags of oven-roasted vegetable chips and Amstel Light beer and spring water to go with Temple's roast-beef sandwiches on rye. Tasty spread. Temple accepted a beer, and Rafi took the water.

"Molina would have a bird if she could see us now," Temple remarked after the first few bites of sandwich, "but not a duck."

"No, she'd have an ostrich," Rafi agreed, upping the ante. "Whole."

"Never a flamingo," Temple added, recalling the Las Vegas visit of concept artist Domingo with his thousands of pink plastic yard-birds.

Enough preliminaries, she thought.

"What's this secret meeting about?" she asked Rafi. "I thought you and Molina had at least blunted the hatchet. You were a great go-to guy at the Oasis celebrity dance contest. Matt and I sure appreciated that; even ol' C. R. seemed to."

"Yeah." Rafi rotated the plastic water bottle between his palms.

Temple was surprised. He seemed a tad nervous. Maybe he wasn't used to talking about his feelings. *Duh!* An Arab-American grad of the L.A. police force from back in the days when ethnic borders were even edgier and bloodier on the streets than today. Guess not.

She prided herself on being able to cross most social barriers since her Minneapolis TV-reporter days. That was a huge asset in her freelance PR business. She decided to let Rafi take his time, and soon he'd be spilling like the *Exxon Valdez.*

"So," he said suddenly, "how do I get the new, Dairy Queen–soft Molina to let me into my daughter's life?"

"Ask?" Temple suggested.

He shook his head. "Too easy for her to give one of her knee-jerk responses. You know how wired she's been lately. Apparently your ex did that to her?"

Temple was startled by another mention of Max, no doubt.

"Your ex-boyfriend," Rafi said more specifically, "that magician guy. He may be gone, but, believe me, he's not forgotten as far as Carmen Molina is concerned."

"Max wasn't . . . forgettable. I thought you ran into him on some of those freelance security jobs."

Rafi shrugged. "Maybe. I ran into a lot of guys on those details. I'd have liked to shake his hand. He did a great number on Carmen and distracting her from her job, which she hates more than anything. Well, you oughta know. You two are always tenser than alley cats on the subject."

"We were not fighting *over* Max. You've got that wrong, just as Molina got Max wrong. She was being a pig-headed cop, sure someone was guilty before she had any more evidence than her instincts."

"Which are pretty sharp," Rafi said.

"You actually admire her? After the way she's treated you?"

"I give her credit, just as I give you credit."

"Well, you don't give me credit for keeping my men. You've implied both Max and Matt might have a love-hate thing going with Lieutenant C. R., she of the untamed eyebrows."

"Untamed? Eyebrows?" Rafi laughed. "Women fight dirty, for sure. At least she doesn't have the untamed love life you've had."

"Me? Untamed? I am so boring and below the radar."

"Yeah, sure, Zoe Chloe." Rafi laughed again. "Look, that's why I'm courting your good opinion."

The word *courting* made Temple seriously leery. "Yeah?"

"You know Molina way better than I do."

"I do?"

"Right. As a woman. I want to take Mariah to that father-daughter dance when she starts junior high in the fall. How can I ace out your handsome, morally superior fiancé for the job?"

"You've got a lot of nerve."

"My line to you, bounced back at me. I'm serious, Miss Zoe Chloe Ozone Temple. If I let another man be there for Mariah because her thirteen-year-old brain thinks he's 'cool,' I've got no chance at ever getting into her life. Unless you think I have no right to be a father to anyone because Molina had such a huge lack of faith in me fifteen years ago in L.A."

"Why did that happen?"

"We were rivals on the force. Minorities and women were put into that position then."

"It was a work problem?"

"Basically. Then she . . . got pregnant."

"Not by herself. But a surprise."

"A shock to the solar system, only she didn't tell me, just held it in and ran. Reminds me of your MIA boyfriend."

Temple wanted to get her back up, then realized Rafi was right. "Max only left Vegas that first time because some international bad guys were after him. He thought staying with me put me in the line of fire, and he was right. A couple of them trapped me in a parking ramp, wanting to intimidate Max's whereabouts out of me."

"From your body language just now, the creeps' pressure got physical."

"That shows? I'd almost forgotten about that nasty incident."

"No, you haven't. Your lips and eyelids tightened. Not much. Enough for a trained observer to notice. I'd say you're lucky they only came calling once. So Kinsella was right to rabbit for the faraway hills. Where'd he go?"

"Canada."

Rafi whistled. "Not easy to pull off on the run. Borders and visas and such."

"Max knew how to vanish. There's got to be a good reason for a pregnant Molina to run."

"Like what?"

"You wanted her to have an abortion."

"Since I didn't know she was pregnant until I saw Mariah some dozen years later, when did I have a chance to dictate what she should do?"

"She knew you would."

"She was wrong. And so are you. She ran because she thought I *wanted* her to have a baby, tricked her into it."

"That's just . . . crazy. From all I've heard, most guys are edgy about fatherhood at first. Especially unmarried, living-together guys."

"Yeah. That's the usual drill. It's a stupid story we both should disown. Her birth control failed. She thought I sabotaged it to make her into a stay-at-home mommy so she couldn't ace me out for promotions at work. She was a twofer. Ethnic and a woman. Management liked to handle 'diversity' by two at one blow. As for the pregnancy, I wasn't ready to go anywhere bold on the relationship front. If I couldn't hack a baby, we could have split. Simple."

"She just took off without notice?" Temple said.

"Yeah. I admit it put me on an auto–self-destruct. She was good. There was no trace. She pulled a total vanishing act. She'd have made a great spy. You don't know how utterly ineffective I felt. Me, a cop."

"She did split, and it isn't simple. What's important is that you want a relationship with your half-grown daughter now."

"Who knew I'd have father tendencies?" Rafi's wry grin grew crooked. "She sure didn't."

"I can see," Temple admitted carefully, "why her disappearing with no word would put you in a years-long tailspin."

"That 'maybe dead, maybe not' question is a bitch, isn't it?" he responded. "Even if you've got someone waiting in the wings this time."

"You don't," Temple said, stung.

"That's just a fact. I'm not blaming you."

"Why didn't you move on and find someone?"

"Let her disappearing throw me into a down cycle? I was a cop. I should have been able to find my girlfriend. It was a double whammy to my self-esteem."

"What changed you?"

"Maybe Zoe Chloe Ozone."

"What? She's an annoying twerp."

"I discovered a couple things doing security at that *Teen Idol* reality-TV house. I liked solving puzzles and I liked watching over annoying twerps who were smart and feisty. I may be wrong, but Mariah really grew up at that thing, didn't she?"

Temple munched chips and sipped beer. "Yes, she did. And so did you."

"Then Mama showed up for the big show with her down-and-dirty undercover cop."

Oooh. Now Temple was doing the observing. Rafi Nadir did not like Dirty Larry Podesta at all. And it was over Molina.

Temple was sure she should be blushing here. She didn't want to think of Molina and Rafi Nadir in bed. She didn't want to think of Molina in bed with a man at all, period, especially that edgy Dirty Larry. You don't get a nickname like that for nothing. Molina should know better. She was the Iron Maiden of the LVMPD, right?

Rafi glanced at Temple. "I've got to follow up on the rapport Mariah and I built at the murder house and now at the dancing competition. That's why I'm asking you to figure a way around Molina. You actually *do* know what that feels like, to be run out on."

"How am I going to influence Molina? She wouldn't believe me about Max . . . not until recently. Why has she turned around on that?"

"Being so quick to judge has cost her. Again. Nah, she doesn't regret leaving me. 'Loser,' she probably figured. All she ever regrets is being wrong. Maybe about Max Kinsella. Maybe even about me. And Mariah. Which is a big step for her. She might even believe I'm human enough to really care about my daughter."

"Of course you are," Temple said. "It shows. On your daughter and on you."

"Yeah? You don't think I'm the pond scum from L.A.?"

"Maybe at first, but not anymore. You get Mariah better than Molina does right now. I think it's this awkward mother-daughter stage. And something is rubbing Molina raw lately."

381

Temple didn't add that maybe the something could be some*one:* Max still, or even Matt. It wasn't human for Molina to be around, or at least know, two such, well, eligible men and feel nothing. But then, Molina hadn't been letting herself feel human for a lot a years, according to Rafi.

"Why," she asked, "don't you just ask Molina for visitation time? You've got a steady job now."

"She'd bite my head off if I asked her the time right now. Carmen is off balance somehow. I don't know if it's a guy or her job or hormones."

"Hormones? She's not *that* old!" Temple said, before she could stop herself from defending her bête noire.

"You've never had a kid. It can do things to your system."

Temple doubted motherhood was that altering, but finding out he was a father certainly seemed to have straightened up Rafi.

"How'd you get that assistant-security-chief position at the Oasis, anyway? That was an impressive step up from temp jobs."

Rafi shrugged the question off, like dislodging an itch between his shoulder blades. "Still knew some guys who could give me a decent recommendation. Guess it was more a question of why than how."

Temple waited. People talked more that way.

"What pushed me to move on, and up, as it turned out, was that last temp job. Guy, uh, got killed on my watch."

"Yeah? Some nut with a gun? You had to shoot him?"

"Nah. This guy shot himself, in a way. It was the guy in the sky at the Neon Nightmare. Bungee-cord act over the dance floor. He shot down from the peak of the pyramid, and instead of bouncing back up, slammed into the wall right in front of me."

Temple's pulse roughened. "I didn't know you worked there. It's a crazy maze of loud music and light, isn't it?"

"Oh, yeah, those damn strobe lights and neon flashes made it insane to see," Rafi said. "And the bosses were freaky and almost invisible. You'd glimpse them coming and going, seeming to slink into those funky black Plexi walls. I did my job interview in a room I never found my way back to again, with a guy in white tie and a woman in a turban."

"Weird. How could you be an adequate security guard in that environment?"

"I couldn't, when it came down to something really serious," Rafi said, his features settling into a bitter mask of self-disgust. "After that bungee cord failed and the magician guy fell, I couldn't find a pulse, couldn't even see what was injured. It was so chaotic. I tried CPR, called an ambulance. The EMTs were right there and whisked him away. They probably kept trying to resuscitate him, but, uh, it was a lost cause, I bet."

"Didn't you check to find out?"

"Where? Hospitals don't provide information like that. Newspapers didn't run a word on the incident. Anyway, he wasn't about to come back anytime soon, or ever, even if he survived that body blow.

"That was a life lesson for me. I saw we were all hanging by a thread, that I needed to hustle and get hold of a better one if I wanted a chance to get to know my kid more before *my* bungee cord ran out of rebound too."

Temple nodded, but her composure was shaken.

Was Max's death Rafi's life lesson?

CHAPTER 33
SYNTHESIZED

Temple drove back from Sunset Park undistracted by what she could see of the coinciding sunset in the surrounding mountains. Nature couldn't soothe a mind and emotions whirling tornado style.

Max must have been seriously investigating the Synth at the Neon Nightmare and had never whispered a word about it to her. After he'd returned from vanishing on her a couple of years ago, he'd promised to keep her in the loop about any threats on his life.

He'd always protected her more than she liked. No more protecting her from his counterterrorism past, he'd promised. They'd figured out what the Synth was — even that there was a Synth — together. Together, they'd mourned the death of University of Las Vegas professor Jefferson Mangel, an academic with a puckish enthusiasm for "magic" and a sense of the mystical in life.

Professor Mangel had been found dead in his classroom-cum-magic museum, inside a drawing of the constellation Ophiuchus, the thirteenth sign of the zodiac, forgotten and dropped centuries earlier.

The ancients named it for the image they saw in those stars, a man struggling with a giant, entwining serpent. That image was not so different from another ancient one for eternity, a circling snake swallowing its own tail. That was called the Worm Ouroboros, in the sense that medieval dragons were often called worms.

Temple was starting to think the constellation's human figure might be female. Jeff Mangel was not the only victim of an unnamed killer cluttering Las Vegas in the sign of the Synth. Wasn't she herself entangled in struggling right now to put Cosimo Sparks's death together with Jeff's, not to mention the parking-lot murder of the retired assistant of Max's magical mentor, Gandolph the Great, aka Garry Randolph, and the spectacular death of Randolph himself (undercover in female garb, no less, to unmask fake mediums) at last Halloween's séance to raise Harry Houdini? So the victims with magical links were Gandolph first, then Jeff Mangel, then Gandolph's assistant, Gloria Fuentes, and now

Cosimo Sparks.

Oh! The personalities, the deaths, the timing, the circumstances, the sign of the Synth's House of Ophiuchus found at the professor's classroom death scene, scrawled in chalk, and at Cosimo Sparks's. They were all tangled up in her head . . . three magic-related men dead and one's retired assistant. All unsolved murders. Now this Phantom Mage at the Neon Nightmare could be another victim. And Max, another retired magician, was missing. Again.

Rafi's comments increased her fears that Max had been trailing the rumored secret society in disguise at the Neon Nightmare. The Synth's calling card was definitely the image of the major stars that formed Ophiuchus. Where the ancients saw tangled human and serpent flesh, Temple had seen the childish sketch of a house, askew, and now holding the splayed stick figures of two dead men, the professor and the Synth magician.

She couldn't let the implications of what Rafi had inadvertently revealed lie there like a dead black mamba. Somebody had to stir up things in the Neon Nightmare snake pit.

As soon as she got home, Temple checked for Louie — apparently out or snoozing somewhere.

Her desk drawer burped up the handy,

dandy table of unsolved murders and purported suspects she'd made and updated to keep victims and possible perps straight, even if one suspect was Max. A quick study of the table showed magic was the undying, unifying theme. She now, thanks to Rafi, had a new highly suspect site to investigate.

WHO	WHEN	WHERE	METHOD	ODDITIES	SUSPECT/S
dead man at Goliath Hotel	April	casino ceiling	?		Max
dead man at Crystal Phoenix	Aug	casino ceiling	?	Resembled Effinger	?
Max mentor, Gandolph	Halloween	seance	?	Cause Undetermined	assorted psychics
Cliff Effinger, Matt's stepfather	New Year's	Oasis	drowning		2 muscle men
Woman	Feb	Blue Dhalia Club	strangled	ligature	arrested
Cher Smith, stripper	Feb	strip club parking lot	strangled		arrested
Gloria Fuentes, Gandolph's assistant	Feb	church parking lot	strangled	*"she left"* on body in morgue	?
Prof. Jeff Mangel	March	UNLV hall	knifed	ritual marks	the Synth
Cloaked Conjuror's assistant	April	New Millennium ceiling	beating or fatal fall	masked like CC or a TV show SF alien	?
Vassar, call girl	May	Goliath Hotel	fatal fall	after seeing Matt	Kitty O'Connor Matt

Temple then attacked her bedroom closet, grabbing a ruffled Reagan-eighties fuchsia taffeta fitted jacket, slim, short Vera Wang skirt suitable for nightclubbing, and her new Giuseppe Zanotti leopard-print suede wedges perfect for the urban jungle.

Temple hotfooted into her spare bedroom-office to raid that closet for a purple suede envelope-style clutch bag with a slim metal shoulder strap. It was flat enough for evening but perfect to hold the Colt Pocket Lite Max had insisted she'd learned to shoot.

The gun was in a closet shoe box (such a TV-show cliché) next to a small, surprisingly heavy box of bullets. The weapon was loaded and the safety was on: no resident kids to worry about, and Louie didn't have an opposable thumb. Finding a firearm that fit her hand, and a trigger she had the finger strength to pull had taken many tries. A tiny twenty-two didn't always fill the bill just because it looked feminine sized. Max had drilled her on proper firearm handling, but her palms still dampened as she lifted the Colt from its sheepskin-lined triangular leather case and put it inside her leather-lined purse. She wasn't used to carrying either one: an ordinary-sized purse or a gun.

The shooting range was months behind

her, but if Max had been the Phantom Mage and had disappeared from the Neon Nightmare, as Rafi's on-scene testimony indicated, she wasn't going there without backup.

Poor Rafi. Witnessing that fall had made him "give up" on private security jobs and indirectly led him into a decent career. Poor Max, if it had been Max. She wouldn't leave the Neon Nightmare tonight without finding that out.

The weight of the small revolver felt reassuring at her hip, where the purse rested. She could keep a hand on the top, as women do in crowds, and be ready for anything. What if Max had never left Las Vegas? What if he was being held prisoner at the Neon Nightmare? Rafi had mentioned the "bosses" coming and going, the place's interior being a black Plexiglas maze, where reflective surfaces and neon almost blinded most eyes.

Temple opened the accessory chest's top drawer. This was for jewelry and bigger accessories, unlike the smaller chest in her bedroom that contained the notorious scarf drawer, where she'd finally stashed Max's ring. She plucked a pair of mirrored sunglasses from the collection stored in shoebox tops. She snagged a rhinestoned raspberry beret to obscure her strawberry-blonde hair, just in case someone knew her.

In the mirror, the effect wasn't at all Zoe Chloe Ozone, amazingly.

"Okay, Retro-Disco Babe," she told herself in the mirror. "We are gonna take the Neon Nightmare by its flaming electric-rainbow mane and shake it until the Synth and what happened to Max Kinsella, if he was there, come falling out into the light of day."

Temple grabbed the Miata keys from the kitchen counter near the tiny entry hall, locked her condo, and headed to where a rearing neon mare surmounted a pyramid crammed with music, mania, and maybe magic and murder.

Sitting in the Miata in the fresh darkness with the top up a block from the Neon Nightmare, Temple finally allowed herself to check the temperature of her sandal-strapped toes, instep, and ankles. Yup, cold feet.

She shut her eyes. The longer she thought about it, the less she liked it.

Her cell phone felt like a magic egg in the palm of her still-warm hand. This was spring in Las Vegas. The desert air was hot and heavy from the hangover of sun-drenched daylight bouncing off all the concrete, glass, and asphalt.

She was bathed in the literal nightmare sign of many neon colors, flowing over her little car like a giant mane. She could leave a message for . . . not Matt in Chicago. Her landlady? No . . . Molina? God forbid. Rafi? No, he knew this place. He could rod right over and stop her. She wanted someone who'd miss her if she didn't turn up, but distant enough to not think much of where she was and what that meant.

Whose number was on her cell phone that she could text?

She settled on Nicky Fontana. "Chkg out Neon Ntmr 4 G's ideas. Disco TB. News at 11."

His phone would record when she left the message — 8:00 P.M. — and he wouldn't bother calling her back or become concerned until after 11:00. Nicky was a casino watchdog. He stayed up at least until midnight every night.

Now. She had been as sensible as a one-woman fury could be. She was going inside that gaudy pyramid, and she wasn't leaving until she had solved the puzzle of the Synth or died trying. Or, better, shot someone in self-defense trying. Hopefully not in her own foot in its flashy leopard-print suede wedge heels. Hey, maybe Bob Dylan of

"Leopard-Skin Pill-Box Hat" fame would write a song about them in her memory.

CHAPTER 34
DALAI LAMA EYES

While my Miss Temple, looking like a floozy, is heading out the front door, I am out my special bathroom exit window, ratcheting up ye olde leaning palm-tree ladder to the Circle Ritz penthouse.

The sinking sun is haloing the distant mountains with a faded neon-rainbow glow, but scenery is not on my mind.

Once I have dropped down onto Miss Electra Lark's penthouse balcony like a ninja, unseen and stealth footed, I pounce down the line of French doors, seeking the loosest hinges. There is always one weak link to everything and everyone, and Midnight Louie is a past master at sniffing them out.

Aha! I pause at an end door. Methinks I smell the blood of a purebred Birman female. Or at least I spot a long, white, airy whisker protruding under the door. It is locked, of course, but this is the same flimsy hardware as on Miss Temple's balcony doors. Back in the nineteen fifties, when this joint was built, the crime rate was as low as the interest rate is now.

I do my patented leaps and twists, and am pleasantly rewarded much sooner than usual, when the locking mechanism bows to my superior strength. Unfortunately, I am at the apex of my leap and enter twisting my torso to land on my feet.

I make an awkward five-point landing — I also take it on the chin when I fall to the carpet — and look up to see a pair of red taser lights gleaming not six inches from my temporarily immobile eyes.

My shivs dig into the carpet as I rapidly scramble up to assume the "Halloween" martial-arts pose, feet clenched and back arched, rear member slashing.

"At ease," drawls an unimpressed female voice. "Where is the fire?"

"What are you doing out in the open?" I wonder.

"Opening the door, dodo," is the tart reply from the agoraphobic Karma, who is usually to be found lurking under large upholstered furniture.

"Uh, *I* did that," I tell her, forgetting you can tell the telepathic or psychopathic . . . or whatever "ick" you want to call her . . . nothing. She knows all, sees all, says all.

"Uh," she mocks, "I *let* you do that. I could sense your neurotic panic all the way from the second floor. It has quite curled my whiskers."

The illumination in here is eternally night-light to accommodate Karma's oversensitive nature, so I have to squint to see that her vibrissae have indeed curled inward at the ends as if under the influence of a permanent wave.

"I did that?" I cannot help sounding a bit pleased.

She sighs, heavily. "I cannot help you, Louie."

This is bad news.

I do not normally buy this psychic hokum anymore than I regularly eat Free-to-Be Feline, but it is true that Karma's breed is descended from the cats that defended the Dalai Lamas in Tibet, back when it was a sovereign and mystical place that harbored legends like the earthly paradise of Shangri-La (from which a naughty lady magician of Miss Temple's and my acquaintance took her performing moniker).

The legends say that the souls of departed Tibetan priests inhabited the beige-colored temple cats. Frankly, they share much in common with the late Shangri-La's performing Siamese, the evil Hyacinth: cream beige body with brown-masked face, brown legs, and tail, and stunning blue eyes, except they are long-haired (and have that uppity longhair air, as if they listen to harpsichord concertos all day on velvet pillows). The legend is that their coloring, especially the four white mitts, were awarded by a god when they tried to save a long-ago Dalai Lama from being killed by mountain marauders.

So I have to keep all this stuff in mind when dealing with Karma, as she is supernaturally sensitive.

"You do not know what I want," I argue.

"Of course I do, Louie. I know what you want before you know it. And I am telling you that had you contacted me *first,* when you sent the clowder to their various far-flung posts, given the fact that you are related by blood to three of them, I could indeed have invoked Bast to lend you the mystical and ancient power called Oneness of Overmind so you could communicate long-distance."

"I am related to *three* of them?"

"I can count."

"Then Midnight Louise is indeed my — ?"

"The product of your littering, yes. And now you are right to fear for her well-being."

"How would we, uh, three, do this Oneness of Overmind thing?"

"I would perform the ceremony, but the effect is only temporary. It would require burning a whisker each and a few drops of communal blood, not to mention the sacrifice of one life apiece."

"Cell phones are much more humane," I say, shocked.

"Had our kind pockets . . . I sympathize with your concerns, Louie. Part of the permanent wave in my whiskers is from absorbing the danger haloing your recently departing human like the scent of death. I hope her recent departure does not become permanent."

"But she has already left, and it will take time to summon the Cat Pack. I need paranormal help."

"And I am giving it to you. I have consulted the stars, particularly the sinister sign known as Ophiuchus, and looked into the future, and I have this urgent advice for you."

"Yes?"

"Run like hell."

CHAPTER 35
ROOM DISSERVICE

"Somehow," Gandolph chuckled as he hung up the room phone, "I doubt a room-service dinner with me will be as enthralling as with your friend Revienne."

"I never said she was a friend," Max objected, using his hands to lift each leg onto an ottoman and stretch out more than three feet of chronic ache.

"The over-the-counter pills help at all?" Gandolph asked, sitting in the upholstered chair.

Max shrugged. "I'm used to the discomfort, but those dank Old World buildings must have been built to make people uncomfortable, like that bloody convent."

"The church probably inherited the manor house a couple centuries ago, and the Magdalen operation was a leftover from the age of Dickens, Max. The Old World was always harsh compared with the New. You've forgotten our small travails when we lived abroad. Daily comfort is an American concept. Think of all the toilet paper American tourists trekked on European tours for decades."

"I spent enough time this unscheduled trip 'roughing it' in the Alps."

"With a hot blonde waiting on you foot and foot."

Max shrugged in surrender. "I'm spoiled. I know it. Speaking of which, I can't believe these 'recovering' IRAers haven't tumbled to the fact that 'Michael' Kinsella is the 'Mystifying Max.' "

"My European counterterrorism associates and I kept your original identity up-to-date all these years. Comfort may not be their game, but subterfuge is. They're way older at it than we are, living right next door to ancient enemies without any massive moats of ocean."

"How the hell — ?"

"According to the record, Michael Kinsella returned to the U.S., graduated from a state university with a . . . biology degree, and got a high-school teaching job."

"I'm amazed. Maybe I should drop back into that phony life. Start over. I do seem to have a gift for biology," Max added with a wicked glint.

Gandolph was perusing a folder. "What

do you want to start with, duck soup or cream of potato?"

"Are you talking about my fakc life, biology, or the room-service menu?"

"The menu. It's quite decent."

"High praise from a gourmand like you."

"How did you like the kitchen in my former Vegas house?"

"Good grief. A memory of that room just flashed through my mind."

"Excellent, Max! Good progress."

"Your online redhead was in it, sitting on your granite-topped central island sipping a bubble glass of . . . probably merlot wine. Not a bad picture. Interesting composition of reds."

"The bubble glass is all wrong! Someone must have added it to the household after I left."

"Could have been me. Bubble glasses are fun magic props to have around the house."

"I'm not catering to your indecisive mood. We're having rainbow trout and stuffed rack of lamb, vegetable mélange, with brandied bread pudding for dessert. I'll order the wines."

"And a Celebrex chaser for my seventy-year-old legs." Max remained silent for a moment. "You know what I'd really love for dinner?"

"What?"

"A Big Mac." Max expected his companion to have a foodie fit over his low-end, high-fat craving.

"McDonald's is everywhere," Gandolph said briskly. "I'll order you one up as an appetizer. You need to get some pounds back on somehow. A man bedridden for more than a month can really lose weight. Perhaps beer will help. We're meeting our next sources in a pub."

"You spoil me," Max said. "I've been an ungrateful boy."

"You've been through as much as you faced seventeen years ago in this very place." Gandolph's smile turned into a thoughtful purse of his lips. "It's good you recalled 'our' kitchen in Las Vegas."

"We're here in Belfast so I can recall my teenage rebel past. Why are Vegas memories intruding in the Irish mist?"

"Because they are all linked, my lad. More than either of us might realize, or like, I fear."

CHAPTER 36
LADIES' NEON NIGHT OUT

A doorman in a muscle T and dated gangster bling bowed her into the club.

"No cover charge, cutie," he said. "Every
night is ladies' night at the Neon Nightmare."

Temple sashayed in, having forgotten she
would be welcomed as cash on the hoof by
a nightclub's management. She usually
looked younger than her thirty years. All
dolled up she probably looked just barely
legal.

Men bought drinks for silly young women
who dressed like they thought they were
hot. Lots of drinks. Good. Temple was here
to pick brains . . . and maybe locks.

Temple had never done the Las Vegas
singles scene, although every bar in town
was a singles scene. She'd moved here with
Max, madly in love. His magic-show ex-
travaganza at the Goliath ran twice nightly,
so they'd played out all their love scenes at

their Circle Ritz condo. It had been a very "married" existence, come to think of it.

Temple apparently didn't look "married." She fended off a couple of middle-aged salesmen-in-suits types who were obviously tourists, and the sale-eager bartenders, because no way was she opening her pistol-packing purse to pay for a drink at this elbow-squashing, people-packed bar.

That would be dangerous, even though she had the safety on. She was beginning to think she had overreacted to the idea that Max hadn't just "gone missing again" but had been here and then never seen again . . . and was possibly really *dead* and she didn't know it. The thought was intolerable.

"Let me guess," a man's voice said on her right. "Whatever you drink comes in a footed glass."

Temple eyed the night's first catch. Around thirty-five, with a face more pleasantly quirky than handsome. She rejoiced to see brown hair gelled into that central pompadour demanded of guys who would be Hollywood hip these days. Even Matt was being threatened with an "extreme makeover" by a radio management going ever more online.

Temple glanced over the guy's shoulder to the gyrating mobs on the dance floor and up into the pyramid's distant dark peak, where stabbing light sabers of neon dueled with electric color.

"You've never been here before," her bar partner guessed. "New in town?"

"Pretty much," she lied. "You too?"

"No. I'm assigned here."

Even better! "Are you a Neon Nightmare habitué?"

"I was right. Footed drinks and fancy French. What can I get you?"

"A wine spritzer?"

"That's for lunch."

"You're right. A Spanish coffee."

His peaked eyebrows became even more pronounced. "You don't do the bar scene much."

"Nope."

"What's in a Spanish coffee, besides the coffee?"

"Rum, Kahlúa, triple sec, cream, and sugar."

"I admire a woman who can hold her calories."

He ordered a beer for himself, surprising Temple. Had she actually drawn a moderate drinker she could pump for half an hour without him making a pass or sliding slowly to the mirror-black floor?

Her Spanish coffee arrived in a footed

glass mug, looking like dark Irish Guinness stout with a head on it. Max-mission appropriate.

"Footed," he pointed out. "Thanks for not proving me a liar. I'm Steve Fox, by the way, boy-wonder programmer. My company sent me out here for three months of skill upgrading."

Temple had left all rings at home. Clutching her lethal purse in her lap with her left hand, she produced her right for a shake. "Temple Barrett. I do PR around town." Okay, she would pull out the cliché: "You come here often?"

"Yeah, as a matter of fact. The company suite-hotel makes one hope for bedbugs for entertainment. This place changes the neon show nightly. They used to have this wildman masked magician on a bungee cord who could do amazing illusions bounding all over the interior. Best free show in town."

Temple sipped the warm, comfortingly sweet foam atop her dark, bitter, strong drink. Her heart was soaring and sinking at the same time. That magic man had to be Max.

"Why aren't they advertising a primo attraction like that?" she wondered aloud.

"Maybe because I haven't seen him in almost two months. Unsung when he performed, forgotten when he left." He eyed her again. "What made you put on the Ritz and come sit at the bar here when you don't want to be picked up? Don't claim you're a habitué. I'd know better."

"Got me!" Temple laughed unsteadily. "I have an assignment, too, writing up trendy bars. I'd heard about your magician, but not that he wasn't performing."

"The Phantom Mage," Steve recalled, sipping his brew. "Kinda hokey name. Smart psychology, though. You didn't expect much and then, *wham!*"

"What was he doing here?" Temple mused, almost under her breath.

Steve had a fox's sharp ears. "Making a buck. You're not going to write about a dead act, are you?"

"I might." Temple bit her lip at the double meaning she heard in Steve's question.

"Drink too hot or too strong? Coffee will keep you awake and rum will keep you happy."

"Exactly right. I better get down to business. Those neon fireworks up top are spectacular. Is that where the Phantom Mage made his entrance?"

"Right. And exit. Now that you say his name again, I guess it suited his act." Steve squinted up into the light show. "I think there are invisible balconies up there."

"Balconies?" That fit with Rafi's seeing people "vanish" into the walls at all levels.

"You know, perches. He seemed to be walking on air at times."

Temple's heart clutched as her left hand fisted on her lap purse. That illusion was right from the Mystifying Max's Goliath act, where he used strobe lights, like some of those that flashed over the dance floor here, to seem to fly.

"These strobe lights are so disco sixties," Steve commented.

"Yeah. They pulse on and off, so people's motions seem jerky."

"Too bad a lot of them *are* jerks," Steve said.

"You don't like the bar scene either."

"No, I'm a nerd, basically. Came here to see the light show and the flying magician. I just drink my two beers and people-watch. I'm heading home soon. You're the first girl I've bought a drink for, Temple."

"You're the first guy I've let buy me a drink in . . . forever."

They smiled at each other.

"You've got someone," he said.

"He's out of town. You too?"

"He's back home in Oshkosh."

Oh-kay. And here she'd been angsting

about picking up guys in bars.

"Will I see 'Temple Barrett' in the next issue of *Out and About in Las Vegas*?" Steve asked.

Temple laughed. "Just a small-type credit at the very bottom, if I'm lucky. Have a nice trip back."

"Thanks. I'll try ordering a Spanish coffee in Oshkosh."

"Good luck," Temple said, "but I don't think that will fly at most bars or restaurants."

"Why not? It's hot and bracing. Just what Cold Country needs. Don't stay up too late."

She sat and digested what Steve had told her after he left, studying the pyramid's flashy interior. The interior was magician-made, *both* smoke and mirrors. Black reflective Plexiglas walls and floors, black mirrors, and bright lights — a giant magician's illusion box. Of course there must be "balconies" along the interior sides. Although this pyramid was hollow, it must harbor plenty of room between the interior and exterior walls for light- and sound-show equipment and maintenance.

The dead body at the Goliath the night Max's magic-show run had ended was found in one of those above-casino crawl spaces. The thought that Max might have been trapped here in a similar situation, and maybe even died here, made her determined not to leave this building until she knew what . . . and who . . . it concealed.

It wasn't impossible that Max was also using the gig as training wheels for a new act. He'd been determined to unmask the Synth, and this was where he'd picked to do it . . . and where somebody got angry or alarmed enough to sabotage his investigation and try to take his life.

Temple sipped her Spanish coffee as slowly as possible to study the possibilities. Apparently her tête-à-tête with Steve had marked her as "taken." Guys might be thinking he'd only left for the men's room. The not-quite-empty beer bottle still sat in front of Steve's empty barstool. That's the kind of escort she liked in a place like this. Invisible.

Great. She was a free agent now. She eyed the dance floor, considered the advantages and disadvantages of performing over an audience's head. When the Phantom Mage came sweeping down, they had to have looked up at the motion. What did they see?

She saw the dance floor as a wall-to-wall mob swept by glaring neon spotlights and winking strobe lights. It wasn't all couples.

Whoever pushed onto the deceptive, reflective surface could gyrate alone, with his or her image in the floor below, or with a cooperative stranger of any nearby gender.

Gosh! She wished things had been this informal when she was in high school and college.

She left two bucks on the bar to join Steve's tip and slid off the high stool, never her most graceful moment, even in wedge heels, and even less so while clutching a purse for dear life. Or death.

The slick floor unnerved her, but she edged onto it, bobbing tentatively. It vibrated with the beat like a subterranean heart. Someone behind her bumped butts. *Oh, rescue me!* She gyrated around and faced a dreadlocked black guy doing the . . . Swim? *Oh, retro me!* Temple swam farther into the center of the dance floor, looking up.

The scene was as psychedelic as she'd heard the sixties were. Lights above, reflections below. You hardly knew where up and down ended. That was Max's magician territory: confusing, sense-flooding, mystifying.

The pyramid sides were a blur of neon flashes. If she'd seen anyone "vanishing" into those walls, as Rafi had, she'd have thought of ghosts and freaked. Steve, sharp left-brained observer, had been right. There had to be perches for a flying magician to rest on before bounding into thin air and back to the wall again.

The impact of man with wall that Rafi had described reverberated with the driving, relentless rock/rap music in her head.

No one could survive that. Unless it was an illusion. Unless it had been Max doing the illusion.

She eyed the apex of the pyramid. Must be five stories. The neon lights at the peak spun around, making her eyes burn and her feet shuffle for solid ground beneath them.

She'd seen PBS shows about the solar system and the galaxies resembling this. Standing here in this mating swarm of loud music and shimmying torsos was like being in a science museum's astronomy exhibition, if you actually looked up and enjoyed the light show.

Temple tuned out the mayhem and watched the signs of the zodiac spinning around the polestar. She realized the image at the apex of the pyramid was a blazing white horseshoe! One shod foot of the exterior night-mare actually "crashed" through the pointed roof to flash all the dancers below. It must be wearing a lucky horseshoe, of course.

Maybe seeing a lucky neon horseshoe was the same as wishing on a star. Temple was acting as a polestar herself. Standing still on the dance floor, she became a fixed point. People grooved all around, not caring what her shtick was any more than they cared whom they danced with or if they did.

Temple tried to picture a masked Max leaping on a bungee cord into this melee, pulling illusions out of his sleeves under all the signs of the zodiac. Look! There was Gemini, the twins, her birth sign. And Cancer, the crab. Then came Leo, the MGM lion. Not really, but in Vegas, was there any other lion on Earth or in the heavens? And Virgo, the virgin, a being as rare as a unicorn on the Vegas Strip. And Libra, the scales of balance and justice. Scorpio, with the curved sting of its tail lashing autumn into winter.

And then . . . Temple didn't recognize the next constellation, or remember what zodiac sign came next. It didn't offer a lot of stars but was rather peaked, like the top of Libra's scales.

The one after it boasted a whole a rash of stars. Oh, that was the centaur shooting the arrow. Sagittarius, the archer. Capricorn, the goat, came next.

But . . . the hoofed centaur followed the scorpion. Temple was sure of it.

So . . . the constellation between Scorpio and the centaur had to be . . . shaped like a leaning house with a pointed roof — *Ophiuchus!*

Why did the Neon Nightmare include the rejected thirteenth sign of the zodiac between Scorpio the scorpion and Sagittarius the archer? Both shot stinging barbs. Ophiuchus combined man and serpent, which could sting as well.

Had Max air-danced beneath this bright and poisonous zodiac and been stung on the fly, falling to Earth and destruction?

Then where was the comet's tail?

Why had such a spectacular death dwindled to mere memory and rumor?

Where was the body?

CHAPTER 37
PLAYING IT KOI

So here I am, at my former PI office, lurking in the canna-lily plants near the Crystal Phoenix koi pond, panting my lungs out so hard I can not even *whisper* "Dixie," much less whistle it.

There was no time to hitch any rides, so I made the trip only on mitt leather, and I have worn my black soles pink. Some consider that a handsome retro color combination, but, let me tell you, it stings!

Luckily, I am too pooped to be distracted by the silken . . . undulating . . . translucent . . . fluttery fins on those plump piscine torsos in the nearby water attraction. Lake Mead may be a few trillion gallons shy a shoreline, but nothing will ever diminish or lower the water level in the hotel chef's beloved koi pond.

I am hoping beyond hope for a rendezvous with Miss Midnight Louise. If she is not here, then my hasty mission to the Neon Nightmare club is doubly vital, for that is the last place I have seen her. So, by the shores of Getchagimme, while the koi beat their fins against the water in an odd familiar rhythm, I hear an internal mantra.

In the land of the Fontanas,
Lives the justice-maker's daughter,
Mistress of the rising phoenix,
And the gleaming goldfish pond,
Born to run with nimble footwork,
Heart and mitt that move together,
She shall run upon my errands,
Midnight Louisa, laughing mocker . . .

Okay, the scansion on Miss Louise's name does not quite work, but she is no Minnehaha, unless she is laughing at me. She would not be laughing now.

My vibrissae snap to immobile attention. I have spotted a familiar black hummock.

Midnight Louise is here on her home turf! Safe and stuffing her face. And here I was worried. . . .

Unfortunately, that still-crouched form is worshiping at the white-shod feet and medically white-clothed figure of Chef Song, arms folded on chest, the usual meat cleaver clutched to defend the precious foreign-named and fat goldfish from any interloper, like me.

I realize a delicate celadon green rice bowl

sits between the kitchen god and worshiper, filled with fresh . . . shrimp or salmon perhaps, or tender slices of beef, or caviar, or octopus.

Preparing to make an end run to snag her attention, I watch the furred one sit up to perform after-meal ablutions. What, no warm, wet rolled-up towel? For shame, Chef Song!

By then the chef is turning away to gather goods to refill the bowl.

The diner strolls off into the canna lilies to finish *his* grooming. It is that big old lazy galoot of a purported father of mine, Three O'Clock! One would think the Glory Hole Gang's test kitchen would suffice for his snacking.

While I eye him contemptuously, *another* black humped form is now worshiping at the about-to-be-refilled bowl.

Chef Song straightens. "You are hungry today, honorable cat."

It is then I notice that he wears a pair of glasses that has slid down his nose, given all the serial kowtows he is making to my kind.

There is no chance even I would assume this latest bowl customer to be Miss Midnight Louise. She is more petite and curls her tail left when eating, and this bozo has a short, stumpy tail. I recall Ma Barker had promised to send some ninjas to patrol the Crystal Phoenix.

Pushing one's face into a full rice bowl is not patrolling.

I can barely contain my impatience. I need to betray my position and go over to interrogate Three O'Clock without the looming, armed presence of my longtime foe, Chef Song. I am astonished he would lavish his bounty on all comers like this, when I am persona non grata.

I should snag a koi on the principle of it, while he is fawning over these street-gang strangers. The current customer also rises, flourishes his vibrissae, and ambles off to cleanse them in the canna lilies' shade.

Before I can make a move, *another* black dude has appeared before the bowl, and while the now-vision-impaired chef is bent over watching the food vanish as if by magic, the dude is taking his turn. *This* is too much to bear.

If Chef Song cannot tell a senior citizen and a street tough from the dainty Miss Midnight Louise, he probably cannot distinguish me as his bitter enemy.

I strut into the open sunlight, stinging my footpads . . . *ouch.*

Nevertheless I march right up behind the current foodaholic. I will either join the chow line or I will bust it up.

Chef Song straightens as he spots me. With

that tall, poofy white hat, he is as formidable appearing as a white Persian with its tail in full battle fluff. In other words, he and his meat cleaver do not scare me.

However, I am apparently so singular I am immediately ID'd.

"You!" he says. "You koi snatcher. You no longer resident. Get away from my private feeding station and pond or I will make minced shallots of your tail."

Our set-to has spoiled the appetite of the latest freeloader, who hisses, spits, and runs for the canna lilies. Good. My posse is on their feet and ready to leave the luncheonette for the real scene of the action.

While Chef Song switches to uttering his own challenges in Chinese, I return full measure of hiss and spit, then show him the business end of my tail root and duck into the thick plant-stalk jungle.

Aaaah. Cool dirt between my toes, even though it will get stuck in my shivs.

"Okay, you worthless chowhounds," I tell my now-assembled troops. "We have a mission. First, Three O'Clock, where is Midnight Louise?"

"I do not know. I just ambled over from the Glory Hole Gang's test kitchen for some real food. Spuds Lonnigan is whipping up his specialty, potatoes, and I am not a meat-and-potatoes kind of guy. Meat, yes. Tater Tots, no."

"You have not seen Miss Midnight Louise, either?" I ask the other two, while a singsong of imprecations continues above our heads and far, far away from our current concerns.

"Bast no, boss," one says, with gratifying respect.

"Not since this old freeloader showed up at our new headquarters," the other adds, indicating Three O'Clock with a quick flick of his shivs.

That is bad mews. Miss Louise should be long back here by now.

"Cut out that palaver," the old boy orders me and his ex's legmen. "I am washing my whiskers. The younger generation has no respect for the civilized formalities."

"No time for cleanup work here," I tell them, "there is a mucho-bad scene brewing at the Neon Nightmare, and we need to join Ma Barker and any minions she may have taken there right away."

"I need time for my lunch to settle," Three O'Clock complains. "I cannot do a long trek and then be ready for fisticuffs."

"There is a shortcut," I explain. "If Miss Midnight Louise had made it back here, she would have put one of you two on guard duty near it. And," I tell the old guy, "no whining.

The entrance to our Chunnel of Timely Crime Fighting is just behind the people-pool area. It is dark and cool and private. From there we can take a secret route into the bowels of the Neon Nightmare."

I consider this a rousing speech to derring-do.

Three O'Clock hiccups and shakes his head. "My bowels are going to feel the earth move if I have to get going without my afternoon nap. After my seafaring life, I find the gentle waves of the subtly shifting koi pond essential and soothing."

I shrug and eye the no-name muscle. They seem to have no digestion issues.

"Stay here and hold the fort, then, Three O'Clock. We need to be off and running to the rescue."

I make a 180 swivel on my four-on-the-floor and take off, to the rewarding skitter of battle-ready shivs digging in behind me. The Cat Pack is on the hunt.

CHAPTER 38
DRINKIN' BITTER BEER

After dinner and leaving the hotel that night, Gandolph led Max to the far edge of the tourist area, until the streets were deserted enough that they heard their individual footsteps.

"Soon," he cautioned Max, unnecessarily, "they will find us."

Almost eerily soon after that, a lone passerby bumped Gandolph into Max, who bumped into the corner of a building leading to a dark, narrow passage. Instantly, they were corned beef on rye toast, sandwiched between two thick, meaty wedges of Irish soda bread.

"Americans abroad, eh?" a coarse whisper crooned.

Now three men clothed in a damp wool scent hedged them in, one in the street, two in the alley.

Max had already taken a visual survey. All three were nearer Gandolph's age than his, so they weren't teenage hotheads unable to get jobs and turning to a bit of street violence if marching Orangemen weren't available to attack.

Like most natives of a damp and cloudy climate, their Irish eyes were lighter than their hair color, which Max judged by their jaw stubble. Their heads were covered with knit fisherman's caps, and they all wore that new and sinister urban fashion/disguise, hoodies, now pushed down into the monk's-cowl position on their broad shoulders, the shoulders of workingmen or professional thugs.

The acrid odors of strong tobacco and ale were their cologne. Their narrowed eyes and tense mouth sets advertised the names of their signature scents: Suspicion and Up to No Good.

Ordinarily, Max would start flailing enough to distract two of them so Gandolph could belly-punch and shin-kick the third to the ground, by which time the second would come stumbling past him and get a disabling blow from the blackjack in the older man's pocket. The other thug, of course, would be out cold by then, flat on the cool cobblestones two centuries old and witness to countless evening attacks of the same crude sort.

Except here, Max was handicapped from the outset, and Gandolph saw no point in making a fight of it. They surrendered to the hard, metal prods in their backs and faded a few steps away from the distant lights and tourists and traffic into the instant isolation of an alley that stank like a urinal.

So much for urban gentrification, thought Max.

"We know a little pub," the same voice purred, with the velvet authority of being well armed.

Max shrugged and Gandolph nodded. They were here to take the temperature of Belfast today. These men weren't muggers, or they'd be out cold and stripped of their paper, metal, and plastic belongings.

Max felt a frisson of fellowship to realize that he and Gandolph were long accustomed to being of like mind without words or gesture. For the second time since he'd awakened from his coma, his veins throbbed with a returning tingle of life and adventure. The first occasion had been with Revienne.

Mostly, he knew he wasn't afraid, as a normal tourist would have been, but . . . pleased.

The "pub" was several blocks' walk through

ever-more-depressing slums. They passed a burned-out, graffiti-slathered office building and a cement-walled shopping arcade as dark as any crypt, before ducking down another alley to a low red-brick building from a couple centuries back.

Uneven cobblestones had Max limping badly by the time they arrived. He relished his obvious problem; it made their custodians careless. A gimp and an old man. Easy prey. For once, Max's height wasn't intimidating but made him appear awkward and unbalanced.

Shoved down some steps into a cellar, they found no warm, red-amber glow of wood and musical instruments and flushed crowds holding topaz-toned pint glasses filled with stout and ale and beer.

A lone bartender studiously refused to look up as they entered. The bar had only one customer, a powerful-shouldered man wearing a peacoat over a sweater and the ubiquitous billed tweed cap, huddled in a corner. Above them, hanging tin kettles and bellows dripped from blackened oak beams. Crude oil portraits of long-dead Irish Republican heroes made a sober row of faces along the dark wood walls.

They were shoved against a smoke-blackened brick wall, hemmed in by two of the shadow-jawed thugs while the third went to whisper to the man behind the scantily equipped bar.

Max pulled out two rough wooden chairs for Garry and himself. By the time they sat, the usual pint glasses filled with dark amber liquid topped by a dispirited frill of foam circled their table, dispensed from the barman's universal round brown plastic tray.

"Not your usual elegant tourist surroundings, eh?" the waiting headman commented more than asked.

Max and Gandolph sipped in tandem and cocked their heads to signal they were listening.

"Came along like lambs," another man chuckled. "You hardly needed all three of us, Liam," they chided their leader.

"Yes," Gandolph said, "we're quite harmless, although not tourists."

"I thought this lame beanpole was the great boy-betrayer, Kinsella," another muttered into his first chugalug of ale.

"Great?" Max inquired with indifference. "I'm a great ale-drinker, 'tis true."

"And blarney man," the leader replied. "The fool has introduced me, but Liam is all you'll know of me."

"And your taste in ales," Max said, nodding at the red-gold brew in their glasses.

"Aye, and you're used to drinkin' yours out of a bottle or a can, like a modern-day traveler," the second man said. "Tourists, Liam, that's what we've netted." And he spat on the floorboards.

Max finally drew the tall golden glass closer to him. "I like to know the name of a man who has ambitions to spit-polish my shoes."

A glowering silence held as all four Irishmen tensed while they made up their minds to be insulted or not.

Liam led again. "Honest Irish spit and sweat is worth ten times an Englishman's piss."

"Then," Max said, "I'd be grateful for names of my drinking companions."

"Just last names; they're all common enough around here," Liam agreed gruffly, after taking a long, considering dip into his very dark ale. He nodded at his cohorts: "Finn, Mulroney, Flanagan. I'm Liam, first and last, as far as you two are concerned."

"And I'm Blarney," Gandolph said, startling everyone, including Max, by breaking his stone-faced-elder silence. "I was darting about Ulster under the dark of the moon before you lot were even out of grammar school. Those surnames could serve well on a music-hall act, but not a one of them was key in the real IRA I knew of old."

Dark-jacketed shoulders shrugged, lifting their sinister hooded hummocks. Max must have forgotten that the Emerald Isle required outerwear even in the spring. No wonder his leg bones ached. He should have bought long johns in Zurich, not designer togs. He wasn't about to consider the image of himself in long johns with Revienne. The reality had been bad enough.

"And what are *you* grinning at, Kinsella?" Finn demanded. "Your last name is not only known but notorious. No laughing matter, even in these namby-pamby 'peaceful' days."

"So the Ulster Easter settlement of ninety-eight is not as settled as some think?" Max asked soberly.

"The IRA fools!" Liam said. "Cowed by the specter of being compared to 'Islamic terrorists.'"

"That nine/eleven slaughter did stir up worldwide revulsion," Gandolph observed mildly.

Shoulders shrugged again, making Max swallow hard to keep his mouth shut. He too had reacted violently from rage and loss and cost of lives, to hear it.

Gandolph was an older, less-fit man, but he plowed courageously ahead.

"'Then, too," he mused in a maddeningly deliberate way, "after nine/eleven the U.S. Irish community had things closer to home to worry about than sending gun money to the Auld Sod, especially the British-run north of it, the nine counties of Ulster."

"Shut your mouth or I'll forget your age," Flanagan said, half rising. His motion made the pints' liquid contents sway like yellow hula skirts.

"Don't spill the beer, man," Mulroney said softly.

"Better beer than blood," Gandolph answered, his expression harder than the parish priest's on confession day. "You're all youngsters compared to me, and I can tell you that you'll tire of blood by the end."

Max was as surprised as the Ulstermen to see Gandolph's steel. He must not remember enough of the man who claimed to have been his mentor, and regretted it for not the first time.

"And the beer?" Max asked. "Does it have a name too, Flanagan?"

As Flanagan sank back down in his chair, the man clawed the glass into his grasp and pulled it to his chest like a miser hoarding liquid gold. "A Bass brew, once made here in Ulster."

Max nodded at Liam's much darker glass.

"And that looks like a Moorhouse's Black Cat."

"Heaven forefend! You've been too long absent from the emerald shore, Kinsella. That nancy brew is tricked out with chocolate and coffee, like a Brit toff would swill."

Max heard himself say, "Blame it on Belfast's annual beer festival, where all the showy brews take home the prizes."

How did he know that? Nobody regarded him as if he were mad.

Although Liam said, "You're daft, man. No workingman drinks those devil-adulterated brews. Only U.S. yuppies."

Again, Max didn't know why or how, but he knew that yuppies were more than over across the Atlantic. He scrubbed his face with a hand.

"What's wrong with your legs?" Liam asked.

"Broke 'em," Max answered.

"Both of them, man? How?"

"Pushed off a mountain," Gandolph said.

"The mountains here are nearer hills," Liam noted.

"Lovely rugged Irish hills," Max agreed. "No, a major peak was my downfall, thanks to someone's unknown hand. Away on the Continent."

"An Alp then, it would be," suggested

Mulroney, sounding suitably impressed.

Max nodded modestly.

The four men eyed at each other. "We know you by old reputation," the spitter known as Finn said, "but you now appear to be as diminished in that respect as we are in ours."

"What reputation?" Gandolph asked, his eyes darting from man to man.

Max stretched his aching legs under the table and watched the men's bodies jerk slightly, like a quartet of puppets sharing the same oversensitive string.

"Easy, boys," he said. "The damp isn't kind to knitting bones."

"That's right," Liam jeered. "You're used to a balmy desert climate."

Max eyed Gandolph. He was the Las Vegas expert as well, given Max's memory was as bum as his legs on certain subjects, like his own past.

"Is there a man among you," Gandolph asked, "that did as much as my friend here at seventeen?"

Silence, then Finn burst out, "He was a wonder, all right, a boy doing a man's work — vengeance for his friend's life. But he was on the bloody wrong side! He betrayed IRA men to the British taskmasters!"

Max was playing a role now, from Gandolph's prompting on the plane trip from Zurich.

"He was a friend," Max said, "that's true, and we were boys, and we stuck our Irish American noses where they didn't belong. But Sean Kelly was more than that. He was my cousin."

"Ah." Liam leaned back in his rickety chair. "Blood."

"Blood," Max repeated, with feeling, and, oddly enough, he felt what he didn't remember. Loss. Rage. Guilt. And, he could reflect now, it must have been driven by a blinding surge of ungoverned testosterone, stirred by the incredibly damaged siren and Magdalen asylum escapee Kathleen O'Connor.

He was back there, at least emotionally, drowned in bitter regrets darker than Liam's oxblood-colored ale. His hands were fists on the table, opening and closing without his will.

Gandolph put a hand on Max's shoulder. "My associate has survived a major accident. So you know who he is and what he did. We know nothing of you. What do you want with us? All that is over and done with."

"Injustice never fades away," Liam said. "It festers."

"We know that," Gandolph said. "We've

432

fought it in our way."

"Yes." Liam swallowed half of his pint at one go and wiped the foam from his mouth with one swipe of his jacketed forearm. "And we are weary and forgotten too. At least, Kinsella, someone cared enough to try to kill you. We can't drum up more than a few callow youths to hurl Molotov cocktails at marching Orangemen."

"What do you want of us?" Gandolph asked. "We're long retired."

"As are we," Flanagan noted.

"We want our due," Mulroney growled, not looking them in the eyes.

"Information," Finn added.

"Odd," said Max, feeling strangely sane and calm again, "that's just what *we* want here."

Liam leaned so far back in his chair it almost tipped over. Almost. Liam knew how to command attention too.

The barman picked up a tray and poured another round into a fresh sextet of glasses.

Now the serious bargaining would begin. Chances were it involved blood and something much akin to it.

Max wanted to think it might be love of homeland and loyalty to one's comrades, but he knew what Gandolph had always thought, always known.

Gandolph knew it was money.

CHAPTER 39
GUY WIRE

Temple was jerked back down to earth by a . . . jerk.

"This is a dance floor, bimbo," a tattooed Asian college-age punk assured her. "Shake something or get off it."

"I'm gonna 'shake' you," Temple said, turning and eeling sideways in dance moves until she finally reached the crowd's fringe.

She wanted to sit down at one of those god-awful bar-height freestanding tables and resurvey the scene from top to bottom-feeder. She held the purse tight to her hip all the way, happy to find a deserted table and sling the heavy bag atop it while she did her Alp-climbing routine to get herself up on a seat and her wedgies, um, wedged onto a crossbar.

It seemed that everybody who was going to hook up here tonight had already done so, so she was relatively invisible and "safe." From her perch she realized that the light works were flashing multicolored tattoos over the dancers and bystanders. The shiny black floor reflected the zodiac-sign patterns.

That made subtle sense. The classic pickup line was "What's your sign?"

Temple almost wished some jerk would approach and ask her that.

"Ophiuchus," she'd answer. "Rhymes with mucus."

Now *that* was a turnoff!

Okay. The Neon Nightmare scene was making her crabby *and* snarky. That's the mood she needed to snoop. She ordered a club soda with a lime wedge from a passing barmaid to secure her place at the table.

Then she watched the sides of the pyramid, with the light lasers glancing off their shiny black surfaces. Looking this hard, she realized the walls weren't all smooth surfaces but a random pattern of black Plexiglas struts crisscrossing the entire interior to break up and further refract the lights.

Max would have been able to play off those fractured surfaces like a rock-climbing wall, particularly if he'd been tethered.

The barmaid returned with the club soda. At least with these high-rise tables and stools, Temple was actually on a level with the waitress's punishing spike heels. Vegas glamour was hard on workingwomen's feet.

"I'm not starting a tab," Temple said, pulling out one of the twenties she'd stuffed down her purse's exterior pocket.

"Struck out," the waitress murmured sympathetically.

"Actually, I'm covering this scene for *Whatsup* magazine, the Vegas Restaurant Association guide."

"Oh, yeah? Really? Then you're like a reviewer?"

"Just like that."

"We only serve appetizers, but they go like hotcakes."

Good thing Temple wasn't planning on quoting the poor girl. "I bet. I'm really reviewing the ambience."

" 'Ambi'-wha? We don't discriminate."

"No, no. I mean the atmosphere. That neon lightning-bolt effect is, er, awesome."

"Oh, right. Awesome."

"Does it wear your eyes out, working in so much flashing light?"

"Naw, you get used to it. Don't even think about it."

"I hear the magic act you had until recently was awesome too."

"Magic act?"

"Guy on a bungee cord, up in the pyramid?"

"Oh, him. Yeah, he was something out of Cirque du Soleil. A high-wire act, only with rebound. You know, at the big hotels." She giggled. "He swept down one night and whisked my tray out of my hands just before I reached my table. Maybe he was a magician, because he bounced around and then set it right in front of my customers. Not a drop spilled."

Temple was impressed. Max must have used the same natural laws of inertia that allow magicians to pull a tablecloth out from under a place setting without upsetting the glass and china.

"What about the bosses here?" she asked sympathetically. "They treat the staff okay?"

"Great. They're almost invisible. Leave it to our floor manager, Craig. I think they're — what do they call them? — 'backers.' They trundle on past the bar and dance floor and sneak up to the offices they have up top that overlook the whole scene. Can't blame them. It must be an awesome view, like overlooking Times Square in a New York City hotel, all those lights and people milling below."

Temple glanced up, agreeing mentally.

It was time she found a different perspective on this case, this scene. A perspective the Phantom Mage had, and the Synth.

438

She gave up her primo seat on the crowded bar floor and headed for the blue neon Restrooms sign off to the side.

She had no intention of resting.

Once there, she took a hard right, putting her back against the pulsing, light-vibrating patent-leather black wall.

It did indeed vibrate.

Cool.

She edged along it, feeling behind her for those unmistakable vibes, hunting the angled crossbars that riddled the surface if you looked hard enough.

It took only a couple minutes to realize she was edging upward, a bit above the bar and dance-floor level. Another two minutes to understand she was ascending a very subtle interior ramp, like the interior of Frank Lloyd Wright's Guggenheim Museum. Or a pyramid.

Give or take a few thousand years, what was the difference?'

The purse at her hip swung with her motions, because both her hands were behind her, searching for some sensitive spot where she could feel a hidden door in the wall and enter the maze the Phantom Mage must have known well, which Max could have mastered.

Could they be one and the same? Maybe.

She was unsure, not knowing if the Phantom Mage, a suggestive name, had hit the wall or pulled off a vanishing act in front of a nightclub full of people and a trained ex-cop. It was odd she'd never read about the accident, but Vegas establishments were used to making bad publicity disappear too.

When she glanced down, she realized she had moved upward to become one of those self-elevating mysterious figures often glimpsed on the fringes of the Neon Nightmare. Neon lights flashed across her fuchsia jacket and red hair, making her part of the artificial night sky. Making her into an object, not a person.

She continued edging upward, trying not to look down and get dizzy.

A spiderweb brushed her ankle.

What was she? An animated broom?

Oh. Another brush. Another spiderweb.

Her ankle almost turned as she suddenly stepped onto horizontal ground.

One of those "perches" Rafi had mentioned.

Temple shut her eyes and felt the flashing lights on her eyelids, the cold heat of their constant stabs on her body.

If one was the Phantom Mage . . . If one were Max . . . If one were one and the same, she might have stood here, on this narrow horizontal ledge, waiting to skydive into the dark below. She would never have done such a thing in her right mind. It was insanely dangerous.

So she took a step backward. Into the spiderweb. And felt the wall behind her swing inward. Her step backward became a stutter of steps as her weight sucked her inside. The purse at her side swung. Only her hand on the top edge steadied it. Steadied her.

Her back was against a wall again, but she was facing sideways to her previous position. The light and noise had vanished, as if she'd . . . passed through a giant cat door in the wall.

Now the airy tickle at her ankles felt familiar. Not a draft, but a wafting, supple furred tail.

Louie? There was nothing wafting and supple, or subtle, about him. He'd have used a claw tip to the anklebone to snag her attention.

Whatever. Whoever. She was *inside* the Neon Nightmare walls, where Rafi Nadir had never dreamed she could go. Had Max done this before her? Did cats see in the dark?

Did they? Because she could use a guide.

Temple edged along the smooth and dark but dimly lit inner corridor, watching the faint reflection of herself opposite. A vague glow of light lit this pathway. She wasn't surprised when the wall behind her again gave way with a tiny click at the same time as a plumy fan wave brushed her knee.

With no fuss and some fear, she turned to face a softly lit room, like the intimate bar in an exclusive — and weren't they all, with today's prices? — Manhattan private club.

This was Vegas, though, and Temple knew she was standing there in the Synth's inner sanctum, at the heart of the mysteries of unsolved murders and Ophiuchus — and Max's disappearance.

Not that anybody other than a pussycat noticed.

CHAPTER 40
GUNS AND GRAVY

"We know," Liam said when all the glasses were a fifth empty, "that you know about the Synth."

Max couldn't help smiling. Until last night, he hadn't remembered.

"Stop yer eternal smirkin'," Finn ordered in this thick brogue. "You've worked as a magician all over the Western world, accident or no accident. Whoever pushed you off that Alp wasn't the only one willin' to kill you. They evidently wanted to shut you up."

"We want the reverse," Liam said, interrupting his cohort. "Tell us what information you want first, and we'll decide then whether we have the patience to tease what we want out of you two or should just beat your brains out for it."

"Our bloody brain tissue," Gandolph said, "would not be noted for coherence, but I see no reason we can't trade fairly here.

443

What you want to know means little to us, and I suspect the doings of Kathleen O'Connor all these years later are of scant interest to you, now that she's dead and buried."

"You know that for sure, old man?"

"Max bore her no good will and has vivid memories of witnessing her crash on a motorcyle. He checked himself that she was dead. The authorities who arrived after his anonymous call concurred, and they buried her."

Max was glad Gandolph could speak for him. He didn't know whether it was strategy or pride on his part that he didn't want these political thugs to know his mind had been more damaged than his legs recently.

"Word is," Liam told Max, with a relishing smirk of his own, "that you bore the lass plenty of love when you first met her all those years ago. Off wi' her in the woodlands of Sir Thomas and Lady Dixon Park, communin' with nature, weren't you, when O'Toole's Pub was becoming beer-soaked toothpicks with a blood chaser?"

Max could wince convincingly at Liam's deliberately harsh words. He didn't remember Kathleen or details of their physical encounter, thank God, but he knew he'd been the virgin in that transaction, and probably unaware of that at the time. The idea of being intimate with such a damaged young woman struck him with double guilt now, though he suspected she'd lured him into it. He knew, from that "Great Unknown Encyclopedia of General Knowledge" still allowing him access, that abused children can become manipulative and even hyper-sexual, convinced that the entire world is a lie and everyone in it a hypocrite and out to prove that to themselves and everyone else.

"She was a beauty, but a notorious slut," Flanagan recalled, with nostalgia. "She'd sleep with anyone, even an American lad who didn't know which side of his pants zipped."

Max's left leg under the table was long enough and his hip and torso just strong enough to hook an ankle around the man's chair leg and jerk it out from under him. The pain was worth the gesture.

Flanagan's rosacea-red face sank under the table like a surprised sunset, as the other three men made fists on the hops-stained wood.

"Have your fun at my younger days' expense, but not at Kathleen's," Max said, his own fists white-knuckled. "We've just learned she was a Magdalen girl before she escaped."

"No lie, man?" Liam exclaimed. "Truth to tell, no wonder she was of a mind to use herself hard. She was the only woman then strong enough to push her way into our patriot game and play a real role."

Flanagan had pulled himself and his chair back to the table. "Peace, man. 'Tis a fact that except for you, she only slept with those who'd give us tip-offs or money. A bit jealous we were, you but a boy from America, and she gave it to you free."

"Free it was not," Max said. "My cousin died in that O'Toole's Pub blast that occurred while she was spending her pinch-penny favors with me."

"Ah, true." Liam nodded into his glass. "It *is* blood indeed that drives you. And guilt. That I understand, and respect. Wealthy and poor Irish Americans may have paid millions before the Northern Ireland Peace Agreement to buy us guns and gravy and information, but even the fiercest of them little remembered what it was to live in a land, your own land for centuries, where you and yours were despised and spat upon and your religion persecuted and your children denied education and civil treatment and every opportunity every day."

"My forebears immigrated to America," Max conceded, aware that his own immediate family was a lost memory to him. Perhaps his Irish heritage was why he'd fallen for a natural redhead like Temple Barr.

"That's just it!" Mulroney said. "Your forebears *emigrated*. Driven out of their own land by famine or force of some other kind, uneducated, unregarded, considered less than the sheep that graze the scant Irish leas."

"Which is amazing," Gandolph noted, "given how the Irish distinguish themselves abroad. Soldiers of fortune, law enforcement, politics, the literary and musical arts. Amazing how any downtrodden people or race always do distinguish themselves when out from under the tyrannical, biased boot heel. 'The world is mean and man uncouth.' I quote the late, great playwright, Berthold Brecht."

"A man of the people," Finn agreed, nodding.

"So tell us more of Kathleen O'Connor," Gandolph said. "We wondered if her dark personal history and agenda sometimes played against even the IRA."

"In what way?" Flanagan demanded.

"Max came to wonder, years later, if Kathleen didn't toy sadistically with him. Now, we think, perhaps with all her lovers.

The price of her body was his cousin's scattered corpse. Max concluded she must have known about that IRA pub bombing ahead of time and let Sean die."

"To torment the surviving lad?" Liam asked. "That would be . . . sick. If so, she wound up betraying our own daring freedom fighters, for we well know what your friend here did to locate the bombers and lead the British soldiers to them. We put a price on his head for more than a decade because of it. Don't think a one of us has forgotten that, as young and foolish an American as he was then and as busted up as he is now."

"I don't ask any quarter," Max said, "now, nor did I then. Patriots always overlook the death of innocents in their own just passion against injustice, though they commit the same sins. Sean and I, we came here to Ulster because we felt that same passion against injustice to our kind. You could have recruited us, instead of making an enemy of me."

"And a relentless enemy you became," Liam admitted. "The Agreement seems to have put a period to the 'Troubles' for good and all, or I wouldn't be talking to you two, but standing over your dead bodies. Yet you boys are turnin' my head around. You're saying Kathleen, our secret weapon, as dedicated as a silver bullet, *used* our secret plans to punish *you* somehow? Why, man?"

"She hated all men," Gandolph said. "And probably the clergy. Did you ever notice a taste for seducing priests?"

"She'd seduce a stump for the cause," Mulroney said, rolling his eyes, "except us boyos. Said she didn't want to stir dissension among us. We got not a bit of it, just the money from her 'adventures.' When the doings in Ulster simmered down, and the U.S. money slowed down even for the alternative IRA after nine/eleven, she was off to any Catholic country she could find to 'recruit' wealthy Irish émigrés her own way, on her back. She screwed her way across the U.S., of course, and Canada, Australia, Argentina, New Zealand, Mexico, South Africa, Brazil, even the Caribbean and Continental Europe."

Liam nodded. "She traveled constantly the last years after the settlement in ninety-eight. Always a faithful source of supply, no matter the mood of the moment."

"And then she disappeared," Max suggested.

"Spectacularly," Liam said. "She was talkin' about sending us a bloody fortune and even a shipment of smuggled assault weapons from Mexico. Had us all salivating. Then . . . the Peace Agreement happened, to the surprise of most of the world, including us."

"The most surprising thing," Max said, "is that the Agreement has worked."

"Nine/eleven did us in," Mulroney said, shaking his head. "Our cause was just, and our people had paid with their lives and souls and hearts over centuries of oppression, but that mass destruction of what would be a fair-size town here, of seeing the same New York City that had finally allowed our immigrants to thrive have its tallest buildings attacked from the top, the very sky —"

"It shook our souls," Flanagan allowed.

"The IRA listened to the widows," Finn said, "our own and others from all over the world."

Max nodded.

"That doesn't mean," came Liam's slow, soft voice, "that we're willin' to surrender what's ours. Guns, yes. Money . . . no. We have our widows-and-orphans fund, with plenty in need, and our own loyal boyos maimed or their minds frayed like denim at the knees."

"You want Kathleen's score," Max said.

Liam's pale eyes glinted. "Correct. You

don't be needin' to put any polish on it, as you see. That money was donated by our American kin. We need it for putting our people right here in Ulster."

"And you think we'd know its whereabouts?" Gandolph asked.

"I think if you don't, you'd know how to find it."

"The woman is dead!" Gandolph said. "My friend was almost killed."

"And why would that be?"

"Some avenging Irish soul from the past, perhaps?" Gandolph was now taking over negotiations.

Max realized they had played these roles before — one leading, one subsiding, always in tune, always partners. He watched the older man as Liam would see him: shrewd, a bargainer, a man with the confidence of unspoken but serious connections and faith in his partner.

Damn! Max thought. *I am a lucky man.*

And he wondered if he'd been as lucky in love recently, and his traitorous memory also had betrayed him there.

"You both know Las Vegas," Liam was saying. "We'd go there ourselves, but we're village boys, as lost there as those bedamned nine/eleven terrorists who wanted

451

a last girly show for all their hatred of the West."

"You're expecting my friend," Gandolph said, "to go back to where he was almost killed?"

Liam eyed Max. "He was 'almost killed' a lot of places and had the nerve to come back here, didn't he?"

"We know and honor loyalty," Flanagan put in. "It's kept us alive long enough to see peace. We just want what's ours."

"What do *you* want?" Liam asked.

"The whole truth about Kathleen O'Connor," Max said. "That woman dogged my life from boyhood on and created plenty of collateral damage."

"You lived to see her dead, man," Liam urged. "Let her go."

"People died because of her. I killed indirectly because of her. Truth is still truth," Max said, "and we haven't found all of it."

"Granted," Liam said. "We can help you find what you want, if you find, and deliver, what we want."

"How are we to know the money is for the community good, as you claim?" Max asked.

"We are all brothers of Erin," said Liam.

"Money is the root of all evil," Max

answered. "Neither my friend nor I need Kathleen's . . . dark dowry. If we find it, we could donate it to the organization of your choosing."

"And ask if we trust all the bureaucrats who run cities and countries any more than we trust you two."

"We'll be in Belfast a while longer," Gandolph said. "I'm sure we can negotiate further."

"And you have other contacts here willin' to lay out Kathleen's trail of broken hearts and blood money?" quiet Flanagan said, slamming a fist to the tabletop.

"Perhaps," Gandolph said. "You of all men know that negotiations are always open and situations change and men's motives and hearts with that." He stirred to get up, being older and more likely to telegraph his intentions.

Liam and his friends leaned tight across the table as the headman spoke. "You're not leavin' until you commit to a deal. We're alone here and outnumber you, a cripple and an old man who's not been out in the field for too many years."

Max stood, pushing the wooden table over on them as Gandolph drew two collapsible metal canes from his trench-coat pockets and snapped them to full length into stiffening steel whips.

By then Max had smashed two pint glasses on the table's downed edge and was holding them like jagged glass fists.

The pair backed to the door, an eye on the barkeep, wary behind his sleeve-polished wooden barrier. The reek of spilled beer steamed up from the damp wood like purified piss.

Max and Gandolph pushed open the heavy pub door with their backs and inhaled the night chill and mist on matching deep breaths.

"They let us go because they can find us anytime they want," Gandolph said, after a deep gulp of air.

"And we them." Max darted his eyes up to the lit-up pub name above. O'Flaherty's.

"It's good to have contacts on both sides of the law," Gandolph said. "Peace doesn't mean total harmony."

"We don't need Kathleen's blood money," Max agreed, "but we need to find out more about where it came from and where it is now. We know she was haunting our backyard recently. Damned if this little set-to hasn't exercised my memory as well as my legs. Don't tell me I'm going to have to go back to Vegas to track down the last bloody acts of Kitty the Cutter and look up that little redheaded spitfire you like so much."

"Oh, Max," Gandolph said, mopping his brow with a fine white linen handkerchief he pulled from a breast pocket. "You'll be the death of me yet."

"Meanwhile, let's get the hell back to our hotel," Max proposed.

"And pick up a Big Mac on the way."

"I hope you're referring to a firearm."

"Sounds like we'd have better luck at that back in Vegas, after all."

Chapter 41
Getting Their Irish Up

Blackie and Blackjack (people are so unimaginative in coining street monikers for strays, but that is how I was named, back in my Palo Alto days) are running alongside me now that we are in the tunnel, aka Chunnel.

"This is a terrific shortcut, Mr. Midnight," Blackie tells me. (I have instructed them in proper protocol and respect.)

"I love all these wall-to-wall billboards," Blackjack adds. "I love to watch people-fights."

"The urge is mutual among species, unfortunately," I say. "But these images are from motion pictures. They form what is called a diorama, and when those tracks are filled with automated vintage cars, the place will be Slaughter City for ignorant cross-traffic. Keep your eyes peeled for rats and cut the chatter. We need to save our wind for a long subterranean journey with a pyramid climb at the end of it."

"Wow, Mr. Midnight," Blackie says. "You sure

know your way around exotic Las Vegas nightlife."

What can you do with a pair of wet-behind-the-ears two-year-olds? Granted, the ear wetness is from grooming, which is commendable, but I could use some second wind here.

"Say, what is that big silver metal door?" Blackjack asks, as I skid to a stop.

"Our path to enlightenment, boys, and reunion with our clan. It is called a 'safe,' but it was not very for the murder victim found inside recently. See that rat hole to the side of it? Dive in there."

"Huh? We are not hungry."

"Look, Blackie, I do not care about the state of your stomach. You should not have been duping the Crystal Phoenix chef and gorging yourselves in Midnight Louise's place. Now I want you two to shimmy-shimmy inside there until you get behind the safe. The rat-size tunnel widens there to boxer size."

"*Ooh,* people-fighting," Blackjack says, sparring with his front mitts.

"I meant dog-breed boxer-size. Just shut up and move."

Both are still street-skinny, which I cannot say for myself. I hope they will push the passage a wee bit wider for me when I bring up their rears. And do not make any smart remarks bringing up my rear. I am not in the mood.

Anyway, I finally writhe my way through, leaving too many excellent side hairs along the trail. Blackjack and Blackie are waiting in the dim light of the tunnel beyond, their eyes gleaming the same eerie green I am told mine do when viewed at the right angle in the dark. I instruct them further.

"We need to be quiet once we reach the big warehouse under the Neon Nightmare. You will hear much thumping and caterwauling and chaos from the nightclub. Ignore it. We will walk secret ways known only to Bast and me."

The luminescent greens of their eyes grow rounder. That is what I need, cowed under-lings. Pity there are no humans I can call on to do the job, but this requires the small and wiry underground fighter.

Really, this mission is getting to be like herding people. Blackie and Blackjack are ever ready to go off task, speculating about the reason for the tunnel, and then *ooh*ing and *aah*ing like tourists when we hit the huge storeroom I anticipated would underlie the Neon Nightmare.

I am not about to waste time explaining a giant neon-sign graveyard to the uninitiated.

"Start climbing, and make it snappy," I order. "This is not a kit playground. This abandoned jungle gym for giants could be dangerous."

Above us, the ceiling that is the Neon Nightmare floor vibrates with the thump of deep bass speakers. Occasional flashes of the nightclub fireworks penetrate the depths.

My two intrepid assistants run under a giant 3-D high heel to hide.

"Thunder and lightning, Mr. Midnight," Blackjack whines. "Ma Barker would never let us out in it."

"Ma Barker is not here, and I am. Would I hide behind a human woman's footwear, no matter how large, like even Miss Lieutenant Molina size? I would not! Now get out and get moving. I need every set of shivs and fangs available."

"Ma Barker runs our clowder, Mr. Midnight," Blackie says. "The rules are rules, and we obey, or we get a home fixing, and I do not mean a nice hot meal."

"Great. I have robo-mice for muscle. I guess I will have to do some home fixing myself."

"*Nooo,* Mr. Midnight!"

I rush the arch where they are cowering and suddenly notice that the two sets of green-eye reflections I am rushing are now . . . three. And the third set has a half-moon on one side.

"Ma Barker *is* here," a raspy voice announces. "B and B, get yourselves back in the open."

"Where are the rest of the troops?" I ask. "My partner is missing."

"Which one?" Ma asks.

"Miss Louise. I have not seen her since we did some reconnaissance here a couple days ago."

"Not good. Where is Three O'Clock?"

"Uh . . ." I cannot betray my threatened gender. "He is guarding the tunnel's other exit at the Crystal Phoenix."

I fix Blackie and Blackjack with a fierce glare and a significant mitt gesture. They gulp and keep their mouths shut.

"What about your human partner?"

"She was headed here, bearing arms."

"They all have arms. We all have legs. What of it?"

"No, Ma. *Firearms.* Well, just one."

"Your red-cream is carrying . . . carrying something besides that giant tote bag of hers? Not good."

"Have you found the secret hallways to the big club room at the top of the pyramid?" I ask.

"We were guarding the exit of this tunnel on the main floor and nearly putting our hearing out," she answers.

"Up above is where I last saw Miss Midnight Louise. That is where the suspect club called the Synth meets."

"Then that is where we will go," Ma says. "Onward Blackie and Blackjack, to join Blackbeard and Blacktop, then it is up, up, and away to the roof on this crazy pointy-topped joint."

Ma Barker as Santa Claus? Please. But she does know how to crack the whip.

So we are soon to be six strong and storming Synth headquarters. I scamper along, newly invigorated. Knowing the headstrong ways of Miss Midnight Louise, I am sure that she is lurking somewhere ahead.

CHAPTER 42
ARMED AND DEAD

Temple felt she had walked onstage in the middle of a play.

Probably the climax of a murder mystery.

She had entered the room between two huge bookcases, putting her in a shadowed niche, and the lights were dramatically dim.

So she kept as still as if in a childhood game of "statue" and took in the scene.

Five people in profile were in the midst of an intense scene, three arrayed on or near the room's furnishings, two in front of a wood-paneled wall that had obviously also concealed a door.

Of the two seated women, one obviously was the femme fatale, the usual slinky brunette. Why were blondes and brunettes always slinky and redheads just . . . cute? The other woman was a chubby Electra Lark caftan-wearing type: electric and eclectic and eccentric in dress. Where Electra spray-dyed her halo of white hair

462

rainbow colors, this lady wore a large paisley turban on her perm-frizzed gray hair.

A Max-tall man about twenty-five years older than he, wearing a chocolate brown suit and rust silk T-shirt, stood by a gas-log-equipped fireplace, the leaping flames making his face a craggy mask.

And then there were the two Darth Vader types in floor-length black cloaks and Cloaked Conjuror full-head masks, holding sleek handguns on the three apparent club residents. Double Darths. Double firepower. How . . . not nice.

Temple's right hand still clutched the top of her purse. In only a few quick motions she could open it and draw the gun. So few seconds and yet far too many; she saw that now. Any movement on her part threatened to uncork the physical violence that was still frozen into verbal exchanges.

Unless . . . she started her moves now and nobody noticed, which seemed most unlikely too. Instead of being armed and dangerous, she could end up being found armed and dead.

Both parties were staring exclusively at each other, the way lovers do. Or haters.

"We know nothing about the money stash," the older woman in the ridiculous turban said wearily. "Cosimo handled all that. He was the main contact with . . . you people abroad."

"If they are the *real* contacts," the tall man said. "Can your gazing crystal tell us that, Czarina?"

The other woman present ignored him to taunt the intruders in a calm contralto. "Did you start by murdering the Phantom Mage?" she asked the masked pair. "Then Cosimo? Now us? That's the way to get your damn stockpile of money, all right."

"The money is not ours," one bizarre, androgynous voice answered. "It was held in trust for our just cause."

" 'Just cause,' " the standing man echoed. "That's a laugh. You needed our magical bag of tricks for the most astounding multi-casino heist in Las Vegas history, and were prepared to pay us 'royally' for preparing and carrying it off on your command."

One of the gun barrels lifted.

"Hal, Carmen," Czarina cautioned in a low, trembling tone, "we're in no position to argue."

"We're in every position to argue — for our lives," said the fiery brunette named, of all things, Carmen. No wonder C. R. Molina hated her given name. "We know nothing of where the funds were kept, or in what form. Cosimo Sparks was our leader, our

464

emissary to you people. And you killed him."

"We did not," the voice of the other figure in Darth drag answered. "That doesn't mean we aren't capable of killing you. Perhaps one of you wanted all the funds — they'd been just lying there for so many years — and killed Sparks in an attempt to get them."

"And then," the other Darth's twin voice suggested, "you moved everything. The cash, the bearer bonds, the guns, and explosives."

"There were explosives?" the brunette asked, astounded.

"Of course, Carmen," Hal answered her. "The actual robbers would have needed them for the heist, and we would have needed them as a distraction to turn the Strip into a bigger sound and light show than the Fremont Street Downtown Experience while the robberies were going down."

" 'Lying there for so many years'?" Czarina asked. "That's absurd. The Synth has been active for only the last three, when Cosimo recruited us and a —"

"There are more members than you?" one cloaked figure demanded.

"None that knew of the scheme or the stockpile of money and weapons," Hal answered. "Only some disgruntled minor prestidigitators we convinced to be part of our 'mystical, magical' alliance, so we'd have 'extras' to deploy for our Grand Strip Illusion, which would be the talk of the nation and the world. We are the Synth, the synthesis that old alchemists dreamed of, the creators of a method to turn base material into gold. Only we were after taking a golden parachute out of the demeaned profession that magic has become in these days of media manipulation."

Temple noticed that the paired gun barrels had lowered slightly. The masked invaders were surprised by what they were hearing. Could the Synth talk itself out of such a double-barreled threat?

"What of this Phantom Mage you mention?" one Darth asked.

Carmen stood, also sensing their confusion. "Only our most prized and recent recruit. He was a marvel. He could have produced the Strip-long illusion you demanded. He maintained his anonymity to the last, but *I* know he was Max Kinsella, playing a double game as himself and this lowly nightclub magician named the Phantom Mage."

Temple felt a gentle tap on her calf and glanced down without moving her head.

Her eyes finally had adapted to the room's dimness. She saw a long black furry tail.

Louie!

No. This was a longer-haired, plumed tail. Midnight Louise had guided her here.

Thanks a lot, sister, Temple thought. *Maybe you can distract them while I claw out my gun.*

"Who the bloody hell is Max Kinsella, and why would anyone want to kill him?" one transgendered voice demanded.

The three Synth members seemed struck dumb, as Temple was. Come on; Max had starred in a major Strip hotel show, billboards and all! True, he'd performed sans surname, but the Mystifying Max had been huge until he had first disappeared two years earlier. Where had these Vader creeps been, on the dark side of the moon?

"Did one of you, perhaps?" the other Vader twin asked.

The entire scene was getting so absurd and Alice-in-Wonderland-ish that Temple was forgetting to be afraid and was getting angry instead. Which was dangerous, but also liberating.

She waited for the Synth's answer — her presence "unbeknownst," as some put it, to the others, making her the third armed but so far invisible person on the premises.

"We don't know," Hal said. "As we told

you, Cosimo was our maestro, our go-between. He's the one who would tell us what to do, when we were called upon. Meanwhile, I guess we felt useful, part of a pending, monstrously amazing illusion, our parting shot to the world that had once applauded us. We were all in the same sorry boat — passé and poor. Cosimo waved his magic words, and we believed we'd get the best revenge — living well. We trusted him."

"And he betrayed *us!*" the pair of Darths said as one.

"I doubt it," Czarina said.

"You saw it in your crystal ball?" a Vader jeered.

"No. I just knew Cosimo. We trusted him because he was a straight shooter." She regarded the leveled weapons. "Oh."

"Perhaps Cosimo was robbed," Hal said. "If you knew of this . . . hidden treasure, wouldn't others of your . . . type also possibly know of it?"

Silence prevailed. Temple was watching a true stalemate. The intruders wanted information, not blood. The Synth as represented here certainly was nothing sinister, although that Ophiuchus and alchemy mumbo jumbo would appeal to anyone with an occult mind, like those drawn to magic. Someone had been playing both ends against the middle, and it was getting obvious to everyone in the room that they all might be the "ends."

Standing there, Temple let the key phrases stamped on her mental tape recorder replay: money and guns and explosives, oh my . . . stockpiled for years, oh my . . . all-time major Vegas heist, oh my . . . a team of magicians providing a distraction . . . just cause . . . bloody hell.

She remembered that some 2001 Al-Qaeda surveillance tapes of Vegas casinos, including New York, New York, with its faux-Manhattan exterior skyline, had turned up from foreign sources years later, and that Mohamed Atta and his 9/11 suicide crew had visited Vegas before the world-devastating plan was put into motion on the other coast. . . .

Terrorists were drawn to Vegas as a target . . . of destruction or bankrolling. Civic powers were always underplaying, perhaps even concealing, that fact to keep the tourists coming.

And . . . years ago, before 9/11 in 2001, before the previous bombing at the Twin Towers in Manhattan, another terrorist group had issued a "dead or alive" Western-version death fatwa on a teenage Max Kinsella for his youthful antiterrorist activities.

The Irish Republican Army, aka the IRA. Temple knew Max's thriller-novel past, but had always considered it a cul-de-sac of personal ancient history. Not a current concern.

The connections jumped synapses in her brain, jumbling around, not adding up to a scenario she could link into anything sensible.

The Synth members were having trouble too.

"Look," said Hal, striding forward, "you've —"

Carry a gun in your purse, and you're depending on crooks to give you time to react.

Hold two guns in your hand and —

The chilling, preliminary double clicks seemed simultaneous with a booming, double-rapping sound. The burnt whiff of firearms discharge in the small room was overwhelming. Temple's hands clapped over her ears before her conscious mind could kick her in the damn-fool shins.

The motion brought every eye to her . . . and then came the sickening sound of clicks from all sides, triggers being pulled to release a hail of . . . not bullets, but —

— hidden doors all around the room springing open at once! A swarm of black

470

screaming figures leaped through them like a circus act of black panthers — a riot of cats hurtling onto Darth Vader cloaks and climbing them, heavy fabric rending with audible groans from the weight of three swarming feline bodies to a cloak. The wearers bent at the knees, screaming as leaping cats clung with all fours to their forearms, while the third attached to each climbed their heads from behind to start clawing the sinister face masks, all the while screaming like, well, tomcats fighting, a sound echoed in double strength by their startled victims.

By then, both visitors' guns had hit the carpeted floor with a *thunk, thunk.*

Apparently the Darth Vaders were all scary masks and no bloodlust. They'd fired warning shots into the floor. Now they were cursing and backing away in tattered cloaks through two of the open doors, pursued by . . . cannibal cats.

Temple had no intention of following the fading Vader invaders, even if they were disarmed. The Neon Nightmare offered too many escape routes. Carmen was eyeing the fallen semiautomatics like a hungry tiger, but the other two were staring at Temple. Temple heard a soft click behind her and felt an opening door bump her rear. She knew it was time for a dramatically astounding exit.

"Sorry," she told the literally shell-shocked Synth members. "I was looking for the restroom. This place is a maze. Anyone ever tell you that? And you have a very bad infestation of really big rats. I won't be coming back."

By then the attack cats had also ebbed into the "maze." Temple backed through the door Midnight Louise had opened, leaving the Synth still immobile and herself in the slightly lambent dark. Which was lit by an honor guard of vivid green irises pointing the way to a presumably vermin-free path downward and out to the main nightclub floor.

She took it and would ask questions later.

At least she knew for sure that Max's magic fingerprints had been all over this place. If he had also been the Phantom Mage, the odds he had died were fifty-fifty. What Rafi had described had sounded too traumatic for any sane person to set up for himself. On the other hand, a master illusionist like Max would want any feigned final exit to look impossible to survive.

CHAPTER 43
MURDER IN 3-D

When Temple awoke the next morning, she felt as if she'd been in that old Memorex tape commercial. "Was it real? Or was it Memorex?"

Her memory felt hung over. The Synth showdown she'd witnessed at Neon Nightmare unwound in her mind like a dream, even though a nightmare scenario involving disgruntled but corny stage magicians, the disbanded IRA, and Max Kinsella was starting to add up to something big.

Her nightclubbing clothes were strewn around the room — not like her — and she was curled into a ball because Midnight Louie's hot, hairy body was plastered against her legs. Surely her eyes had been playing tricks on her in that creepy, dark lightning-struck nightclub with its network of secret passages.

She couldn't have really seen Midnight Louie cloned to the ninth power and in frantic attack mode, or any Darth Vader clones either.

Temple decided to reach out to the real world. First she checked her iPhone for messages.

Matt had called and left a long, sweet, sexy missing-you message that had her kicking Louie out of bed to run to her computer to download it for future replay on rainy days and the next time Matt was out of town.

Then . . . darn! Nicky Fontana's message wanted her to attend a fancy-dress gala command performance at Gangsters at 4:00 P.M. Temple checked the bedside clock and groaned. Eleven A.M. already!

She quick-dialed Nicky to question the wisdom of plowing ahead with the Chunnel of Crime and got her marching orders instead. Yes, the police were totally okay with them "test-driving" the vintage cars rail-run. The vault and environs had been released as a crime scene and the Olympic games could be held there, as far as Detective Ferraro was concerned.

No, there was no progress on the Sparks killing, but the police seemed to find everything involving the Glory Hole Gang, "Concrete Boots Benson," the Chunnel of Crime, and cats too outré to deal with. Just don her glad rags and get over to Gangsters for the dry run.

Temple, exhausted and confused after her intense night before at the Neon Nightmare, knew a PR person must be on call around the clock, especially in Las Vegas. Holding a "dry run" near a bar and restaurant named Speakeasy's was a contradiction in terms that tickled her funny bone, and she much needed something distracting at the moment. Besides, Nicky was her boss. He was so jazzed about introducing the installed 3-D Chunnel run. Previewing an ambitious new Las Vegas attraction was an invitation Temple couldn't refuse, even if several pesky mysteries simmered behind the scenes.

She decided to consider touring the Chunnel a welcome break in her investigation, especially now that she'd penetrated the Neon Nightmare–Synth connection. She replayed Matt's message, showered, microwaved an individual pizza and gulped it down, raided her closets for a slinky, black-crepe thirties tea gown and some kicky heels, replayed Matt's tape, and by three thirty was riding the cocktail carousel down to Gangsters' lower and most lurid depths.

The Chunnel of Crime was fully gussied up for company now. It resembled a subway tunnel without any stops except beginning and end. Black-and-white gangster movie stills wallpapered the tunnel sides. These bigger-than-life scenes of movie mayhem would appear almost animated as the limos glided past on tracks. The blowups also served as background "sets" for the 3-D filmed scenes of vintage movies Santiago had projected onto both sides of the tunnel.

For now, only one side was activated, so the trial-run spectators could stand against the clear opposite wall to watch the rail-adapted vintage cars glide by like the showboats of style they were.

Some were elegant conveyers of moneyed mobster kingpins; others looked like they'd been grabbed on the run outside a just-robbed bank. Almost all of them were shiny basic black with slit-windowed and cavelike passenger compartments. Until now, Temple had never realized that the automobile designs of early decades emulated the closed, private-to-the-point-of-paranoia urban carriages of the nineteenth century. People today were used to full exposure, more than ever, with every cell-phone camera a potential online media nexus.

The cars' exuberantly accessorized exteriors were a different matter.

Even the lowlier cars sported bubble fenders and running boards. They had Bugsy-eyed headlights sitting up high and lonesome above twin chrome horns and fog lamps, alongside dazzlingly large vertical chrome grills, almost like horizontal harps. Some big-city mobstermobiles screamed "sleek and expensive." Others hoarsely declared "Clyde Barrow's hijacked budget back-road Fords." Some were pricey Packards and Buicks, according to Nicky, who introduced the lineup like a proud father. One was a gorgeous dark purple Hudson Terraplane.

"Did they have stretch limos in the gangster days?" Temple dared to ask.

"Since before the real Depression, little girl," Macho Mario replied. "I've ridden in a beauty like that Hudson, only it was painted a rich cream color. That car was class. Black is for funerals."

"Cream is too visible for a getaway car," Nicky pointed out.

"Since nineteen twenty-eight," Eduardo Fontana said, bending down to answer Temple's question. "That's when the stretch limos first came in. There are plenty of the oldies still out there. We picked up some for this light-rail gig. Our own street chauffeuring business relies on creating new lavishly customized stretches with a Vegas theme."

Temple nodded, having seen the mind-blowing old and new selection in the car service's parking lot.

"These smooth rides-on-rails are perfecto," Santiago proclaimed, his white tropical suit blossoming into the Fontana's dark pin-striped midst so he looked uncannily like a ghost of the brothers' usual selves. "In South America, older American cars are treasured."

Temple swallowed her natural comment. She could picture Santiago being driven around Vegas in a white stretch 1961 Cadillac limo with chrome fins from here to eternity to match his ego.

Meanwhile, Macho Mario was playing the tribe elder and escorting the renovation's main forces into various cars.

"Here." He gestured the five booted and bejeaned former miners, who looked the most at home in a dark tunnel, into a six-seated thirties Ford. "You Desert Rat Pack boys can ride in the Longhorn-mobile." He gestured to the pair of chromed steer horns riding the car's narrow hood.

Nicky joined the diminishing knot of guys surrounding Temple. She was surprised the Fontana brothers and Glory Hole gang had gathered around her and Santiago, when not thirty feet away, Van von Rhine stood with her statuesque blonde classmate from

Swiss finishing school, Revienne. *Two sleek blondes should attract more men,* Temple thought, *especially the charm-spreading Santiago.*

Hey, Temple thought again, *Van had snagged the first Fontana brother to ever wed.* Opposites do attract, and Revienne seemed born to snag another bachelor Fontana brother. Then Temple would have a fourth bridesmaid for her so-far-fictional wedding party. Better to dwell in the future than the confusing past.

She cocked her head and cast an inquiring glance from Eduardo to Revienne to Eduardo. "I'm surprised you and your bros aren't making a beeline to that foreign honey."

His head shook almost imperceptibly. "She's taken."

"How do you know?"

"That's my job. I work in a 'people' business."

"She says she's single."

Eduardo discreetly elbowed his nearest brother, temporarily known as Ralphie the Wrench, in the, ah, elbow. When Ralph looked his way, Eduardo shifted his eyes sideways to Revienne.

"Nice icing, but no go, bro," Ralph murmured, smartly shooting his suit sleeves to

479

reveal the onyx links on his baby's-blush-pink shirt cuffs.

Fontana Brothers were so cool.

If guys unafraid to wear pink were wary of Revienne, it explained why Temple found her troubling. It seemed the woman was watching them all, Temple especially. Temple must be imagining that, because she was not the type people took seriously enough to watch. Which was their mistake. So maybe Revienne was not just foxy looking, but foxy sharp.

Temple glanced back as the last Glory Hole Gang scuffed boot heel disappeared into the vintage Ford. They'd never had the money their old associates, Boots and Jersey Joe, had cheated them of, but then they were here, still kicking and cooking; Boots was just a bizarre museum piece, and Jersey Joe, the ghost of a sad, reclusive bankrupt.

Temple's heart warmed to see the Glory Hole Gang together again, jazzed on a new enterprise at their ages, a recognized historic part of the Vegas scene, worthy of a prime seat at the pre-pre-pre-opening run of this groundbreaking new attraction.

Nothing really got lost. Even Boots had experienced his new day in the sun, if a bit too literally. And, thanks to his supposedly hidden loot, Jersey Joe Jackson had remained a force around the Crystal Phoenix long past his death.

Heck, with all the dead actors resurrected for these still and moving media effects, this could be considered a zombie jamboree. The party certainly was of mixed company.

Lined up along the dark place where dark floor met dark fauxstone tunnel wall was Midnight Louie . . . and Midnight Louie and . . . Midnight Louie and . . . Midnight Louise with the waggly, fluffy tail.

Maybe Temple's suddenly misty vision was turning Louie into multiple images. She wasn't surprised to see him. He often decided to go everywhere that Temple went, and his coat was black as coal. His last command performance with the Cat Pack had been stellar.

She was sure Macho Mario wouldn't have a free car to usher Louie and Louise and pals into. Three O'Clock Louie she recognized on second thought. He had finally moved his center of operations from Lake Mead to the Glory Hole Gang's Gangsters suite and the Speakeasy bar and restaurant.

She recognized from the Neon Nightmare the cat among them with the half-masted eyelid. Poor thing. She'd take it home to the Circle Ritz if she could catch it . . . which didn't look likely from the battle-scarred condition of that eyelid.

"Okay," Macho Mario announced behind her, addressing his nephews, "boys, you climb into the stretch nineteen thirty-seven purple Hudson Terraplane."

"There are eight of us," Julio's deep voice objected.

"Bend your knees and scrunch. Besides, purple complements that girly pink in your pinstripes."

"Ah, Uncle Mario," they moaned in chorus.

"Guys are secure enough these days to wear pink and carry mother-of-pearl pistols," Ralph said.

"Only on Broadway, boys, only on Broadway. Now, scat!"

Temple turned to watch. It was like loading up a clown car, all those tall, lean, butch but modern and sensitive Fontana brothers, crouching to enter the Tom Wolfe–extravagant Chrome-Covered Purple-Flake Streamline Baby, baby!

Revienne should be so lucky to have such a ride.

Temple took a step forward to get into the next free car, a totally cute black thirties number that was tiny and low-slug but all bubble curves, when Nicky's hand on her arm held her back.

"Getting whisked away by your own publicity plans?" he asked softly. "Let Van and Revienne ride in that petite mobster motor."

"But . . ." Temple watched two smooth blonde heads duck inside and sighed. "Oh. Yeah. It suits them."

She had to admit, blondes seemed made for black gangster cars. Maybe she could hitch a ride on a Mickey Rooney jalopy with a rumble seat.

"We're the ones who orchestrated this trip down memory lane," Nicky went on. "You, me, Santiago, and, of course, Uncle Mario as a rep of the old days, will bring up the rear."

"Right," Temple agreed, no longer carried away by her own hype.

Count on Nicky to save the best for last. The next car was to drool over. It was the always-elegant-and-deadly black, of course, with whitewalls and a running board and dainty, classy, cuff-link-size touches of chrome here and there and everywhere, like diamond jewelry on wet black velvet.

Nicky gestured Santiago in first, so Temple had less far to crawl in. Santiago doubled over, but his wool-silk suit blend didn't wrinkle, just as his face never did. So mahogany rich and dark and *sooo* smooth.

Nicky bent to take the opposite seat, his uncle easily managing to follow. Macho Mario had inherited the Fontana empire when short and stocky genes ran in the family, before the next generation got their cod-liver oil and vitamins and added a few inches to better show off designer Italian tailoring.

Temple bent only slightly to walk into the commodiously high seating area. Before Nicky could draw the door shut after her, a wave of Cat Pack oozed inside to circle Temple's bare ankles — and help show off her black-satin forties-style strappy platform heels, which matched the car with their rhinestone-buckled ankle straps.

She giggled.

The Cat Pack tickled.

"Well," said Macho Mario, eyeing the four black cats. "Some people think these things are unlucky, but I say, at least we've got personal protection against those dirty rats we saw down in the tunnel at the empty Jersey Joe Jackson vault. I always said Jersey Joe was all hotel and no capital. And his Action Attraction never got tourist traction. This will be the first time the old fool made money in Vegas, instead of hiding it."

Santiago seemed uneasy about the foot-level feline honor guard. He shook out his pale, exquisitely flared boot-cut pants legs and muttered, "Black cat hairs," with a shudder. "Not unlucky, only tasteless."

He moved to edge away from his window seat, but Nicky put a hand on his arm.

"Better stay put. We're not using seat belts yet. No time to install them in these vintage honeys before the trial run. Hang on, we're moving!"

The cars were indeed starting up, but it was a smooth, *whoosh* sort of thing, no "road feel" that Temple could discern.

Oh, wow. The ride was so smooth and creamy, while the film images projected on the static poster images on the tunnel walls created this jagged, wild, video-game double-action scene that was instantly adrenaline pumping and absolutely hypnotizing.

Santiago might be a prima donna pain, but his media work was . . . magic!

Temple leaned her head closer to his to see out the dark-tinted side window, mentally dodging bullets and tough talk, looking Edward G. Robinson in the eye as he aimed a big pistol right at her, and then a bullet sound whizzed by in an echo of harmless but heart-rate-upping *rat-a-tat-tatting*. She'd only been so sound-surrounded at a Cirque du Soleil show, when massive timpani drums had everyone's seat bottoms and pulses throbbing into breath-catching heart-attack mode.

Her pulse was leaping now, but in a good way, a live-entertainment high. She was feeling breathlessly alive, as if they were all escaping the past and daily life and death. What a pseudorush.

Then the tinted window she was craning past Santiago's sharp, sun-baked profile to see through, viewing the visual wonders, turned 3-D. The scene morphed. She was staring into a face hanging in space outside the tinted car window, a face that was a combo of the Joker's twisted clown visage from *Batman* and the talking Magic Mirror from *Snow White*. Its features, almost Silly Putty human, seemed totally real. They moved in their own space and plane, and reassembled into . . . Jersey Joe Jackson's.

Temple was amazed Santiago had reached that far back into local history. Jersey Joe's name was known, but you'd only see his photographed face on Internet sites, if you bothered. As she had.

Now a voice whispered, inside the car interior, right next to them all.

"Welcome to my 'Chunnel of Hidden Treasure.' If you come to rob me you will find only empty vaults and busted dreams, but if you come to enjoy the ride, you'll get more than you bargained for. . . ."

At that, the facial image dissolved into a younger, plumper visage, a face suspended over a formal winged collar and tie. It reminded Temple of some slot machines that featured a magician's face and disembodied white gloves laying out the video poker cards . . . and now here came the gloves, protruding their fingers into the actual passenger compartment. *Oooh, spooky!*

Only the cards it laid out were tarot cards.

"The magician, oh my," the face said, in stagy tones, white gloves flaunting the card in question.

It was amazing how the bones of the face pushed through the window glass, as if it were only a cellophane cerement. Temple cringed back as an actual tarot card flipped into the limo compartment. Louie reached out a clawed forefoot and snapped it down to the carpet, anchoring it with a sharp nail.

She stared at Santiago, wondering. Had he *used* this multimedia display to program something personal?

The echoing voice filled the car interior.

"Magic never dies," it pronounced. "Am I mere bones in a morgue or a disembodied voice on a manipulated movie screen? Does it matter? I live, I speak, I watch, I intrude. I am the ghost in the machine. I live to avenge untimely deaths. Murders. I take vengeance."

Temple jerked back, surprised.

What a lifelike effect. What a gruesome segment. Maybe too scary for the public . . . She'd have to mention that to Nicky and Van. *Whoa!* She had goose bumps, though. Super effective.

Oops, Temple thought. *My lord, it resembles an actual, animated death masque. Not exactly promotable.* Temple was betting the wax sculptor who'd created the Boots concrete memorial had accomplished the model for this filmed resurrection.

"Where is the money?" the eerie voice intoned from the 3-D death masque. "Follow the money. It was in the vault. Then I ended up there, dead. Stabbed."

Temple knew by the prickling of her thumbs that something wicked this way comes. . . .

Actually it was by the prickling in her panty hose, had she been wearing any. She could feel the cat hair around her calves flaring and prickling instead of tickling.

And cat claws in three-four time, kneading warning into the unseen black carpet on the car's floor.

She had to admit she hadn't expected this demo ride to be so . . . ghoulish, so in your face.

So . . . like from a major historical theatrical masterpiece, like *Hamlet.*

"The play's the thing," to prick "the conscience of the King." The king . . . of chutzpah?

"This is absurd," Santiago objected. "This part is not of my creation. This is a cheap fright show. I demand you restore my immortal and elegant Rat Pack figures — Sinatra, Dean Martin, Sammy Davis Jr. They had charisma, talent, a deathless magic."

"Like Cosimo Sparks?" Nicky asked. "He was a stage magician once, still dressed like a magician of the old school, in white tie and tails. Was it hard to stab him through that starched shirt?"

"I? Santiago?" His chiseled features tightened with dismay instead of warming with rage. "How dare you! I am internationally renowned, as you well know. I am not some cheap . . . gangster, stabbing someone with a . . . shiv."

Midnight Louie leaped up between Temple and Santiago and issued a low rumbling growl, the likes of which she had never heard from him. It gave her chills and forced Santiago cringing into the corner of the car. Louie was a big cat, and every black hair was puffed out like hackles as he stared at Santiago, until the man blinked and looked away.

"Get that wildcat away from me," Santiago snarled in turn, his head turned into the car window as if about to kiss the now-frozen grotesque face of Cosimo Sparks.

"We'll get you away," Macho Mario assured him, "for a lot of years in prison."

Midnight Louie leaped onto Temple's lap, so she tumbled over sideways, just as Nicky and Macho Mario pulled major iron from their shoulder holsters. Like guns. Like big guns. Like they were ready to use them for real.

Santiago tried to lurch somewhere, his hips slamming Temple's back into the hard leather seat, his hands meshing with the taunting 3-D face in the car window.

He'd worked this audiovisual magic. He knew it was an illusion, a high-tech, amazing, and breathtaking illusion — didn't he? Magicians like Max and Cosimo Sparks knew illusion from reality. Santiago, mystic architect, did not seem to know.

His hands crashed through thick tinted glass as they sought to touch, to stop, to strangle the dead man's image, spraying blood and sharp shards, some maybe of bone.

Temple cringed against the seat back as the whole Cat Pack clan joined Louie in surrounding her with a moat of fang and claw, and she felt boas of black cat fur wreathing her torso.

And lots of sharp claws braced on her — *ow!* — thighs.

Macho Mario and Nicky grabbed Santiago and pulled him onto the opposite seat, stuffed immobile between them and two gun barrels.

The window image had vanished. Only the faces on the graphic tunnel walls flashed past, and then the steel vault, all impressive metal facade and empty significance.

"That's the wrong vault," Santiago shouted. "That vault is a substitute. It's empty. It's not supposed to be empty."

"Nor are you," Nicky said, producing handcuffs from his jacket side pocket and wrapping Santiago's back-pinned wrists as Uncle Mario kept the gun at the man's chest. "You're just another empty suit, Santiago, running a scam to feed your greed. And we Fontanas hold the key to your past and your future. *Arriba!*"

"Thanks for taking us for a 'ride,' " Macho Mario chortled, holstering his revolver once the man was manacled. "Brings back the bad old days in the most delightful way. Unfortunately, modern times are not in favor of 'offing' bad apples on the spot. We have Detective Ferraro and other officers of the law waiting at the other end to take you into custody for killing Cosimo Sparks. Thanks for the really thrilling ride."

Scowling and handcuffed, a silent Santiago remained bracketed by the Fontana family while the car rushed past the effects he'd created.

Temple, upright again, with four cats for seatmates, leaned across to whisper into Macho Mario Fontana's ear.

"I'm surprised you'd let a girl go along for the action and danger."

"Ah, Nicky told me you'd get more violent if we didn't than if we did," Macho Mario whispered back. "The detective did whisk Van and her long-stemmed girlfriend out of harm's way."

"Santiago could have been armed," she admitted, leaning back to her side of the car.

"Only by his massive ego," Nicky put in. "He thought he was home free, and also free to hunt a second vault's cache to his heart's content."

"And, besides," Macho Mario said, reaching inside his jacket, which made the haughty Santiago flinch, "I have a little something —"

Temple pulled her feet in tight as the black boa gathered close to her and emitted a ganglike growl.

"Not to worry, little lady and little kitty cats." Macho Mario extended a long cream envelope to Temple. "Here's a gift certificate for a big little shopping spree at Gangsters Moll Mall for any damage our ride here might have done to your rolled-down hose."

He managed to sneak in a pat on her bare knee as she took the envelope. His thick, still-jet-black eyebrows rose. Macho Mario hadn't realized hose was passé for modern, comfort-driven women.

"Uh, sorry for ruffling your . . . fur, Miss Barr," he said, hastily reclaiming his hand before any of the four cats could snap it off, and sending Nicky an apologetic look.

Macho Mario Fontana might be old mob, but he had no idea who possessed the important fur not to ruffle in this gangster car, Temple thought, looking down and smiling on a constellation of green, and one set of gold, cats'-eyes.

That would be Midnight Louie and the latest hot new gang in town, the Cat Pack.

Chapter 44
On Thin Ice

After uniformed officers had hauled away the urbane and protesting Santiago, who claimed he had lawyers on three continents and would use them to sue everyone in Vegas involved in this travesty, Detective Ferraro asked "the principals" to remain behind, while the Glory Hole Gang and the Fontana brothers — the elegant Revienne escorted in their midst — took the trio of Chunnel elevators up to the exit on the Crystal Phoenix's landscaped grounds.

Nicky and Van and Temple and Uncle Mario had no such luck losing their accompanying four cats, who ignored police wishes and stuck around, sometimes quite literally. Midnight Louie and Louise shadowed Temple and Van, while Three O'Clock glued himself to Nicky's pant leg. Uncle Mario had somehow ended up with Ma Barker at his feet, favoring him with frequent upward but off-eyed glances that were either admiring or murderous.

"I hope you enjoyed your *Columbo* moment, Mr. Fontana," Ferraro began.

"Of course," Macho Mario beamed. "It was a pleasure to nail that phony."

"I meant Mr. *Nick* Fontana," Ferraro said. "That was a risky stunt, but it was worth shaking that cool customer up for interrogation. I had no idea Miss Barr would be on board for it."

"She pushed her way into the car. What could I do?" Nicky asked innocently.

"You couldn't overpower her?"

"You don't know women, detective. The smaller they are, the more tenacious. They don't call those stiletto heels for nothing."

The detective eyed Temple's spike heels. "I guess those are oddly fitting today."

She immediately got the allusion. "Because Cosimo Sparks was murdered with a very thin dagger, like a stiletto?"

"And how do you know that?"

"Just . . . guessing from the context." She'd never squeal on Coroner Bahr. She wasn't a dirty rat.

"Pretty clever," Ferraro said, turning to Nicky. "You got the evidence?"

Nicky reached into his breast coat pocket and pulled out a tiny tape recorder, not a firearm. "He didn't actually confess, but he was pretty rattled by the dead man's rerun appearance in his own media show. Broke the car window."

"Glad the blood on his hands is his own doing," Ferraro noted, pocketing the tape.

"Well said," Nicky answered. "I'm just glad the Glory Hole Gang is cleared."

"What?" Temple demanded. "Have I been totally out of this loop? They were suspects?"

"You should be 'out of the loop,' " Ferraro said, his lean face stern. "I've heard a bit about your civilian snooping. Not to be encouraged. Yeah," he finally admitted, "they were mixed up with Jersey Joe Jackson and his stolen silver dollars and rumored hidden stashes of other assets through the years since the late forties. We couldn't come up with a motive for Sparks's murder other than attempted robbery."

"Not Sparks's attempted robbery?"

"Could be, and Santiago could have come on him cracking the safe while inspecting the tunnel before the vault was opened, but why would a rich guy — and he is — kill someone for an empty vault? It looked more like money from the past was involved, with those few silver dollars found in the vault. When we searched the old boys' suite . . ."

Temple's jaw dropped and she stared at Nicky.

He nodded confirmation. "The police asked, so we got them all out of there on a pretext."

"How could anyone think the Glory Hole guys . . . ? They're in their eighties."

"Greed never dies, Miss Barr, you should know that." Ferraro's lip quirk could have been the start of a smile. "Anyway, we found an ice pick among their test-kitchen supplies. It looked as clean as a whistle and new as a store-bought razor blade, but forensics found Santiago's DNA on it, which was easily obtained from all over the media wizard's Fontana Suite."

"Why would Santiago kill Sparks?" Temple asked. "Greed is a pretty broad category."

"For some reason, Santiago could have been looking for Jersey Joe's treasure, now that he was in the vicinity."

That just lay there, as linguistically lame as it was as a motive for murder.

"What about the hesitation marks on Cosimo's body?" Temple asked.

Ferraro frowned at her as fiercely as he had at Midnight Louie. "You have some inside access to the forensics report, Miss Barr? I thought Lieutenant Molina had enough of your fringe investigations."

"I was a reporter, Detective Ferraro. I hear things."

Midnight Louie chose that moment to take a long stretch up the detective's pant leg. His full-length reach was awesome, almost crotch-high.

Ferraro stiffened like a frozen haddock, winced, and gazed down into Louie's big green eyes. Louie's big black claws had probably pricked through his lightweight slacks fabric into his skin, but very delicately.

"I hate cats," Ferraro said, "almost as bad as amateur dicks. Get this one off me, and I'll overlook your possession of police information," he told Temple, never breaking Louie's stare.

"Louie! Down!" Temple ordered, as if he were a dog. She wasn't sure how he'd react to that indignity.

Louie held his pose and Ferraro's gaze for a long, deep moment of mutual standoff, then dropped back on all fours.

"We won't keep you, Detective," Nicky said. "We'll, uh, read all about it in the *Review-Journal.*"

Ferraro turned to go.

Temple spoke. "What if those 'hesitation marks' on the body were *prod* marks?"

Ferraro turned back, looked at her, at

Louie, and then nodded. He knew a bit about prod marks personally now.

"Good point. Sparks failed to find the loot, and once Santiago saw the empty safe, he thought he'd been deliberately led astray and tried to 'prick' Sparks to give out the 'real' location of the Jackson treasure. For some reason, Sparks couldn't, or wouldn't, then Santiago lost it, like he did in your car," Ferraro said, nodding at Nicky.

"Frankly, despite his DNA on the ice pick, the motive is all iffy and airy-fairy, and I doubt we'll convict. Where did Santiago run into this slightly eccentric retired magician? Why would a sophisticate like him buy this bizarre Jersey Joe Jackson hidden-money rumor, and then kill over it? Right at the site of his brand-new toy about to debut. He would have had to have had a lot more visceral motive than a rich man's unending greed to go through all that."

"I don't know," Temple said, who thought she did, "but he was in and out of the Glory Hole Gang's suite and test kitchen next door to his like a neighbor with a borrowing fetish. I saw that while I was visiting the old boys briefly."

"At least," Ferraro said, "your ultrasenior-citizen friends are in the clear. If I were you, I'd leave it at that and be happy."

Temple nodded quickly. "You're right, detective. All's well that ends well."

He actually grinned, but it looked forced. "We're in agreement on that."

She turned to Nicky when it was just her, him, Macho Mario, and Midnight Louie again.

"I can't believe you engineered that stickler detective into letting you take Santiago for a 'ride' to his arrest."

"It was a hard sell," Nicky admitted.

"And you didn't even tell me? I'm your PR person, Nicky. That was . . . cold."

"I only told Uncle Mario, and I had to do it that way."

"Well, letting Santiago luxuriate in his own setup and then slipping in a whole new scenario — how'd you do that, anyway?"

"Please. Vegas is teeming with special-effects people. You got the dough, they got the go. But the police demanded secrecy."

"I get that, but why the big production?"

Nicky waggled his handsome head from side to side and shrugged with his hands in his pockets like a misbehaving twelve-year-old.

"The police came to me with their evidence and suspicions. It was all as thin as an ice pick, but I knew a high-profile arrest couldn't go down at the Crystal Phoenix

Hotel itself. People sleep there. You can't have them thinking murderers are floating around. Van would kill me!"

Macho Mario nodded soberly. "Definitely."

"So . . . ," Nicky said, "down here it fits. It's all part of the ambience, right?"

"I suppose there's a certain poetic justice to Santiago riding the rails to his own arrest."

"You can work with that? I mean publicity-wise?"

"I can work with that. Publicity-wise," Temple said. "You know, I'd just like to sit down here in the car seat and collect my thoughts."

"Van wants all us Crystal Phoenix folks up in the Jersey Joe Jackson Ghost Suite for a cocktail calm-down in half an hour or so."

"Just folks?"

Nicky glanced down at the four cats still swarming at Temple's ankles.

"My brothers will bemoan the black cat hair on their usual pale and expensive Ermenegildo Zegna suits, but two of these four felines have lived at the Phoenix, and the quartet does seem to be the new Cat Pack in town. So sure, bring on the dander."

On those not-feline-flattering words, Nicky grabbed his uncle's arm and they headed for the elevators.

Temple sat, unsatisfied and uneasy.

Yes, it was good Santiago had been unmasked as someone criminal. Even now, he might not be fully unmasked. What if he'd been one of the foreigners in the Synth club room?

Whew. The Synth and its schemes remained a conundrum that could go any of a dozen ways. Whether the Synth's extravagant mass casino heist scheme was a group delusion or they were being used by terrorists, it was best to keep them out of the limelight until some real evidence existed. The secret underground link between Gangsters and the Crystal Phoenix and Neon Nightmare needed to stay that way for a while too.

Temple was sure the new Cat Pack would be patrolling it for rats of any variety now.

Maybe stopping and arresting Santiago would end all the plotting. The Synth had lost their real leader, Cosimo Sparks, but had he been truly linked to a larger scheme, or playing some game of his own? The silver dollars and rat-snatched bearer bond proved the vault had once been full of filthy lucre. Had it been hoarded IRA money, though? And where had the guns and explosives gone, if so? Had Sparks gotten greedy or scared and decided to move the hoarded IRA money? Had he just found a Jersey Joe Jackson hoard and had he been trying to save the Synth's Neon Nightmare investment? Or was he a true loyalist to the last-gasp alternate IRA cause, trying to protect its holdings from elements who'd raid it? Had he died rather than give Santiago the location of the moved treasure? Or had he simply known . . . nothing? And died because of that?

If Temple kept quiet about all these unsettling questions, maybe Max Kinsella's name would never need to come into it. And he was the last thing she needed on her mind with a marriage to plan.

Besides, Detective Ferraro had been dubious a solid case could be made against Santiago. As long as all these questions remained unanswered, Max's possible connections to all and any of it remained unknown to anybody but her.

Unfortunately, that put news of his fate in a similar limbo.

Might it be better for all concerned for the situation to stay that way?

Forever.

Beside her, Louie, surrounded by his triplets, meowed plaintively.

"Right," she told him. "The old-time

gangsters knew that sometimes 'mum's the word.' That's 'meow' to you.

"I'll keep quiet about your street gang connections and we'll all move forward. And you can be ring bearer again."

CHAPTER 45
DA DENOUEMENT, DUDES

I have been the life of the party before.

I have also been the death of the party, if the party in question deserved it.

All in the line of duty, defending my partner and her interests, whatsoever they may be.

I must say, she is sufficiently grateful. Although my not-inconsiderable contributions to subduing crime in Las Vegas and meting out punishment are often overlooked by officialdom (this was even a problem for Mr. Sherlock Holmes), my Miss Temple never fails to see that I get in on the celebratory party.

Hence, we are all gathered in the Jersey Joe Jackson Ghost Suite at the Crystal Phoenix, where a feast of gourmet appetizers is laid out for the guests of honor: yours truly, Pa Three O'Clock, Ma Barker, and the kit chit, Miss Midnight Louise.

A bunch of Fontanas also happen to be present, and the Glory Hole Gang. Actually, Miss Van von Rhine, being the hostess from whom all good things edible and drinkable flow at this affair, and my roomie are the only females present, the Midnight family femmes excepted.

Apparently, Miss Van von Rhine's hot blonde foreign friend, Revienne, had a headache after all the Chunnel of Crime ride excitement and is dining quietly in her room. Fine. Leaves more for me and mine.

And what a spread the Glory Hole Gang helped lay out! The overgrown members of our party are nibbling from a long table with some foodstuffs the Cat Pack is being polite about and leaving for demolishment later.

Along a classy plastic runner on the vintage carpet are exquisite Asian dishes tricked out with exquisite tidbits of world cuisine, including anchovies à la orange, shrimp and liver with sautéed giblets, and catfish in a sauce of liver and milk.

Maybe not *your* menu, but right up my alley.

"The Jersey Joe Jackson Ghost Suite is filled up to the gills," Miss Temple notes.

I do like her figure . . . and figures of speech. "Gills." *Aaah.* I foresee a leisurely midnight dip at the koi pond.

So does Chef Song, who is presiding over the buffet table and knifes me a sharp warning look. I am reminded that the kitchen is among the most likely places for an "accident" in the house, and that a kitchen tool was the murder weapon in this case.

"Stifle yourself," Midnight Louise hisses in my ear. "This is the family 'coming out' party at the Crystal Phoenix. There shall be no crude fishing expeditions."

"Look at that cat's poor eyelid, Nicky," Miss Van von Rhine croons, bending low to examine Ma Barker's puss.

I squint my eyes shut. Miss Van von Rhine will get four in the first three epidermal levels from Ma for that liberty.

"I know a great eye surgeon for that," Miss Van von Rhine goes on, speaking directly to Ma, "if you would consent to drop by my office with Midnight Louise and let me treat you to Gangsters' new spa for a facial and even maybe a tummy tuck. We will have a plastic surgeon on hand for Botox and laser eye lifts."

Eek! A tummy tuck is *my* mark of honor for surviving a premature surgical attempt on my, er, fur balls.

I am amazed to see Ma Barker erupt in a purr and rub on our hostess's ankles.

Female! Thy name is vanity! What a traitor.

Whilst I am stewing about the turn of events — I seem not to be the object of every eye — Miss Midnight Louise slinks up to me again.

"Good job, *mein* papa. Who knows what that South American terrorist would have done to our poor human associates had we not been there to staple his treacherous suit lapels to his epidermis through his trachea."

Females can be so visceral.

I do see how Ma Barker, after her harsh street life, might be ready for the Queen for a Day treatment. As for my esteemed pater, Three O'Clock has drifted to sleep with his whiskers in the catfish pâté. Pater is in the pâté. What a family! I could die.

"Louie," says my Miss Temple, "it has been a busy day, and I think you and I should head home to the Circle Ritz."

Sweeter words were never spoken. I cannot wait to hit the solo sack with her and have my . . . tummy tuck scratched. I am the exclusive sort.

Meanwhile, there are some tiresome matters, always as clear as a crystal phoenix to me, that the humans always have to settle.

"What made you suspect Santiago, Nicky?" my Miss Temple asks.

"Actually, my brilliant wife. Van, do you want to explain?" He turns to her with a bemused smile.

She shrugs charmingly. "It was nothing. Merely my broad knowledge of international finance."

Macho Mario barks out a laugh at the word "broad," which evokes cocked shivs in the

Midnight family females, not that anyone biped would notice.

"I always say, Nicky," he predictably says, "if you do not have it, marry it."

Mr. Nicky Fontana is a modern dude and knows to give credit where credit is due. "And how did your superior knowledge save the whole project and remove the blot of a murder rap from all my nearest and dearest? Dearest."

"You . . . flattering phony Santiago, you," Van answers with a smile. "Temple came to my office and asked me to explain bearer bonds, after we found that one . . . 'rat dropping' in the tunnel.

"I explained that they had been a convenient way to do international transactions and were available for up to ten thousand dollars apiece. The investment was poor because they often did not earn interest, and their usage is being phased out as we speak."

Nicky frowns. "We knew any valuables found in a Jersey Joe Jackson stash would be . . . out of date."

"Yes. Of course, dear."

Uh-oh. That is the prelude to a forthcoming contradiction.

"However," Miss Van von Rhine goes on in that sweet, reasonable, feminine way that always stiffens my hackles into boar bristles, "bearer bonds are worth the loss of interest to international illegal parties who need ready cash. In fact, despite the colorful update of Gangsters attractions, we Americans have been pikers in the 'gangster' stakes since Prohibition was reversed, at least north of the border, as Las Vegas is."

"Agreed, my dear niece-in-law," Macho Mario rumbles from his kingpin seat on the chartreuse satin chair, which is usually my private throne.

I guess I will submit to age before beauty. This time.

"Anyway," Miss Vanilla goes on in her tooth-decaying way, "bearer bonds have remained popular in South America, which made me wonder why a North American rat was playing Foosball with one. Upon further studying of the document in question, I saw that it was dated."

"It *was* in Jersey Joe's locker, albeit it was otherwise empty," Eightball O'Rourke puts in, while chowing down on a caviar cracker. "He has been gone since the seventies."

Ouch! Not true, especially *here* in the Ghost Suite. And maybe now!

The hairs on my backbone are standing up and singing "Clementine." And I cannot even carry a tune, much less wear a size-nine boot or carry a bearer bond. I do so hate to see humans of my gender rushing toward their doom, unless it is Santiago.

"The bearer bond was dated nineteen ninety-seven," Miss Van puts in, as if we should all get it now.

"So it is a teenager," Macho Mario disparages. "It is still worth the ten thou. That is a pretty good baccarat-room tip in these times."

Are mine the only vibrissae that are reaching for the ceiling in this room? Can Macho Mario be that behind the times?

Yes.

Miss Temple takes up the theme. "What was a major world event in nineteen ninety-eight, one that was actually positive?"

There is a long, long silence. Nobody remembers much by years, only by personal ups and downs.

"Uh . . ." comes a lone, cautious response from a Fontana brother. Ralph, the second youngest to Nicky. ". . . Windows Ninety-Eight?"

"Good answer!" Miss Van responds. "But not relevant."

Frankly, the last thing on the Fontana brothers' minds is being relevant, and the whole clan heaves a sigh of relief.

"And," Miss Temple adds, "on the pesky international front, the peace accord in Ireland."

"What should peace have to do with this

mess here today?" Macho Mario asks.

"After what Temple told me she learned at the Neon Nightmare, a lot," Miss Van von Rhine says. "I will let her take up the narrative."

"I do not want a 'narrative,' " Macho Mario says. "I want an answer to who killed who, so long as it is not a relative, and why."

"Commendable," Miss Van says dryly. "I will let Temple continue with what she risked life and limb to learn at the Neon Nightmare."

Macho Mario frowns. "Her knees did seem to be dry and nubbly today."

My Miss Temple rolls her eyes. "It is not what happened in nineteen ninety-eight, it is *how* what happened in the Irish peace process that year that made the U.S.'s nine/eleven attack so earthshaking over there. I did some research and —"

"— And I hope this is not another boring TV news thing," Macho Mario says.

"I will cut to the chase," Miss Temple says. "On record, there is only one 'beneficiary' of nine/eleven, as admitted by the Dean of Saint Anne's Anglican Cathedral in Belfast. He cited the 'worldwide revulsion against terror it sparked.' As American dollars to support the IRA cause vanished almost overnight, the dean concluded for the Protestant side that 'We here in Ireland are perhaps the only beneficiaries of nine/eleven.' "

"What do the Irish have to do with it?" Macho Maria demands. "Gloomy northern folk with a jones for justice and music and alcohol hard and soft, like their heads."

"Yet they did what almost no one in the world has managed in recent decades, Uncle Mario," Nicky says. "They made peace."

"And because of that wonderful step forward for humanity," Temple says, "the core of this whole puzzle of murder and magic was a war chest."

I yawn and make my way to the buffet. I see that this is going to be a talky party, and I prefer rebuilding my strength to social chit-chatting. I have a lot to face in the future: having both Three O'Clock and Miss Midnight Louise hounding me when I visit the Crystal Phoenix and Gangsters and the additional stress of Ma Barker crowding me near the Circle Ritz.

And having someone sleeping in my bed again, when Mr. Matt comes back.

I am starting to feel very crowded by family on all fronts. Maybe I should just move! I could run away and join the Big Cats and the evil Hyacinth at the circus, or more realistically, the Fontana brothers at Gangsters. Nobody crowds them.

Do not worry for one minute about Midnight

Louie not landing on his feet in some lavish and satisfactorily lethal new situation. Yes, sir, I have more options than a trader in pig futures.

CHAPTER 46
CLOSING CALL

"Back to the hole-in-the-wall pub with the alternative IRA chappies?" Max asked, after Gandolph had thoughtfully shut his cell phone.

Max was reclining against one of the made-up beds' headboard, his stockinged feet and legs stretched out on the goose-down coverlet.

They were digesting an informal but fine dinner they'd had at a restored restaurant on the square: pepper steak with béarnaise sauce for Max, and pan-fried monkfish with curry-mango sauce for Garry. The after-dinner coffee had been dark and rich, and the Bailey's Irish Cream liqueur that accompanied it absolute heaven: Irish whiskey and cream that would draw any cat in the world away from looking at a queen.

"Back to the alternative IRA," Gandolph confirmed, "if you can move your lazy after-dinner Irish-American frame."

"Barely," Max admitted. "You know, that's one 'memory' that came to me after the coma: after-dinner coffee with you when I was young and green and listened to everything you said as gospel."

"Good. The way to a man's memory is through his stomach, then." Garry stood, slapping one of Max's feet. "Come on; Liam sounded excited. I think the scent of money has recharged his desire to deal. We can take the Mondeo."

"And drive down that rat hole of unrestored slum streets?" Max asked, rising.

Gandolph fetched their black trench coats, bought on the square, from the narrow hotel wardrobe. The night often misted. "Yes. My GPS has the coordinates, and I checked the computer maps for routes. That'll spare your legs, at least."

"Modern spy ware," Max mocked. "I've been retired too long."

"Not long enough," Gandolph said. "We're in this only to name and disarm your would-be murderers. I don't want you back in the counterterrorism game. It's totally new, more brutal, and not happening in our bailiwick anymore. One last round to ensure your future safety, and then we're retired for good."

Max nodded. "Agreed. Four votes from

me and my damaged legs and brain."

"Recuperating, Max. Not damaged."

"No," Max said, struggling to stand while shrugging into the hokey trench coat. "Not damaged as Kathleen O'Connor was, glory be. Lead on, Macduff."

Gandolph laughed. "We've got something from these guys or they wouldn't have called! We can tell them some Las Vegas legend in repayment. Maybe give them the location of Ted Binion's now-empty vault."

Max laughed. "You're bad, Garry. I wager these Old World types never heard of that. A hidden, secret underground vault in Las Vegas. It sounds like Nancy Drew."

"Then Temple Barr would be in on it," Garry quipped back.

Temple Bar or Temple Barr? Max produced a crooked grin. At least that name was securely etched on his memory now. Too bad the woman wasn't.

Gandolph was now a geographical magician, Max admitted to himself.

The Mondeo was parked down a narrow street, where its black body color vanished into the ill-lit night. Yet they were only a two-alley walk on rough stones from the bar. Max had his fists in his coat pockets and his head down against the coat's turned-up collar. He might look like a skulker, but it was bone-chilling weather, not that cold to a Midwestern-boy but cutting deep with the dampness.

"I never thought I'd welcome the sight of this place," Max said, holding the unwelcoming thick wood door open for his senior partner.

"If this is useful, with what we know from the Magdalen asylum, we can head home to sunshine and slot machines."

"Was I ever a gambling man, Garry?"

"Only with your life, Max. Only with your life. Which is starting anew now, believe me."

Max nodded, caught up in his old friend's sense of achievement. A life all came down to a D. H. Lawrence title, didn't it? *Friends and Lovers.*

Max was so mellow he was able to look on the dour set of disenfranchised revolutionaries with a historical distance. Their battles and time and temper were over. Here, at least, it was a new and more peaceful world.

This time Max and Garry bellied up to the bar and brought their pints to the table, not as prisoners, but peers.

Brusque nods around the scarred table were a somewhat sheepish welcome.

"You're walking better," Liam observed.

Max didn't mention he'd walked less far to get here.

"What have you got?" Garry asked. "Something 'fresh,' you said."

"Oh, fresh, all right," Liam answered, lifting his glass. "Fresh as County Antrim cream."

Max and Garry exchanged glances as they sat. That sounded good.

"First," the leader said, "we want something for the pot from you."

Gandolph nodded. "You may have heard Las Vegas was founded by American mobsters."

"Aye. Not the Irish mob. The Italians and the Jews."

"The Irish aren't much for the desert," Max put in.

"Unless we're pounding railroad tracks through it."

"That would be the Chinese out West," Max said with a smile. "The Irish stuck to the mines and the East Coast."

" 'Suckin' up the coal dust into our lungs,' " Mulroney said, quoting an old work song.

"Desert dust in Las Vegas, lads," Garry said. "Sometimes gold dust, but more often silver. If you check the Web, you'll see there's been news of a hidden vault opened under a Las Vegas hotel."

"Empty," Liam sneered. "You think I don't get the news of the world hourly?"

Max was astounded, and thus was gagged from saying anything to back up Gandolph.

"Still . . ." Garry went on, "there's a Vegas cadre of magicians —"

"Magicians?" Finn hooted. "We're to be interested in a gang of magicians?"

"You should be, because a lot of deaths over the past two years or so could come to lie down like lambs at their feet, and they may roar like lions before this hidden-vault business is over. Such a vault was found a decade ago in the desert, loaded with collectible American silver dollars worth millions. Millions, lads. Wouldn't that do your 'charitable' causes some major good?"

"A treasure hunt is what you're offerin' us instead of solid information?" Flanagan said.

Liam put a hand on Flanagan's sweater-clad arm. "Our American sympathizers gathered millions and millions in treasure for our cause over the decades. This lad and his cousin came here almost twenty years ago because they were afire with our just grievances. I've never doubted the sincerity of our American cousins. Do you, Michael

Kinsella, swear that there might be something to this Synth and its hidden treasure?"

"I've trusted this man with my life since he whisked me away from your lot," Max said, "after I found and triggered the O'Toole's Pub bombers in the name of my slain cousin." He regarded Gandolph with complete sincerity. "I believe that every word he's told you now is true."

"You betrayed our kind and our cause, but not your kin and kith," Liam said. "In our old days there would be a blood price, but in these new days, we cannot deny it's no more than we would have done."

"So," said Gandolph. "We'll return to Vegas and endeavor to find your lost promised fortune. What is this . . . jewel . . . of information you have for us?"

"Kathleen O'Connor is your lost jewel, yes?"

"If you speak in terms of long-delayed vengeance," Max said.

"Hard to get over kin betrayed and slain, is it? And ye've only had twenty years of it, lad."

Max nodded, soberly. These men had truly had cause. Centuries of it, enough to no longer feel like men, but trapped, snarling animals. If he and Gandolph indeed found Kitty the Cutter's last savagely patriotic stash, they'd send it to the widows and orphans of Ulster, both sides.

He glanced at Gandolph, knowing his unilateral resolve would be honored there.

"All right, then," Liam said, hunkering down over his pint and lowering his voice. "You've proven your mettle to me. We asked around, as you wanted. We asked about Kathleen O'Connor. No man who saw her forgot her. Some didn't wish to speak of her, defending her to this very day. Some spat at the mention of her name. One, only one woman who is our liaison to the charities knew of her."

Max and Garry leaned in and strained their ears to hear Liam's soft conspiratorial tone.

"She's contributed to the charities within the past year."

Max reared away, almost physically seared by the implications. "No. I saw her dead."

"I don't know what you saw, man, but she put forty thousand American dollars of bearer bonds into the widows' and orphans' coffers within the past three months."

"How do you know it was she?" Gandolph asked, his grammar precise even during the stress of hard bargaining.

"Because Rose Murphy, one of our longest, loyalest supporters, said it came in from a name Kathleen used to use. From the U.S."

"And what name was that?" Max asked.

"Rebecca."

Max tensed again. He and Garry and Liam knew from the documents that was Kathleen O'Connor's name in the Magdalen asylum.

"Just Rebecca?" Gandolph asked. "A lot of women bear that name. How can you be sure it was Kathleen, then?"

"Not just Rebecca. Rebecca Deever. That was the code name she used for all her U.S. activities after she left the homeland. Even I recognize it from 'donations' and weapons shipments before the bloody 'peace accord.' 'Twas from her, no doubt. Even I didn't know about these last decade's sendings. She went around me and my associates. Directly to the women. You see, it worked both ways, Max, you and Kathleen. We IRA men blamed her for inflaming you so much our bombers were tracked down by your vengeance."

"Then she did know O'Toole's was scheduled to be hit while Sean was there?"

Liam shrugged. "Should have. You understand, man, we were as mad at you for bein' with her at the time as you became angry with yourself. We never understood why she spent her time and self with you."

"Causing heartache and guilt and murderous jealousy," Max said. "That was the only real 'cause' that drove her, setting men against one another over her and enjoying the mayhem. She was avenging herself on the entire male sex, and Irishmen particularly."

"For the years at the Magdalen asylum," Finn suggested.

"And," Max reminded them, "for that recorded teenage pregnancy and the baby taken away, never to be found."

Liam nodded, eyeing his fellows. "We played into her hands as well, then."

"So does it matter, then, whether the money is from her or her ghost?" Max asked. "Isn't that where you intend any money Kathleen raised in the States to go? To your widows and orphans?" He kept his voice disingenuous yet silken.

"Mostly," Liam whispered back, "but we do have our own priorities, even now. Remember. You've promised to help find her stash of cash. Even if she's not still alive, there's a backup pile of it, and we deserve every bit of it."

"You certainly do," Gandolph said abruptly, with Oliver Hardy emphasis. Max marveled that his own mind could remember eighty-year-old Laurel and Hardy comedy routines, but not the tragedies of his recent life.

Gandolph put down his pint glass and sat back. "A fair bargain. We want her; you want her amassed foreign treasure. We still both need each other, but mostly we — Michael and I — need to get back to the States to hunt her and the guns and roses and money she promised you."

At Gandolph's prodding, Max rose.

He felt like a walking zombie. Nothing settled. He'd been prepared to bury Kathleen O'Connor as an old enemy dead and gone for both their benefits. Now he had to deal with her resurrected and still poisonous? Did forgiveness go that far? Recovering terrorism money for shaky, defanged terrorists? What was Gandolph thinking?

Probably way ahead of him and his on-off memory.

Max swaggered to the pub door, because it was either that or limp. Gandolph was right behind him.

Then the door crashed inward with a crowd of dark-coated men behind it . . . five, by an instant count: the two ex-IRA men they'd met with and three more of that ilk.

He and Gandolph had led them here, for sure.

"Out of the way," Gandolph shouted, pushing Max into the wall and then through the open door behind the incoming newcomers. The room behind them exploded with Irish curses and splintering wood and glass as the two gangs met full force.

Max was out in the misty night, scrambling over the slippery-damp cobblestones, his hand rushing Gandolph along with him to the sanctuary of their car.

He grappled the keys from his pants pocket as he ran and used the unlocking device to open the doors from twenty feet away. The customary beep sounded like a siren in the echoing, hard empty streets of Belfast.

He shoved Gandolph around the Mondeo's rear and into the passenger side. The older man clutched his computer and briefcase to his chest as Max leaped around the car's front, then slammed himself into the driver's seat, gunning the engine and careening down the left side of the narrow way. No headlights, no seat belts, no time.

The wheels screamed around a corner, into the so-far-deserted dark.

They heard muffled voices bursting out into the night and the choked sound of at

least two cars or vans hastily starting behind
them.

"Damn!" Max's fist pounded the steering
wheel.

"Damn for the interruption or because
Kathleen may still be alive?" Gandolph
grunted, with frequent interruptions, wrestling to buckle his seat belt while keeping
hold of his precious computer and briefcase.

"Damn everything," Max muttered,
watching his side and rearview mirrors.
"There they are," he exclaimed, as the
inside of the car was washed with a streak
of headlights from the rear.

"I can get up a street map of this section,"
Garry huffed, opening the laptop and making keys cluck like chickens.

"I haven't time to crane my neck and eyes
at small-screen maps," Max said in frustration.

A screech of corner-turning wheels at an
upcoming deserted cross street made him
suddenly veer into the right lane . . . the
wrong lane for this city.

Behind the Mondeo, a black Morris Mini
crammed with men streaked forward
fast . . . and toward the front fender of a
crossing Ford Focus. Max squinted into the
rearview mirror, watching both cars swerve
away from a collision. He lurched the

Mondeo into the proper left lane as a pair of high, bright headlights riding behind a sustained horn was about to smash into them head-on.

"Oh, my God, Max!" Garry averted his face. "I'll expire from cardiac arrest."

"*They* had the near miss, not us," was Max's reply. "Why did the ex-IRA raid the alternate IRA, and why they are now both after us?"

"Money. Kathleen was a master money-maker, and both sides see no reason to let any hidden funds go to the other, or to foreign pilgrims like us seeking something as intangible as closure."

"We wouldn't keep any of that money, but give it to a common cause," Max said.

He jerked the steering wheel and car down another side street, which turned out to be one-way the wrong way. He gunned the motor to shorten the time exposed to a head-on collision. Another cross street flashed by, with oncoming cars from both ways. Both drivers hit their brakes, and both cars spun sideways.

"Duck!" Max cried, as bullets slammed the Mondeo broadside from both directions. He covered the steering wheel with his crossed forearms and hit the gas so the oncoming cars would be shooting at each other.

A seat belt would have kept him from banging up his legs and head in this seesaw maneuver. Too late to buckle up now.

Max heard the driver's window shatter and felt a hot *zing* of air behind his head as his forehead jerked toward the windshield. He braked reflexively.

His right foot reversed the slowdown with a to-the-floor shot of gas. The Mondeo jack-rabbited forward. His forehead bounced briefly off the windshield. He leaned back hard and applied the brakes to the floor again.

The two pursuing cars were spinning into each other's now-bullet-riddled frames with engines steaming as they crashed in a glassy, metallic shower of body parts.

Max released a huge breath. "Close call. Are you all right?"

He glanced over, glad to see Garry upright in the seat. The passenger-side window was shattered too.

"We need to dump this car and hoof it to our hotel to decamp ASAP," Max thought aloud. "Good thing you belted yourself in. I almost gave myself another memory concussion, but I'm okay. I think."

Something tickled down his right forehead, making his eyelashes wet and sticky. Head wounds bled. Awkward, but not serious.

His hands and feet tingled as if they'd been "asleep" at the wheel. His knees and hips felt jolted, but solid. Best to get going while his body was still numb and couldn't tell him where it had broken down until he was committed to moving it, to running.

"You take the briefcase," he told Garry. "I'll manage the computer. What's the matter? Is your seat belt jammed?"

Max brushed the blood from his forehead, checking the rearview mirror. He heard a distant siren.

"Come on, we've got to move." He grabbed Garry's shoulder.

The older man was staring straight ahead. *He should be moving by now,* Max thought. He'd always been Max's goad, not the other way around. Max focused on the shattered window haloing his friend's familiar profile. Ruby red mixed with the diamond-edge crackle pattern shining in the light of a semi-distant street lamp.

No. . . .

His stunned brain replayed the moment. The bullet that had shattered his window, meant for him, to stop their escape, had sped by a millisecond behind his head as the brakes jolted him forward, no seat belt to impede his reflexive motions.

Garry, belted in, held still, became the perfect target.

Now Max could see the small round hole in the grayish hair at Garry's temple.

"No!" he cried, ripping Garry's seat belt out so hard it gave at the door mount.

He pulled the old man's body onto his shoulder, shedding bloody, blinding tears.

No, no, no. Not this loss too. You up there, take it back!

Garry — the name ran through his hobbled brain in a rhythm like a song — *Garry, I hardly knew ye.* Again.

Move, Max. The voice came out of the aching, blinding despair in his head. *No matter who, no matter what. You've got to move on. Mourn your losses later. Move now!*

"Why?" Max asked the empty car interior. "This isn't a mission to save anything but my sorry past. Garry, I won't leave you. You've never left me."

And his faltering memory hadn't resurrected all he'd known of the living man. Maybe it never would, now.

Listen to me. No matter how bad the situation, you have only one option. Always. Action. Move, Max!

"Why am I remembering your advice

531

now? When it's too late. It's too late, Gandolph. I can't do a damn thing about anything. That fucking seat belt!"

His voice and questions filled his mind, the car. There were no answers but the mantra that Gandolph had planted in his head over the years, released like a long, old-fashioned tape recording.

Trust me. Move, Max. Move on. It's what you'd want if the situation were reversed. Let it go. Let me go.

"No. Your body. Who will claim your body? Buried and forgotten like a Magdalen asylum woman? No!"

A vehicle was rushing into the shattered night of broken cars and men, flashing blue lights.

The Belfast police.

Max, for God's sake, move!!! Find out what you must, do what you must, what we determined we must do. Find Kathleen O'Connor, if she's there to be found. Tell her "Sláinte" for me. Then find your heart's desire.

Max pulled the torqued driver's-side door open, grabbed both legs, and kicked them out as battering rams against the balky steel, hoping they'd break again. The door creaked agape. And Gandolph's body slid farther into the driver's seat Max was abandoning.

He let a calm thought cross his mind, then

grabbed the laptop and briefcase, Gollum's "my precious" times two. He'd read *The Lord of the Rings,* even if Garry claimed he hadn't.

Everything they'd learned, that Gandolph had learned, for his sake, rested inside these fragile cases, one of paper and leather, one of pixels and plastic.

Max pushed himself up, out of the Mondeo's stuck-forward seat, into the clean, misty night air. The sirens screamed louder, and blue lights washed over the street like a Kmart special offering capture and unanswerable questions.

He needed escape and survival.

With no glance back but in his heart, Max lurched down the empty wet cobblestoned street, unerringly finding the shadows and blending with them. He knew he could operate under the dark of the moon with the best of them, but he had a long way to go as just a crippled shadow of himself.

CHAPTER 47
MOVING ISSUES

"Matt!" Temple rejoiced into the cell phone as she recognized his voice. "You won't believe what mayhem we've had here, solving the Chunnel of Crime murder."

"Mayhem in Vegas," he answered. "What's not to believe?"

"Right now, I want to hear all about *The Amanda Show* appearances and the family soap opera," Temple said.

"Oh, it is a soap opera, way more exciting than anything currently on TV. But I've got other news, something that could really remodel our lives."

"Oh?"

"For the better. I'm getting tired of working night shifts."

"I can live with that."

"That's just it. We don't have to. *The Amanda Show* producers have offered me my own, ah, gig."

"Your own gig?" Temple felt confused.

"You don't sing. . . . Is it the dancing?"

"Lord, no. It's what I do. Talk to people."

"A talk show?"

"Right. A daytime talk show. No more me rushing out before midnight six nights out of seven like Cinderfella."

"But . . . you *are* Mr. Midnight."

"When we're married, I want to work normal daytime hours, like you do."

"Talk shows are tricky, Matt. Eighty zillion more have gone down than have made it."

"The *Amanda Show* producers think it's time to bring on a guy who isn't Jerry Springer. Something more substantive. They say my Q-ratings go through the roof whenever I'm on Amanda's show. The time's ripe for a spin-off with Oprah's retirement coming up. That's a seismic event, and opportunity. Don't you see, Temple? We could be together more."

"Well, yeah. That's great, Matt! I just couldn't believe it at first. That's right about Oprah. This is a major, major offer. Dinner at the Paris Eiffel Tower restaurant for that!"

"Tony Valentine, my agent, will be rarin' to go on this. And we can do the wedding in Chicago, because we'll need a house here. Not too suburban. You don't want a long commute."

"Chicago? Living there?"

"Yeah. Of course."

"Wouldn't Vegas be a great talk-show city, lots of celebrities buzzing through?"

"This wouldn't be the usual celebrity gab-and-promo fest. I'd do something similar to the radio counseling, only on a TV screen during the daylight hours."

"The Circle Ritz . . ."

"We can keep my unit. Visit."

"My job. The Crystal Phoenix."

"Chicago has big hotels too. I'm sure your PR ideas will knock 'em dead around here too."

"Literally?"

His laughter made the phone vibrate in her palm.

"I'm sure you could find a murder or two to solve here."

"The Chicago winters . . ."

"We both grew up in winters like that. Look," he said, "this has to be a joint decision. But it's such an amazing opportunity. The show would be structured to do people some real good."

"Elvis will miss you."

"That's another thing. No more eerie call-ins."

"And . . . Midnight Louie."

"He can move."

"He couldn't own the town, like here."

"Maybe he'd have to hold down your condo, and we'd visit. Anyway, I'll be home in a few days and we can discuss it. I have to stay on for more talks. I admit I was bowled over by their presentation. A whole conference room, huge TV screen, network VPs. Then there's the latest mind-blowing wrinkle in my family. We'll talk when I'm not semi–out of my mind from pressure on all sides."

"*Ooh.* Sounds like a trip full of surprises."

Temple clung to the phone, trying to calculate all the pros and cons of leaving Las Vegas.

"Too much to discuss on a phone call," Matt said again. "I just couldn't wait to tell you. We'll find what works best for both of us. Love you."

"Matt, I am so happy for you. I love you too."

The line went dead, and Temple felt something pressing against her calves. Talk about pressure from all sides.

She looked down.

Midnight Louie looked up with solemn green eyes.

"That was Matt," she told him. "How'd you like to be the biggest, baddest get-around-town dude in Chicago?"

She was not to know what Louie thought of that. The phone rang again. She wondered what Matt had forgotten to mention.

The voice wasn't Matt's. It was strange and fuzzy, as if coming from a bar or a street corner or a distant star.

"Can you hear me?" it asked. "The line is fading in and out."

"Barely," she answered, wondering if she should just hang up on a crank caller.

"You're supposed to know me," the voice was continuing. "Sorry if I sound slurred. I'm calling from Northern Ireland, wouldn't you know? Yes, I've been drinking. That's what we Irish do at wakes, even private ones."

She was about to end the call, except something in the distorted voice rang disturbingly true. It went on.

"Hang up anytime you're feeling bored. I've got two recently broken legs that will ache in this blasted damp weather for the rest of my life if I stay in the damned country, and I'm a wanted man, anyway.

"I've got a case of amnesia, where all I'm remembering is a bit about the IRA, a dead woman named Rebecca, or a possibly live one named Kathleen, and a crew of crazy-ass has-been magicians who think they belong to a secret society called the Synth.

"'The man who was my only family for half my life is dead, as good as assassinated, and I suppose I'm next on the list. I don't know if there's any point for anything but another three fingers of Black Bush whiskey, but I've been told by the only man I ever trusted you're a pretty smart and gutsy girl, and the Las Vegas weather would be better for my legs and my lungs, if not my long-term 'health,' so I have a decision to make as to where I'll live and die or if there's any point to the years in between those states.

"I don't know anyone now, here or any-where, who knows anything about me but enemies.

"They tell me my name is Michael Aloy-sius Xavier Kinsella, and I know I need to get the hell somewhere else fast. I guess there's only one question to ask or answer before I decide where.

"Is it possible . . .

"Do you . . . love me?"

Temple had slowly slid down from shock until she was sitting on the hard parquet floor, her back braced against the sofa front, her legs and feet disappearing into the thick long hair of her faux-goat-fur rug.

Midnight Louie was now sitting right beside her, his soft, warm, sturdy bulk brac-ing her side and shoulder on the left side, the heart side.

There was no time to dither. She heard a hard-breathing silence on the other side of the world, from the other end of the satellite high in the sky, up there with Ophiuchus looking down and almost shaking the stars out of the sky from laughing at muddled mortals and that nasty upraised third finger of fate that seems to direct all the traffic in the universe.

She had no options either. So she listened to her voice break the silence and say three little words.

Three little inevitable, critical, dangerous, life-altering little words. She sighed and spoke them.

"Come home, Max."

TAILPIECE:
MIDNIGHT LOUIE DECRIES
SEX AND GORE

Actually, I do not decry sex. I am actively trying to acquire it, but the pool of possibilities continues to shrink during a politically correct age. Also I am turning up too many female relatives lately. I actually have begun to miss the evil Hyacinth, the late Shangri-La's Siamese magician's assistant.

All of my assorted human associates have been distressingly dull and monogamous, until just lately, which is not setting a good example for my species.

Nor am I against Al Gore. I am all for saving the planet and its many glorious species, every one, including my sorely tried larger cousins, the Big Cats. And no one can say I have not done my personal part for overpopulation.

What I do object to is "all gore," the profligate and gratuitous use of truncated human body parts to pander to the popular taste.

It is bad enough that eaten-away legs figure

in this last case. A floating severed arm on semipublic display does not polish the badges of the German or British police forces, even if it is from the last century.

My species is not known for shirking blood and guts, since we are carnivores, something we try to downplay in our domestic lives. We are only carnivores because nature has honed us for thousands of years to eat on the run.

Clearly, we can be rehabilitated.

Humankind I am not so sure about. Certainly, recent turns of events abroad put Kitty the Cutter in a whole new light. I must also take the powers-that-be to task for putting our absent Las Vegasites through so much misery and danger. I expect the usual murder victim, deserving or not, but I do not expect to lose anyone really nice. This is fiction, after all! I do not want it to be "a tale told by an idiot, signifying nothing"!

Wait a minute! Ignore that last, borrowed turn of phrase. Sometimes I get carried away. I tell a good part of this tale, and I am not implying I have an idiot bone in my body or hair in my coat.

Anyway, since Mr. Gandolph the Great was falsely thought murdered in one of my earlier books, during the Halloween haunted-house séance to bring Harry Houdini back from the dead, I am hoping for a second resurrection.

It may be too much to hope that my heedless collaborator is listening to my druthers. She is part and parcel of a savage breed.

Homo sapiens is notorious for playing with its kill, as witness the watery end of poor Boots or the vicious slaughter of the St. Valentine's Day Massacre, an ironic piece of mob violence if ever there was one.

Me, I do indeed think there should be a mob museum in Las Vegas or even elsewhere; in fact, several of them. The public thirst for gory details should be satisfied and showcased, so the rest of us natural-born carnivores do not look so bad.

Very Best Fishes,

Midnight Louie, Esq.

If you'd like information about getting Midnight Louie's free *Scratching Post-Intelligencer* newsletter and/or buying his custom T-shirt and other cool things, please contact Carole Nelson Douglas at P.O. Box 331555, Fort Worth, TX 76163-1555, or at

www.carolenelsondouglas.com.   E-mail:
cdouglas@catwriter.com

TAILPIECE:
CAROLE NELSON DOUGLAS
MEDITATES ON MOBS

As usual, you have hit the nail on the head, Louie. The more lurid elements of life and death sell like *gangbusters*. And the fact is that very word derived from the federal raids to capture mobsters emphasizes that it's always easier to glamorize the baddies than the goodies.

The mob era that still lingers was built on greed, power mongering, and bullying, as were the centuries-long Irish "Troubles." Hearing a British couple's deliberately public, bigoted remarks against "the Irish" in an Irish hotel during a college trip spurred me to start my first novel, *Amberleigh,* on my return to the U.S. that very fall.

What I've read of the nineteenth-century Irish diaspora, when the Irish were literally starved out of their own land and driven to emigrate, illustrates the lengths of brutality that bullying will go to. The Magdalen asylums are another. A year or so before the Good Friday Agreement between the Northern Ireland factions, I spent a gala convention banquet spellbound, hearing my dinner partner, a Roman Catholic widower rearing three children, talk about the spirit-shattering hardships of living in Protestant-dominated Ulster. Such institutionalized, mean-spirited bullying can't be underestimated as one of the most dangerous and savage human traits.

Those of us who love and adopt animals often save them from bullying situations. I write about cats because their storied "independence" means they will leave unkind or even "not perfect" situations. I write about dogs too, but I find their natures too tragic to address in darker terms. As animals with a pack organization and alpha and beta rankings, they're always vulnerable to bullying by their own kind and others. As are humans. I've never seen a cat that wouldn't run from abuse if it could. Dogs and too many abused women and children don't share that gift, the instinct to be solitary for self-preservation's sake.

Apparently, Kathleen O'Connor did.

ABOUT THE AUTHOR

Cat in an Ultramarine Scheme is the twenty-second title in **Carole Nelson Douglas**'s sassy Midnight Louie mystery series. Previous entries include *Cat in a Topaz Tango, Cat in a Sapphire Slipper,* and *Cat in a Red Hot Rage.* In addition to tales of her favorite feline, Douglas is also the author of the historical suspense series featuring Irene Adler, the only woman ever to have "outwitted" Sherlock Holmes. Douglas resides in Fort Worth, Texas.

The employees of Thorndike Press hope you have enjoyed this Large Print book. All our Thorndike, Wheeler, and Kennebec Large Print titles are designed for easy reading, and all our books are made to last. Other Thorndike Press Large Print books are available at your library, through selected bookstores, or directly from us.

For information about titles, please call:
(800) 223-1244

or visit our Web site at:
http://gale.cengage.com/thorndike

To share your comments, please write:
Publisher
Thorndike Press
295 Kennedy Memorial Drive
Waterville, ME 04901